Praise for the novels of "awesome talent"*
Kathryn Shay

SOMEONE TO BELIEVE IN

"Kathryn Shay is an awesome talent who gets better, if possible, with each new story. *Someone to Believe In* is a wonderfully written, emotional, and extraordinary read, and truly deserves a five-star rating."　　—*Affaire de Coeur

"Once again, Shay shines in this starkly realistic story . . . This powerful story will stay with readers long after they finish the book."　　　　　　　　—*Booklist* (starred review)

"Shay's writing trademark is taking seemingly impossible relationships with almost insurmountable obstacles and developing them into classic tales of true love, which is exactly what she does here . . . Another highly complex, compelling, and thought-provoking novel written by one of the best."　　　　　　　　　　　—*Fresh Fiction*

"An exceptional book as well as a gripping page-turner. Ms. Shay is surely a masterful storyteller who weaves a mesmerizing tale . . . Run to your nearest bookstore and grab this book off the shelf. *Someone to Believe In* is truly a powerful, emotional book to read."　　　—*Love Romances*

"This star-crossed love story has passion, intensity, and likeable characters . . . Powerful."　　—*The Romance Reader*

"A riveting tale . . . The characters are well-developed and complex, with imperfections and quirks that make them easy to relate to."　　　　　　　—*Romance Reviews Today*

continued . . .

TRUST IN ME

"[This] powerful tale of redemption, friendship, trust, and forgiving shows once again that Shay knows how to pack an emotional wallop." —*Booklist*

"An unusual and compelling tale . . . I don't know when I have become more involved in a novel's characters and story." —*The Romance Reader*

PROMISES TO KEEP

"A wonderful work of contemporary romance, with a plot ripped straight from the headlines." —*New York Times* bestselling author Lisa Gardner

"Emotion, romance, realism, and intrigue. A love story that you'll never forget . . . a plot that will hold you on the edge of your seat, and an ending that you'll remember long after you turn the last page." —*New York Times* bestselling author Catherine Anderson

MORE PRAISE FOR KATHRYN SHAY

"Master storyteller Kathryn Shay pens an emotionally powerful tale that leaves you breathless. Woven into this riveting plot are wonderfully written characters that grab your heart and don't let go. Bravo, Ms. Shay." —*Romantic Times* (4½ stars)

"A fantastic treat . . . Filled with heartbreaking action, but it is the lead characters that turn this plot into an insightful read . . . Kathryn Shay pays homage to America's Bravest with another powerful novel . . . [so we might] share in their passions and adventures." —*Midwest Book Review*

"Super . . . The lead protagonists are a charming duo and the support characters add depth . . . Kathryn Shay's tale is a beautiful Christmas story." —*Painted Rock Reviews*

CLOSE TO YOU

KATHRYN SHAY

BERKLEY SENSATION, NEW YORK

THE BERKLEY PUBLISHING GROUP
Published by the Penguin Group
Penguin Group (USA) Inc.
375 Hudson Street, New York, New York 10014, USA
Penguin Group (Canada), 90 Eglinton Avenue East, Suite 700, Toronto, Ontario M4P 2Y3, Canada
(a division of Pearson Penguin Canada Inc.)
Penguin Books Ltd., 80 Strand, London WC2R 0RL, England
Penguin Group Ireland, 25 St. Stephen's Green, Dublin 2, Ireland (a division of Penguin Books Ltd.)
Penguin Group (Australia), 250 Camberwell Road, Camberwell, Victoria 3124, Australia
(a division of Pearson Australia Group Pty. Ltd.)
Penguin Books India Pvt. Ltd., 11 Community Centre, Panchsheel Park, New Delhi—110 017, India
Penguin Group (NZ), 67 Apollo Drive, Mairangi Bay, Auckland 1311, New Zealand
(a division of Pearson New Zealand Ltd.)
Penguin Books (South Africa) (Pty.) Ltd., 24 Sturdee Avenue, Rosebank, Johannesburg 2196, South Africa

Penguin Books Ltd., Registered Offices: 80 Strand, London WC2R 0RL, England

This is a work of fiction. Names, characters, places, and incidents either are the product of the author's imagination or are used fictitiously, and any resemblance to actual persons, living or dead, business establishments, events, or locales is entirely coincidental. The publisher does not have any control over and does not assume any responsibility for author or third-party websites or their content.

CLOSE TO YOU

A Berkley Sensation Book / published by arrangement with the author

PRINTING HISTORY
Berkley Sensation mass-market edition / February 2007

Copyright © 2007 by Mary Catherine Schaefer.
Cover art and design by Springer Design Group.
Interior text design by Stacy Irwin.

ISBN: 978-0-425-21450-3

BERKLEY SENSATION®
Berkley Sensation Books are published by The Berkley Publishing Group,
a division of Penguin Group (USA) Inc.,
375 Hudson Street, New York, New York 10014.
BERKLEY SENSATION is a registered trademark of Penguin Group (USA) Inc.
The "B" design is a trademark belonging to Penguin Group (USA) Inc.

PRINTED IN THE UNITED STATES OF AMERICA

10 9 8 7 6 5 4 3 2 1

CLOSE TO YOU

ONE

Secret Service Agent C.J. Ludzecky and her three colleagues hustled into New York City's Memorial Hospital on the heels of the Second Lady and the vice president of the United States. Though she kept her emotions at bay when she was on the job, C.J. couldn't help but empathize with Bailey O'Neil, the vice president's wife of two years. She remembered well the night her own father had died in an institution far too similar to this one. She'd been fifteen, and she and her brother, Lukasz, had taken it the hardest, probably because they were the oldest of his eight children. Briefly, C.J. wondered how Bailey's brothers were faring. Embedded in her memory was the image of holding a weeping Luke in her arms. His vulnerability had crushed her. She considered saying a prayer for this family, but dismissed the notion; she didn't believe in that anymore.

The group of six reached the admittance desk and were met by a man dressed in an impeccable suit. "Mr. Vice President. Ms. O'Neil. I'm sorry to meet you under these circumstances. I'm James Jones. I manage New York Memorial."

Bailey and Clay shook hands with the administrator. "Thank you for coming in at this hour," the vice president said.

C.J. watched Clay slide his arm around his wife's shoulders; Bailey leaned into him. They had to be the most demonstrative political couple she'd ever encountered in the six years she'd been with the service. Their open affection for each other was often a topic of discussion among the who's who in Washington—much of it not always kind. Since Bailey was four months pregnant, Clay was even more attentive than usual.

As they spoke with the doctor, C.J. scanned the forty-by-forty hospital reception area. The other three agents did the same, though her partner, Mitch Calloway, who headed the Second Lady's detail, and Tim Jenkins, the special agent in charge of the vice presidential force, moved in close to the protectees.

"I'll show you the way." The hospital administrator glanced at the agents, then back to the Second Couple. "All of you, I guess."

Calloway looked over at C.J. About forty, he had shrewd brown eyes and dark hair accented by a touch of gray at the temples. Nodding to the other side of the room, he signaled her to take note. A striking redheaded woman was arguing with a . . . uh-oh, a man with a camera. Damn it, how had the media gotten wind of the vice president's midnight trek on Marine Two, the VP helicopter, from Washington to New York? And how did they get past the uniformed guards at the entrance to the hospital? True, the service hadn't had time to do any advance work because this was an emergency. But, still . . .

Irked, C.J. strode across the area. When she reached the pair, their disagreement was in full swing.

The female stood tall on her three-inch heels. Apparently she was digging them in. "I said no, Ross. We're not intruding on them. We're leaving right now."

"Yes," C.J. said, drawing herself up to her full five-eight height. "You are."

The cameraman, a wiry wrestler-type, peered over half glasses at her. "Yeah? Who says?"

Brushing back the tailored jacket of her black suit, C.J. exposed her semiautomatic, then flashed her badge. They could guess who she was by her suit and the American flag pin on her lapel, along with her earpiece, but a little show of force never hurt. "The United States Secret Service. No media here, hotshot." She shook her head and let her usually even temper spike. "Can't you people be humane for once? This is a family emergency."

"First Amendment gives us—"

The woman stepped forward, sending a fall of auburn hair into her eyes and perfume wafting toward C.J. "I'm Rachel Scott. Our TV station, WNYC, got a tip that Vice President Wainwright and his wife had arrived in town and were headed to Memorial. But we won't intrude. Obviously a family member is more ill than we anticipated. We'll be leaving."

"Thank you. I'll follow you out." C.J.'s comment was neutral, as she'd been trained in responding to questions.

Don't confirm or deny the press's comments. Usually they're on a fishing expedition. If you agree with them, they'll phrase it like you said the words. Her first boss, David Anderson, had given her good advice on all aspects of being an agent. He'd been her mentor, until he turned on her, which still made her furious, except that it led to her working with Mitch in the D.C. field office. When Mitch had gotten into the coveted VPPD, the Vice Presidential Protective Division, he'd often called on her to substitute for agents or when extra protection was needed. After a year, one of the Second Lady's personal agents cycled out in the customary rotation of agents, and Bailey had asked for C.J. to join their detail permanently. That was how she'd come to such a plum position with not even a decade in the service under her belt.

Because she saw to it that the press exited through the front door without taking any detours, and turned them over to the uniformed agents standing post outside, C.J. had to find her own way to the CCU. As she traversed the corridors, she said into her wrist unit, part of the service's restrictive radio network, "Reporters are history. I'm on my way back."

"Understood," Mitch said. "We're at the CCU with Bulldog and Bright Star."

Code names were given to protectees, usually indicative of their personalities. Clay Wainwright was known for fighting relentlessly for the rights of others, and Bailey was a standout on the Hill because she didn't play politics.

The smell of *hospital* assaulted C.J. as she made the trip upstairs. Antiseptic, ripe food and something best left unidentified abused her senses. She remembered the odors. She associated them with death. For Bailey's sake, C.J. hoped her own visceral reaction was wrong this time.

Her three colleagues, Clay and Bailey were in the corridor outside of CCU talking to a doctor whose tag read, Edward Crane, *Chief of Cardiology*. The vice president of the most powerful country in the world commanded top people's attention. C.J. came up next to Mitch, who threw her a quick nod.

"Mr. O'Neil is resting now. We've given him a sedative." The doctor's voice was soothing. "We've run some tests to assess his condition and make a determination on how to proceed. I've called in our best cardiac surgeon and his team." Glancing at his watch, he added, "I expect them any minute."

Bailey leaned into Clay. "What's the prognosis?"

C.J. had to smile, despite the circumstances. Though she'd only been the Second Lady's permanent shadow for a few months, she'd followed the news accounts of the woman's whirlwind career as the wife of the vice president. It was public knowledge that Bailey and Clay had a history; first, as a young district attorney, he'd put her in jail for harboring a criminal. After that, for almost a decade, they'd disagreed on the best way to stop youth gangs, and had battled out their different views in the newspapers. But two years ago, when they were assigned to the same task force by the governor of New York, they'd fallen hard for each other, and thumbed their noses at the political world. From what C.J. understood, they'd fought like hell to be together. In any case, Bailey O'Neil was a perfect role model for teenage girls and women alike. C.J. truly valued her assignment protecting the Second Lady, even though there had been some nasty gossip about how she'd gotten the position.

The doctor continued analyzing the patient's condition. "It appears Mr. O'Neil had a major heart attack. Your brother tells us he had the classic symptoms—chest pain, shortness of breath, discomfort in his arm. Mr. O'Neil, the son, called 911 and administered aspirin, which helped."

"Will Pa be all right?" Bailey asked, her voice shaky.

"We won't know that for a while. We've already done some tests to determine the amount of blockage. It wore him out, and made him anxious, which is why he's sedated. The cardiologist and his team will determine the extent of the heart trauma and a course of action when they get here."

"What might that include?"

The doctor glanced to Clay when he asked the question. "It depends on the amount of blockage. It could mean angioplasty, or some form of surgery. But we're getting ahead of ourselves. I hate to commit, Vice President Wainwright, until the surgeon can give us his opinion."

A woman who'd hovered behind them—she wore a hospital badge that read Janice Denny—cleared her throat.

"I'll show you to the private waiting room. The rest of your family is there, Ms. O'Neil."

Bailey frowned. "Can I see Pa first?"

"Yes, of course." The doctor's smile was sympathetic. "One person at a time is allowed into the room. He's alone now, as your mother took a break. Try not to wake him up."

"Hold on." Mitch spoke with the air of a man used to being obeyed. "An agent will have to accompany Ms. O'Neil."

"Into the CCU?" the doctor asked.

"Yes, I'm afraid so."

"Isn't that a bit excessive?"

"We didn't have time to do thorough advance checks on your personnel or the hospital rooms themselves. If the press downstairs knows we're here, others could, too."

Tim Jenkins stepped forward. His kind eyes and boyish charm were deceptive. He said with the authority of an SAIC, special agent in charge, "One of your team should go to the waiting room and check the area out while Ms. O'Neil is in with her father. We'll stay here with the vice president until you let us know all's clear."

"I want C.J. to come with me," Bailey told them.

The Second Lady accepted the protection of the Secret Service willingly. Only the vice president was required by law to have it. On occasion Bailey let it slip in conversation that it was hard for her to have the agents around all the time. But she knew they were needed to protect her and her children, especially because she was so high profile, due to her gang work in New York. And she did her best not to take her annoyance out on the agents. Mitch had told C.J. horror stories about presidents like L.B.J. mistreating his protectives, and even some vice presidential wives trying to dodge the service's watch over them.

C.J. stepped forward, her face blank. "Whatever you want, Ms. O'Neil." Agents always addressed the protectees formally.

The doctor opened the door to the private CCU room, a privilege given to them because of the patient's relationship to the vice president. When the doctor moved back, Bailey and C.J. stepped inside. Bailey stood by the door and stared at the bed. Then she grasped C.J.'s hand. The Second Lady was such a toucher, it often surprised C.J.

Still, C.J. squeezed her fingers. "It's all right. Go on over."

A nurse sat in a chair in the corner. C.J. followed Bailey and stopped a discreet distance away, while Bailey sat down at her father's side. Machines at the head of the bed beeped and whooshed; the soft sounds of muted phones and footsteps filtered in from the corridor.

"Hi, Pa," Bailey whispered, lightly touching Patrick O'Neil's limp hand. There were tears in her eyes. "It's me, your girl. I'm here in New York, and I'm going to stay until you get better." Some sniffling. "I love you so much. Please, come out of this. Get better. I'm not ready for you to leave us yet." She placed a hand on her stomach. "Clay and I are having another boy. We're going to name him after you." She kissed her father's head. "Please, Pa."

Before she lost control, even a modicum of it, C.J. averted her gaze. She was used to quelling her personal feelings, though she'd known this trip to New York would test that skill. Ever since she'd joined the Secret Service, straining her relationship with her family and being subjected to unfair rumors among the agents, she'd hardened her heart. Getting weepy and sentimental about the situation had no place in her life now.

AIDAN O'NEIL stood by a window in the private waiting room with its stuffed couches and subtle lighting, staring down ten stories at the taxis and stalwart motorists who braved New York City in July at midnight. When he heard a commotion behind him, he steeled himself for this encounter. He'd been holding it together, but he knew Bailey's arrival would test his strength. And right now, he was afraid he'd fail miserably.

Pivoting, he watched his baby sister come into the room; he had to smile at the sight of her. The Second Lady of the United States of America was dressed in jeans and a light blue top that revealed her just-beginning-to-swell stomach. Her hair was in a messy braid. The vice president wore jeans and a sweater.

Bailey rushed to their mother; the two women hugged, then Bailey sat down and held Ma's hand. Before long, Aidan's brothers approached them. By order of age, they embraced their sister. Aidan grinned thinking of the nicknames Bailey had given them all. Patrick, the oldest, enveloped Bailey in his strong arms. He was physically bigger than the rest of them, but had the same dark hair, blue eyes and Irish wit they shared. He was dubbed The Fighter. Dylan, the next oldest, sported the broadest shoulders, which dwarfed Bailey when he kissed her head. She called him The Taunter. Tall and lanky, Liam, The Manipulator, held Bailey in a death grip. Also the most sensitive of them, he wiped his eyes when he drew back. There were murmurs among them.

Aidan noticed the bodyguards lined up like soldiers behind the foursome. He'd met all of them but the woman, who'd been permanently assigned to Bailey three months ago. The men were about his height, a touch over six feet, and muscular. She was around five feet eight, with steely blond hair pulled off her face. Standing poker straight in her black suit and severe white blouse, she rarely took her eyes off Bailey.

When his sister spotted him on the other side of the room, she broke away from their brothers and approached him.

Please don't let me break down. It wouldn't be good for her.

Bailey enveloped him in an embrace. She smelled the same, like lilacs, though she felt a bit heavier with the weight of her pregnancy. They shared the long hug wordlessly. No need to talk. The two of them were still as much on the same page as they'd always been, despite her sojourn in D.C. for two years. Finally they drew back. When he caught sight of tears on her cheeks, he wiped them with his thumbs. "Hormones wacky again, B.?"

"Yeah." She cradled his cheek in her palm. "You don't have to be so strong, you know. You can cry, too."

"I've had my moments."

"It's bad, isn't it? The guys are putting up a front for Ma, but I can tell they're really worried."

He'd heard the EMTs. *Myocardial infarction.* Which meant part of the heart had died. "Yeah, honey, it's bad."

"You were with him?"

Aidan felt his pulse pound like a thousand drums. Of anyone, he could tell this woman the truth. But he wouldn't lay it on her now. "Uh-huh." He glanced over Bailey's shoulder to the female agent standing by the door. "I haven't met your new watchdog."

"What? Oh, no, you haven't." She turned and smiled at the woman. "C.J., come here."

Long strides brought the agent to them. C.J.? What the hell kind of name was that for a girl? The fairer sex should be named Adriana, Lorena, Sophia.

"C.J. Ludzecky, this is my brother Aidan. He's the youngest of them."

A small smile softened the agent's mouth. "Nice to meet you, Mr. O'Neil."

He snorted. "Better not call me that, darlin', or you'll have the four of us doing a heads-up. Make it Aidan."

"Thanks, but I prefer Mr. O'Neil."

He noticed she didn't offer her own first name. What was he supposed to call her, Agent Ludzecky? Shit, what the hell did it matter? Where was his *mind*? His father lay dying in a hospital room right down the corridor and Aidan was wondering about formalities.

Clay came up to them and gave Aidan a bear hug. From their open affection for each other, a spectator would never guess Aidan had once decked the future vice president in Bailey's living room because he thought Clay was playing her. "You okay, buddy?"

"Yeah."

Clay touched his wife's shoulder. "You have to sit down, honey." She didn't move. "Now."

"I want to know what happened first."

Clay nudged Aidan. "Help me out here."

"Let's sit and we'll talk."

They chose a furniture grouping away from the others; Aidan took a chair and Bailey and Clay sank down onto a sofa. Again, the agent stood several feet away.

"Where, when and how?" Bailey asked. "Paddy didn't have details on the phone."

To stem the rush of guilt, Aidan took a deep breath. "Pa and I were in the back room of the pub." The O'Neils owned and ran Bailey's Irish Pub on MacDougal Street. "We were having a beer, watching over Shea and Mikey." The sons and daughters of his brothers often accompanied their dads to work. A bedroom/play area was set up in the back, and the adults took turns staying with them. Though Aidan was the only sibling who'd never married, nor had kids of his own, he often babysat. "We were talking and watching the end of the Yankees game."

Aidan swallowed hard. Ever vigilant, and because she knew him too well, Bailey would sense something in him if he wasn't careful with his words; she could be a pit bull when she wanted information. "We got into it, like we do sometimes. As usual, Pa got himself stirred up. And then he clutched his heart. Started to sweat. He said his arm was feeling funny." Damn it. Aidan's voice cracked on the last word.

Because he could still see his father, furious at him . . .

"You want to leave the pub? To take *pictures*?"

Aidan had kept his professional goals from his father for a long time, but he'd decided that night the subject needed to be broached. "Pa, it's more than taking pictures. I wanna be a photographer full-time, to do that with my life. I don't want to work at the pub anymore. Besides, if I leave, Dylan and Liam can give up their second jobs."

Long ago, his father had made it clear he expected his sons to take over the family business. Aidan knew the need to keep them close was because he'd already lost one child. Since none of the boys had ever balked, it had worked for everybody. Until now.

"You can't make a living taking pictures, son."

Usually, Aidan was careful to quell his anger at Pa's dismissal of his talent. This time it had bubbled to the surface, probably because Pa had voiced one of Aidan's insecurities—deep down, he felt inadequate about going out on his own. Still he fought for the chance. "Damn it, Pa, I can. I've worked at it since I got out of college. I've sold photos to a lot of different magazines here in New York. Last month, I won this prize, and was contacted by . . ."

He never finished explaining the Ansel Adams international photography prize he'd won, and how he'd been offered a probationary job at a reputable photography magazine because of it. The heart attack had come fast and furious, taking down his big, robust father within seconds. Mother Nature could strike vehemently, and that night she'd been in top form.

Bailey asked, "Aidan? Are you all right?"

"Yeah, sure."

His sister shook her head, rose and knelt before him. She grasped both his hands in hers. "A., you're not blaming yourself, are you? We all get into it with Pa. Your fight was about the stupid Yankees."

"Watch your mouth, girl. The Yanks are sacred ground."

"Aidan." She squeezed his fingers.

"No, I'm not feeling guilty. I feel bad, though."

She studied his face until Clay came to her side. "Up, woman."

"I'm not an invalid, Clay. For God's sake, I'm pregnant."

"I know. But you need to rest. Now get up and sit on that couch. Put your feet on the table."

His sister stood and squared off with her husband. Usually Aidan loved to watch these little tiffs, but not tonight.

Clay cut it off at the pass, anyway. "Sweetheart, it's going to be a long night." His tone was tender. "Conserve your energy."

She leaned into him. "All right. Before I sit, though, I have to use the ladies' room." She peered down at Aidan. "But we're not done with this."

"Okay. Go for now."

Aidan knew he'd tell Bailey the truth eventually, but for tonight, no one but him needed to deal with the fact that he might very well have killed his father.

Two

DAWN WAS BREAKING, but C.J. surveyed the waiting room area with crisp alertness. Bailey was sound asleep, stretched out on a couch, her head resting on the vice president's lap. Clay had propped his legs up on a table, his own head thrown back; he was dozing, too. At six a.m., most of the O'Neils were either sleeping or resting quietly with their thoughts. Liam had his arm around his mother, holding her close. The support and love in this room was tangible. It made C.J. sad to be around what she once had and lost, by her own making.

When the homey scene became suffocating, she crossed to Mitch. "I'm going to the john."

Wide awake, he rubbed his hand over his stubbly jaw. "Do me a favor?"

"Maybe. If you're nice."

Even though he was the head of Bailey's detail, and technically her boss, she could tease him because they had a special bond. He was one of the few people in the service who knew her whole history. Since he'd once been in the interrogation division, over the four years she'd known him, he'd dragged everything out of her.

"Check up on Aidan. He's been gone a half hour."

"You don't think he's in any danger, do you?" Kidnapping of a protectee's family was always a looming threat. However, the danger was usually to the spouse and children.

"No, I don't. But like I said at CCU, since the media was here, other people could know we're in town. Grayson"—another of Bailey's agents—"is checking the morning news to see if our presence here is public knowledge. I'd feel better keeping track of this whole family for a while."

"Sure. Any idea where he is?"

Dylan had awakened and was crossing to the coffeepot. He stopped by them. "I overheard you asking about Aidan. My guess is he's in the chapel."

That surprised her. It shouldn't, though. These people were Irish and Catholic. Not unlike her Polish family, who prayed before every meal and went to church every single Sunday.

C.J. hit the ladies' room, then went in search of the chapel. She found a small one down the corridor from the private waiting area. The space housed only eight pews, an altar and a wooden cross. On the outside walls were stained-glass windows. Like many churches, candles scented the air. Aidan sat in one of the pews, his shoulders slumped and his head bent, his blue thermal top stretching across broad shoulders. She was about to go inside, when she realized he was talking.

She should leave—he was safe—but she didn't. For some reason, his words, spoken aloud, mesmerized her. So she stepped into the shadows and blatantly eavesdropped.

"I'm sorry." His voice was sandpapery. "I didn't think . . . I didn't know . . . Oh, hell, I knew Pa would be pissed that I wanted to leave the business. He has this thing about keep-

ing us boys together, but I thought he'd understand. I expected he'd fuss, but in the end, he'd give me his blessing.
Damn it!"

C.J. hadn't ever heard anybody swear at God.

"If you let him be okay, I'll stay. I'll forget about the
stupid prize. The chance to do my photography full-time. I
promise, I . . ."

As she listened to his words, caught the hoarse tone of
his voice, C.J.'s throat got tight. She was well acquainted
with the kind of deal he was trying to make with God.
When her brother was a Secret Service agent, she'd done
the same thing. *If Lukasz is okay, and calls this Monday
like always, I'll go to Mass an extra day . . . If he comes
home for a little while, I'll be nicer to the twins.* And then
that heart-stopping time he'd been undercover trying to
ferret out suspected school violence and was beaten badly
by some punks . . . *Please, please, God, if you let him re-
cover, I'll stay in New York and take care of* Matka.

The last was a promise C.J. had broken. Lukasz had
gotten better, then the roof caved in a few months later
when she told her family that instead of continuing her
work as an interpreter at the UN, she had new career plans
she'd been putting in place for months. Because they
couldn't understand her choices, she entered the service
under strained circumstances. Her contact with her family
now was limited, though she was on the Ludzecky e-mail
loop, which she read vigilantly but didn't post much. What
could she say? For the same reasons, she didn't go home to
Queens much to visit.

Apparently, the weeping man in the front pew had also
tried to find his own way by breaking off from the family
business, and now felt he caused his father's heart attack.
That was dumb, but guilt, C.J. knew, could be as irrational
as hope.

She moved in the half-open doorway, which made her
presence known.

He turned around. "Who's there?"

"Agent Ludzecky. I've come to see if you're all right."

No answer.

"Mr. O'Neil?"

"Come in a minute."

Again she hesitated. The *thing* inside her that made her a top-notch agent—knowing when to check out someone in a crowd, when to put herself in front of Bailey or the kids, when to draw her piece—stirred inside her. Talking to this man alone wasn't a good idea. Still, she made the short trip down the aisle. He scooted over, signaling for her to sit. "I'll go back . . ." His face blanked. "Oh, shit, has something changed with Pa?"

"No, no. My partner wanted me to check on you. We're being overly vigilant because there was a reporter in the reception area when we came in, and"—she shrugged—"we'd rather be safe than sorry."

"Glad to hear that. My sister's welfare is vital to me."

She wanted to comment on how close they seemed, but didn't. *Stay detached*, she warned herself. *Stay distant from these people who were filled with so much love it was palpable.*

As if he knew her thoughts, he said, "We're so close. It's spooky sometimes."

Smiling, she remembered Luke's words . . . *Christ, Cat, you can read my mind. That's spooky.*

Aidan glanced over at the woman beside him. He'd watched her during the night, was intrigued by her demeanor. And he'd appreciated the distraction from his own worry over Pa that she'd provided. "Do you have a family, Agent Ludzecky?"

For a minute she'd relaxed, but now the starch stiffened up her body again. "I, um, yes. Of course, I do."

"Where?"

"Where what?"

"Where are you from?"

"Here, New York. Queens."

"Will you see them this trip?"

She'd been staring ahead, but now she looked at him. "No, I don't have time off like regular people. I . . ." She stopped herself, as if she'd said more than she wanted to. "It's not protocol to talk about my personal life with you."

Her brows were thick, unplucked and wheat colored. Up close he could see that her eyes were a light brown, almost amber, with flecks of green sprinkled in. Their shape was unique. He wanted to photograph just those eyes.

He said finally, "Surely your . . . code, or whatever it is, doesn't mean you can't make polite chitchat."

"It's recommended we don't get friendly with protectees or their families."

"I can't believe Bailey lets you get away with that."

A chuckle escaped her. "No, she doesn't like distance. But mostly it's the little ones . . ."

When she trailed off, Aidan seized on her slip. "How are my niece and nephew? I assume Anika is taking care of them tonight." Their German nanny was a delight and Aidan loved to flirt with her and make her blush.

"Yes, she is."

"I helped raise Rory, you know. You call him Bruiser, right?"

"You shouldn't know that," she said scowling. Code names were supposed to be kept from the public and press.

"I do. Apt name."

She seemed to smile in spite of herself. "We had him designated as Buddy, but he found out and wanted a manly name. He's a pistol." C.J. shook her head, looking more woman than agent. "He hounds the vice president to tag along with him. Mr. Wainwright takes Rory everywhere he can and the staff has to scuttle to accommodate them. They love the kid, of course; he's become sort of a mascot at the offices."

Since she was more comfortable with this topic, he

pursued it. "How about Angel?" He winked at C.J. "Blue Eyes, right?"

Her gaze narrowed on him.

"I hate that I don't get to spend much time with her."

"She's beautiful." So was Agent Ludzecky's face, when it got all soft and feminine, like now, as she began talking about Angel. "She's into everything since she got the hang of walking. And running."

"Bay called me when she took her first steps. Angel did that late, didn't she?"

"Yes. That's because everybody *does* everything for her. I remember when my sister Elizabeita was born. We all jumped when she wanted food or a toy . . ."

"Elizabeita is a beautiful name. What does C.J. stand for?"

"Huh?" Shoulders tensed. Agent Ludzecky resurfaced.

He wondered what kind of woman hid beneath the light wool suit, was tucked away in the knot she'd pulled her hair into.

"I asked what C.J. stood for."

Abruptly she stood. "I should be getting back. I—"

Someone came to the doorway. They both turned around. C.J.'s hand slipped inside her suit coat and Aidan caught a glint of silver at her hip.

One of Clay's agents, Jenkins, stood poised in the back of the chapel. Aidan had spent some time in his presence and liked him. "Aidan, Ludzecky, come with me."

Alarmed, Aidan bolted up. "Is, is . . ." He reached out and grabbed C.J.'s arm. Clutched it.

"Everybody's fine. The cardiologist is ready to talk to you. His team has a diagnosis."

Aidan's body felt ready to implode. "Any good news?"

"I don't have that information. Calloway radioed me when I went to do a sweep of the halls." Jenkins walked halfway down the aisle and his eyes narrowed on Aidan's grip on C.J.

She said, "Come on, Mr. O'Neil. Let's go see what's happening with your father."

"AS YOU KNOW, Mr. O'Neil has had a heart attack. The problem is in two of his arteries—one is ninety percent closed, the other is completely blocked." Dr. Hargrove frowned. "Our recommendation is that surgery be performed this morning."

Liam's mother, Mary Kate O'Neil, grasped onto his arm. "So soon?"

Glancing at his watch, the cardiac surgeon nodded. He was a tall man with a shock of salt-and-pepper hair, kind brown eyes and an air of authority, which felt good right now. "The team's here. We can get started ASAP."

"How serious is his condition?" Liam asked, thinking about the frailty of human life. Three years ago his wife, Kitty, had succumbed to cancer. Though the pain had dulled, and he could get up in the morning now without having to force himself from the bed, he was worried about his family weathering yet another loss if Pa didn't make it. The fact that his full-of-piss-and-vinegar father might die just about broke his heart.

"Mr. O'Neil needs a double bypass. There's significant risk from any surgery," the doctor told them. "But there's more risk for your father if we were to leave his condition unattended. I've done hundreds of these operations—they're fairly routine now. And he's in decent shape for a man nearing seventy."

Next to their mother, Bailey leaned into Aidan, who had his arm around her. The blond Secret Service agent stood across the room. Bailey said, "Dad walks every day."

"And eats right. I make him," their mother added.

"All that's going to help his recovery." Dr. Hargrove looked to Clay. "I take it you're comfortable in this waiting area. Do you need anything sent up?"

Clay glanced at Bailey. "We're comfortable. Mrs. Denny is helping the agents with food for us."

"For security reasons," Mitch put in, "we don't want to spend time in the cafeteria. Besides, the food has to be checked or brought in specifically for the vice president."

The doctor looked surprised. Liam wasn't. Once Clay had been elected, he'd studied up on the protection available to his brother-in-law and sister. Given 9/11 and also Bailey's gang activities, both she and Clay received special attention. In addition to their personal agents who were inside the room, two others had stood as sentries in the corridor, while agents in uniform were outside the hospital. Cleary, his twelve-year-old, would've gotten a kick out of seeing them—he was fascinated by Bailey's position as wife of the VP. Not so with Mikey. Since Kitty died and Bailey moved away, the boy was getting more and more introverted. And now Pa was sick. Liam shuddered thinking about the effect of his father's illness on his younger boy. Since Bailey left town for Washington, a semiretired Paddy O'Neil had stepped in and spent more time with his troubled grandson.

Mary Kate clasped Liam's arm. "The little ones? They're taken care of?"

"Yes, Mama," Patrick said. "Brie's got Cleary and Mikey, and our kids." Pat's wife was a godsend in an emergency. "And Hogan's with his mother." Dylan's ex wasn't around much, but she was in town this week. At thirteen, his son Hogan was torn about his mother's absences, as he had been when they were together.

"With the new baby, can Brie handle everything?"

"We got help, Mama."

Things still weren't right with Liam's oldest brother and his wife, Brie, either. They'd been separated for more than a year. Then she'd gotten pregnant after she hooked up with Pat one night, and they'd reconciled—sort of. Liam and Brie were close; she was a big help with Mikey, and because of proximity, he knew about the strain in their relationship. It was obvious Paddy was having a hard time.

"Can we see Pa before his surgery?" This from Bailey.

"Of course. You can go in one at a time." The doctor nodded to Clay. "Except for you two. Your bodyguards can accompany you."

Clay shook his head. "That won't be necessary. Our agents have swept CCU and are in the corridor now. The nurse has also been checked out. They can stand post outside the door."

Dr. Hargrove glanced at his watch. "Make it fast. We need to prep him within the half hour."

Liam's mother went into the CCU first, and the others settled on various couches. Over the next half hour, they visited Pa. When Liam's turn came up, he went inside the room with hesitant steps. His big, strong father was attached to machines and his color was grayish. Pretending to be cool, like he always did with his family these days or they'd hover, he sat in the chair next to the bed. "Hey, Pa."

"Son." His father reached for Liam's hand. Blue veins stood out on his skin, which had gotten leathery with age. "How's Mikey?"

"He doesn't know about your heart attack yet."

"I'm worried about him. How he'll take this."

So am I. "You worry about yourself. I'll take care of my boy."

"Too much loss," Pa mumbled, closing his eyes.

Liam leaned over and kissed his father's head. "Rest, Pa."

When he returned to the waiting room, he noticed Aidan, standing by the window, staring out as the city woke up. Liam crossed to him. "Your turn, buddy."

Aidan shook his head. "I think I'll hold off. Don't want to tire him out."

"Something's wrong." Liam kept his tone calm. He'd been watching his kid brother through the night. "Spill it."

"I'm worried about Pa is all."

"Nope, it's more than that."

Blue eyes full of pain focused on him. "I did something. I can't talk about it."

"Is it about Pa?"

Aidan nodded.

"Can you talk to Bailey?"

Though sometimes it rankled, the other brothers pretty much accepted Bailey and Aidan's special bond. They were only a year apart, and they'd gone to college in Rochester together. Paddy and Liam never went on with their education after high school, though five years ago, Dylan surprised everybody by getting a degree in journalism from Columbia without anybody in the family knowing he'd been attending classes.

"I'll talk to her about it. Later."

"I think you should see Pa."

"Not now."

Remembering his own searing loss, Liam touched Aidan's arm. "You may not have another chance, kid. I think he's going to be all right, but you can never tell."

His brother's eyes misted. "You're right. I know. I . . ."

"I'll go in with you, if you want."

"They said one at a time."

He nodded to C.J. "She went in with Bailey when they first got here."

Aidan gave a boyish shrug and some of his charm seeped out from his grim exterior. "Yeah, but you're not as pretty."

"She's pretty?"

Aidan shook his head. "Gotta start noticing those things again, bro."

"I know, I will. Now let's go see Pa."

"All right."

They headed out together, passing the agents. He guessed the woman was pretty. For thirty-six months and three weeks, Liam had been in a kind of frozen state, an emotional suspended animation. He never noticed women. But acknowledging the agent's looks might signal his coming out of it.

Which scared the hell out of him. Like frostbite warming up, he knew the return of these feelings was going to hurt. But he banished the fear. His family needed him now and he'd put their welfare first.

THREE

"YOUR DEAL, KID." Patrick drummed his fingers on the table when Aidan hesitated. "Come on, get with the program."

Dragging himself from the thoughts that haunted him since last night at nine when his father had crumpled to the ground before his eyes, Aidan picked up the cards and began to shuffle. The swish of the deck seemed loud in the quiet room.

They'd all tried sitting around, had dozed some, but once the four-hour operation began at eight a.m., none of the O'Neil brothers could sit still. Dylan had suggested playing euchre. Aidan glanced over to see Bailey was asleep again. Pregnancies tired her out. Agent Ludzecky was also catching some winks. Mitch Calloway was standing near the table watching them play and periodically scanning the room. Bailey's two watchdogs had been taking turns getting some rest. He wondered what kind of life they led; from what he'd heard about the profession, he was glad it wasn't his, or anybody he was involved with.

One card, two cards, three, four, five. Lucky him, he turned over a jack of spades. Paddy passed. Dylan said, "Pick it up. I'll take it alone." That meant Dyl had a great hand if he didn't need the right bower and could kick his partner out of play in order to earn four points instead of two.

Aidan watched as Dylan demolished his brothers. Listened to Patrick swear. Liam mumble. Dylan gloat.

Over all of it, he heard the chief of cardiology's words. Pa had fallen back asleep after Aidan got out an apology and a kiss on the forehead. Just as he and Liam exited the room, they'd seen Dr. Hargrove at the nurse's station and Liam had pounced. His brother loved facts. He'd been an information junkie when his kids were born, had learned everything there was to know about Kitty's ovarian cancer and had studied up on the Secret Service when Bailey had become the Second Lady.

Liam approached the doctor in his typical low-key manner, something Aidan couldn't muster if you'd bribed him with a date with Julianne Moore. "Dr. Crane. I was wondering if you could tell us the procedure for the operation."

Everyone was quick to oblige the vice president's family. Aidan had stood by, listening to the detached way the doctor described the invasion of his father's body . . . the prep involved sedatives, muscle relaxants, anticoagulants and pain meds, IVs to the neck vein and bladder. Then they'd put tubes down his throat: one into the windpipe for the respirator, one in the stomach to collect fluids. The most gruesome part was the cutting of the sternum—Aidan had flinched when he'd heard the sound of the saw on a medical TV show. Then they'd cool the heart—how did they do that?—clamp the aorta, making holes in it. Simultaneously, another team would be working on removing two veins from Pa's leg to bypass the blocked spot, to detour the blood. He guessed he'd known open-heart surgery didn't correct the heart disease, but circumvented it. A lot like Aidan lived his life, by detouring around problems.

"Four points, bro." Dylan was trying to look at ease, but he kept glancing to the door and shifting his seat.

Patrick stood. "I can't do this anymore. I'm goin' for a walk."

Of all of them, Patrick had the most volatile relationship with their pa. It had something to do with the one time Pa strayed when their parents were separated, and the daughter he'd had with another woman. Pa didn't know about Moira until her mother died, and she'd come to live with them when she was fourteen. Moira and Bailey had gotten close, which was why his sister eventually got into fighting street gangs, as Moira had been a member of the GGs, the toughest New York girl gang. Patrick never forgave their father for what he considered Pa's infidelity. Aidan had been too young to know the ins and outs of it, and had just been glad when Pa came back.

Aidan looked over at his mother, who was sturdily built, with graying hair that had once been a deep auburn. Aidan had never admired her more than when she'd taken Moira in and treated her like family—and insisted the children do the same—for the short time Moira lived with them before she was killed in prison.

Aidan sensed someone come up behind him by a movement of the air, a faint female scent.

Calloway eased away from the wall and glanced at his watch. "You only slept an hour, C.J."

"It's enough for now."

"Suit yourself." Mitch crossed to the couch to stand behind it.

"She's out," C.J. said to no one in particular.

"Wish I was." There were grooves around Dylan's mouth and eyes. "I'm whipped. I was up the whole night before the attack covering a story."

C.J. didn't ask what else Dylan did for a living so Aidan

said, "We all work at the pub, and three of us have part-time jobs. Dylan does a column for a weekly news-magazine called *CitySights*."

She didn't ask for elaboration.

"Liam's a short-order cook for breakfasts at a diner nearby." He also cooked for the pub at lunch, got dinners ready, then went home to be with his kids for the evening.

The agent remained stone-faced, so Aidan didn't tell her what he did, and she didn't ask. It irked him for some reason. He liked women who were interested in him. Most women probed and prodded to keep his attention. Shit, she wasn't a woman, she was a robot. Again, the notion made him pissed off. A little human kindness was called for here. So he faced her with an attitude. "You could show some interest in our lives, Agent Ludzecky."

Mitch glanced over sharply. His brothers stared at him in shock. Why not? Bailey had dubbed him The Peacemaker of the family because he charmed the pants off everybody. Now he was acting like a first-class jerk.

She wasn't fazed, though. She said simply, "Unless it relates to guarding the vice president's wife, nothing about any of you is relevant."

That made him even madder. He threw back his chair and stood. Somewhere, he knew he wasn't angry at Agent Ludzecky, but at himself, and his father for ignoring warning signs. Hell, he was mad about life in general. Knowing that didn't stop him from going on the attack. "That family you mentioned earlier? Are they relevant?"

It was just a flicker. In those eyes that sparkled like good brandy. Then it was gone. Without a word, she turned and walked back to the couch. Positioning herself where she could see her charge, she folded her arms over her chest and looked straight ahead.

His brothers dispersed, and Aidan went back to his post by the window.

After a brief time, Agent Calloway came up to him. "Do me a favor." This didn't sound like a request. "Don't make a personal attack on one of my agents again."

Aidan was about to apologize when the surgeon entered the waiting room.

"WE HAVE a plan." Bailey's eyes were dancing with pleasure. And something else. Mischief. C.J. had seen that look before and it usually spelled more work for the service. The Second Lady's schemes often created a logistics nightmare. Like the time she decided to have a kids' Halloween party at the vice presidential residence on Observatory Way. She'd dressed up as a witch and insisted the vice president come as Frankenstein. She would have had the agents in ghost and goblin garb if she'd had her way. Thankfully, the Secret Service director had put his foot down. Though the whole thing had been fun to watch, the agents had scurried around all night, checking out parents, who were also in costume, coming and going.

"I don't think I want to hear this." Patrick, the oldest brother, leaned against the wall of the private room where his father had been transferred four days ago. Looking stern, he said, "Your plans spell trouble, lass."

C.J. glanced at Mitch. He shrugged, but she could tell he knew something about this, which was why she and Mitch were in the room for this family discussion.

The patient, who among themselves the service had begun calling Pa O'Neil to keep him and his son straight, shook his head. His color was better and his blue eyes alert. "What is it, girl?"

"I think we should all go to Clay's and my cottage on Keuka Lake for your recuperation. Or at least part of it. We'd need to be back at the beginning of August so Rory can go on the Boy Scout camping trip with Liam and Mikey."

Bailey and Clay still planned activities for Rory with the

O'Neil family, and those, too, had to be covered by the Secret Service. This camping trip required an agent to go along. Jerry Grayson had been designated, as he was male, and an outdoorsman.

C.J. had never been to the Wainwrights' secluded lake residence—hardly a cottage—on two acres of land in the picturesque Finger Lakes, though she'd seen photos and schematics of it in her VPPD training. She'd studied the layout of the house and grounds on her own time. The building itself wouldn't be hard to secure. As with each of the presidential and vice presidential private residences, the taxpayers' money had been spent to make the place safer by installing things like bulletproof glass on the banks of windows, a Fort Knox–type security system, closed-circuit cameras on the roof and fenced-in perimeters. The lakefront posed a problem, though. No one could control the waters themselves. When the vice president was on site, they'd need even more agent coverage.

"Define *us all*," Dylan said.

Bailey glanced at her husband, who gave her an encouraging nod. "Well, Mama and Pa, of course. Me and the kids would go with you."

From the corner where he stood, Liam frowned. Bailey smiled at him, as if she knew what he was thinking. "We could take Mikey, Liam. He's on summer vacation. I could spend the whole month of July with him. It might make up for missing me so much."

"That'd be great, Bay."

Having heard Bailey on the phone talking to her nephew Mike countless times, C.J. knew there was a bond between them; from what she'd picked up, the kid was having trouble since Bailey went to live in Washington.

"And Mikey could see firsthand Pa's doing fine," Bailey continued. "He didn't take the heart attack too well."

"What about Pa's rehab?" Patrick asked.

"Well, he's finished with Phase One." Which was hospital

care, advice about diet and exercise and medication decision making. "Phase Two can be done at the lake. We'll
have a private nurse come in three times a week to monitor
his physical progress and hire a therapist to work on his exercise plan with him, at least for a while."

Bailey's father grasped her hand. "I can't afford that, lass."

"I know, Pa. But Clay and I can."

Pa O'Neil was about to object—C.J.'s own pa would
have been outraged by the suggestion—when Bailey
played her first card. She placed her father's hand on her
belly. "Little Patrick in here wants his grandpa to get the
best care."

Still, Pa seemed unconvinced.

Clay stepped forward. "Actually, Patrick, you'd be doing me a favor. Bailey was supposed to go to Zanganesia
with me in a week on a goodwill tour."

"Where is that?"

"On the northwest border of China." He shot Bailey a
stern look. "I've thought all along that the travel might be
too much for her but couldn't convince her to beg off."

The emotion on the Second Lady's face wasn't faked.
Travel abroad was dangerous for the president and vice
president. The security was a nightmare. Three advance
visits by the service preceded any trip, and between those
and the number of agents needed for the travel itself, huge
amounts of man- and womanpower were required. So far
C.J. hadn't gone on one of these trips with the Second
Lady.

C.J. shook her head. And she hadn't planned on going
this time because Clay was fudging the truth. He and Bailey had fought over her going with him. Zanganesia had
been overrun with youth crime, and just after Clay took office, the prime minister had come to the United States and
sought out Clay's advice for cleaning up the small Asian
country. Many of Clay's suggestions had been imple-
mented and the country was getting back on its feet.

Because of her background with youth gangs, Bailey had been in on the discussion and wanted to take this trip with Clay, but when she got pregnant he opposed her going along. In the end, Bailey agreed not to go because of the jet lag a trip like that would cause and the always-lingering danger of native militants with a grudge against the U.S. They didn't tell Pa the issue had already been resolved, though.

"I'd rather have my daughter here in New York than in Asia, too." Pa O'Neil scowled. "What would I do up at the lake? It's out in the middle of nowhere."

"Not really, Pa. There are towns at either end of the lake. You'd rest. Visit with your grandkids. You complain you don't get to see Rory or Angel enough. Anyway, you're not gonna be dancing till dawn in the city. You have to take it easy anywhere you'll be." His daughter grinned. "You and me could fish, too. Like we did when we went up there before."

Not good. Fishing would require a lot of detail work.

Mary Kate O'Neil crossed to the bed and touched her husband's arm. "I could cook and take care of the kids." She glanced at her daughter. "You wouldn't be bringin' that nanny, would you?"

"No," Clay said. "I suggested Anika come along, but Bailey thinks she should have the time off to visit her family."

"I can take care of my own kids." Bailey surveyed her brothers. "But I *do* think one of the boys should go with us."

"Why?" Aidan asked. He still seemed grumpy and out of sorts. His attack earlier on C.J. had been unwarranted, and seemingly out of character for the guy, but she was able to ignore his remarks and cutting tone. Though it did smart a bit, probably because he'd hit bull's-eye about her family. She'd steered clear of him the last few days, and hoped *he* wasn't the one to go to the lake with them.

"Pa could need help," Bailey explained. "Lifting heavy stuff, that kind of thing."

"You'll be surrounded by Secret Service agents." Aidan again. "They can lift whatever."

"That's not their job," Clay put in. "Besides, Pa's needs might be personal at first and one of his sons should be there to assist him."

The oldest, Patrick, looked thoughtful. "Liam could go with Mikey. Cleary's going to the special computer camp for a few weeks. When he's home, Brie could take care of him, or Liam could bring him up there."

Dylan said, "We'd have to find a replacement cook at the pub first."

"Doesn't matter if you could. I got my other job mornings." Liam's brows knitted. "I could come up on my days off. Maybe even take some extra vacation."

Again, the oldest brother scowled. C.J. had learned how much responsibility he shouldered. "I'd go, but me leavin' the pub would be even harder."

"And I can't abandon Hogan now." Dylan's voice was strained when he talked about his son. "With Stephanie in town, he needs me around as a buffer."

Everybody looked to Aidan. "I work at the pub," he said weakly.

"My boys are off for the summer," Patrick put in. "Sinead's graduating high school. And Sean's fifteen. They could take up the table waiting you do, the heavy stuff. Me and Dylan can do extra shifts bartending and Bridget could come in a few extra hours."

Bridget was a part-time cook and bartender, C.J. knew. The service had checked everybody out who had a connection with the vice president's family.

Bailey zeroed in on Aidan. "You could take pictures at the lake. Think of the shots you could get on the water. There's some quaint areas near the cottage, too. Unbelievable landscapes. The magazines that publish your work will love the change of scenery from New York photos."

Pa O'Neil harrumphed.

Shoving his hands in his pockets, Aidan rocked back on his heels. "I guess I could do it." He glanced at Mitch. "I assume you two would go?"

"Them and more," Clay added. "There are agents up there already. To guard Jon before he left for France."

Clay's twenty-two-year-old son by a former marriage was going to study at the Sorbonne for the summer and had taken a break at the lake for a few weeks before he left.

"The agents who were guarding him made sure the cottage and the trailer on the property were secure for his visit. They swept the town, too. They'll stay on so we don't have to redo that security. And, since we'd prefer not to broadcast Bailey's location, people will think the security contingent is at the lake still guarding Jon."

Though the public knew the whereabouts of vacation homes for protectees, like Camp David, Mondale's spread and Reagan's ranch, the government tried to keep specific vacation plans on the QT.

"It'll get out eventually that Bailey's in residence, but she'll have some peace for a while, and be safer."

"I'll be plenty safe with C.J. and Mitch."

Mitch said, "Agent Ludzecky and I can cover Bailey, Angel and Rory. We'll bring in two more special agents for relief, and a few more uniforms to join the agents there."

Again, Aidan shook his head. "It sounds like a lot of work."

Giving them the infamous Calloway grin, Mitch shrugged. "We don't mind, do we, Agent Ludzecky?"

She minded. A lot. First, she preferred the routine. Protecting Bailey was easier in Washington or even at the New York town house. Second, she didn't like close-proximity details. They could be smothering. And spending time with this happy family would be hard for her personally. She shot a glance at Aidan. Not to mention *him*. They were at odds for some reason. But it was more than that. She had that feeling again, niggling at her. *Stay away from this guy.*

Hell. She also admitted to herself that she didn't want to be in the New York area because her own family was here. Her brother Luke lived only an hour from Keuka Lake. What if they found out she was nearby? Would they seek her out? Worse, if she was in the vicinity for any length of time and didn't call them, they'd be mad as hell. Even *Matka*.

"Agent Ludzecky?" Mitch's tone was all business.

She said only, "Of course we don't mind. When do we leave?"

FOUR

Dumping his gear on the taupe leather sofa that hid a pullout bed, Mitch surveyed the ground floor of Clay Wainwright's *cottage* on Keuka Lake. "This basement's nicer than my place in D.C."

"I wouldn't exactly call this a basement." C.J. yelled out her answer from across the hall, where she was stowing her things. "It's nicer than my apartment, too."

The ground floor had been specially built to function as the command post for the Secret Service. When more space than the six-person trailer on the back property was needed to house agents, some bunked down here. The room Mitch would occupy had a corner desk area with a fax/copier/phone system, the service's interactive radio network and monitors for the closed-circuit TVs, as well as the pullout. It was the center for agent communications, where they contacted the outside world and each other. Opposite that space was a room with another couch and pullout bed, where C.J. would sleep. It sported an exercise area, with a treadmill, punching bag and free weights.

The entire cottage was a showplace. The sketches she'd studied hadn't done it justice. Built into the side of a hill, this lower level had two rooms, a big bath and a sunroom facing the lake, with a walkout to its own stone patio. The main floor had rooms in the back and a larger sunroom and deck affording the breathtaking panoramic view. The lapping of the water on the shore, along with the smell of the seaweed and surrounding earth and grass, permeated the entire house.

When C.J. finished unpacking, she crossed to Mitch's side. "What time are we meeting with everybody?"

"Twenty-one hundred."

"We'd better get upstairs." She tugged at the collar of her white starched shirt. "It's hot in here."

"The air-conditioning isn't on but the windows should cool things off soon."

There were rows of windows on each side of the downstairs and floor-to-ceiling ones in the sunroom, all bulletproof. There was always some debate about whether the windows should be opened, but the Second Lady loved fresh air, and she usually won out.

They climbed the staircase to the first level. The sunroom up here was filled with overstuffed furniture and a wood-burning stove. Behind it was a huge kitchen with a center island the size of a bed, gleaming appliances and warm chestnut cabinetry. Off that was a dining area, behind it a bedroom and bath where Mr. and Mrs. O'Neil would stay. Tucked in a corner was the vice president's den. Upstairs were two small bedrooms and the Wainwrights' suite.

The huge banks of first-floor windows were open, letting in a warm breeze. Everyone wandered into the sunroom by eleven, except Aidan. Bailey had settled on one of the nubby white couches with a sleeping Angel, dressed in a pink romper and sprawled half on her mother, half on the cushions. Rory was playing a video game with his cousin

Mikey. Though the two of them were the same age—
seven—and had the O'Neil looks, Mikey seemed younger
and more fragile than Rory. Ma and Pa O'Neil were on the
other sofa, sitting close. The Wainwright family black Lab,
Hower, named after former Republican President Dwight
D. Eisenhower, whose foreign policies Clay admired, lay
in a pool of sunshine near the window.

Bailey addressed Mitch. "Ready to start?"

"Your brother's not here."

"Yeah, I am."

Turning, C.J. saw that Aidan had come down the stairs.
He wore simple navy trunks and a light blue T-shirt that out-
lined muscles she didn't know he had. Nice ones. His dark
hair—a bit long—caught the rays that peeked in through the
windows. "I was changing so me and the guys can hit the
water after we get our orders."

Mitch chuckled. "We'll be brief." They'd already done
some groundwork, assigning rooms, talking about the security alarms and the closed-circuit TV for the outdoors.
"We have a few more ground rules, and want to fill you in
on what we found out in our advance visit."

"Advance visit?" Pa O'Neil asked.

"As Vice President Wainwright mentioned in the hospital, before the protectee arrives on-site, a team of agents
goes in to check out the area: to get the lay of the land,
touch base with local law enforcement, sweep the house,
secure the grounds. We already had much of this completed because of Jon's stay at the cottage, but things were
rechecked for Ms. O'Neil's visit. Since you decided so
quickly to come up here, and Jon's visit required a different level of background checks, we have the bare minimum
advance work done and will continue to receive information, particularly on the Watch List."

At the parents' questioning look, Mitch explained that
the Watch List was crucial to security. It was composed of
people residing in the area who might have reason to harm

either the vice president or Ms. O'Neil. The service would check out any people who've been released from jail that might have a grudge against either of them. They also took note of any known criminals in the area who had nothing to do with the two of them.

Aidan asked, "Should Rory and Mikey be hearing this?"

"I'm afraid so," Mitch answered. "They need to be on their guard." He smiled easily. "Rory's used to this."

"Not Mikey." Aidan crossed to where the kids were sitting and dropped down next to his nephew. "You okay, buddy? This scare you?"

"I'm okay." He nodded to the TV. "I'm beating Rory."

"Nuh-uh."

Aidan locked a hand around Mike's neck affectionately. Despite her pique at him, C.J. could appreciate his sensitivity on how this discussion might affect the boy.

"Did you find anything new on the Watch List?" Bailey asked, brushing back Angel's damp hair.

Mitch scowled. "The NRA group that meets in Hammondsport, the town on the west end of the lake, is still grumbling about the vice president's vote on the last gun control bill."

C.J. added, "And we're constantly checking on the ramifications of some of the controversial things you've done since becoming Second Lady, Ms. O'Neil. And before."

The air literally stilled. The O'Neil family wasn't totally aware of what the service did to keep their daughter safe—and why. The agents tried to be careful not to alarm the family. "Before?" Ma O'Neil asked. "Like with the gang stuff?"

"Yes. Ms. O'Neil made some enemies previous to becoming the vice president's wife."

Bailey cocked her head. "Far as I know, the GGs are out of commission." She bit her lip. "And the person arrested for Taz's murder is still in jail, right?"

Taz Gomez was a girl Bailey had tried to get out of a gang. Instead, the gang had killed her.

Mitch leafed through his notes. "Yes, Mazie Lennon's in jail. She was the only one indicted. Other GGs were rounded up, but they weren't with Lennon when she killed Taz, either. Some of those kids were sent to minimum security prisons, and some were let go. They're scattered all over now; the few homegirls left in the city don't appear to be involved in gang activity."

The Second Lady focused on her mother. "The guys at ESCAPE"—the anti–youth gang organization where Bailey used to work—"have kept me up on most of that, Ma."

"Typical," Aidan said. "My sister can't quite give up her wings." He was referring to Bailey's nickname, the Street Angel.

"Let's spell out the rules for the month," C.J. suggested. "Then you can be on your way."

"They're simple." Mitch addressed the kids first. "Listen up now, Rory. Mike."

The boys stopped playing and sidled in close to Aidan. He tugged Mikey onto his lap. The movement roused Hower, who crossed to Aidan and got a few licks on his face. Aidan ruffled the dog's fur.

"Rory, you, your mom and Angel can't go anywhere outside of the house without one of us."

Rory threw his sleeping sister a disgusted look. "All she ever does is crash into things when she walks anyway. She can't go nowhere alone."

"Well, this is for you, then. Usually it will be Agent Ludzecky or me accompanying you. Sometimes the agents on the second perimeter, Agent Gorman, or Agent Grayson, might fill in during the day. Other agents are here for night duty. They'll stay awake while we sleep."

He went on to explain the setup of guards: The president and vice president had three perimeters of security around them. One either inside the house or stationed at the door outside, or accompanying them in a car. At the lake, there were two agents posted near the security fence, and patrolling the gated-in area around the house. Finally, uniforms were responsible for the outer perimeter of the property, and covering the lakefront, along with the cameras on the roof.

Aidan gave a low whistle. "That must cost a bundle."

C.J. shot him an annoyed look. Though there was nothing exactly deprecating in his tone, he seemed to have a lot of criticism rolling off his tongue. It made her say, "I would hope you'd think it well worth the cost, Mr. O'Neil."

"Of course I do!" he snapped.

"In any case," Mitch continued with a frown, "we'll try to remain as unobtrusive as we can. C.J. and I will be either right outside the house, or in the basement command post. Unless there's an immediate threat, then we'll stay right in the room with Ms. O'Neil and the kids."

C.J. studied the little boys. Mikey had turned his face into Aidan's chest. Rory was fiddling with the remote. "Do you understand all this, Rory?"

"Yep. Outside I gotta be with you or Mitch." His eyebrows lifted. "Daddy will paddle my butt if I don't."

Bailey frowned. "We never spank you, Rory!"

"Daddy said he would. If I went *any*place alone."

"I'll be mad, Ror, which is worse. Like the time you followed Hower out of Uncle Patrick's yard while Agent Calloway was by the swings with Anika and Angel."

"Oops." Rory slapped his hands over his mouth, his eyes alight with the devil.

"And you have your panic button, right?" C.J. asked.

"Huh?"

"Your 'help me' button," Mitch explained. He was more used to this detail than she was. And better with the kids. For a minute, the image of her nephews and nieces flashed through C.J.'s mind. How long had it been since she'd seen them? She caught Aidan staring at her and averted her gaze.

"I got it." Rory pulled out a chain from inside his T-shirt. Hooked to it was a small oblong device that when pressed, alerted the agents that something was wrong. Bailey and Clay had them, too. "Do I have to wear this swimming?"

"No. Either Agent Ludzecky or I can hold it."

In a half hour, they finished with the details. Seeming somewhat dazed, Ma and Pa O'Neil went to sit outside on the second-level deck.

"Can we *go* now?" Rory asked.

"Yes. C.J. will be with you."

She narrowed her eyes on Mitch. "What will you do?"

He looked to Bailey. She said, "I'm going to lie down out here in the sunroom with Angel."

"Okay, I'll be in the command post. We still have to update our list of area residents."

"Looks like us guys got Agent L." Aidan faced her. "We'll wait till you change."

"Change what?"

"Your clothes."

"I'm not going to change my clothes."

"You'll die of heatstroke out there in the sun this time of day."

"I'm fine."

"You're kidding, right?"

Exasperated by his pushiness, she looked to Bailey for help.

"Sorry, C.J. I agree. As a matter of fact, this might be a good time to tell you that those suits have to go. I want the agents to dress casually while we're here." She addressed Mitch. "Like last summer."

"Ms. O'Neil . . ." C.J. began.

"C.J., I've agreed to everything you want us to do. We're going to be sensible and careful. We'll obey your rules. But it'll be more normal, especially for Ma and Pa and Mikey, if my agents wear summer clothes appropriate for the lake, like they have before."

C.J. glanced down at her suit. "I don't have any other clothes with me, except for workout gear."

Mitch shrugged. "The rest of us do. Those of us who've been up here before. We know Ms. O'Neil likes it this way. And we were hoping we could dress down again."

"Then C.J. and I will have to go shopping. My treat," Bailey said yawning. She moved Angel to the inside of the couch and slid down next to her. Discussion of the matter was apparently over.

"Come on, C.J.," Rory said, grabbing for her hand. "Let's go."

She sighed, thinking this assignment wasn't going to be an easy one. At least not for her. She was beginning to feel more a part of the family than a guard posted here to protect them.

"SWIRL ME around, Uncle Aidan." Rory's voice rang out in the crystal-clear afternoon amid the whoosh of the waves and the purr of the boats. Somebody on a jet ski whizzed by and waved to them. Aidan waved back. When he turned, he saw Agent Ludzecky had come to the edge of the dock and was checking out the skier through binoculars. They shaded her eyes, but he didn't need to see the expression in them. Her entire body language spoke for her—alert, poised, ready to swing into action at any moment. For the life of him, he couldn't understand why that . . . vigilance irritated him.

Picking up Rory, Aidan swung him around, then dropped him in the lake. Dunked, Rory surfaced easily because the water was only to his chest. Mikey stood on the dock, a few feet away from C.J., Hower nuzzling at his side. He looked forlorn. "Want a swirl, Mike?" Aidan asked.

Shaking his head, he knelt down and petted the animal, buried himself in warm doggy fur. The kid was not doing well. Liam said that since Pa's heart attack, Mikey was reverting back to the behavior he'd demonstrated in the weeks after Bailey left for Washington.

"Can I dive off the barge, Uncle A.?" Rory glanced up at C.J. "I can swim. But I gotta wear my vest." This nephew was fearless, outgoing, risk taking. A lot like his mom.

Before Aidan could answer, Agent Ludzecky did. "No, Rory. You can't swim to the barge unless I go with you."

"You don't have a suit on."

Aidan rolled his eyes. After the exchange with Bailey about clothes in the house, Aidan had caught up with her downstairs.

Did you even bring a suit?

Um, yes.

Shorts?

She'd raised her chin defensively. *I said I didn't bring casual clothes. I only brought a suit in case I need to go into the water with Rory.*

If you feel self-conscious about wearing it in public, you can borrow a T-shirt from me.

I'd never wear your clothes.

She'd looked so horrified, he said, *Women usually like that offer from me.*

I'm not a woman. I'm a federal agent . . .

Shielding his eyes from the sun, Aidan also looked up at her. "I can watch Rory. And we'll put the life vest on him, like he said."

"No. I'd have to get the boat out to check the barge first. Then I'm required to follow you out."

"Isn't this a little excessive? No one's around."

"First off, anyone could be hiding on the other side of that barge ready to pounce."

Remembering that the danger to the vice president's family was mostly kidnapping shut Aidan up.

"Second, somebody could come by on the lake, like that skier."

Rory glared at her. He was used to restrictions by now,

but he was a little boy and didn't like them. "Go anyway, Uncle A. Do a cannonball for us."

She shook her head. "You can't do that, either, Mr. O'Neil. You have to watch Mikey by the water. Rory's my sole responsibility."

"You can watch me and Mikey. We're little." Rory's tone was turning whiny. "And we'll be good."

"No, Rory. I have to focus on you."

"For Christ's sake, can't you give an inch? The whole month'll be ruined if you're this much of a stickler."

Still, she hesitated.

"I'll stay on the dock, I promise," Mike said. His chin was down and it was obvious that he knew he was causing problems. "You can watch Rory in the water."

"Come on," Aidan said, even more irked that she was causing Mikey grief.

"I guess I could get in the water with him while you swim out." She nodded to Mike. "Stay down at this end of the dock, okay?"

"'Kay." He trudged toward the shore with Hower at his heels.

C.J. shrugged off her jacket, revealing her holster and gun. Aidan could see the chain for Rory's panic button around her neck. Then she took off her shoes, socks, and rolled up her pants and shirtsleeves. She had nice calves and arms, finely toned. Agent Ludzecky was in good shape.

When she was in the water up to her knees, Rory said, "We'll count."

"Count?"

"It's a game. To see how fast I can get out there." Aidan arched a brow. "You remember games, don't you, Agent Ludzecky?"

C.J. was miffed now. "Just go."

Squinting into the sun, she watched the path Aidan took. He was a strong swimmer. He had back and arm muscles that made his long powerful strokes impressive.

C.J. looked away from the disturbing sight and focused on Rory, keeping a peripheral view of Mikey on the dock. She'd committed a breach of protocol by allowing her attention to be divided and wasn't happy about it. But she *had* been strict since they got here, and she could see that it was making the O'Neil parents nervous and the brother angry. Besides, the talk had upset Mikey, which she hated to see. To compensate, she stationed herself equidistant between him and Rory. The water was warm and she liked how it lapped around her legs. Combined with the breeze, and the adjustment of her clothing, she felt a lot cooler.

Rory was counting but it was obvious he was growing bored. Mikey and Hower were on the grass, playing fetch the stick. Liam's son seemed comfortable with animals, probably since he didn't have to talk to them. C.J. remembered how one of her sisters, more quiet than the others, related to their dog, Yenko.

In a few minutes, Aidan reached the barge and hiked himself up onto it. He waved to them. Rory waved back, and yelled for Mikey to look just as Aidan did a cannonball into the water. The splash caught Hower's attention; the Lab began barking and jumping up and down, then galloped to the far end of the dock. Mikey followed him.

"Mike, don't—"

The warning came too late.

Mikey reached the end of the dock.

Hower lashed around. The front of his torso hit Mikey.

Who fell into the over-his-head water and went under. C.J. pressed the panic button around her neck, then dove into the shallow water and swam the short distance to Mikey, who'd floated to the top. Plucking him out of the lake, she saw blood on his forehead. He was logy. She grabbed him up to her chest in a carry.

It took only seconds to get to Rory. Encircling him with one arm, still hefting up Mike with the other, she dragged them both toward the shore. As deadweight, Mikey strained the muscles in her arm and shoulder.

By the time she got to the grass, Mitch had arrived. "What happened?"

"Mikey fell off the dock into the water. He must have hit his head on the wood." She stretched the little boy out. "It stunned him, I guess."

"He's conscious. The cut doesn't look too bad."

"My head hurts." The kid's voice was raspy.

"You're okay, sweetie, we're here to help you."

"I want my mommy." His mother had been dead for three years. He reached for C.J.'s hand. "Mommy."

She swallowed back the emotion.

Mitch's breath evened out and he knelt down. "Where the hell is Aidan? Why wasn't he watching Mikey?"

"He swam out to the barge. I was watching both boys."

"Your only responsibility is Rory."

From behind, she heard, "I talked C.J. into keeping an eye on Mike." She turned to find a dripping wet Aidan had come up to them.

Mitch zeroed on her. "Let's take care of the boy, then you and I need to talk, Agent Ludzecky."

FIVE

AIDAN ENTERED the second-floor sunroom and found his father alone, feet propped up on a hassock. He seemed to be gazing out at the water, but when Aidan moved closer, he could tell Pa had been dozing. Though he'd gotten stronger in the ten days since his surgery, he still slept a lot. At least he was more independent. At first, Aidan had to help him shave and wrestle with his clothing. Bathing had been the worst—especially trying to keep the incisions dry—and Pa refused to let Ma or the nurse help. Sometimes Aidan still assisted him because they were afraid Pa would fall. The weakness would come and go.

During their time together, Pa had never accused Aidan of causing his heart attack and Aidan would rather have a root canal than bring it up. The guilt was gnawing at him, though, which was probably why he was behaving like a jerk with Agent Ludzecky. After what happened with Mikey, he needed to make amends with her.

Pa opened his eyes. "Hi, son. Sit a while."

Dropping down on the sofa, Aidan stared at his father.

The four o'clock sunlight streaking in from the windows highlighted the signs of age in his face. "How you feeling?"

"Good. Good." The look Aidan gave Pa had him saying, "All right. The incision in my leg hurts like holy hell. And it itches. It's driving me crazy. The god-awful chest one isn't even as bad."

"I heard that's true with open-heart surgery." He didn't tell Pa, but Liam had e-mailed him some information on what to expect in recuperating from the procedure.

"And I'm still fucking exhausted most of the time."

His pa didn't normally swear like this. "All that's to be expected."

"Yeah, I know. That's what the nurse who came today said, too. She examined Mikey." He shook his head. "The secret agents had a bio on her a mile long. Wouldn't be surprised if they frisked her."

Did they do that? Aidan thought briefly of what it would be like to be frisked by Agent Ludzecky.

"They gotta be careful."

Pa nodded to the lake. "I saw what happened out there. I was sittin' right here watching the whole thing."

"I shouldn't have left C.J. in charge of Mikey." He felt a surge of panic that something could have happened to the boy. And gratitude to Agent Ludzecky that it didn't. "The kid doesn't need to get hurt on top of everything else."

From the corner of his eye, he saw Pa study him. Aidan had been born on Pa's birthday—this fall, Pa would be seventy and Aidan forty—and they had a special affinity Pa didn't seem to have with the other boys. But they butted heads, too. "Mikey could have fallen just like he did if you were there."

"I guess. I put her in an awkward position."

"Hmm."

"Calloway was pissed."

He'd heard her and Mitch from the stairs leading to the

ground floor. *Why did you do that? You're such a stickler for details.*

She hadn't even defended herself. *I was wrong. I made a mistake.*

You did. A pause. *Don't let it happen again.*

Will there be a letter in my file?

No! Jesus, C.J., I'm not that much of a prick.

She'd chuckled, a warm, feminine sound. Combined with how she looked soaked from head to toe—he'd vote her queen of a wet T-shirt contest—made Aidan shift on his feet to a more comfortable position.

You're not a prick at all. I promise, I won't do anything so stupid again.

"She get in trouble?" Pa asked.

"Uh-huh." Aidan fiddled with the newspaper on the table. "I tried to explain things to Calloway but he wouldn't discuss it with me. I told him it was my fault."

"What'd he say?"

"That nobody was to blame but Agent Ludzecky for making a poor decision. She should have known better."

"They're damned uptight about Bailey and Rory."

"I'm glad about that. But I had no idea how bad the constant surveillance was on a day-to-day basis. The times Bay's come home, we didn't live with it because she stayed at Clay's town house. Still, I want what's best for her."

"Oh? And what *is* best for me?"

Bailey had come into the room, cutting off any private discussion between him and Pa. Dressed in a white cotton sundress, her belly sticking out some, she looked cute as hell. But worried.

Pa smiled at her. "That your secret agents are overprotective."

"*Special* agents, Pa."

"Bay, about what happened on the dock?"

Crossing into the room, Bailey stood behind Aidan, put her hands on his shoulders and began to knead them. "Not your fault. Not C.J.'s, either. I'm mostly worried about Mikey."

Pa smiled reassuringly. "The nurse said the head wound was superficial."

"He's so fragile, though."

After discussing Liam's son, Pa stood. "I'm gonna go find the boy. Keep him company some. Maybe make a fishing date."

When Pa left, Bailey circled the couch and sat close enough to Aidan to take his hand. Hers was cold and seemed small in his.

"You sure you're not worried, B.?"

"Not about that."

"About what?"

"Clay called." Her eyes misted and she glanced away. "He's going to Zanganesia at the end of the week."

He squeezed her fingers. "You knew he was leaving, honey."

"When he goes, it's a different story. And who knows how people there feel about his influence on their anticrime policies."

"They're probably glad they live in a safer place. The prime minister thinks he walks on water."

Pique came quickly to her face. "If it's too dangerous for me, then it is for him."

"He's not pregnant."

Her head back against the couch, she stared up at the ceiling fan creating a soft whir. "Sometimes I wish we weren't who we are."

"The Second Couple?"

"Uh-huh. If he and Mark Langley get reelected, I've got six more years of this. Then who knows?"

"You mean Clay could run for president."

"I don't even want to think about that. This whole discussion is making me crazy. Let's talk about something else."

"Sure, sis. What do you want to talk about?"

For a minute she watched him like Pa had. "Why you're feeling guilty about Pa's heart attack."

"Who says I feel guilty?"

"Your eyes say it. Your body language. Come on, tell your favorite sister what you think you did."

Edgy, he got up and walked to the windows. The lake was calmer now, the sun gilding its surface. In the midst of such beauty, he said the awful words. "I'm responsible for his heart attack, B. I almost killed Pa."

THE NEXT MORNING, C.J. sat at the desk in the command post, still stinging from Mitch's reprimand, though he'd been fine since the whole thing with Mikey and Rory happened yesterday. Nonetheless, she hated to screw up. This job was all she had and she was determined to do it well. But instead of completing the form before her on the computer, her mind wandered to Aidan O'Neil. She'd stumbled on him twice, but had pulled back without being seen.

She'd come in the house two nights ago after a run and found him and Pa out in the sunroom, arguing about Aidan having to help him bathe. The older man had been grumpy and out of sorts, and seemed embarrassed about needing his son to take care of his personal hygiene. Aidan had resorted to joking. He began telling stories of Pa bathing *him* when he was little and the funny things that had happened. It had put the older man at ease, and made him smile, especially the story about the time Aidan had rigged the faucet to spray in every direction and flooded the entire bathroom.

Then, she'd come upon him and Bailey talking softly on the couch in the sunroom. He'd been comforting her. His hand had soothed down her hair, then he'd drawn her head on his shoulder. The two of them reminded C.J. of herself and Lukasz. Her brother had often hugged her like that.

Their closeness had been one of the most precious things in her life; she hadn't realized how much she missed it until she was around Aidan and Bailey.

Forcefully putting Luke and the O'Neils out of her mind, she got to work filling out the incident form required by the headquarters anytime something went awry on a detail.

"I can't believe I did this," she grumbled as she recorded the information on the computer. "I was so stupid."

"It was because of me."

Swiveling in the desk chair, she found Aidan standing in the entryway as if he'd been summoned by her thoughts of him.

She calmed her pulse and cocked her head. "What's because of you?"

He grinned, and she could see how an ordinary woman would be swept off her feet by just that smile aimed at her. Thank God she was immune.

"I heard you talking to the computer. I talk to my cameras that way. It's an aberration, you know."

She gave him a weak smile and shifted in the seat. She didn't want to talk to him, worse yet, be friendly with him.

Then he sobered. "It was my fault that you were watching Mikey, instead of Rory, C.J. I badgered you into it." He held up his hand. In it was a bunch of wildflowers—an explosion of different colors of yellow.

"What are those?"

"A peace offering."

For a brief moment, joy fluttered in her heart. When was the last time anyone brought her flowers? She bit her lip to keep back the loneliness that hit like a train wreck in the night. "I . . . thank you but those aren't necessary."

"Flowers are always necessary when a man does something wrong."

She arched a brow.

"What?"

"Just that most men I'm around don't easily admit they've made a mistake."

"Who said this was easy? It's killin' me, darlin'.""

"Still, I can't take them. My job . . ."

"Keeps you from accepting them from me. Fine." There was a snap to his words. Then his brows raised, as if he'd just thought of something. "Consider them a gift from Mikey for pulling him out of the lake." He winked. "It'll be our secret."

He was flirting with her. Jesus.

"Mr. O'Neil, please, this isn't protocol."

Aidan could tell he'd knocked her off balance. The man in him rejoiced—damned if something about her appealed to him as much as she annoyed him. But the fair person he was surfaced. He'd come here to apologize. "Okay, okay." He gestured to the desk. "So everything's all right? I didn't get you in trouble?"

"I made a mistake." She spoke in her agent voice. "No one got me into anything. Besides, Mitch is fair. He saw it for what it was." She watched him. "How's your sister doing? With the vice president leaving Friday?"

She was changing the subject. He decided to go along with it. "Bay freaks when he travels in a foreign country. It's why she wanted to go with him, even though she came to her senses about the baby." He shook his head. "Who'd have thought? Bailey's fiercely independent. She'd have died before she'd depend on a man that much."

"Sometimes, it's wise to count on yourself."

"Is that how you live your life, Agent Ludzecky?"

The question made her shoulders tense. "That's not something I care to discuss." Cold voice, even colder stare. "Especially with you."

"Don't you ever get tired of the isolation?"

She prickled ever more and nodded to the computer. "I have to finish this." Her voice held the edge of dismissal.

"All right."

He started away. This hadn't gone exactly as he'd planned. He'd thought to soften her with flowers and an apology, but the usual bribes didn't work with her like they did other women. In fact, she wasn't like any other woman he knew. Pity the poor sap who brought her flowers for real.

"I CAN'T believe you agreed to this after what happened yesterday." C.J. stomped over to a dresser, removed her wallet from a drawer and slammed it shut. She was getting ready to go *shopping*, for God's sake.

Mitch lounged on the sofa. He'd changed from his khaki cargo shorts and red knit polo into a suit, since they were going off the cottage grounds. "Security isn't compromised. We have a plan in place for this. We'll go in the Suburban. It's a hard car." Their specially outfitted vehicle for transportation at the lake included a relatively impenetrable body, bulletproof windows and government-designed tires. "Bailey shops at Beach Fashions all the time and the people are used to the drill. The store was swept this morning, and will be closed until we get there and while we shop."

"Everybody'll know she's in town."

"We can't keep her whereabouts a secret the whole summer. Besides, the store personnel know to be discreet if they want the Second Lady's business. They never publicize when she shops there. In turn, they get to advertise they've been chosen to provide her clothes. If they blabber, that perk is deep-sixed."

C.J. stuffed her wallet in her back pocket. "Shit, I don't even want new clothes."

"Talk to Bailey."

"I tried. She won't budge." C.J. scowled. "Besides, she's worried about the vice president's trip. I don't want to cause her any more grief."

"This will distract her." Mitch raised his brows up and

down. "Me, too. I can't wait to see you in something skimpy."

"First off, skimpy is not my style. Second, you've worked out with me a million times. Seen me in shorts and a tank top."

"I meant *girly* clothes."

"Oh, God."

Mitch studied her. "C.J., you weren't always so conservative, were you?"

She stilled in the act of shrugging into her suit jacket. "Um, no. Lukasz used to tease me about my girly clothes, as you put it."

"Ah. The legendary hotshot Special Agent Luke Ludzecky. You see him much?"

"Not enough. He's living in upstate New York with his wife. He's a teacher now, like her."

Her friend was thoughtful. "How far away from him are we?"

"About an hour."

"You going to call him?"

"Maybe."

"Hmm."

"Hmm, what?"

"You don't take to heart the gossip that you got a break in the service because of him, do you?"

"It bothers me some. But mostly it's the stuff with Anderson that's made me circumspect. Even in clothes, which I seem to have *no say over* right now!"

"Anderson is a son of a bitch."

"He's your buddy."

"Doesn't make me think he's any less of a bastard because of what he did to you."

"Look, can we not get into this now? I got enough problems."

"All right. Let's go shopping."

They left the room and passed by the sunroom. "Where'd the flowers come from?" Mitch asked.

"Um, Mikey." She kept her tone neutral. "As a thank-you gift from fishing him out of the lake."

"Hmm," he said again.

She refused to look at the pretty yellow blossoms that were even fuller today.

Once they piled into the car, Grayson drove the Suburban down the winding lake road to Beach Fashions. Mitch rode shotgun. Bailey sat behind Mitch, because the protectee had to be in sight of the two people in front. C.J. was behind Grayson and kept scanning the landscape of trees, foliage and cottages that scrolled by.

As expected, no cars graced the parking lot of the clothing store in Penn Yan, the town at the east end of the lake. Their police had blocked off the street with construction vehicles and detoured traffic. Two of the cops approached the Suburban.

The female opened the door and Grayson jumped out to make a final sweep. She slid inside and turned a dazzling smile on Bailey. "Ms. O'Neil. Nice to see you again."

"You too, Sonia. You look great. Did you ever see Aidan's photos of you from the last time we were here?"

"Yeah, he sent me some." The redhead raised her brows. "He with you this trip?"

"Uh-huh."

"Tell him to call me."

C.J. had overheard the O'Neil boys talk about their affinity for redheads. This woman sported beautiful auburn hair and green eyes. C.J. bet flowers worked on her.

Grayson knocked on the window. "All set."

Like the trained professionals they were, the four of them hustled Bailey out of the car and into the store.

The place was a study in femininity and made C.J.'s fists curl. It smelled of potpourri, the kind Lizzie had in her apartment. The walls were painted peach, with soft oak tones on the floor. Swags of silk hung all over the freakin' room.

"Ms. O'Neil. So nice to see you." The store owner gushed, and her assistant looked starstruck.

"Hello, Mary. Thanks for accommodating us again."

Grayson and Sonia the Cop stood by the door. C.J. and Mitch flanked Bailey.

"What can I show you?" Mary asked.

"As I said, the trip isn't for me this time around." She caressed her belly. "Nothing fits but maternity wear, I'm afraid. We need some casual clothes for Agent Ludzecky."

The woman turned to C.J. "What size are you, Agent?"

Geez. She didn't want to talk about this in front of everybody. "Um, a twelve."

"You don't look it."

"I weigh more than you think." *And that's nobody's business!*

"Come with me."

The woman led her to a corner where pants were stacked on peach painted shelves. C.J. picked out two pairs of navy shorts. From the tops, she snagged white T-shirts. That should do it.

"You'll need some loose shirts, Agent." This from Mitch, who was sitting down next to Bailey on a couch. His face was all smirky and smug.

The Second Lady said, "C.J., pick out some *colors*."

"Huh?"

"Those shorts are okay, but get them in yellow. Or pink."

C.J. rolled her eyes and added pink to the pile. She started for the changing room, when Mitch called out, "Your gun, Agent Ludzecky?"

"Oh, sure." Man, her brain was mush from so much estrogen floating in the air.

The shorts fit, and she had to admit, the pink ones were pretty. The blouses fit, too, but the T-shirts were too small. The proprietor brought back the next size. And more pants—this time light-colored capris. And a dress.

"What's this?" she asked of the fragile yellow confection.

"Ms. O'Neil picked it out. She wants you to try it on and come out."

"Oh, Lord."

"You're lovely, dear. And that yellow will go so well with your hair and coloring."

C.J. sighed. Minutes later she stepped out into the store, wearing the dress and feeling . . . exposed.

"Wow!" Bailey said. "You look beautiful."

At the entrance, Grayson's mouth dropped.

Mitch whistled, and said, "You clean up real good, Agent Ludzecky."

C.J. caught a reflection of herself in the mirror and her brows shot up. Because in the glass stood the old C.J., before her estrangement from her family. Before David Anderson almost ruined her career.

She'd forgotten what that woman looked like.

SIX

THE CAMERA came alive in Aidan's hands. He made it move, breathe, then burst with brilliant consummation when the lens snapped. Once he told Bailey that holding his Nikon or his ES Digital was like having a woman in his arms. Instead of being insulted by the sexist remark, she put him in his place with a hoot of laughter, and a snide, "You gotta work on your love life, A."

He'd laughed, too, though in truth, he did feel an intimacy with his cameras. Not a sexual connection, of course, but a connection he never felt with anything else. He called each camera *she* and, as he'd told C.J., he even talked to them like they were alive.

And his love life was just fine, thank you very much. He adored women—especially his sister and mother—had female friends through the years and enough girlfriends to satisfy him. Sure, he wished he'd find a woman he could settle down with. Particularly since he was going to be forty in September. But that would happen any day now.

Peering through the lens of his digital—he'd brought

that to the lake because it was easier to work with——he focused on a patch of wildflowers like the ones he'd brought to the stiff and formal Agent Ludzecky. She wouldn't accept them as a gift from him, but he noticed the bouquet was still on the table in the sunroom where she could see it every day. As he photographed some daisies, a doe and her fawn came into his viewfinder. They were picking their way through the wet grass and dewy flowers. It had rained last night, a sudden fierce outburst, and this morning, just after dawn, the grounds were slippery, especially way out here on the edge of the Wainwright property. His feet planted firmly in his hiking boots, Aidan snapped the button in rapid succession, but he was waiting for his special shot, the one his gut told him would be a prizewinner. It came, like it always did, a crystalline moment when he would wield his magic. The doe bent her head and pressed her nose to the fawn's. And as always, when he captured a stunning image like this, his throat got tight, his heart beat faster, his skin prickled. He chuckled. Not unlike being with a woman.

"There you go, sweetheart," he whispered to his camera. "That's it . . . good girl. We got it, don't you think?"

He wandered through the woods, remembering the picture of Bailey and Angel that he'd taken yesterday. His sister had been outside in a lounge chair, with the baby on her lap. They'd been reading, when Angel turned her face to her mother and touched her nose to Bailey's. He could juxtapose that shot next to the one he'd just taken. Too bad he wouldn't be able to send *that* picture to the magazines that published his work. Though Bailey wouldn't have objected, he'd vowed not to use his sister's position to further his career.

What career? he thought miserably. Last night, he'd called *Inside/Outside* magazine and turned down the job he'd been offered, because that offer had caused him to talk to Pa, and put in action the chain of events that led them here. Guilt had kept him from following his dream. That and an innate worry that he wasn't, in the scheme of things, talented enough to make a living at photography.

Forcefully, he shook off the notion and hiked down the slope leading to the water. On the edge of the property beyond the fenced-in gate, he studied the shore. Sometimes, interesting stones washed up. Once, he'd gotten a dynamite photo of a good-sized, perfectly formed white stone, striated with black. He'd photographed it, then took the stone with him. He'd given both to Ma for Mother's Day and they occupied a place of honor at the pub. Though he didn't show his parents as many pictures as he did Bay and the guys, he used some of his best shots as gifts for them.

As he scanned the beach, his gaze caught on a series of footsteps on the muddy shoreline. Odd, as there were No Trespassing signs everywhere; and nobody should be down here. Then he remembered—it was probably the *secret agents*, as his pa liked to call them.

"Okay, baby, let's get this." Aidan took several pictures of the footprints. He turned when he heard a motor. Six a.m. was early for people to be out on the water. He photographed the boat, too. And the horizon. Salmon pink gave way to lighter rose, to shades of yellow as dawn came like a peacock, displaying its full colors. Talk about breathtaking.

Deciding he'd had enough, he made his way back to the house. It was a hike, and by the time he got there, he was dying for coffee. He unlocked the gate with a security card he'd been given, and as he neared the lower outdoor patio, he caught sight of a figure on it, facing the lake. He was too far away to see who it was with the naked eye, but when he lifted the camera and zoomed in, he got a clear view of Agent Ludzecky through the lens.

Her blond hair was a riotous mass around her face and shoulders; holy hell, he didn't know she had so much of it. She wore a tight-fitting tank top and even tighter pants that ended at her calves. And she was moving . . . he recognized the routine as yoga. Gut instinct urged him to snap the camera . . .

Head high, arms at her side, legs rooted to the ground, she looked like a Greek statue . . .

Arms overhead . . .

A graceful bend, almost a dive . . .

Up again, facing the sun, chest forward, sternum high . . .

On all fours . . . arms out, she raised her butt up . . . held the position a long time. Aidan was impressed.

Standing, she faced the side, bent, put weight on one leg and one hand, lifted the other leg; her top hiked up even more. Through the zoom, he could see an expanse of creamy bronze skin. He felt like a voyeur, but kept snapping.

By now his mouth was dry.

When she stood, then arched her body into a backbend, her breasts thrust up into the air. They were sculpted, firm.

And Aidan's whole body tightened.

Mesmerized he watched and snapped, watched and snapped until she finished her routine.

Still at a distance, he tucked the camera into his pocket, sank onto a stone and stared out at the water. Coffee forgotten, he felt another need pulse through him. A very male need.

He remembered her words. *I'm not a woman, I'm a federal agent.*

Cocking his head at his camera, he said, "No way, Ms. C.J. Ludzecky. You are a woman through and through."

The notion was disconcerting.

JUDY GORMAN, the agent who worked with Jerry Grayson on the second perimeter, didn't like C.J. Having grown up with six younger sisters, C.J. could sense other women's hostility toward her like she often sensed trouble in a crowd. Ana, the sister closest in age to her, once told C.J. she had too many brains and was too good-looking for any females but those in her family to genuinely like her.

C.J. suspected, though, that Gorman's animosity had other origins. She'd been an agent longer than C.J., and had only worked her way up to substituting occasionally on the VPPD. She hadn't even gotten a permanent relief shift, as Grayson had, until now. Mitch said she'd asked him point-blank why C.J. was chosen over her for the prestigious detail. Mitch had told her that in his estimation, C.J. was a better agent than Gorman was, and also that Bailey had requested C.J. The Second Lady's slight incensed Gorman so she took it out on C.J. C.J. guessed she might have felt the same way, especially since there were already rumors about her and David circulating through the service. And then there was her connection to Luke.

So it was with trepidation that she approached Judy Gorman outside the front door. "Gorman, could you take over for me for a while? Grayson's covering for Calloway. We want to work out."

Dark eyes registered on her. The woman would be pretty without the scowl, as her hair was a nice reddish color and her features petite. "Of course, Agent Ludzecky."

C.J. thought about making an overture of friendship to Gorman, but she decided against it. This was one person it was better to keep at a distance. "Thanks." She was about to walk away when Gorman asked, "She pay for those clothes?"

Glancing down at her white shorts and pink boxy shirt, C.J. replied honestly. "We're still arguing about that." Maybe she should try for friendly. "You brought your own clothes, I see." She nodded to the agent's denim capris and white shirt. "I didn't know Ms. O'Neil would require this."

"Because you haven't been around long enough."

Bingo.

C.J. shook her head. "See you inside in ten."

Her thoughts were still preoccupied with Gorman as she jogged down the steps to her room and changed. They'd been at the cottage for four days and things were settling into a routine, so she and Mitch decided they could pick up with their workouts. C.J. had been doing yoga, and both she and Mitch had run daily, but they missed their usual boxing matches. She was tugging on one glove when Mitch walked in.

He was dressed in plain gray shorts and a tank top. "Hi, babe."

"Babe?"

"Hey, you look like a babe in those new clothes."

"Not really my style."

"Yeah, yeah, same old, same old." Crossing to her, he picked up her other glove and slid it on. Tied both. Their usual gloves were fastened by Velcro, but the ones stowed here had strings. Grabbing his own, he turned and looked out the window. Knocked on it. She heard him say, "Aidan, we could use your help." He held up the gloves.

C.J. sighed. She'd managed to stay away from the guy since he gave her the flowers that bloomed with abandon in the sunroom. Their civil encounter yesterday—though she tried to stay distanced—made her even more wary of him. And she'd caught the appreciative male look in his eyes when he first saw her in her new duds. Why couldn't it be somebody else out there this morning?

He came inside, sweaty and flushed. He was dressed in running clothes: Perspiration beaded his face and soaked his clothes. Sipping water, he gave her a quick once-over. She turned away from the look and jabbed the punching bag.

"What's going on?" he asked.

"C.J. and I are working out, but we need somebody to help with my gloves."

"Sure, okay." From the corner of her eye, she saw him scowl. "You got height and weight on her. Doesn't seem an even match."

Oh, terrific, now he was going to play caveman. He probably thought women swooned over that behavior, like they did when given flowers.

"Stick around and you'll change your tune."

"Maybe I will."

She felt self-conscious as she adjusted her head gear and raised her hands in the traditional boxer's stance. Mitch did the same.

A few testing punches on Mitch's gloves; his hit hers a little harder. Then she landed a quick one on his shoulder, causing him to stumble backward. His dark eyes narrowed, and she paid for getting in the first serious jab with a series of hard hits on her gloves. But she got an opening to his biceps. The blow made him recoil.

Rules were to stay away from the head, but he clocked her on the temple by mistake. "Sorry," he mumbled, not breaking his concentration.

"Jesus," she heard from their spectator.

She managed to get in a few more hits of her own, and lost herself in her the contest. Sweat poured into her eyes, and she felt her body heat from the inside out.

Groans. Mumbles. The smack of leather hitting leather.

A buzzer rang. Mitch held up his hands. "Time." They went about twenty minutes, but it was a workout.

C.J. moved her shoulders, kicked out her legs. "Already?"

He chucked her under the chin. "You're one tough cookie."

Grinning, she pivoted to find an unsmiling Aidan watching her. "Are you two nuts?" he asked.

Calloway laughed and held up his gloves in front of Aidan. "It looks worse than it is."

"I doubt it." He undid Mitch's gloves and yanked them off.

Mitch wiped his head with a towel. "Keeps our reflexes at top speed, and us in shape." He turned to C.J. just when the fax machine clicked on. "I've been waiting for this. Aidan, can you help C.J.?"

"Yeah."

Her colleague disappeared into the other room and C.J. faced Aidan. She hoped he'd untie her gloves and be done with it. He came closer, his head cocked to the side, his gaze narrowed in on her shoulder. After a moment, he reached out and ran his fingers along her rotator cuff. "You have a bruise."

His touch was gentle, butterfly soft, but C.J. felt it zip through her.

"Um . . ." He ran his hand down her bare arm, to a place above her elbow. "Here, too."

His gaze met hers. His eyes were so blue, like the sky behind him, but with a black ring around the iris. She never noticed that before. He smelled like man and musk.

He didn't say anything, but left his hand on her. She swallowed hard, liking the feel of it.

"You should stick with yoga." His voice was rusty sounding.

"What?"

"Yoga. It's better for you than getting pummeled like this."

"I didn't get pummeled." The import of his words sunk in. "And how do you know about yoga?"

"I saw you doing a session this morning."

"At six a.m.?" The fact that he'd watched her unnoticed made her warm inside. She felt her face flush even more.

"I was out on the grounds taking pictures."

"I didn't see you."

"You weren't on duty. I told Grayson where I was so he didn't think a stranger was prowling the grounds. Everybody was safe."

Safe did not feel like an appropriate word. Particularly because his hand was still on her. "Get my gloves off."

Flecks of darker blue flamed in his eyes. "Since you

asked so nicely," he said, grabbing her wrists with both hands. "What's with you? You're prickly as hell again today."

She lifted a glove to her mouth to untie it with her teeth, but he batted her hand away. "I'm prickly because, with the exception of the flower thing, you've been criticizing me since I showed up as your sister's agent in the hospital. About staying aloof. About not caring enough. About my vigilant view of protection. And now about boxing."

He stared down at her gloves, then started to undo them. When he was finished, he tugged them off, and surprised her by grasping one of her hands. "You're right. I've been on you. I have no idea why." His grin was devilish. "Usually, I have a way with women."

She stepped back. "Well, spare me that, and your snide comments, will you?"

"Christ, you don't budge at all."

I can't afford to with you. She stuffed the thought, and was prevented from volleying back something mean because Mitch appeared at the door with a paper in his hand and a scowl on his face. "We got a problem."

"WHAT'S GOING ON?" his sister asked as soon as she entered the first-floor sunroom. "And why didn't you want Ma or Pa or the kids in here?"

"Sit down, Ms. O'Neil." Mitch had thrown on a sweat suit, as had C.J. "We just received a disturbing fax."

"About Clay? He hasn't even left yet for Zanganesia yet."

"No. This has nothing to do with the vice president."

Bailey sank onto the couch next to Aidan. "What is it then?"

"A member of a former New York City girl gang has relatives in Penn Yan."

"I'm confused. ESCAPE keeps a database. I told you, Joe and Rob stay in touch with me. Word on the street is

that all the GGs are accounted for. We went over this before. Mazie Lennon's in jail. The rest are leading produc-
tive lives either in New York or they've left town and are
off our radar screen."

"She isn't a GG. She's a member of Anthrax, another
defunct girl gang. The advance team didn't go deep enough
first time around because your visit was unplanned. They
only checked the known GGs in the area. We've gone
down another layer and found one of the Anthrax gang
member's relatives up here."

"What made you do that?"

"Actually, C.J. suggested it. She worked in the Intelligence unit in New York."

"Did you get girls out of Anthrax, Bay?" Aidan asked.

"No. They were pretty impenetrable, mostly because
they were an arm of a boy's gang. But the GGs gave the police information on them, enough to bust up Anthrax six
months later."

"There's more." Mitch's tone was grave, making Aidan
move a little closer. "The girl who has the relative up here
is Annie Oh."

His sister grasped onto his fingers.

Aidan could feel the tension in her. "Who is she?"

Bailey turned to him. "Remember the night Clay stayed
over and I asked you to come and get Rory for preschool."

"Because you were out helping Taz."

Sadness shone in Bailey's eyes. She'd loved that girl.
"Annie-O—her homies shortened her name to a zero—is
the girl who was squaring off with Taz that night and
wounded her with a knife."

"She sounds dangerous." Aidan scowled over at Mitch.
"Does she live with her aunt here?"

"No." Mitch again. "We tracked her to the city. She
doesn't appear to be involved in any gang. As a matter of
fact she's working in a diner. She finished high school and
is taking courses at a community college in the city."

C.J. zeroed in on Aidan. "Her aunt and uncle bought the property in town two years ago."

"Do you think there's a problem with that?" Bailey asked.

"If Annie-O does still have gang connections, and her aunt or her cousin Sasha, who lives here, too, mentions that Bailey's in town, Annie could retaliate against Bailey for indirectly shutting down Anthrax."

"Damn it." Aidan squeezed Bailey's shoulder. "We should go back to the city."

Bailey shook her head. "Let's not buy trouble. If Annie-O's clean now, there might not be anything to worry about."

A memory niggled at Aidan. "I saw something this morning. I didn't think much of it, until now."

"What?" C.J. asked, her gaze dark. She'd gotten majorly ticked off because Aidan had watched her do her yoga practice; her reaction was pretty stupid, in his book. He wondered what she'd do if she knew—over his dead body—that he'd taken pictures of her.

"There were some footprints on the outer edge of the property, in the mud. It had rained, so they were visible."

"Why the hell didn't you tell us this before?" C.J. asked.

Everyone in the room looked startled at her outburst. Her pretty brown eyes widened. "Oh. Oh, God. I'm sorry. I didn't mean to speak to you like that, Mr. O'Neil."

He could make an issue out of this. Bailey would side with him. Agent Ludzecky would be in hot water. But he remembered how Mitch chided her for the mistake she'd made with Mikey and Rory their first day here, which was partly his fault. Besides, he didn't want to get her in trouble even if *she* had gotten under his skin.

"Forget it. I should have told you sooner." He faced Mitch. "I took pictures of the prints."

"You did? Why?"

"I shoot a lot of different things. Sometimes, the smallest

natural occurrence can be a great photo." He thought of C.J.'s breasts. And determinedly avoided her gaze.

"I'll need the film."

"They're digital. I'll run the pictures off my computer."

"I can do that," Mitch said. "Give me the disc card."

No way was he letting the Secret Service near those pictures of C.J. "It's okay. I have time."

Mitch quirked a brow. The agent was smart and savvy and knew something was up. "All right, let's do it together now on your computer."

Aidan stood. "I'd rather do it myself. I'm picky about my work."

Mitch started to object when there was noise at the front entry door. Both agents went on alert and automatically moved closer to Bailey.

Then they heard, "It's all right, Gorman, I'm here to see my wife."

"It's Clay." Circling around C.J., Bailey bounded out of the sunroom and into the kitchen, where the vice president of the United States stood. Several agents hovered in the background. Though she was four months pregnant, Bailey ran across the room and hurled herself at him, encircling his waist with her legs. "Clay!"

Smiling broadly, he grabbed hold of her. "Hello, love."

Aidan saw his brother Liam behind Clay. Knowing the agents would be distracted now, he took the opportunity to creep out of the sunroom and hurry upstairs to his printer. With any luck he could download the photos, delete the ones of C.J. on the card and be back before anybody missed him.

SEVEN

LIAM SAID, "You need competition."

Rock in hand, Aidan snorted and glanced over his shoulder. The expression in his eyes reinforced Liam's suspicion when he first arrived at the lake. Something was up with his brother.

"Yeah, I guess." He nodded to the pile of stones at his feet. "Bet you five."

"You're on." Bending down, Liam picked up a smooth, flat stone. "Me first."

He threw the rock. It skimmed the water, making tiny splashes along the way, and went far enough to be a contender.

"Beginner's luck."

"Sore loser."

Aidan took his turn. His stone dribbled along the surface. "Shit."

As they alternated skimming, one of their favorite childhood games, they made small talk. Liam was one of those men—all the O'Neils were—who could discuss things easier if they were doing some activity.

Finally, Liam got to the point. "What's going on with you, kid?" Though he was only two years younger, Aidan always seemed more youthful than him. And these days, Liam felt like Methuselah.

"This secret agent stuff is wearing thin."

"Secret agent?"

A chuckle. "That's what Pa calls them."

"They seem nice enough. I liked Calloway right from the start. Don't know the other one."

"She's prickly as hell."

"Prickly?"

"Yeah, defensive, irritable. She balks at everything Bailey wants."

"I see Bay won on the clothes. Agent Ludzecky's a fox in them."

"Tell me about it."

His arm in the air, Liam halted. "Is this about her?"

His brother faced him. "Let's sit. I brought out a cooler."

Crossing to the dock ahead of Liam, Aidan took out two Coors from the Styrofoam box. The pop of the aluminum cans resounded in the seven o'clock evening air.

Liam stared at what was promising to be a gorgeous sunset. "You should photograph the horizon."

"I take too many pictures for my own good."

"All right, spill it. You're acting weird."

"I was up early this morning taking pictures."

"I know. Everybody went nuts about the footprints."

After Aidan provided a set of pictures and a disc, Clay's team got right on it. They had Aidan show them the way, only to find the prints had been washed away by the water. Then they'd enlarged the pictures on their supercomputer and studied them.

"I guess they can't be too careful with Bailey and Rory's safety."

"So what's the problem?" Liam probed.

"After I finished shooting, I came upon Agent Ludzecky on the ground-floor patio this morning."

"And you had a fight?"

"No, she didn't know I saw her. She was practicing yoga. I took some pictures of her."

"Without her knowing?"

"Yeah. So what?"

"You know *so what*. That's why you snuck out as soon as I got here. You deleted the shots of her?"

"Yeah, from the card."

"No harm then."

"I downloaded them to my computer. I couldn't . . . make myself get rid of them."

"Aidan, Jesus, get to the point. This is worse than the first time you wanted to know where to buy rubbers." There were few secrets growing up in the O'Neil household.

"What I saw in those pictures stunned me, Liam. It was like a lover had taken each shot. They were sensuous. Female." He cleared his throat. "Sexual."

"And it turned you on?"

"Fuck, I was hard all day."

Liam laughed out loud. He rarely did that anymore, and it felt good.

"Not funny. I don't even like the woman."

"So? Remember Julie Johnson? You hated her guts because she was such a snob, but she was your first time."

Aidan laughed, too. "I guess."

"Besides, C.J. seems likable enough to me. She's devoted to Bailey and the kids."

"I know. But as I said, she's prickly." He sighed. "I can't get the pictures out of my mind, though."

"And now when you see her, you're gonna remember them."

"I wish Bailey hadn't made her buy those clothes."

"Poor guy. Having to look at a chick like that all day."

"Up yours."

Liam clapped a hand on Aidan's shoulder. "Tell you what. After Mikey goes to sleep, why don't you and I go into town? There's that little Mexican place with good music and spicy food."

His brother stared over at him. "Sounds good. I need to get out of here."

"Maybe that pretty little cop will be around. What was her name?"

"Sonia. I'll call her." He cocked his head. "I could see if she has a friend."

Liam hesitated. "Not sure I'm ready for that."

Now, Aidan clasped *his* arm. "Liam, it's time."

Once again the thought of moving on after Kitty's death terrified him. "I don't know."

"You gotta try."

Liam glanced up to the deck off Bailey and Clay's room. His sister was standing there with her husband. They weren't kissing; Clay had Bailey's back to his chest, his arms around her, and they were watching the sunset. For a minute, Liam was struck with such longing it almost leveled him. He and Kitty had had that kind of connection and closeness. In spades. Sometimes, he missed it so much it was like he'd lost a limb when she died. Overall he was doing better, but at moments like these the ache was so bad, it sucker punched him.

Which was why he said, "Okay, call your cop and see if she has a friend. I'll give it a shot."

ON THE main floor of the cottage, C.J. sat with Tim Jenkins, Clay Wainwright's special agent in charge, drinking coffee. She tried to concentrate on the schedule he'd made for Clay's visit, but her mind kept wandering.

It had been a joy to witness the reunion of the vice president and his wife, though they'd only been apart for ten days. The two of them practically shimmered when they were in the same room. Add to that Clay's imminent trip to Zanganesia, even C.J. was moved by the sight of them together.

"What time are you off?" Jenkins asked.

C.J. glanced at her watch. "Right about now. Conklin's taking over. You?"

"Six a.m. Not that they'll emerge from their suite."

No snide comments were made about the vice president's whereabouts. After spending a few hours with Rory and Angel, Clay had said he wanted to have dinner with Bailey in their suite—something they often did up here, she gathered—and not to be disturbed unless Rory or Angel needed them. Grandma and Grandpa volunteered to put Rory to bed and Angel was already out cold. Privacy for married couples was difficult with so many agents around, and no one thought much of Clay's manipulation to get time alone with his wife.

"They're nice people," Jenkins said.

So was he. She watched his youthful face that belied a sophisticated agent. "How's your wife feeling?" Celia Jenkins was expecting their third child.

Jenkins's smile was a mile wide. "Good. I don't see her enough, though."

"You really quitting the VPPD after this term, even if Clay gets reelected?"

"Yep."

"Will you cycle back in?"

"No. It's time for me to leave the stress of this kind of job in the service. I've got feelers out at the New York office. You worked there, didn't you?"

"Uh-huh. It's a great place. Lots of freedom. Exciting work." She wouldn't have left if it hadn't been for David, but she didn't tell Tim that.

"If I work there, I can commute from Connecticut. We just inherited Celia's family home. She's already moved in so the boys can start school there in September. I'm going up on my days off."

"I'm glad, Tim. This life's hard for married men."

"It is." He took a bead on her. "What—"

Mrs. O'Neil appeared in the doorway. "C.J., could you come upstairs?"

C.J. bolted out of her chair and felt for the gun at her back. "Is something wrong?"

"Nothing like that. Rory's being a brat. He won't go to bed unless we let him play some game on the computer. We don't even know what he's talking about. I didn't want to disturb Bailey." Worry marred her brow. "And Paddy's getting agitated with the boy's antics."

The front door opened and closed and Conklin came in. "Sure, Mrs. O'Neil. My relief 's here, anyway."

After signing off with Conklin, C.J. followed Bailey's mother upstairs. Rory and his grandpa were outside the kids' room, and the door was closed. Mikey was probably asleep.

Mikey, who, since she'd rescued him, hovered around C.J. like a lost puppy. He'd shyly come up to her after the accident, taken her hand and whispered, "Thanks for saving me." The boy's face was so sad it had won her heart. Despite her resolve to stay detached, she'd bent down and scooped him up for a hug. Since then, she made a point of spending time with him when she was off duty. Even grumpy Uncle Aidan had thanked her for the extra attention she gave the boy.

"What's going on, Rory?" she asked. He was cute in his Spiderman pajamas.

"I wanna play *Goodnight Guys*."

"Don't have a clue what that is," Pa O'Neil said. He did look tired.

Though they rarely did any personal chores like babysitting or running errands for protectees, C.J. said, "I'll take care of this. Why don't you two go to bed?"

"Who'll put him down?"

"She can." Rory was pouting now and his eyes turned mutinous. C.J. had seen that look, and what came after. It wasn't pretty.

Crouching, she stared Rory in the eye and showed no fear. "If I find that game on the computer, and let you play for a few minutes, will you promise to go right to sleep?"

"Uh-huh."

She stood. "Go ahead, I can handle this."

With relieved looks, the O'Neils headed downstairs to their quarters. She glanced toward Rory's room. "I don't want to wake up Mikey."

"The game's on Uncle Aidan's computer."

"Oh. Do you think he'd care if we used it?"

Had she ever asked a dumber question? Rory would say no, no matter what. Well, too bad. Aidan had invaded her privacy this morning. So why should she care about using his computer?

They went inside. The room was larger than Rory's. And it was neat, except for the stuff dumped in the corner, on a cot that had been set up for Liam. Funny, she would have pegged Aidan as a slob. Hell, she didn't know the guy at all.

Except that he liked redheads. All the O'Neil brothers did. Bailey had teased him and Liam about picking up a couple in town. When she heard they were meeting the pretty cop and her girlfriend, Bailey went in for the kill in typical little sister fashion. C.J. remembered taunting Luke like that. For some reason, tonight she didn't find it funny; the thought of Liam's and Aidan's dates didn't . . . feel good.

As she sat down and booted up the computer, it was like he was in the room with them. His scent—some aftershave—lingered in the air. It was really sexy and reminded her of tangled sheets and long lazy mornings in bed. Sometimes, when she had these physical associations, like this smell or the feel of a man's hand on her, she was startled by the loneliness they brought out.

That's it, she was just lonely.

You don't have to be. No man in sight, but you've got a family to spend time with.

She should call her sisters. Better yet, her brother. As she'd told Mitch, he lived only an hour from the lake and though they were at odds about her being in the service, he'd come right away if he knew she needed him. Satisfied with that option, she concentrated on the game and let it distract her.

The *plot* consisted of a series of people trying to sleep and various things that kept them awake. The player had to chase around the intrusive element and destroy it. After beating out the distraction, an image of the person tucked cozily in bed came on-screen, making sleep look desirable. By the time Rory finished playing, he was yawning.

"Time for bed, Champ."

"That's what Daddy calls me."

"I guess I got it from him."

"Carry me."

C.J. smiled and hefted him up; he laid his head on her shoulder. The sensation was wonderful. Warm child, solid weight. Once again she thought of family. Only this time it would be hers: a husband. Kids. A normal life. Geez, what had gotten into her?

When Rory was settled in bed, she started to go back downstairs but as she walked by Aidan's room, the screen light beckoned like a beacon. Must be the computer hadn't shut down. She went inside, and sat on the chair. About to press End Program, she caught sight of an icon in the lower left corner. Lake Pics 7/07. This was July 2007. Would they be ones that he took this week? Against her better judgment—the feeling that she should stay far away from this man still lingered in her consciousness—she booted up the pictures.

Logically, C.J. knew it was impossible to fall in love with a man through his photographs, though in the past she'd felt an intimacy with painters and writers when she saw or read their work. These pictures, though, captured Aidan's essence as much as the subjects. Whimsy: a shot of a doe and its fawn. Excitement: the bursting sunrise. Oh. He'd taken several of Bailey and Angel. After seeing them, C.J. couldn't stop herself from continuing. With each shot she got a look at Aidan's heart. His soul. His mind. Because of that, she began to feel like she was intruding and it made her uncomfortable. She was just about to close the program when she accidentally hit the mouse and it went forward. Another photo appeared on the screen.

"Oh, my God, how dare he?"

AS THEY PULLED up to the house in the car Aidan had rented to use at the lake, Liam lapsed into bust-your-brother's-balls mode. "I can't *believe* you came home with me."

"Yeah. I can't believe it, either. Dancing's always like foreplay to me."

Liam shut off the engine but didn't get out. "That cute little cop was all over you on the floor. Why'd you leave her high and dry?"

"Damned if I know."

In the dimness of the car's interior, Aidan could feel Liam study him. This brother, in particular, could read him well. But, thank you, God, he also had a sensitivity the others didn't; he knew when to joke and when to be serious. Dylan and Paddy way overstepped that boundary. "Does this have anything to do with what we were talking about earlier tonight?"

"Maybe." He ran his finger along the rubber framing on the window. "It goes against my principles to sleep with one woman when I've had the hots for another all day . . . and maybe longer, I'm thinking now."

"We're in sync on that one."

Disgusted at himself, Aidan reached for the door handle. Liam exited, too. They started up the driveway. The night was still, and the crickets were going at it, big time.

"I wonder what C.J. stands for?" Aidan asked.

"Cute Jill?"

Aidan laughed. "Cuddly Jane?"

"Come-to-me Judy?"

As they reached the house, they were having fun with the silly repartee. But they stopped short when they saw an outline of a person on the swing. Oh, fuck. C.J. Aidan hoped she hadn't heard them kidding around about her name.

Dressed in a lightweight black running suit with a star and "The United States Secret Service" emblazoned on the left upper corner of her chest, she had her hair pulled back in some kind of tie and was sipping from a mug. It smelled like coffee. She didn't have an earpiece in, which meant she wasn't on duty.

"Hi, C.J." Liam smiled ingratiatingly. "Enjoying the night air?"

"No." She glared at Aidan. "I'm waiting to talk to you, Mr. O'Neil."

"Told you not to call me that, darlin'," he teased. "There's another standing right here."

"Save your charm for some redhead."

Uh-oh.

Liam moved away. "I'll leave you two alone." He grasped the doorknob, but turned back. "Thanks for talking me into coming tonight, A. It was fun."

"I'm glad." Aidan's voice was full of feeling. He truly hoped Liam would rejoin the living. He'd seem to enjoy the company of the female cop that Sonia had brought along.

Thoughts of the two women vanished as Aidan leaned against the porch railing and watched the moonlight shimmer on C.J.'s hair. His fists curled at his sides; he wanted to yank the tie out in the worst way. Tunnel his hands through the thick mass. "What can I do for you, Agent Ludzecky?"

"How about a walk down by the lake?"

Holy shit, was she asking what he thought she was asking? She'd sounded jealous earlier with that redhead remark. Man, this could be his lucky day. "Sure."

Leaving her cup on the table, she took the lead around the house and spoke to one of the guards standing post on the back deck. There were more agents stationed all over the grounds tonight because Clay was here. C.J. preceded Aidan down to the lakefront. It struck him that she was used to being first. Ferreting out the danger. Placing herself in its way. A fierce streak of displeasure went through him at that thought.

The water slapped the shore and the breeze was cool down here near the dock. Aidan slipped on the thermal green long-sleeved shirt he'd tied around his neck. "Want to sit?" he asked.

"No, walk." Again, she headed down the beach and didn't stop until they hit a copse of trees, putting them out of sight of the agents around the house and the outdoor cameras. Oh, this just kept getting better and better.

The crickets were more noticeable near the trees and the moonlight even brighter at the shore. When she turned to him, her eyes were sparkling and her face was lit. With lust.

Blood lust.

"How dare you invade my privacy this morning?"

"What? Jesus, I thought we rang this bell." At her stony stare, he threw up his hands. "I wasn't spying on you. I happened to catch you doing yoga. It's not a federal crime." He grinned and tested her biceps. "You looked great, by the way. You're in terrific shape."

Stepping back, her eyes widened. "Don't *flirt* with me. We talked about this when you brought me the flowers. Just treat me like an agent."

"Sorry, what was I thinking?"

"You tell me. Exactly what you *were* thinking when you took pictures of me without my consent?"

It rarely happened, but for a second, Aidan was speechless. Then the ramifications of what she said sank in. Like any man worth his salt, he went on the offensive. "How do you know I took pictures of you?"

"It doesn't matter."

"It matters to me. You must have snooped on my computer."

"And found pictures of *me*. Pictures that were . . . lewd."

His jaw dropped. "Lewd? What are you talking about?"

"They were . . ." She looked away, sputtered. "They were blatantly sexual."

Remembering how he'd captured the thrust of her breast, the gentle curve of her spine, a patch of skin—and what those images did to him, even now, just thinking about them—he flushed. But damn it, he didn't do porn. "They were sensuous photos of a female subject, yes. But I don't take lewd pictures."

"This is a complete breach of ethics on your part. Photographing a federal agent without her knowledge. Not to mention the security issues. Damn it, the agents at the front desk at headquarters in D.C. come out and make people delete pictures they've taken of our *building*. You can't go around photographing the agents who are protecting your sister."

"I took pictures of C.J., the woman. Not the agent."

Crossing her arms over her chest, she arched a brow. "We've discussed this before."

"I know, I know, you're not a woman up here."

"Right. Best you remember that and keep your hormones under control."

Sometimes women just said the wrong things to guys. Like now. He stepped forward and invaded her personal space. He was a head taller than her, and had weight on her, but she didn't move. She simply stared up at him with those brandy-colored eyes, which were fiery in the moonlight.

"What does C.J. stand for?" he asked silkily.

"Not Cuddly Jane." Her tone was blistering.

"You weren't meant to hear that. Or see the pictures. I . . ." God he hated apologizing. "I'm sorry if this upsets you." He refused to lie and apologize for the photos themselves. He wasn't one bit sorry for having taken them.

"Somehow, that seems insincere."

"Shit, you invaded my privacy, too. How did you find the pictures anyway?"

"Rory wanted to play *Goodnight Guys*. Your parents didn't know how to set him up on the computer. My finding them was accidental."

"So were my pictures."

"You don't take pictures by accident."

"I couldn't help myself." He grinned, with the memory, and all right, with the fact that he could keep flustering her. "You were so beautiful in the morning light. Almost ethereal."

"Forget about what I looked like this morning, Mr. O'Neil."

"Say my name."

"*What?*"

"Say my name. Just once."

"This conversation is over." She tried to move around him, but he grasped her shoulders.

"Take your hands off me. Attacking a federal agent *is* a crime."

Okay, time to switch tactics. Time for some of his legendary charm. "Got your handcuffs hiding under this suit?" he asked, tugging the shiny silver ring on her zipper. "You could tie me up. Have your way with me."

He saw her swallow hard. Saw her chest rise and fall. And saw her eyes go heavy lidded. Her reaction, so blatantly aroused, shot right to his groin. *He* reacted without thinking. He yanked the tie out of her hair and tunneled his hands through the thick blond mass. Released from their bond, the strands felt like silk and smelled like heaven.

"What do you think you're—"

His mouth closed over hers to shut her up. But his intention changed the minute their lips touched.

He didn't taste. Didn't sip. Didn't tease. Instead, he took. And, after a few seconds of hesitation, she gave. She leaned into him. Pressed her body against his.

So he deepened the kiss. Hungry, and hard, he kept his hands in her hair but tangled their legs. He bit her lip, soothed it with his tongue. Did the whole thing over again.

She wasn't passive. She locked her hand on his neck. Drew him down and angled his head for better access.

After a long time, his mouth left hers and he kissed his way down her jaw to her neck. Bit the soft flesh there. His hand slid between them and closed around her breast, which was hot and heavy in his palm.

She moaned.

"Tell me your name," he whispered. "Please."

Buckets of cold water couldn't have doused the moment quicker than his words. As if they made her realize who she was, what she was doing, she stiffened. Drew away. Pressed her palms on his chest and stepped back. She said, "Oh, my God," and clapped her hands over her mouth.

It took him a minute to come out of the haze of desire. "Don't be upset."

"Upset?" She was watching him like he was a predator.

"Look, I'm not the only one who was involved in that kiss. You were practically climbing up me."

She wiped her mouth, as if that could erase what happened.

He grasped her arms. "C.J., honey, it's okay. We're two consenting adults. Unmarried." At least he thought they were. "Aren't we? You aren't . . ."

"Do you have any idea what would happen to my career if anyone saw us doing this down here?"

He scowled. "I suppose it's not protocol, but I can't believe it'd be a big scandal. In that Clint Eastwood movie about the Secret Service, the agents had personal lives, even relationships with other agents." He remembered something. "And Liam told me that Susan Ford married the Secret Service agent assigned to protect her when her father was president." He grinned. "They must have done some of this"—he swiped at her mouth—"while he was guarding her."

She moved back even further. "Chuck Vance left the agency right after he got involved with Ford. Under a cloud, I heard. In any case, this isn't what I want."

Wounded male pride surfaced. Damn, what was with this woman? "You seemed to want it a few minutes ago." Again, he stepped closer. His tone was silky when he whispered, "Shall we give it another shot and see?"

"No!" She sucked in a heavy breath. "We don't even know each other well enough to be doing this."

"I know you."

"No, no, you don't."

He went on as if she hadn't spoken. "You're a hard worker, you take your job to heart. You try to be tough, but you're a marshmallow where Rory, Mikey and Angel are concerned. You *are* argumentative, and stubborn, a little uptight, but I can handle it. That's enough to know I want to pursue this thing between us."

"*Proszè!* Please," she repeated in English. She placed her hand on his chest. If she'd been angry, or pushy, he might have pursued it. But she looked frightened. And vulnerable. "You don't know the important things about me. My background. My history."

Shocked by the anguish of her plea, he said simply, "Then tell me."

Her face turned up to him, he could see the sadness on

it. "I can't. We'll forget this happened." Circling around him, she walked away.

He turned, but let her go. He thought of the movie he referred to earlier, *In the Line of Fire*. Sitting on the steps of the Lincoln Memorial, Clint Eastwood watches Renee Russo walk away and wills her to turn back to look at him, because it would mean she was interested.

Aidan didn't follow Clint's lead. He didn't wish for that. Because he'd been moved by C.J.'s vulnerability, and, oddly, he wanted to protect Agent Ludzecky.

From himself? What a crazy thought.

EIGHT

THE SNIDE comments, the innuendo and the outright slander from her past haunted C.J. during the dark hours of the night. The same taunts came back as she ran along East Lake Road, her feet slapping the pavement with ruthless determination. She'd taken a longer break to run this emotional marathon and still she hadn't outdistanced her demons.

Hotshot Agent Luke Ludzecky is her brother. How else do you think she got into Intelligence after her rookie year in New York?

Of course she slept with Anderson. The Washington field office doesn't take just anybody. I hear his wife found out and insisted Ludzecky be transferred. He pulled strings to get her a plum job and keep her quiet.

There's got to be something going on with her and Calloway. The woman has a track record . . .

And so C.J. could predict the D.C. gossip if she let herself get involved with Aidan O'Neil. *Yep, Ludzecky seduced the Second Lady's brother. Gotta give her credit, she knows how to get to the top and stay there.*

Well, the former rumors might have circulated in Washington, but the latter would never make the rounds. C.J. had no intention of seducing, or being seduced by, a black-haired Irishman with sexy blue eyes and muscles to die for. And lips that made her forget her name.

As she took a slight incline, the sweat poured off her, not because of the late afternoon sun, but because of inescapable thoughts about how those blue eyes had looked at her for days before the kiss. How those muscles pulsed under her hands last night. And how that mouth had taken hers with a raw possessiveness that should have put her off but thrilled her instead.

He was right. She'd been a willing participant. She'd not only allowed his advances, she'd urged him on, took the lead, become wholly steeped in him. Physical sensations had swamped her, and she let herself drown in them.

Why the fuck had she done that?

Because in some ways, despite what she'd said, she *had* gotten to know him in the last two weeks. He was unselfish with his father, tender to Bailey, attentive to the kids. He had a great sense of humor, though he did have a stubborn streak and was arrogant as hell. But he'd tried to appease her with flowers, which showed he had *some* common sense.

Stop it! she chided herself. You're just lonely. You hate how this job has isolated you from everyone, men included. And you're not used to being cut off like this.

C.J. had been a normal teenager and college student, having fun with guys, sleeping with a chosen few, getting serious a couple of times. Once she'd joined the service, she thought she could continue in that vein until she met someone she would make a life with. She'd dated in New York, had one significant involvement with a teacher, but it had been too hard on him: the long hours, the travel, the danger of her job when she was recruited for protective duty at the UN.

Then the debacle with David had caused her to be gun-shy in Washington. Finally she'd given in to the need for male companionship there, but nothing ever stuck. That had to be it. This was just another example of normal healthy female hormones asserting themselves.

Feeling marginally better, she saw the house up ahead come into view. Aidan had been out for the entire day, and she hoped he wasn't back yet. The car he'd rented was in the driveway next to the service's black monster of a Sub-urban, but he hadn't taken it when he left. Who had picked him up? Probably sexy Sonia.

Good.

That was good.

It *was*!

Instead of entering the first floor, C.J. jogged around to the back, hoping to get inside and shower because she smelled like the inside of a gym bag. She'd just entered the ground level when she heard Mitch's voice from upstairs. "Agent Ludzecky, can you come up here?"

The use of her title alerted her that this wasn't an idle request. Grabbing her gun from the locked drawer by her bed and sticking it her waistband, she took the stairs two at a time. She reached the first floor and found everyone was in the sunroom. Clay and Bailey sat on the couch with the kids. The brothers had taken chairs. And Hower, the dog, stood at attention, his tail wagging, as if something impor-tant was happening here.

One person stood out from the rest. C.J. froze at the sight of him. The wonderful, fabulous, terrific sight of him. His face was inscrutable. She was rooted to the ground.

"Don't you dare not come over here and give me hug, Caterina. Do you hear me?"

As she watched Lukasz smile, she heard, "Ah, so it's Caterina . . ." and "Who the *hell* is this guy?"

She ignored the comments and flew across the room. Luke caught her up in a bear hug strong enough to break her ribs. She felt his solid strength, his big, safe body, his familiar smell. *"Brakuje mi Ciebie."*

"Me, too, Lukasz." She'd missed him so much.

"Kocham Ciebie."

"Kocham Ciebie."

Finally Luke drew back but held her by the shoulders. "You're a mess, *bopchee.*"

"What language are they speaking?" This time, she recognized Aidan's voice.

Reality dawned.

Drawing away from her brother, she turned to Mitch. His smile told her he knew Luke's identity. But he said, "We caught this character trespassing on the grounds. He wouldn't tell us who he is. We brought him here because he said he knew you."

"You recognize him, don't you?"

"Yeah. The legend. It's why I didn't frisk him."

Aidan stepped forward. "And what legend is that?"

For the first time since last night, she looked at the man who had kissed her senseless in the moonlight. Today, his face was full of thunderclouds. Luke took her hand and she squeezed it. "Everybody, this is Luke Ludzecky."

"You're *married*?" Aidan got out, his tone horrified.

"I'm her brother." His voice amused, Luke anchored his hand at her neck. "Her big brother."

"What were you doing sneaking around the grounds?" This from Jenkins, who stood poised next to Mitch. He wasn't angry, just curious, so Mitch must have filled him in.

"I wanted to see how good a job my baby sister and her colleagues were doing up here."

Clay Wainwright seemed amused by the whole thing. "So how good are they?"

"They caught me, didn't they?"

The vice president smiled. "That's reassuring."

On the couch next to him, Bailey grinned. "This seems like quite a reunion. Want some privacy?"

"We'll go downstairs." C.J. glanced at her watch. "I have a half hour left of my break."

"Take the afternoon," Bailey told her. "The others can cover for you, right, Mitch?"

"I was just about to suggest that. Go ahead, C.J."

"If you're sure." She really wanted to spend time with Luke.

"Go."

Nodding, she led her brother downstairs. But not before she saw's Aidan's glare level on her.

AFTER C.J. took a quick shower, she joined Luke on the dock where he waited for her. His dark blond hair was windblown as he stood out by the lake, staring at the water. Dressed in denim shorts, hiking boots and a T-shirt that said "Corning East High Spartans," he still resembled the young agent who went undercover in a high school to ferret out some suspected violence, lost his heart to one of his *teachers* and quit the Secret Service to marry her.

Coming up behind him, she slid her arms around his waist and leaned into him.

"You smell better." His voice was husky and laced with humor.

"I know." She held on tightly. "God, it's good to see you."

He pivoted around, his face serious. "I can't believe you cut yourself off like this. From me. And from the rest of the family."

One thing about Luke, he never minced words. And he didn't know the meaning of *tact*. Of course he'd jump right in. But she didn't want to fight with him.

"Let's sit."

Kicking off their shoes, they dropped down onto the dock and put their feet in the water. The feel of it was warm and soothing after her punishing run. "I didn't cut myself off. I read the family e-mail loop regularly."

"And rarely post."

"What would I talk about, Luke? My daily activities? I respond when something significant happens to somebody. That's enough."

"You should go home more."

"I go to Queens now and again."

"Last Christmas for a day. You didn't even stay overnight. It's July. You haven't been to see them since."

"I had lunch with Elizabeita when she came back from Oxford. And I spent time with Ana when she brought little Donuta for a visit."

"I didn't know about that. Still, you're in and out of New York all the time." His tone was scolding, but this time it didn't make her bristle.

"I'm working when I come here."

He picked up her hand. Held it. "Tell me the truth."

And there is was. Just like when she slept with a guy the first time. When she first fell in love. There was a bond with this sibling that she didn't have with the others. So she said honestly, "You know the answer to that."

"How could you do this *me*?"

"Luke, when I signed up for the service"—just as he'd *re*signed—"you had a fit. You blew up at me, we had that huge fight, and when you couldn't make me do what you wanted, you didn't talk to me for a month."

"I know. I apologized for that. After I cooled down."

"When I started on the VPPD, you flipped again. They all did."

"*Matka* does not flip."

Matka. The embodiment of motherhood with her house-dresses, bun, sturdy shoes and a heart as big as Texas. "All right. She got sad. Which was worse."

Luke watched a fish making splashes in the water. "They thought it was over. The worry. The fear. Then you hooked up with the Wainwrights . . ."

"I know. And it killed me to hurt them even more."

"Yeah, it killed me, too. It's one of the reasons I quit."

"You quit so you could be with Kelsey Cunningham."

Seriousness vanished. "The love of my life." A smug grin. "At least for now."

Something in his tone. "What?"

Undiluted joy shone in his eyes, the exact color of hers, when he looked at her. "She's pregnant. We're having twins, both girls."

"Oh, my God. Oh, Luke, congratulations." She threw her arms around him and hugged him again.

He raised his eyes to the heavens. "I'm destined to be surrounded by women my whole life."

"I'm so happy for you."

"Thanks, baby."

They talked for a few minutes about how Kelsey was feeling.

"Okay, back to you. Listen, you can stay in the service and do what you have to do, but see your family more."

"It's so strained, Lukasz. No one says anything outright about this detail, except Lizzie of course, but you can cut the tension with a knife when I go back there."

"Talk it out with them."

"I tried. They started to sound like Pa."

Stash Ludzecky. Whose displeasure with Luke and stereotypical expectations of C.J. had far-reaching effects on both their lives.

Luke said, "He meant well."

"Don't give me that shit. He was too hard on you. And me."

"I joined the service to please him. To show him I could be straight."

No response.

"And you joined to prove girls didn't need to be teachers or nurses."

Her shoulders sagged. "Does it matter, Luke? I'm here now. And I like my job. A lot."

"I thought you'd stay in the Intelligence unit in New York. With your UN background, you were a natural."

"So did I."

"There were rumors when you were transferred."

On their brief visits, they never talked about her job. When she left the New York office, she just said she needed a change. So they never discussed the gossip before.

"How did you hear them?"

"I use my service connections to find out about you."

"Like you did today. From who, by the way?"

"Joe Stonehouse."

"Talk about legends." Head of the National School Threat Assessment Center for a while, Stonehouse set the benchmarks for stopping school violence and saved thousands of lives. Luke had been on several assignments with him. "I could never figure out why he quit. He was revered."

"For love, honey. Just like me."

She shook her head. "What'd you hear about me?"

"That you had an affair with your boss."

Her face heated and she felt the familiar indignation well inside her. "I didn't."

"I was pretty sure of that."

"But David Anderson would have."

"What does that mean?"

"As far-fetched as this seems, he fell in love with me."

"Shit."

"He said I had to leave the New York field office because he was afraid his contact with me would affect his marriage."

"That's fucking nuts. You could have sued him for sexual harassment."

"I know. There were a thousand reasons why I didn't. I was young and inexperienced. I was afraid. And I liked him, Luke. Along with his family. He had little girls. I couldn't make public his actions and ruin his life."

"So you let the rumors go."

"Those and the ones about you."

"Me?"

"Yep, that I got where I am—into the VPPD—because I had a hotshot agent for a brother, and because I slept with David."

"Shows how little they know. I was a thorn in the service's side."

"They begged you to stay."

"I'm sorry, Cat."

"You know what? In the end, it was a beneficial move. And I made out great despite the gossipmongers. I work on the vice presidential team. I love being around Bailey and the kids. This is a terrific assignment."

Luke's scowl alerted her.

"What?"

"Aidan O'Neil."

She felt the blush creep up her neck.

"You better be careful."

"Of what?"

"Don't bullshit me. He's the one with the runner's body. Hair a little long?"

"Yeah."

"He wanted to rip my throat out when you hugged me and he didn't know I was your brother. Something going on there?"

"No."

"After what you just told me, you can't afford another opening for people to criticize."

"I know that. Nothing's going on, Lukasz."

Standing, Luke pulled her up. "You never were a very good liar." He kissed her nose. "Just be careful, baby. Now, let's go for a walk and I'll fill you in on the details of having a wife pregnant with twins."

* * *

MESMERIZED, AIDAN watched her from the upstairs window. Right before his eyes, she'd transformed. For a few minutes, the night before, he'd gotten a glimpse of that woman inside the agent. As he'd held her in his arms. As he'd kissed her. But this was different; in the light of day, he could observe the metamorphosis unhindered by the darkness that had cloaked them.

She was as graceful as a gazelle as she walked toward her brother in pink capris and a pink shirt. She was all soft and womanly as she hugged him. Laid her head tenderly on his back. When she turned, even from this distance, he could see the love on her face. He imagined this was how he looked around his family.

And she kept touching her brother. Fingers on his arm. Holding his hand. Resting her head on his shoulder. This was the real woman . . . Caterina. The name fit her. His hands itched to capture the myriad facets of her in his camera.

All night long, Aidan had considered leaving her alone, as she'd asked. In the past, he'd been able to forgo what wasn't good for him, usually without much regret. And he certainly never pursued females who weren't interested in him. Not that there were very many.

But seeing what kind of woman C.J. could be when she completely let down, he realized that no matter what he told himself, of even what was best for both of them, he wasn't going to roll over and play dead.

He was going to go after her.

NINE

"Ms. O'Neil? Are you all right?"

Bailey looked up and C.J. saw that the Second Lady's eyes were red. It was just after six in the morning and most everyone in the house was asleep. C.J. had returned from her run and heard someone walking around on the first floor so she'd come up to investigate. Bailey was alone in the sunroom, staring out at the lake. "Yes, I'm fine."

"You're up early."

"Clay left." She sniffled. "Look at me, I'm a wreck."

C.J. stood at the room's entrance. "Is there anything I can do for you?"

"Get a cup of coffee and come sit with me for a bit. Keep me company." Although Bailey always tried to draw her into conversations, most of the time C.J. managed to avoid them. When she hesitated, Bailey said, "You're not on duty for another hour."

"I need to shower and change after my run."

"Please."

Damn it. Chitchat wasn't good, especially when C.J.

already felt too involved in this family. But geez, the woman was hurting. "All right." After pouring herself a mug of coffee, she dropped down in the chair across from Bailey, self-conscious in her gray shorts and tank top.

Under normal circumstances, Bailey O'Neil was a beautiful woman, but pregnancy made her skin even more vibrant. Despite her obvious upset, she still glowed, sitting in the early morning light in her icy blue pajamas. "I'm sorry you're upset about Mr. Wainwright. Our people will do everything they can to make sure he's safe over there."

"Foreign travel is dangerous."

C.J. knew stories of presidential and vice presidential foreign travel fiascoes. One in particular was the Nixons' goodwill trip to Caracas. Upon arrival at the airport, hordes of demonstrators jeered at the then vice president and his wife. They began throwing bottles and stones at them. The Secret Service formed a tight perimeter around the couple and got them into the limousine. After traveling only a few blocks, the motorcade ground to a halt due to makeshift roadblocks; demonstrators swarmed the limo with pipes and clubs, battering the car. The service managed to get them away, though this was a closer call than they'd ever experienced.

Of course, C.J. had no intention of telling this to the Second Lady.

"Mr. Wainwright is a careful man. Tim Jenkins and his team are used to traveling vice presidents."

"He promised he'd minimize working the ropes there." Many times protectees got out of the car and shook hands with bystanders. This was a nightmare for Secret Service agents who stood behind them, sometimes having to hold them back by their belts. Clay Wainwright was outgoing by nature, often venturing into the crowd, befriending staff at the embassies and giving impromptu speeches.

"They'll make him wear a vest and curtail his activities."

"Which he hates." Bailey sighed. "I thought about trying to talk him out of going. I read a book on first and second ladies. Nancy Reagan interfered all the time with her husband's foreign plans. The Secret Service said if they wanted a trip canceled, they'd go to the wife."

C.J. knew Bailey could persuade Clay to do almost anything for her. The vice president was putty in her hands most of the time. "You didn't do it?"

"No. He really wanted to go. He feels a sort of mentorship for what they've done over there with juvenile crime."

"As do you."

"Yeah. We fought about my going. But he was right." She rested her hand on her slightly rounded stomach. "Usually I'm a lot more sane about things. I knew I shouldn't go. And he *should*. The damn pregnancy is making me irrational. And vulnerable, which I hate!"

C.J. smiled. "So did my sisters. I remember when Ana was carrying Donuta. She was an emotional wreck. Luke seemed to be the only one who could calm her down, and he wasn't around much."

Bailey cocked her head. "What does *Kocham Ciebie* mean?"

Swallowing hard, C.J. just stared at her.

"Luke said that to you, and you said it back."

"It's *I love you* in Polish."

"You're close to your family?"

"I, um, need some more coffee." Uncomfortable, C.J. stood and crossed into the kitchen.

Unfortunately, Bailey followed her. "C.J.?"

She turned around. "Ms. O'Neil, it's not protocol to—"

"Loosen up today, please. I try to respect the distance you want to keep, though I'm not sure why you do it. You know as well as I do agents get close to the protectees. Jackie Kennedy adored Clint Hill."

"Because he jumped on her in the motorcade when Kennedy was shot."

Bailey placed a hand on her arm. "Wouldn't you jump on me if there was an attack? Or take a bullet for me?"

"Of course. I'd do anything to protect you."

The Second Lady smiled and glanced behind her. "Then sitting outside with me isn't too much to ask."

Instinctively, C.J. knew she wasn't going to win this disagreement. And truth be told, since Luke left she was missing him and her sisters a lot. When they were settled in cushioned chairs at an umbrella table, Bailey looked at her expectantly.

C.J. said, "Yes, I'm close to my family."

"Your brother especially? I sensed a bond."

"We're closest in age." She shook her head. "We shared everything when we were growing up."

"Clay told me about his reputation in the Secret Service."

"He kept everybody hopping. He never quite fit the standard image of an agent."

"He calls you Caterina."

"All of us have Polish names."

"All of you?"

"I have six sisters."

"Six? Wow. I thought having four brothers was a big deal. What are their names?"

Because Bailey was smiling instead of fretting about her husband, C.J. decided to keep distracting her. "There's Lukasz, me, Ana, Sofia, Paulina, Antonia, Magdalena and Elizabeita. Now *she's* a handful."

"The youngest?"

"Uh-huh. When she was sixteen, Luke was on an undercover assignment and got hurt. Lizzie tracked him down through the phone call he made to us. She had to see for herself that he was really all right."

"That must have caused a stir."

"Everything she does causes one."

"What's she doing now?"

"She went to Oxford on a Fulbright scholarship and is a curator at the Met." C.J. shook her head. "She's the smartest of us all."

Bailey stared out at the water. "I love having a big family. I love my brothers. I don't know what I'd do without them."

C.J.'s heart bumped in her chest.

"What?" Bailey frowned. "Oh, I'm sorry. You don't get to see your family much." Her face brightened with a little of the old Street Angel peeking out. "You could take some time off to go see them when we're in the city. I know you've never done that, but you should start."

"Thanks. Things are really strained among us now. They balked at my joining the service. It got worse when I joined the VPPD."

"I can understand why. It would kill me to think of one of the guys in danger."

Unable to resist, C.J. gave her a knowing look. "I imagine they felt that way about you when you worked for ESCAPE."

"Yeah, I guess. It was something I had to do, though." She was thoughtful. "Like you, I imagine. I do understand you, C.J." Bailey's gaze was diverted by something behind her.

A morning-deep male voice said, "Hi, ladies."

"Hey, hi, A., come join us."

C.J. turned and saw Aidan had come out onto the deck from the kitchen. He was tousled from sleep and sexy as hell, bare-chested and wearing Gap pajama bottoms. Nodding to her, he crossed to his sister, leaned over and kissed Bailey on the cheek. Then he pressed a palm on her stomach briefly.

Out of nowhere, a scenario hit C.J. Of Aidan kissing *her* good morning. Cradling *her* stomach in his hand. She stood to banish the very real images. "I need to get changed. I'm on duty soon."

Aidan arched a brow. "Don't leave on my account."

"I'm not."

Aidan watched C.J. hurry away from him. *Running scared* came to mind. He grinned at the evidence that he could affect her that way.

His sister watched C.J. leave. "She's an interesting woman."

Having decided not to put Bailey in the middle of this thing between him and C.J., he dropped down onto a chair holding a mug he'd brought out of the house. "Is she?"

"She has six sisters. All younger."

"Oh, God, can you picture it when they get together?" He sipped his coffee. "Must be like a beauty pageant."

"You think C.J.'s pretty?"

"Sure, don't you?"

"Yes. But you usually go for redheads, like Sonia. Speaking of which, you came home the other night. I asked Liam about it before he left, but he told me to talk to you."

"That's not gonna happen."

"Why?"

"I, um, don't know."

"You're, um, lying to your favorite sister."

"I don't know why, B. I'm not as anxious to see her as I was last summer."

Bailey was quiet, which was never a good sign. Finally she said, "Something going on I should know about, A.?"

"No."

"I—"

The phone rang, cutting off the conversation. "That might be Clay." She picked up the cordless she'd set out on the table. "Hello."

Aidan watched her face.

"Hey, Suze. How are you?"

"Go ahead and take it," Aidan told her, standing.

"Just a second, Suze." She put her hand over the mouthpiece. "Don't leave."

"All right." Aidan wandered over to the railing and

stared out at the water while Bailey talked to Suze Williams, her former coworker at ESCAPE. Reaching into his pj's pocket, he pulled out his digital camera and began snapping pictures of the way the waves crashed on the shore. But his heart wasn't in it. He was preoccupied with Caterina Ludzecky, with the six sisters and one brother she adored.

The brother who'd sought out Aidan before he left yesterday. . .

"Hey," Luke said to him when he'd found Aidan on the dock. Not by accident.

Aidan had been taking photos of a mama duck and her ducklings right near the shore. He'd turned to see Luke looming behind him. The guy was a powerful presence, even though he was a couple of inches shorter than Aidan. "Hi."

Luke aimed a smile at the ducks. "Cute." He shrugged. "My wife's pregnant."

"Congratulations. Your first?"

"Uh-huh." Luke stared at Aidan, making him shift on his feet. "I don't know if I should say anything."

"About your wife?"

"No, about my sister."

Aidan turned away so Luke wouldn't see the guilt in his eyes. He raised the camera again. "Bailey really likes her. She's a good agent."

"She's a good person."

"Is she? I don't know her very well."

He thought he heard the brother snort. "I don't wanna see her get hurt here."

Lowering the camera, Aidan frowned. "Agents put themselves in harm's way by just taking on the job."

"I mean personally."

Silence seemed the best course, so he kept his mouth shut.

"And reputation wise."

Because he remembered decking Clay in defense of Bailey one time, Aidan said, "I feel the same way about my sister."

"Then I guess we understand each other."

Aidan wondered what C.J. had told Luke. Were they as close as he and Bailey? Would she have confided her feelings for Aidan? How else would Luke know to come and warn off Aidan? Now that was something to think about.

"Have a safe trip back," was all Aidan said.

Luke headed toward the house without answering . . .

"Aidan?"

He pushed away from the railing and rejoined his sister. "How's Suze?"

"Really well. ESCAPE is flourishing."

"Do you miss it?"

"Sometimes. I've got a lot going on, and I think I'm doing some good things for kids in Washington." She gave him an impish grin. "I miss the hands-on aspect, though. And the excitement."

"Now why doesn't that surprise me?"

She smiled. "Suze is getting an award from the National Women's Rights Museum in Seneca Falls on Friday. They're recognizing women who've overcome the odds—impoverished backgrounds, dysfunctional families, crime. She's coming to the lake to see me after the ceremony, since it's only an hour from here."

"That's great." He saw the glimmer in her eyes. "What?"

"I'd like to go to the ceremony."

"Did she ask you to come?"

"Of course not. She knows what a production it is to take me or Clay anywhere. I'd surprise her."

"Is that possible without weeks of preplanning?"

"Anything's possible."

"The big guys won't like that, sis."

"I can handle them."

Aidan wished he felt the same about the Secret Service agents. Well, one in particular.

MITCH HAD BEEN scowling all morning. So C.J. said, "I think it'll be safe. We've done impromptus with the family before."

"Impromptus?" Aidan asked.

They were all sitting in the main-floor sunroom. The noon sky had turned dark, and the wind whipped the water below them. Rain banged against the windows. Bailey and Aidan had sought out C.J. and Mitch about midmorning. They'd been debating the trip to Seneca Falls since then. The dog, Hower, sat at Bailey's side, like a guard, too.

Mitch explained the term. "It's when a protectee visits a place in an apparently spontaneous stop, but it's preplanned. Usually this kind of thing is done for publicity purposes and photo opportunities. Like the president going to an ice cream stand to get pictures of him in an ordinary setting."

"Then we can go?" Bailey's eyes lit. Gone was the grim expression in them earlier. C.J. hoped they could pull off this little excursion. The Second Lady could use the distraction.

"I'd rather not." Mitch was giving it one last try. "We don't have time to execute much of an advance trip. Two days means only cursory scrutiny." Mitch shrugged. "Can't you just be content with Ms. Williams visiting you at the lake afterward?"

Instead of becoming the haughty vice president's wife, Bailey gave Mitch that endearing smile of hers. C.J. guessed they were good to go to Seneca Falls. "Mitch, I know this isn't what you want to do. But I so seldom argue against your judgment, can't you compromise just once?"

Mitch looked to C.J. She gave her honest opinion. "No one will be expecting her. Only a small group will be at the museum. We've got two days to run enough checks on the other women being honored, people who work there, residents in the area. The Syracuse field office will jump at the chance to help out. Overall, I think it would be okay for her to go." She watched him. "What's bothering you most about this, Mitch?"

"Two things. Those footprints Aidan saw at the lake. We still don't know if they were from somebody checking out Bailey and the kids. Second, there's a former Anthrax member's family in the area. I'd rather not give anybody who might be checking us out for an AOP"—an attack on the principal—"by leaving the grounds."

Aidan's brows raised. "Did you and Caterina find anything out from my pictures?"

She rounded on him. "Please don't call me that. It's either C.J. or Agent Ludzecky."

Folding his arms across the chest of the white T-shirt he'd put on, Aidan leaned back against the wall. "Why? It's your name. A pretty one, by the way."

"Aidan." Bailey's tone was short. "Don't pick on her." She asked C.J., "*Did* you find anything?"

"They were small, almost like a kid's." Standing behind the couch, C.J. turned to Mitch. "Are you afraid they're Annie-O's prints?"

"Well, she's Asian, so her foot size could be small. But there's been no sign of her up here. We did extensive checks on the aunt and uncle, who's a cop. They aren't even close to Annie-O's family."

Mitch frowned again. "The jury's still out on the daughter, Sasha. Parents don't always know what their kids are doing."

"There's no indication anywhere that Sasha is friends with Annie. And from our reports, Annie's gone straight anyway. She's working at a decent job."

Bailey said, "Mitch, I really do want to go to Seneca Falls. Please make it happen for me."

"All right. I'll get an advance team out there right away."

C.J. brightened. This would be great. "I'll go. Gorman can fill in here for me."

"No, I'd rather head the advance myself. Gorman can fill in for me."

Shit. She thought she could get away from Aidan for a while. "Sure, okay."

"I'll go down to the ceremony with you," Aidan announced.

Bailey looked thoughtful. "Pa and Ma can't watch both Rory and Angel."

"I'll have to insist you don't bring either of them," Mitch told her, his tone exasperated.

"Then it's settled. You should stay here, A. Help out with the kids."

"He definitely should stay." Mitch eyed C.J. speculatively, so she added, "Mr. O'Neil isn't strong enough yet to do everything here. And Rory's a handful."

Aidan shrugged. "Then it's settled."

"Come on, C.J., let's get to work on this." Mitch glanced outside. "Grayson's on the second perimeter, Ms. O'Neil. He's even closer to the house because of the rain. C.J. and I will be in the command post downstairs."

Rising when he did, Bailey grasped Mitch's arm. "Thank you. For listening to me."

He smiled. "I can see why the vice president doesn't stand a chance with you."

Bailey laughed out loud, a nice sound to hear.

C.J. and Mitch headed downstairs and entered the office area over on his side. He shut the door and turned to her. "Okay, *Caterina*. What's going on?"

"Going on?"

"Don't bullshit me. The vibes between you and Aidan O'Neil are wacky. Has something happened between you two?"

"What makes you say that?"

He lifted a hand and extended a finger. "Number one, he *yelled* at you in the hospital for no reason. Second, you jumped on him about not telling us about the footprints. Totally out of character for you and improper behavior toward a protectee's family. Number three, O'Neil looked like he was ready to take Luke down when he didn't know Luke was your brother. Now, this *Caterina* shit and your inappropriate tone of voice with him over that."

C.J. watched her boss, and her friend. Should she confide in him? He knew about her past and he'd never let her down before. Instead, he'd helped her over the bumps. But an image of David Anderson superimposed over Mitch. *He* was her friend. She'd trusted *him*. And he'd pulled the professional rug out from under her. So she said to Mitch, "Nothing's going on here. I don't like the guy much is all."

Mitch's gaze turned steely. "I thought you trusted me more than this."

Her jaw dropped at his response. Before she could respond, he turned to his desk. Without looking at her, he said coolly, "All right, Agent Ludzecky. We've got an advance detail to plan."

TEN

"FISHING'S GOOD, isn't it?" Pa was making small talk as they sat in Clay's seventeen-foot boat in a cove where the trout were biting because the morning storm had churned up the fish in the lake. The water was choppy but not enough so they couldn't take the boat out. And the sun was shining.

"Yep, great." Aidan gave his father a genuine smile. Dressed in a loose shirt and shorts, his dad sported a fishing hat, complete with lures and hooks decorating it. Aidan wished he could photograph him, but it wasn't a good idea to resurrect all that now. Picking up a can of beer, he sipped it. "Too bad Bailey couldn't come with us."

"I'm worried about her goin' down there to the museum."

"She'll be safe, Pa. Mitch is leaving in the morning, but he already has the Syracuse field office setting things up in Seneca Falls. He and C.J. will stick with her."

"Hope so. Can't say I like havin' my girl in the limelight like this."

"She could be First Lady someday."

"Oh, Lord." His eyes widened and he gripped the pole. "Hey, I got one. A *big* one."

"Want me to help?"

"I'm not an invalid."

Biting his tongue, Aidan watched his pa reel in a decent-size fish. With the others they'd caught today, they had enough for dinner. "Ready to head back?" he asked.

Pa looked tired. Had they stayed out too long? "In a minute." His father took a bead on him. "It's not your fault, you know."

"You being tired?"

"The heart attack. Because we fought."

"Oh, yeah, I know that."

"Don't get me wrong, I think you should stay at the pub. Do honest work. But the argument, it didn't cause this." He tapped his chest with his fist.

"Sure it didn't."

"You're not a good liar, boy."

Aidan busied himself with the motor. "Let's head back."

Pa shrugged. "Suit yourself."

As they traveled to the cottage, the wind picked up and waves increased in size and intensity. Aidan was thinking about what his father said as he steered the boat into its slip between the dock and next to Clay's cabin cruiser. He set the cooler of fish on the dock, then leapt out.

"Toss me the line," he said to Pa. When he had the knot secured, he held out his hand. "Come on, I'll help you. The water's getting choppy."

"I said, I ain't no invalid." When Pa was tired, he got cranky. "Wish people would stop treatin' me like one."

Aidan stepped away.

With one foot on the dock Pa was about to hoist himself out when a gust of wind rocked the boat. The momentum carried Pa with it. He toppled backward, went down hard. And cracked his head on the edge of the middle wooden bench.

"What . . ." Aidan jumped back into the boat. His father didn't move. He lay on the bottom, his arms to the side, feet out. Eyes closed. Still. Very still.

Aidan froze, unable to act.

There was a thundering of footsteps on the decking. He felt the boat sway and then a quiet, "Aidan, move out of the way." Sun blinded him as he looked up. It took him a minute to identify C.J.

"I have training. Let me in." Her tone was gentle but firm enough to have him scrambling back.

She said into her wrist unit, "Call 911, Mitch. Mr. O'Neil's had an accident out on the dock."

Kneeling down close to his father, she got a good look at him. "He's unconscious." She put her fingers on the pulse at his neck. Opened his mouth and peered inside. Lifted his eyelids. As if by rote, she said, "Airways aren't blocked, he's breathing steadily."

"What can I do?"

"Find me blankets."

He located some in the storage area under the seats and brought them to C.J. "Shouldn't you check the back of his head? He hit it pretty hard."

"The last thing we do is move him." As she spoke, she rolled up blankets and wedged them on either side of Pa's head, then she covered him with one. She checked his pulse again, just as he started to come around. "Mr. O'Neil, can you hear me?"

"Arrgh . . ." His father's eyes opened. He squinted.

"Can you see me?" C.J. asked.

"Blurry."

"How do you feel?"

"Head hurts. Dizzy."

"Just lie still. Help will be here soon."

Aidan dropped back on the vinyl seat, his heart still thudding in his chest. He saw Bailey hurrying down the dock with Mitch. Sirens screamed in the background.

"Oh, my God." Bailey reached the boat and stood over them. "Oh, Aidan, what happened?"

C.J. answered. "He fell trying to get out of the boat. He's got classic symptoms of a concussion. But he's awake and breathing evenly. That's all good news."

Bailey leaned against Mitch.

Two paramedics hustled down the dock. Aidan felt a pull on his arm.

"Come on," C.J. said. "We have to give them room."

Like a man in a daze, Aidan climbed out of the boat. He went to his sister and slid his arm around her, for his comfort as well as hers. Together, they watched the medics get in the boat . . . talk to his father . . . put a neck brace on him.

"Why are they doing that?" he asked.

"In case of a spinal injury." C.J.'s tone was gentle again, but she couldn't dilute the message.

Bailey moaned. Aidan sucked in a breath.

"It's not likely," C.J. added. "He was moving around some. The brace is a precaution for everybody who falls like this."

Soon, his father was on a stretcher and the paramedics were hiking up the slope with him.

"I'm going to the hospital," Bailey said. "I won't argue about this."

Aidan felt sick, couldn't respond.

Mitch nodded. "All right."

"Do you want to come with us, Aidan?"

"No."

Bailey frowned. "Then see to Mikey, will you? He got upset when C.J. radioed in."

"You're in charge here, Agent Ludzecky." Mitch's voice was strained. "Gorman's with Bruiser and Blue Eyes now. We'll take Grayson and two uniforms with us; the others will stand post on the second perimeter."

A flurry of activity got Mitch, Bailey and the guards on the road. Aidan dragged himself upstairs to find Rory and Mikey. They were in their room, staring out the front window.

"Uncle Aidan," Rory yelled, racing toward him. "What happened?"

Though he felt like he was going to puke, he gave the boy a reassuring hug. "Papa fell getting out of the boat and hit his head."

"Grandma says Papa's got the hardest head of anybody in the family."

A small smile. "There you go. He's going to be fine."

"Why they taking him to the hospital?"

"Just to make sure he's okay. He was sick a little while ago so they're being extra careful."

Setting Rory down, Aidan crossed to Mikey, who hadn't spoken a word, just stood by the window watching them. Aidan knelt down in front of his nephew.

"Hey, kiddo. Did you hear what I said about your grandpa?"

Mikey nodded. His eyes were somber like they'd been for months and months after Kitty's death.

"Honest, Mike. Papa's gonna be okay. You believe me, don't you?"

"Where's Daddy?" he asked.

"He'll be up to the lake again soon. Meanwhile, I'm here." He stood and took Mikey's hand. "Why don't you guys come with me to check on Angel?"

"'Kay."

Aidan and the boys played with the baby until she started to fuss. He set Rory and Mikey up with a DVD on his computer and had just rocked Angel to sleep in Bailey's room when a phone rang. C.J. came to the door with the cordless in her hand. "It's your sister."

His throat worked hard. "You talk to her."

She looked at him oddly, then spoke into the phone. "He's rocking Angel, Ms. O'Neil." A long pause. "Yes, yes, I'll tell him."

Clicking off, she set the phone on the table by the door and approached him. He didn't say anything. Finally she bent over, took Angel out of his arms and laid her in the port-a-crib they used sometimes. Aidan sat where he was, staring ahead.

C.J. waited, then knelt in front of him. "Your father's fine. I tried to convince you of that at the dock, and now it's confirmed. He has a slight concussion. Sometimes the paramedics don't even take the person to the hospital when that's the extent of his injury. But because of your father's heart attack, they wanted to check him out. Everybody's on their way back. He's fine. Just a bit of a headache." She smiled. "Ms. O'Neil said he's ornery, but that wasn't caused by the concussion."

Aidan didn't react. When she stepped back, he rose and walked out onto the upper deck off the bedroom. Bracing his hands on the railing, he peered out over the lake. The wind whipped around him and he shivered. Now it was hitting him. He tried to battle it back—the fear, the nausea, the guilt.

Then he felt a hand on his shoulder. More of the ice cracked. "Don't," he said.

She didn't move her hand. "It's not your fault."

C.J. didn't know about the argument that had caused his pa's heart attack. "That line is wearing thin."

Sidling around, she managed to come between him and the railing. "He *fell*, Aidan."

"I should have . . ." Shit, his eyes stung, so he closed them.

"Tell me."

"I tried to help him out of the boat. He wouldn't let me. I should have insisted."

"From what I've observed, O'Neil stubbornness runs in

the family. Once one of you has something in your head, nobody can change his mind."

That lured a smile from him. "Still. He's recuperating from heart surgery. I should have found a way."

"He had an accident. A very common one."

Aidan made a disgusted cluck of his tongue. "I didn't even know what to do."

"When a family member is injured, people often freeze."

"You knew what to do."

She shrugged a shoulder. "Ten-minute medicine."

"What?"

"All agents are trained in medical care. We call it *ten-minute medicine*. We know what to do in the approximate ten minutes before help arrives."

Another weak smile.

"Don't beat yourself up. Your father's fine. He'll have a few symptoms—headache and the like—but nothing serious."

"He didn't need this."

"No. But you didn't cause it."

He wanted to believe her. Her certainty calmed him some.

They heard commotion downstairs. Aidan didn't move. C.J. said, "I think he's home. Go on down and see for yourself."

He nodded, but again, he didn't step back. She stood there, close. Her eyes were warm as she watched him. Then she reached up and drew him to her. He let himself fall into her arms, be reassured by her strong embrace, her sensible advice. After a few moments, he drew back and started away.

Halfway down the stairs, he admitted that one simple hug was a lot more meaningful, and a lot more dangerous, than the kiss they'd shared that night on the beach.

* * *

HER PALMS were slippery from exertion, but C.J. gripped one of the free weights she'd found in the closet and did another arm curl. Her muscles strained with the effort; needing the outlet, she continued. By exercising, she could force herself to concentrate on the physical and not think about what had happened yesterday with Aidan.

Setting down the fifty-pound weight, she stood, picked up two forty-pounders and, holding them at chin level, squatted. Her quads screamed after three reps. She did another. She'd just completed the fifth when she saw Aidan come to the doorway. He looked better today, rested. His hair was damp as if he'd just showered and there was a nick on his jaw from where he'd shaved. In his hand was a bunch of wildflowers, this time purple, and in a vase.

"I suppose those aren't from you, either," she said, trying to lighten the mood.

"Nope. From Pa." He set the flowers on the table.

"Thank him for me."

Turning, he nodded to the weights. "Should you be doing that alone?" His tone was gentle, solicitous, no longer challenging, making him a hundred times more dangerous. C.J. was used to head-on confrontation; she was a rookie in soft seduction.

She finished the last squat, set the weights down and dropped to the floor, bracing her arms behind her. "Not really. Mitch usually spots me."

His brow furrowed and there was a stiff set to his shoulders. "Can you take a break? I'd like to talk to you."

Grabbing a towel, she wiped her face. "About what?"

"First, I wanted to thank you again for what you did yesterday with Pa."

"How is he?"

"Fine. He wants to see to you today when you have the chance. He's grateful, too." He hesitated before he said, "You're winning the O'Neil men over one by one."

"I was just doing what I was trained for."

Aidan shrugged, wandered over to the window, stood by it. "I was wondering about Bailey's trip. I'm worried about her."

"Mitch will make sure the bases are covered. And I'll be there, too."

The sky outside made his blue gaze intense. The navy T-shirt he wore with jeans magnified the effect. "Have you gotten an update today?"

"Yes. Mitch is bringing in the Syracuse staff and the local police this morning to brief them. Some agents from the field office will be at the ceremony undercover. Cops will be posted around town and the park itself."

"Everybody will know something's going on with the police out in droves."

"We won't be able to keep it a secret that Bailey's in Seneca Falls. Mostly when a protectee travels, we worry about people knowing ahead of time and having the opportunity to put a plan in place."

"To hurt her?" His voice was raw. This was a man who loved deeply.

"An enemy might want to do that, and Bailey's made some in this area of the country. We have to be realistic about that. But with the family of the president and vice president, we're concerned about kidnapping, not someone doing bodily harm."

She didn't go into the details of preplanning an alternate route out of the museum in case someone tried to get to Bailey, or stationing an agent at the nearest hospital and making sure the protectee's blood type was in stock, or the myriad other things that could go wrong. Aidan was worried about his sister.

"Don't be upset. We're good at what we do, Mr. O'Neil. We'll keep her and the kids safe."

There was a flicker of amusement on his face, momentarily replacing the concern. "You called me Aidan yesterday."

I know. "Did I?"

"Uh-huh."

Giving him an innocent look, she said, "Does that answer your questions about this trip?"

"For now."

When he didn't move to leave, she finally had to ask, "Anything else?"

"Yeah. Are we going to talk about the elephant in the room?"

She rolled to her feet, needing to be his height for this discussion. "What elephant is that?"

"You know as well as I do what I'm talking about."

Crossing to the table, she busied herself with her gym bag, pretending to search for something. She caught the sweet scent of the flowers from here. "No, I don't."

He drew her around. "Something's been happening between us since day one. Then the kiss by the lake blew my socks off. But yesterday, after Pa's accident, cinched it. There's more than a physical attraction between us. We connect. We have feelings for each other, Caterina."

She could deny it. But she didn't. She didn't even object to his use of her full name. Intuitively she sensed that wasn't the way to handle this. Honesty was the best now. "Are you really grateful for my help with your father? And for keeping your family safe?"

He scowled at the non sequitur. "Of course."

"Then let me do my job without distraction."

"I'm a distraction? Only a distraction?"

She didn't respond.

"At least admit there's something between us."

Her heart beating at a clip, she prayed she was doing the right thing. "All right, I admit it. But under no circumstances can I give into it."

"Because of your reputation?"

"Partly. Some things have happened in the past that have hurt my standing in the service. Trust me when I tell you any relationship with you will be the straw that broke the camel's back."

He grasped her arm. "Tell me about that. I want to know everything about you."

"No. That isn't going to happen." She hated the pleading tone in her voice. "Can't you do this for me?"

"I honestly don't know."

"Then this might tip the scales. You *are* a distraction, Aidan. And because of that, we'd be endangering Bailey and the kids by pursuing anything between us. By having a relationship. Don't you want your sister safe?"

"Of course I do."

She took his hand off her arm, held it in hers, felt its strength. "Then please, for all our sakes, for all those reasons, forget any connection we've made, or might make." She cleared her throat. "And any *feelings* you or I might have for each other."

He stared at her a long time. She prayed he'd listen to her. Finally, his expression bleak, he said, "All right."

C.J. should be happy, relieved. But her heart ached like somebody had stomped on it.

Raising his hand, Aidan brushed back a stray lock of hair. "Too bad, Caterina. It could have been really good."

He walked away then, leaving C.J. to feel she'd just thrown away something very rare and very precious. Something she may never find again.

ELEVEN

❧

THE NATIONAL WOMEN'S Rights Historic Park and Museum stretched over seven acres of land in the small town of Seneca Falls, New York. It was built on the site of the now-famous Wesleyan Chapel, where three hundred women had gathered in 1858 to declare their independence and worth as citizens of the United States. That meeting was the kickoff to the nineteenth-century women's rights movement, which eventually led to female suffrage. C.J. swerved the black Suburban into the parking spot Mitch had roped off for them in the back, near an entrance closed to patrons. Her coworker said the advance trip went well, and there was adequate security in place.

From inside the car, Bailey pointed across the way. "I want to see the Wall."

C.J. smiled into the rearview mirror. Today she dressed in her suit, and she felt more comfortable. Other than what had happened with Aidan, she was almost back to her old self. "Of course."

She spoke into the wrist unit. "Be advised. Bright Star is on the horizon."

Grayson, one of the three agents accompanying them, slid out of the front seat and opened the Second Lady's door. He and the others formed a perimeter around her as she exited. In her earpiece, C.J. heard Mitch's voice. "Arrived right on time, Ludzecky."

"I'm a good driver."

"How's Bright Star?"

"Excited to be here." More softly she said, "Me, too. I love the significance of this place."

"You would."

"Bright Star wants to see the Waterfall Wall."

"Be better to get her into the building quick."

"Not going to happen."

Outside in the sunshine, wearing a dark blue skirt and matching top, Bailey looked more pregnant today, and more vulnerable. While one agent walked ahead and two behind, C.J. moved into step beside her.

"Ever been here before?" Bailey asked.

"Yes. My brother brought us here when we were old enough." The memory made her nostalgic. "You?"

"Uh-huh. Though three of my brothers have never set foot near the place." She smiled. "Aidan and I drove down when we were in college. He was taking a women's studies course." She winked at C.J. "He always was interested in studying the female sex."

C.J. pictured Aidan walking the block along a five-foot wall of granite that was scripted with the Declaration of Sentiments, the women's version of the Bill of Rights. Water trickled down its surface. Bailey stopped and ran her fingers over the words *We hold these truths to be self-evident. That all men* and *women are created equal.*

"Just reading it makes me weepy," she said. "Those women were so brave to do this."

"Elizabeth Cady Stanton's husband left town that day. A lot of women's husbands refused to let them come."

Bailey turned to C.J. "It's important to marry someone who supports the rights of women and would have embraced this conference."

C.J. couldn't let herself think about husbands and babies and men who would support women wholeheartedly. There wasn't a man alive who would be able to accept her job.

Was there?

The wall turned a corner and stretched out for another block, displaying the names of the original women in attendance. The sun sparkled off the stone. C.J. and the other agents scanned the area. When people began to arrive for the ceremony, she said, "I think we should go inside."

"All right."

Mitch met them at the door. It was startling to see him dressed in his agent suit after weeks of casual garb. There *were* agents in street clothes scattered throughout the site, though. She and Mitch were the official Secret Service personnel, obvious to the crowd, but operatives from the field office were stationed in the museum itself and in the theater where the ceremony would be held. Once inside, C.J. felt more comfortable.

A woman met them at the door. "Ms. O'Neil, I can't tell you what a surprise and pleasure it is to have you here."

"Thank you." Bailey read her tag. "Mrs. Olsen. Is Suze Williams here yet?"

"Yes."

"You didn't tell her, did you?" Bailey had asked the organizers not to alert Suze that she was attending the ceremony.

"No, but the presence of your agents might tip her off." She nodded. "Follow me."

Making their way through the ground floor, they bypassed the bronze statue grouping of Susan B. Anthony, Stanton, Frederick Douglass and others who'd fought for women's suffrage and civil rights. The winding staircase led them upstairs. Along the wall were posters celebrating women and their accomplishments through the ages. C.J. felt a swell of pride in her gender, along with a reaffirmation that she and all women had a right to choose their own lifestyles, regardless of what men thought.

They entered a small room off the theater. A black woman with chiseled features and savvy eyes turned when the door opened. C.J. knew Suze Williams had been in a gang, then spent her entire adult life trying to keep other girls from making the same mistakes as she had. "Oh, my God, Bay?"

"Hi, Suze."

"What are you . . ." She rushed across the room and threw herself into the Second Lady's arms. "This is so sweet."

When C.J. saw tears in both the women's eyes, she smiled. The work the service had done to clear the path for Bailey to attend the ceremony was worth it. Once again, such obvious female closeness made her miss her sisters.

Ten minutes later, they were in a small auditorium, ensconced in their seats. Bailey's designated spot was off to the side, near an unmarked door leading to a secured hallway that would provide an alternate escape route, if necessary. Mitch and C.J. flanked Bailey, while undercover agents were in the back and front. One posing as a museum's employee sat facing them onstage. Another as a security guard stood a few feet away.

Though C.J. kept scanning the crowd, it was fun to watch the ten women receive the plaques to be put in a newly erected display recognizing women's struggles to overcome adversity. Tough Suze Williams had a mile-wide grin through the whole ceremony.

When it ended, Bailey stood along with the others and put her fingers in her mouth. And whistled! C.J. had to hold back the laughter. Mitch didn't even bother and guffawed at the sight of the wife of the vice president of the

United States behaving in such an unseemly manner. She'd never have done this in D.C.

The reception room had been swept clean an hour before they arrived, and no one was allowed in until the ceremony was over. There were agents everywhere in here, and again, Mitch and C.J. flanked Bailey. Suze came up to her. "It was nice, wasn't it?"

She and Mitch stepped a discreet distance back, giving the two friends a bit of privacy. C.J. studied the room—about fifty by fifty feet; chairs and tables were set in groups of six. There were three exits and several windows. About fifty people gathered to congratulate the women who were honored. Several men were among them. Nothing out of the ordinary or suspicious.

Crowd scanning was intense; being responsible for determining who might be dangerous was nerve-wracking and C.J. felt her shoulders and neck tighten. Since this trip was unannounced, the potential for attack was minimal, but she'd been taught to expect the worst.

In the back of the room was a man with video camera panning the interior. There was something about him . . . not the camera itself because a lot of people were filming this, but something else. She stepped close to Mitch. "Video camera at three o'clock. Guy with a scruffy beard and bandana. Half glasses."

"I see him. What's up?"

"Don't exactly know." Though she couldn't explain why, her instincts went on red alert. And agents never ignored their sixth sense. "I'm going to work my way over to him. Something about that guy seems . . . familiar."

As C.J. started across the room, a woman came up to the man in question. She was dark haired. Tall. She spoke to him, and when C.J. was halfway to them, they ducked out a side door. By the time she maneuvered the crowd and reached the hallway, there was no sign of them. Into her radio, she said, "They're gone."

"All right." Mitch's voice was serious. "Let's see if we can get Bright Star out of here."

"Good idea."

The appearance of the man and his companion niggled at C.J. on the way home. She was sure she'd seen them before.

THE SUN on his face woke Aidan. He was sprawled out on a mattress, his head buried in a pillow. When he opened his eyes, he realized he was naked beneath a sheet, and in somebody's bed other than his own. The bright light escalated the drums pounding at his temples and he winced. His mouth felt like stale cotton candy. Sighing, he forced himself to turn over.

The other side of the bed was empty, but there was an indentation on the pillow. Sonia. He closed his eyes and tried to recall the series of events that brought him here.

Last night, he'd come to town. He was feeling guilt about his father, and rotten about the promise C.J. had wrung out of him.

Then please, for all our sakes, for all those reasons, forget any connection we've made, or might make.

All right.

Since Aidan was a man of his word, he meant to keep that promise. He'd decided not to mope about it and had hit San Jose's about eight. Sonia showed up after her shift and all he could recall was some sexy salsa dancing and drinking margaritas. A lot of margaritas. What the hell else had happened?

After hitting the john and dragging on his jeans, he found Sonia in the kitchen. He remembered the last time he'd seen C.J. in a kitchen, dressed in shorts and a tank top that had him hard in seconds. No reaction today though.

"Hi."

Glancing up from the newspaper, her dark eyes were amused. "Hey, lover boy."

Lover boy? So that must mean . . .

He poured himself coffee and sat across from her. "So," he said, trying to sound casual. "Was I any good? I drank a shitload."

"You were amazingly . . . unsatisfying." Again the smirk.

"I don't usually drink this much."

"Who's Caterina?"

"Excuse me?"

"You called me Caterina."

"Oh, hell." Calling a woman by another woman's name during sex was unconscionable. He wanted to kick his own butt.

"Don't look so horrified. You were about to pass out when you said it."

"After?"

Lazing back in her chair, she smiled. "You're such an easy mark. The guys at the station would eat you alive."

"What do you mean?"

"Nothing happened, Aidan. You were drunk as the proverbial skunk."

"I woke up naked in your bed."

"About all you could do was get your clothes off. Just before you passed out, you said, 'Goodnight, Caterina.' "

"That sucks."

She gave him what he called her cop's glare. "Are you involved with someone else? I don't poach."

"No." He sipped his coffee and decided to be honest. "There was someone, but it turned out she wasn't interested."

"Aidan O'Neil got dumped? The world might as well end right now."

He gave her a sheepish grin.

"So, she out of your life?"

"She was never really in it."

"Fine by me." Sonia stood and stretched. She was dressed in her navy uniform. "Then you can make last night up to

me. There's a family picnic for local police officers and firefighters tomorrow. It's right on the beach, at a park across the
way from your sister's place. Come with me. Maybe you can
take pictures for us." She crossed to him, and from behind,
placed her hands on his shoulders and bent over to his ear.
"If you don't drink, we can try this again."

He grasped her hand. "I'd love to do the pictures. The only
problem might be that Liam, my brother, is leaving tomorrow
and his son is always sad when Liam goes back to New York.
I'd planned on spending time with him. And Rory."

"Bring them."

He frowned. "Rory requires protection."

Kneading his shoulders, she laughed aloud. "The place
will be crawling with cops. One agent ought to do it."

Maybe Mitch would come. No way was he bringing
C.J. *Caterina.*

"You're on."

A half hour later, he pulled into the driveway of Clay's
cottage and sat for a minute in the car. Sonia said that after
he passed out, she'd called here last night to tell them Aidan
wouldn't be coming home. Liam had answered. Still, everybody would know where he was. Maybe that was for the
best. C.J. would see he meant what he said. He just hoped
he hadn't hurt her.

Bailey, Liam and the boys were in the sunroom, putting
together a jigsaw puzzle. Angel was in the kitchen with
Grandma, who was trying to feed her something slimy and
green. Fresh coffee and baking dough filled the air. The
dog jumped up and began to bark when he came into view.
When he scurried over, Aidan took a minute to pet him.

"Hi, everybody."

His ma looked up. "Hrumph."

At almost forty, he still got this reaction from her whenever overnights and women were concerned. Crossing the
room, he kissed her cheek and ruffled Angel's hair. The
baby banged her spoon on the tray.

"You smell like a brewery." Ma's tone was gruff but she squeezed his hand.

"What's a brewery?" Rory asked from the porch.

"A place where they make beer." Liam's tone was teasing. "Uncle Aidan fell into the brew last night."

Mikey asked, "Did you almost drown? Like me?"

"Almost," he said significantly. "But not quite."

Liam's brows shot up. "Get *out*."

"Can it." He came into the room and sank onto the couch next to Bailey. "How was the trip?"

"Great." Bailey smiled. "Suze is skimming stones on the lake with Cleary if you want to say hi. She's going back tomorrow with him and Liam."

Mikey moved in close to his dad and put his head on Liam's shoulder, buried his face there. Liam encircled his arm around the boy. "You can come back with us, honey, if you want. It's only another week before everybody goes home."

"Papa's taking us fishing."

"And we're goin' out with Uncle Aidan tomorrow," Rory said. "You promised."

"How would you like to go to a picnic across the lake? There'll be other kids there, playgrounds, fireworks at nine."

At his family's questioning looks, he explained the situation.

"Cool," Rory said. "All cops."

"And firefighters." Mikey was in awe of those guys.

"We have to ask Mitch," Bailey warned.

"Can C.J. come?" This from Mikey. "I'll go if she does."

Bailey grinned. "I think that can be arranged."

Liam shook his head. "Man, would I like to be there to see those fireworks."

* * *

THIS IS GOOD, C.J. told herself as she accompanied Aidan, Rory and Mikey across the water to a park on the opposite side of the lake from the Wainwright place. The air was warm, the breeze cool and the day crystalline. She'd managed to convince Mitch that watching Aidan with his girlfriend wouldn't bother her at all. The girlfriend he'd spent the night with twenty-four hours after he told C.J. he wanted a relationship with *her*.

Mitch had confronted her directly.

"You sure you can do this right? Keep your focus on Rory?"

"I'm perfectly capable of watching Rory by myself."

"You won't be by yourself. Gorman's going. And two uniforms. That's not what I meant."

"What did you mean?"

He'd braced his foot on one of the deck chairs and draped his arm over it. "Level with me, and I won't ask again. Is there anything between you and O'Neil?"

She could be honest about that now. "No."

"I need to know for sure."

"I said no, Mitch, several times. Drop it."

And so she'd locked herself into today.

He manned the boat, which bumped and slapped the water; Rory was at the wheel with him. He'd offered a try at the helm to Mikey, but the boy wanted to be with her. He was glum, after his dad and brother left, and so C.J. sat him on her lap. He leaned against her and didn't talk; she kept scanning the lake through her Ray-Bans. And forced herself not to think about what Aidan had done with the pretty cop the night before.

Judy Gorman was up front with him and Rory. And she was practically drooling over Aidan. Why wouldn't she? He looked great in dark green swim trunks, a yellow T-shirt matching the stripe down the side. His legs were corded with muscle, as were his arms. His hair was being tousled by the wind.

So was hers. She left it down because she wanted to conceal the earpiece. Also dressed casually in yellow capris and a boxy yellow blouse over a matching shirt, she wore white canvas sneakers with the outfit, which would have horrified Lizzie, who was a fashion plate these days. But C.J. might have to act quickly on her feet.

Aidan's husky laughter drifted back to her. It made her heart ache. With blinding clarity, she wanted that laughter directed at her. No, no, that wasn't possible. She'd been the one to tell *him* it wasn't possible. Hugging Mikey close, she braced herself for the day.

The park was filled with cops and firefighters when they exited the boat. Mitch had talked to both department captains, and they said about seventy people would attend the picnic. The police captain also assured Mitch that several of his men had volunteered not to drink any alcohol since Rory would be there. It would provide an additional layer of protection.

As soon as they arrived, C.J. contacted the agents who had gone over earlier and would stand post at the perimeter. "Be advised. Bruiser is on-site."

"Read you," Al Girard said.

Zeke Conklin checked in, too.

They'd just reached the picnic area when Sonia spotted them. She popped up from the table where she sat with the guys and headed toward Aidan. As if she had the right—of course, she did—she embraced him and gave him a full-mouthed kiss on the lips. He smiled down at her, but drew back some. She looped her arm with his and moved in close. C.J.'s insides contracted and she looked away to scan the crowd.

"Can we go over there?" Rory asked C.J.

Twenty yards down, a slip-and-slide was set up. "Sure can, Champ." C.J. held out her hands. Mikey took one and Rory the other. Gorman, who'd been instructed to wander the group looking for anything out of the ordinary, did so. Aidan followed Sonia to the keg.

The sun beat heavily on them as it was in the eighties today. Already wearing their bathing suits, the little guys were cute on the big lime-green vinyl tarp, spouting water from holes in strategic places. Mikey giggled as an unexpected spurt hit him in the face and Rory laughed when he went down on his rump. She was standing close to the edge, arms folded over her chest, when a big-shouldered guy with a head of dark hair approached her. He gave her a friendly smile. "Hi, I'm Jim Connors. We met when the Wainwright contingent hit town. Agent Ludzecky, right?"

"Captain Connors. I remember. Hello."

"Want something to drink?" He held up a Coke in one hand, bottled water in the other.

"I'll take the water, thanks."

"Thank you for coming with the guys."

"It's what I do."

He popped the tab on his Coke and sipped as he watched the kids. "Those two are mine." He pointed to tiny tow-headed girls edging their way toward Rory.

"They're beautiful." She smiled. "They must take after your wife."

"Hmm. She would have been proud of them."

C.J. cocked her head.

"She died two years ago in a car accident. Funny, I was the one with the dangerous job."

"I'm sorry."

The captain was quiet a while. Finally he picked up the conversation. "So what's it like being a Secret Service agent?"

Technically, she shouldn't talk to this guy, but when a pickup volleyball game was called, Aidan came into view just beyond the boys. So she talked to Jim Connors about her job, relating the positive things.

Still, her gaze kept drifting to Aidan, who was on the same team as Sonia. It was his serve, and his muscles bunched as he punched the ball over the net, snagging three aces in a row. After he sent across a spike that hit the ground like a bullet, Sonia jumped on him and locked her legs around his waist. C.J.'s throat hurt and she took another slug of water.

Jim Connors asked, "Aren't there any drawbacks to being an agent?"

C.J. watched Sonia plant a big kiss on Aidan. "About a million."

THIS WAS A colossal mistake. Aidan had been miserable all day long. Every time Sonia touched him, kissed him, made a remark to him, he worried C.J. might see it. Be hurt by it. He'd tried to keep himself from looking for her, but he couldn't. Every time he turned around, he searched the area to see where she was. Once, she'd lifted up a wet Mikey, and afterward, the damp T-shirt under her blouse clung to her. He watched Jim Connors, the macho police captain, engage her in conversation. Flirt with her. Was she flirting back? Hell, she shouldn't even be talking to him while she was on duty.

And twice she was close enough for Aidan to see her face tighten when she caught sight of Sonia's petting. He felt like a complete scumbag for making her stand by and watch him with another woman, but he hadn't seen the day shaking out like this.

Which was why, when C.J. excused herself and put Gorman on Bruiser duty, he followed her around to the bathroom cabins. She headed straight to the women's side, and he waited behind the rough-hewn building. When she came out, she startled, and her hand snapped to her back. To her gun. The gesture reminded him of who she was.

"What are you *doing* lurking out here? You should never sneak up on an agent. I could have hurt you."

Leaning against the building, he asked, "Have I hurt you today?"

She didn't question what he meant. "No, of course not."

"You were watching me with Sonia. I saw your face."

For a moment, a flicker of pain shadowed those beautiful amber eyes. "You've done exactly what I asked you to do. I'm not one of those women who says one thing and means another."

Women. Not agent.

"I know. But today sucks. I didn't realize it would play out like this."

"It's fine. I'm fine." He was starting to believe her when she added, "Anyway, you seem like you're having a great time. Like last night, I imagine."

"Looks can be deceiving, Caterina."

"What does that mean?"

"I didn't sleep with Sonia."

"I didn't ask." Then she said, "You were out the whole night."

"Still, I didn't."

"I've got to get back." She started to sidle around him, but he stepped in her path and grasped her arm. She stopped, focused her gaze on his hand caressing bare skin that had no right being so soft. She swallowed hard. When she looked up at him, her pupils were dilated. He got a glimpse of her T-shirt and he could see her nipples harden. At his closeness. For a moment, she was all woman.

"Please," she whispered hoarsely. "I told you I was fine. Now let go of me."

He stepped back and she hurried away. Her ramrod stance, her stiff shoulders confirmed what he already knew.

That they were both kidding themselves.

TWELVE

ON TUESDAY MORNING, C.J. was surprised to circle around the house and find yet another O'Neil brother visiting his sister. Dylan. He swerved up in a snazzy red Fiat and unfolded from the small car. He was taller than Aidan, with a rangy build that reminded her of Clay Wainwright's. His hair was stylishly cut, and his sunglasses prevented her from seeing his eyes.

He gave her a once-over. She felt uncomfortable in her denim capris and white T-shirt. "Why Agent Ludzecky, you're transformed."

"Hello, Mr. O'Neil. I wasn't aware you were visiting today." She scowled. "How'd you get in?"

"I charmed Millie at the gate." Millie was a uniform.

At her raised brows, he chuckled. "*Kid-ding.* I phoned Bailey earlier and the guards were expecting me." His brow furrowed and he removed his glasses to reveal troubled eyes several shades darker than Aidan's. Same shape, though. "I've got something you guys and Bay need to know about."

They'd begun to walk toward the house. Bailey swung

open the front door just as they reached it. "Dyl. I'm so glad you're here." She hugged him, said, "Come on in," and held his hand the whole way to the sunroom.

Mitch came up the stairs just as they passed them. "Hi, Dylan. Something's wrong, isn't it?"

"I'm not sure. It might not be too bad. I just thought I should drive up and tell you about it."

Pa and Ma O'Neil came down the corridor to greet their son with big hugs and smacking kisses. Aidan wandered in from the deck, wearing cargo shorts and a boxy checked shirt. The brothers embraced, too.

"What's up?" Aidan asked.

Holding out a DVD case, he faced Mitch. "This ran on the eleven o'clock news last night, which I routinely tape. It might compromise Bailey's safety."

Mitch took the box from Dylan, crossed to the DVD player and put the disc in the machine. Aidan dropped down on the couch next to Bailey.

C.J. recognized the anchor woman, Rachel Scott, from the hospital when Pa O'Neil was admitted. She wore a lovely peach-colored suit, styled hair and perfect makeup. "Good evening. I'm Rachel Scott with a special report on our very own Big Apple girl, the Second Lady, Bailey O'Neil." She grinned for the camera. "We've followed Ms. O'Neil's life here in New York since her marriage to Clay Wainwright. After her highly lauded work getting kids out of gangs, it appears she didn't quite forget her old friends when she moved to Washington as the wife of the vice president."

The woman's voice continued over a video clip. "After canceling her trip to Zanganesia, Ms. O'Neil was spotted in upstate New York. We caught a glimpse of her at the National Women's Rights Museum on Friday."

On-screen, the camera panned the buildings on the site. Bailey was shown exiting the car, and a clear shot of C.J. came on. There was footage of them walking side by side along the Wall. They looked like friends out for a stroll.

The camera zeroed in on their faces, and C.J. was laughing.

"Ms. O'Neil's friend, Suze Williams, received an award, at this renowned birthplace of women's rights."

Suze was shown onstage getting her plaque, then the camera switched to Bailey—and caught her whistling. Scott chuckled and said something about Bailey being *real*.

"Don't tell Suze's connection with ESCAPE," Bailey whispered, clutching Aidan's hand. "Please."

"Ms. Williams received the award for overcoming her own street gang past and going on to help get kids out of gangs today."

There was a shot of Bailey and Suze hugging at the reception. At least they didn't mention the name of the organization.

"Damn," C.J. said, "that's who they were."

Mitch shook his head. "The ones you pointed out."

Dylan straightened. "This is the bad part."

A panoramic view of the lake filled the screen. "Ms. O'Neil is staying at the Wainwright cottage on Keuka Lake, a gated site no one is allowed near. Our camera did catch a long-range view of the cottage. But here's the jackpot: some pictures of the Second Son."

"Oh, shit." This from Aidan.

There was video footage of Aidan and the boys in the boat, coming across the lake. Of them arriving at the park. Aidan carrying Rory.

Still shots of C.J. watching Rory, and smiling. C.J. frowning in the direction of Aidan. Jim Connors handing her a bottle of water.

More shots of Rory. Of Aidan.

Another view across the lake from the park zeroing in on the Wainwrights' cottage.

"She might as well have drawn a map for anybody interested in Bailey's whereabouts." This from Dylan.

Aidan said, "Bay, I'm sorry. I never thought we'd be seen."

"Why should you?" She looked to Mitch. "How bad is this?"

"I'm not sure. The location of the cottage wasn't a secret to begin with, though we've kept news media away from the gated grounds. But it wasn't publicized that you were staying here now. And I don't like having your exact whereabouts broadcast to several million viewers. Worst case, anyone with a grudge might get ideas from hearing this newscast. Best case, people drive by, or more press could pester us at the outer perimeter." He looked to C.J. "We could go back to New York now. The town house is a more secure location."

Frowning, Pa said, "I promised Rory we'd go to the fair Saturday. We'd do the pond fishing thing together."

Bailey's eyes flamed, and C.J. got another look at the old Street Angel. "I won't be sent running by the press, Mitch."

"I suppose we could increase security around the perimeter." Mitch's tone was reluctant.

C.J. added, "It's only until Sunday."

Mitch waited a beat. "All right."

As he took the disc out of the DVD player, Dylan's face was dark. "Scott must have what? Found out you'd be in Seneca Falls?"

"How would she have done that?" Bailey asked.

This time, Mitch scowled. "She must know people in the area or at the Women's Rights Park. It's highly possible she's covered events at the museum before. The advance team wouldn't have gone unnoticed when they went down, and somebody could have caught on and alerted her."

"So she's there to catch pictures of you, then she what?" Dylan shook his head. "Trailed you back here, camped out and followed Aidan and Rory over on a boat?"

"Or used the zoom lens from the other side." Mitch didn't appear to be too upset. If he was, fair or no fair, they wouldn't be staying.

Dylan seemed the most disconcerted. C.J. remembered the talk about his column in *CitySights* and how he sought out people abusing their power and hurting others in the process.

"Dyl," Bailey said. "This isn't a big deal. She didn't do anything to harm us."

"Let's hope not." The tense set of his jaw and his rigid stance made C.J. realize that this O'Neil brother was someone to be reckoned with.

Over his shoulder she saw Bailey lean into Aidan. He kissed her head and whispered something to her.

Then again, C.J. thought, Dylan wasn't the only one.

SUNSET ON the lake was almost a physical experience. Through his camera lens, Aidan caught the pinks and reds and yellows forming a watercolor sky. On the deck chair behind him, his brother sipped a beer. "Blow up one of those shots for me. They're winners."

"Sure." Aidan stuffed the camera in a case at his feet, then turned and dropped down into the other chair they'd brought out. Dylan handed him a beer. "So, how's it going with Hogan?" Aidan asked.

Dylan's brow furrowed. Mostly, this brother was low-key, and often a wise guy, but when something got his back up, he bristled like a porcupine. His ex-wife could flick that switch in a second. "Acting out. Stephanie left him alone yesterday to meet with some of her outside investors, and he was bored out of his mind in her apartment."

"What'd he do this time?"

"Took a bus to the Village. By himself." Hogan was thirteen. "My guess is he bought some pot."

"I thought that was a onetime thing."

"His mother brings out the worst in him. Jesus Christ, I hate when she comes to town and insists he stay with her. It's like ten steps back for him." Raking a hand through his hair, he shook his head. "I was glad to get away for an overnight because we were close to coming to blows."

"Why didn't you bring Hogan?"

"I wanted to. But Stephanie pitched a fit. I caved. So did he, the poor kid."

"Sorry. Anything I can do?"

"Maybe spend some time with him when you get back to the city. He digs his uncles." Dylan looked down the shoreline. A figure was approaching. "Who's that?"

"Bailey's agent, C.J."

"How can you tell? She's far away."

"I don't know. Being around her, I guess." Aidan made an effort to control his tone of voice, and anything else which might clue Dylan in. His brother took no prisoners in the razzing department. That's why Bailey had dubbed him The Taunter. "You think Bailey's in any danger?" he asked, changing the subject.

"Probably no more than usual." Dylan dug the label off the bottle with his fingernail. "That reporter rankles me."

"She's a looker. And has red hair. Maybe you're just attracted to your type."

"Hmm. *Our* type." As C.J. drew closer, Dylan said, "Though blond's looking mighty fine to me right about now."

"Yeah, she's okay."

"I'd like to get in *her* pants."

Aidan controlled the impulse to tell Dylan not to be crude about C.J. Or to punch him in the face.

"Women with guns and handcuffs are a turn-on."

"Can it, Dyl."

"Bet she's hot in the sack. All that pent-up emotion. She has to stifle everything. I wonder what she's like when she lets off stream."

She's wonderful. Aidan didn't trust his voice to respond.

"Think she likes being on top? I'll bet she—"

"Shut up, Dylan."

"Huh?"

"I said shut up. She's a federal agent and you shouldn't be talking about her like she's a piece of fucking meat."

Dylan laughed, deep and from his belly. It took Aidan a minute to know that he'd been had. "So that *is* the way the wind blows. I kinda figured. Don't think you're gonna get anywhere with her, little brother. Now me, I could—"

Aidan stood and kicked back the chair; it slammed against the wood of the deck, resounding in the night air.

His brother looked over at him. "Oh, man, this is worse than I thought."

"I said, shut up about her."

"Yeah?" Now Dylan stood. "Who's gonna make me?"

"You sound like a kid."

"You sound like an adolescent boy, mooning over some cheerleader." Dylan straightened his shoulders. "And for the record, I'll say what I want. Whenever I want. You certainly aren't gonna stop me."

They got into it sometimes, him and his brothers. Looked like this was going to be one of them. When Dylan turned his back to walk down the deck, Aidan lunged for him. He got him in a headlock from behind.

Dylan bucked. "What the hell?"

"*I'm* gonna make you."

Again the condescending laugh. Before he knew it, Dylan hooked his leg around Aidan's, breaking his neck hold. Aidan started to go down, but grabbed Dylan around the waist. The reaction unbalanced them both and they fell— right off the dock into the lake.

They hit the water hard, went under and came up sputtering. "Jesus Christ," Aidan said, shaking his wrist in front of him. "I got my new watch on."

Dylan looked down. They were knee-deep in seaweed. "I'm wearing expensive boots. You shit."

"Me?" He wiped the hair out of his eyes. "You started it."

Then they both burst out laughing. They did sound like little boys and were men enough to admit it.

"What's going on here?" C.J. stood on the dock in her jeans and T-shirt over which she'd thrown a white sweater. "What are you guys doing?"

"Sunset swimming." Dylan winked at her. "Want to join us, pretty lady?"

C.J. scowled. "Have you two been drinking?"

Dylan glanced at Aidan. "Not much. My brother just needed cooling down." He grinned. "A lot, from the looks of things."

Aidan grabbed Dylan's arm. "Be careful what you say here."

Dylan pushed on his chest sending him back into the water; Aidan surfaced swearing. He attacked Dylan from behind and brought them both under again.

As they surfaced, he heard C.J. say, "Little boys. Jesus." She walked away.

He and Dylan dragged themselves out of the water and sank down dripping into the grass. They watched the waves lap for a while. Dylan sobered. "Seriously, if something's going on, maybe I could help."

Aidan shook his head. "Nah, it's hopeless. Just don't rag on me about it, okay?"

"Okay."

"And stay away from her. No more of this 'pretty lady' shit."

"Sure." He stood and held out his hand to Aidan. "Race you to the copse of trees."

Rolling to his feet, Aidan said, "You're on," and took off.

Sometimes, it was better to act like a little boy than deal with a grown man's problems.

C.J. STARED at herself in the mirror. The white towel turbaned her head and accented the tan she'd gotten from being outside with the O'Neils these four weeks. Because of her light complexion, she usually avoided the sun, but the bronze tone of her skin looked good on her. Glancing down, she took in the pink she wore. Not her style, too frilly, but she was getting used to bright colors. Well, it all would end tomorrow. They were going back to the city on Sunday.

Tugging the towel off her head, she began rubbing her hair dry. The past week had been hard in a lot of ways. First, all the agents on the VPPD were tense, given the knowledge that the whole world knew where Bailey was staying. Though they tried to hide it from the family. But sending for field agents to help around the perimeter of the cottage had added an extra layer of security, dispensing with the illusion that this was just a regular vacation. Even C.J. had been lulled into feeling the latter. She was going to miss Ma O'Neil's cooking, Pa's grumbling about the nurse's visits and exercise regime, which Aidan had done with him after the first week.

Aidan. After Dylan left, he'd been quieter than usual. She grinned as she plugged in the hair dryer. He'd been so cute with his brother. Their scuffle reminded C.J. of her sisters. They used to wrestle each other to the ground and dunk each other in the neighborhood swimming pool. At least C.J. had decided one constructive thing: She had to see them before she went back to D.C. It was another effect of being around the O'Neils. Which was an additional reason to return to New York—C.J. was acting out of character. Not being herself. That and the fact that even though Aidan kept to his promise to leave her alone, there had been a connection with him all week—a sizzle when they brushed past each other; catching each other with a long glance; smiles now and then. The exchanges were filled with a longing that she hoped nobody else would detect.

Except for this morning, he'd stayed away from her. She was off duty and having coffee down on the lower patio that the O'Neils never frequented. He'd found her there.

He was wearing his Gap pajama bottoms and a T-shirt. Her whole body reacted to the sight of him . . .

"Good morning."

"Hi." She had to clear her throat. "You're up early."

"I was hoping to catch you alone." He dropped down at the table with her and sipped from the mug he'd brought with him.

C.J. waited for him to explain why.

"The fair's today. We're going home tomorrow."

"Yes. It'll probably be good to be back in your own routine. Your own place."

Hurt flashed across his classic features. She noticed things then . . . the curve of his jaw, the straightness of his nose. A little dimple to the left of his mouth. His beard was bristly and she had a quick fantasy of touching it—or it touching her. Intimately.

"I have to ask you again. One last time."

Raising her chin, she stared at him.

"You sure this is what you want? To cut off ties between us?"

"I am."

"Be honest, Caterina. If things had been different, what would be happening now?"

"Things aren't different."

"Answer the question anyway."

"No."

Emotion filled his face. "That's what I thought. So I'm asking. One more time. Can we try to find a way to pursue what we're feeling?"

"No. I told you what would happen to me professionally if I got involved with a protectee's brother." Because that felt weak now, she added, "And as we said before, I can't be distracted by you while I'm trying to watch your sister and her family."

He didn't look convinced.

"And there's something else we've never discussed."

She shook her head, thinking of the company joke—if the service wanted you to have a family, they would have issued you one. "You couldn't live with what I do. You and your brothers are so macho. It's hard for any of you to let me lift something heavy or drive the car when you're in it. How could you stand by and let a woman you cared about put herself in danger?"

"It would be hard. I know that."

"It would be torture."

"Maybe I wanna try."

"I'd never let you."

"Why?"

She'd stood. "Because I do care, Aidan. About you." She stared down at him. "But I don't want this. I'm not going to risk it. For personal reasons. Because of Bailey. And for your own welfare. So, if *you* care about *me* at all, you'll leave it alone. Like you promised."

He nodded. Then rose, too. Before he left, he ran his knuckles down her cheek. Her heart constricted in her chest at just that light touch. "Good-bye, Caterina . . ."

Staring at herself in the mirror, C.J. drew in a deep breath. She'd stored the feel of that butterfly caress in her memory bank and summoned it now. "Stop it!" she told herself and concentrated on finishing up in the bathroom. She came out fully dressed.

Mitch was standing in the hallway. "Took you long enough," he said. "I think you're turning into a real girl."

"Bite me."

He headed down to the john.

"Mitch?"

He glanced over his shoulder.

"Do you think today's a good idea? Going to the fair?"

"I'm not sure. But the O'Neils have been troupers this week, and Pa O'Neil really wants to do this fishing thing with Rory and Mikey." He shrugged a shoulder. "We've got the field agents covering the grounds. It's safe enough."

"Maybe."

"You don't think so?"

"My gut tells me no." Then again, her instincts were going haywire this week. "But you're probably right."

"We'll be careful."

"Yeah, sure. That's our motto, right?"

"Something else wrong?"

"No, I'll just be glad to get into town"—she tugged on her pink shirt—"and out of these."

He grinned, a very male one. "I'll miss seeing you in those clothes, *Caterina*."

She swallowed hard at the use of the name. She said again, "Bite me."

THIRTEEN

SNAPSHOT OPPORTUNITY number one: Ma standing over a counter full of quilts, pointing to one with pink and red as the primary colors. Bailey, her hand on the carriage where Angel slept, rocking it back and forth, shaking her head. Looking through the lens, Aidan smiled. He knew what would happen here. Bailey wouldn't be satisfied with any of the quilts and Ma would end up making her one for little Patrick.

Snapshot opportunity number two: Rory, Mikey and Pa in a small boat out on the pond, near which the Penn Yan Summer Fair had been set up. All three held fishing poles. The two boys wore hats like Pa's. Rory's face was animated, then shocked when he got a bite. Aidan snapped and snapped. Pa talking to Rory, Rory concentrating just like Bailey, reeling something in. Aidan got a great shot of Rory holding up a decent-size fish. He yelled something to the occupants of the boat just a few feet away. In it, C.J. sat with Gorman, and both women clapped.

The sun glistened on C.J.'s hair and reflected off her

dark glasses. He zoomed in, could see she was laughing. "Ah," he said, speaking to the camera. "Isn't that about the most beautiful thing we've ever seen?" He took photo after photo of her, happy and grinning for a change.

Snapshot opportunity number three: Angel awake now, pink-faced and pretty in a summer dress made of white eyelet. She sat on Bailey's lap, clapping her hands as the small train circled around the tracks. Aidan grinned and took shots of Mitch and Grayson, stuffed into tiny seats in front of and behind them on the train.

Snapshot opportunity number four: He couldn't resist. Knowing this was probably the last opportunity he'd get to photograph her, he caught C.J. in several stills: eating a hotdog with Rory and wiping mustard off her face; squatting down and talking to Mikey, and the little guy looking glum. Something C.J. said made him smile. C.J. climbing into the roller coaster with Rory. He'd heard her say she had a cast-iron stomach and loved to go on the rides.

Through the lens, he saw his whole family unite, flanked by agents. Ma and Pa headed to a table the agents had held for them, and Bailey and the kids walked toward the small Ferris wheel, which rose up about forty feet in height. Bailey got into a car with Mitch. Damn, should she go on that thing while she was pregnant? He took a shot of Rory, jumping up and down, pointing to the ride. Mikey sidled into C.J. and clung to her legs. C.J. said something into her radio, probably to Mitch. Then Gorman got in a car with Rory. People slipped in between them. Four seats later, C.J. led Mikey into one with her. She looked around when she was settled and her gaze seemed to zero in on Aidan, standing off to the side, chronicling this day—and her.

He lowered the camera and headed to the nearest booth. He'd take more pictures in a few minutes, but right now, she was just too hard to watch.

* * *

MIKEY MOVED in closer to C.J. as the Ferris wheel bumped and started. "This gonna be okay, C.J.?" he asked.

"Sure is, buddy."

"You're supposed to watch Rory."

"He's only a few cars away. And Gorman's with him." Mitch was close by in the seat with Bailey.

"'Kay." He gripped the bar. "Mom used to take me on the rides. She said Daddy's a chicken."

Her heart went out to the little boy. She hugged him to her, while she surveyed the grounds. Nothing out of the ordinary, unless you could spot the myriad plain clothes agents infiltrating the crowds. She said into her wrist unit, "Things look normal, Mitch."

"Yeah, to me to." Mitch glanced up and over his shoulder and waved to her. Bailey caught the action and followed suit.

"Gorman, things all right?" Mitch asked into the radio.

"Bruiser's fine. Me, I hate these things."

C.J. sat back and tried to enjoy the ride. At first, it didn't move too fast as the attendant was still letting people on. One bump up and she could see Aidan, standing by a booth, shooting basketballs. When the ride began to move in earnest, it picked up speed. They went full circle twice, and she saw him walking away from the booth carrying a white teddy bear with a pink ribbon around its neck. Before her mind spun a fantasy about him giving the bear to his girl—her—C.J. averted her gaze. On the next several rotations, she purposely didn't look for him.

The grounds were getting crowded. Lines were forming at the Ferris wheel. On the last cycle C.J. noted there were too many people packed together to feel secure. It was time to go back to the cottage.

"Crowds," she said into her unit.

"Yeah, I see." Mitch and she were usually in sync on these things. "We'll leave as soon as we're done here."

The Ferris wheel slowed, then stopped for people to exit

their cars. C.J. zeroed in on Bailey's. It reached the bottom, and Mitch helped her out. She was smiling, turned and waved to Rory, who was still in the air. He rocked the car, and she heard Gorman say, "Be still, Rory. My stomach's had all it can take."

Bailey waved to Mikey, who was even further up; he waved back and rocked their car. C.J. laughed.

Rory's car reached the bottom. He climbed out. C.J. was about twenty-five feet up as she watched him and got a closer look at Gorman. She scowled. "Gorman," she said into her radio. "You're a little green."

"I'm fine," the other woman snapped.

Mitch had gone through the exit gate to the left and followed Bailey over to the picnic table with Ma, Pa, Angel and four uniforms.

The crowds obscured anyone's view of Rory except for hers and Gorman's. Rory raced ahead of Gorman, who suddenly stopped and darted off to the side.

"What the hell, Gorman?"

"Sick," she said.

Her senses heightened, C.J. said into the shoulder unit, "Mitch. We got a problem," as Rory turned left toward the exit gate. He was still in the area about midway between the outer fence and the Ferris wheel, but he was by himself. "Bruiser's alone, headed for the exit gate." Around cupped hands, she yelled down, "Stay right there, Rory."

He stopped and looked up at her; she kept her eyes trained on him as her car moved down again to twenty feet above the ground.

From the crowd waiting to enter the ride, two boys hopped the fence and converged on Rory. They grabbed Rory's hands and headed for the gate. Rory started to scream and one of them, in the guise of a hug, clapped a hand over his mouth and pulled him close. He squirmed but they held on.

"Ferris wheel exit," C.J. yelled into the radio. "Bruiser's in trouble. An AOP. Everybody go. AOP."

She saw the uniforms with the O'Neils bolt up to stand in front of Angel and Bailey, their bodies blocking the family. As required, they all stayed with her.

Mitch raced to the fence. Into his radio he shouted, "All agents, to the Ferris wheel."

But the agents couldn't penetrate the crowd waiting to get inside the fence fast enough. The two boys were dragging Rory away and came just beneath her car, about ten feet out from the ride.

C.J. didn't wait. She said to Mike, "Hold on, honey. Grip the bar tight. I have to help Rory."

She was already up on the seat when he said, "I will."

Taking in a deep breath, C.J. leapt from the car, down twenty feet and landed right next to the three of them. Her ankle crunched, and pain shot through her leg, but she managed to grab Rory, throw him to the ground and cover him with her body.

Shouts. Yelling everywhere.

Agent voices . . . a touch on her face.

Then the world dimmed.

"SHE'S COMING around," someone said out of the darkness.

C.J. stirred, then moaned as the movement set off jackhammers in her head. She lay still; when the pain abated, she opened her eyes. Fuzzy images. She blinked. Clearer. Mitch was standing over her. Bailey and her father were behind him.

Then she remembered. "Rory?"

"Is safe with several agents behind locked doors in the cottage."

Her lips burned. She licked them. "Thirsty." She tried to sit up, moaned, sank into the cushions.

Bailey came around Mitch, holding a cup. "Here, have a drink."

Once again, when she moved her head, pain splintered

through her. She fought it. The water felt cool on her parched lips and throat. "Did you catch them?"

"No," Mitch said. "We didn't even know who we were looking for. The agents who managed to get through circled you and Rory and ignored everything else."

SOP. Standard operating procedure. The Secret Service's job was not to catch perpetrators, but to safeguard the protectee. Afterward, the whole matter would be turned over to the FBI.

"Rory told us what happened on the ground." Mitch's voice was gruff. "What you must have seen from above."

"I could tell what was happening. Two boys . . ." She coughed and took some more water.

Mitch finished for her, "Approached Rory. Grabbed his hands. He couldn't get to his panic button and tried to scream, but they covered his mouth. Then you jumped out of the sky."

"I didn't know what else to do." Oh, God. "Is Mikey okay?"

"He did what you told him." Mitch grinned. "They're calling you Superwoman."

"No."

"You are to me." Bailey took C.J.'s hand. "You saved my son from kidnapping."

"Just doing my job." But she squeezed Bailey's fingers. "What happened with Gorman?"

"She stepped off to the side to toss her cookies. No blame there. What else could she do?"

C.J. asked for help to sit up. Once she was braced against a mound of pillows, she frowned. "Mitch, was it my fault, for going on the ride with Mikey?"

"No. He was with another special agent. The operatives right outside the fence were trying to get to the exit gate and got trapped in the crowd. I should have had them stationed inside, I guess, but I didn't want to draw any more attention to who was on the ride."

"I won't listen to this," Bailey told them. "You've protected us as well as anyone could."

"Yes, ma'am," Mitch said dryly.

A little more calmly, but there was anger there, she finished, "Nobody's to blame but the two boys who went after Rory. Young boys? Why?"

"The FBI will find out." Mitch touched Bailey's arm. "I promise."

The door flew open and Luke stalked to the bed. He seemed controlled on the outside, but C.J. knew from his eyes that he was worried. Bailey stepped back and he took C.J.'s hand. After studying her, he shook his head. "Leaping off tall buildings? *Proszè.* Didn't I teach you anything?"

She remembered then. She and the girls had gotten into a superhero phase, capes and all. Luke had tried to control them, without telling their parents. "Good practice, all those years ago for today."

Leaning over, he kissed her forehead, then searched her face, frowned and turned to Mitch. "What're the extent of her injuries? You hadn't seen the doctor when you called me."

"Sprained ankle. Bad blow to the head, probably a concussion. Various scrapes and bruises. That shoulder she landed on has to be sore as hell."

"Jesus." He stared down at her. "I hate that you're in this business."

"*Nie.* Not now." She looked to Mitch. "When can I work?"

"In about two weeks, the doc said."

"That's too long. I'll be—"

Bailey cut her off. "You need to recuperate fully, C.J. You can stay at our town house in New York or go back to your place in D.C. Whatever you want to do. But you're following doctor's orders."

Luke straightened. "She's coming home with me."

"To Corning?"

"No, to Queens. You're gonna recuperate with *Matka*. I'll stay for a while. And the girls will be in and out."

Her heart bumped a bit in her chest thinking about spending time with her family. Then her mood plummeted when she remembered the strain between them. "I don't know, Lukasz."

"*I* know." He leaned over and kissed her again. "They need you there, baby. So do I."

Maybe she needed to be there, too. Leaving the detail for a while had the added bonus of getting her away from Aidan.

Surreptitiously, she surveyed the room. Pa was hovering in the background. But Aidan was nowhere in sight. She convinced herself she wasn't disappointed. "All right, I'll go home. For a while, maybe not the whole two weeks."

"We'll decide once you get there."

C.J. must have dozed off, because when she awoke, it was dark outside and she was alone. Or at least she thought she was by herself until she saw a figure emerge from the corner. She could see him in the light sneaking in from the hall.

"It's me, Aidan. Don't get scared."

Feeling woozy from medicine they'd given her, she mumbled, "I'm not scared. I'm glad you're here." She pushed herself up. Her head was better and her stomach wasn't roiling anymore. "Can I have a drink of water?"

Coming to the side of the bed, he switched on a small light and dragged over the high patient's table. On it, along with a pitcher of water, was a bunch of wildflowers, pink this time. As he poured her a drink and got a straw, she nodded to the vase. "I know. They're not from you."

"Nope. From Rory. For obvious reasons."

She grinned at the running joke. While she sipped, he smoothed his hand over her hair. She was too tired, too raw and in too much in pain to stop the caress. The same was true when she finished drinking and he sat down on the mattress and took her hand. "I saw the whole thing." His voice cracked on the last word.

"Oh. I'm sorry, that must have been hard for you. You and Rory are so close."

His eyes flared with . . . anger? "No, I didn't see what happened to him. Nobody did but you because he was surrounded by the crowd. What I *saw* was you leaping off that Ferris wheel like some kind of Wonder Woman."

"I didn't know what else to do."

"You were so brave."

"I was just doing my job, Aidan."

His expression was tender. And sad. "I know."

She didn't want to ask why he hadn't come earlier, but she couldn't summon any inner strength right now. "Did you, um, go home with Rory?"

"No, I didn't come to the hospital, either. I couldn't. I knew everything I felt for you would be obvious and you wouldn't want that." He swallowed hard. "The paramedics said you were all right, so I went home and hiked the grounds until I could barely breathe."

She squeezed his hand. "I'm sorry. It's good, though, that this happened."

His eyes snapped; she could see them even in the dim light. "Tell me how it's good that you look like you went a few rounds with Mike Tyson."

"Because now you have firsthand knowledge of what it would be like if we let our feelings go further. Imagine living your life watching me do things like I did today, which are part of my job."

When she'd first gone to the academy, she'd seen the tape of when Tim McCarthy was shot in the stomach protecting Ronald Reagan. She wondered if McCarthy's family had witnessed it on live TV.

Aidan kissed her hand, then brought it to his cheek. The tenderness of the gesture made her eyes mist.

He swallowed hard. "You're right. I couldn't watch you do those things."

Knowing her face revealed the same bleak sense of loss, she whispered, "I care about you too much to allow that to happen."

"I'm staying for a while. Just tonight."

"I want you to." She felt her eyes close. Heard him drag a chair, probably sit. Then he took her hand again and held it in both of his.

She drifted off, thinking this was the closest they were going to get to sleeping together.

FOURTEEN

FBI AGENT Jack Masters fit his name. If Aidan were interested in taking pictures ever again—and he wasn't because he'd taken one too many while staying at the cottage—he'd make Masters the subject of a photo essay on the typical FBI agent. Dressed in a suit like the ones worn by the Secret Service—when they weren't in fucking lake clothes—Masters sat across from Mitch and Bailey and Gorman, who'd taken C.J.'s place for two weeks while she recuperated in Queens. Masters had come down to New York today from Penn Yan to talk to Bailey. Since Clay was still in Zanganesia, Bailey had asked Aidan to be at the town house for the session.

"This is what we have so far, Ms. O'Neil." He referred to a red file. "No one except Agent Ludzecky seems to have seen the two *boys*, if indeed they were boys, which we can't assume, jump the fence and go after Rory."

"No one?"

"Most people crowded around the entrance. Few were at the exit, where he was headed."

"What about the Ferris wheel operator?"

"He was getting people off the ride, one car at a time. The FBI got to the scene within hours, but from what we could gather, people weren't paying attention to what went on inside the fence. Rory told us he couldn't yell out or make a scene because one of the kidnappers put a hand over his mouth, and then scrunched his body—Rory's term—to his own." Masters shook his head. "The only thing anyone remembers very well is Agent Ludzecky playing Supergirl by jumping off the damn ride. Unfortunately when something dramatic like that happens at a crime scene, it's all people remember." He looked to Mitch. "How is she, anyway?"

"Recuperating fine. She's enjoying her time at her mother's house."

Which was more than Aidan knew. He'd had no contact with her since Saturday night in the hospital. Son of a bitch!

"Did you get anything off of Rory's clothes?" The Secret Service had confiscated the kid's shirt, pants and hat to analyze it for traces of the kidnappers.

"We got one strand of long black hair."

Bailey touched her head. "Mine? I know the Secret Service took my hairbrush for a sample."

"Both are at headquarters as we speak, undergoing DNA testing. If it's not yours, we can find out a myriad of things from forensic testing and genetic genealogy, including sex and ethnic origin."

"Have you checked out anything related to Bailey's gang activities?" Mitch wanted to know. "We're worried about the presence of the Sanders family on the lake."

Masters nodded. "We're going over their background again to find out if there's a connection between the aunt, uncle or daughter with Annie-O, the Anthrax girl. So far—just like your people, Mitch—we haven't found any. We'll go see Annie-O while we're in New York to make sure she's what she appears to be these days."

"What about the GGs?" Aidan asked. "Could the kidnapping be linked to them?"

"Still out of commission. But we tracked down the core group again—about ten of them, with names like Buzzy Iverson, a girl called Locust—just to make sure. So far, no luck with them, either. We're checking into juvenile records now. The cops remember some underage girls hanging out with the older kids. They must have gone through juvenile court."

"Then their records will be sealed," Bailey said.

"Given what's at stake, the Freedom of Information Act and the Patriot Act, I'm sure we can convince a family court judge to release them. But first we have to find out who they are."

His sister leaned back and cradled her stomach. "I can't believe my gang activities would surface after all this time."

The FBI agent shook his head. "Unfortunately, your stay at the lake was on the New York news. Gang members have a long memory, Ms. O'Neil. You know that. If they're still on the wrong side of the law, no telling what the reminders of you might have generated."

Poor Bailey, Aidan thought. It seemed her life would never be simple. Thinking of C.J., Aidan decided maybe nobody's was.

MIKEY ENTERED the pub's kitchen where Liam was putting the finishing touches on his Irish stew for tonight. The boy had always liked being around the homey scents of food and the warmth of the hearth.

"Dad?" His son's face was serious again. For a few weeks, when he was at the lake with Bailey, Mikey's mood had lightened, but since he got back to the city, he'd been keeping to himself again. There was a disturbing sense of stillness about him.

"Yeah, Mike?"

"Is somebody gonna try to kidnap me?"

The spoon in Liam's hand clattered onto the steel stove-top and he whirled around. "What are you talking about?"

"Some guys almost got Rory. Cleary says they could come after us."

Hell, the effects of the damned lake trip were wide-spread. They'd all returned to New York three days ago as if they'd been to a funeral instead of on a vacation. Cross-ing the room, Liam hefted up his seven-year-old, gave him a hug and sat him on a stool at one of the counters.

"Sometimes Cleary just likes to get your goat, Mike. You know that. Nobody's coming after you, I promise."

The boy was owl-eyed. "They did Rory. We saw it again on TV."

Goddamn it! The footage of the near kidnapping—mostly C.J. Ludzecky jumping off the Ferris wheel—was on the news. Rachel Scott hadn't been finished when she filmed Bailey at the museum and Rory at the picnic. Dylan, espe-cially, was angry at this woman's constant publicity of their family. Not quite as angry as Clay, though, when the FBI had gotten through to him in Zanganesia and told him what had happened at the fair. He called Bailey to make sure she was all right and was livid about Scott.

Grasping Mikey's shoulders, Liam stared into his eyes. They were so like Kitty's it broke his heart. "You know Aunt Bailey's husband is the vice president."

"Yeah, 'course. The kids at school think it's cool he's my uncle."

"Some bad people don't like politicians and want to hurt their families. It's why Bailey needs so many agents with her."

Mikey's eyes got watery and he wiped stray tears with the hem of his T-shirt. "Is Aunt Bailey going to get hurt?"

"No, honey, she's got excellent people protecting her."

"Not C.J. anymore. She jumped off the Ferris wheel to save Rory." A hitch in his voice. "*She* got hurt."

"Only a sprained ankle and a bump on her head." He smiled at the boy. "You like C.J., don't you?"

"Uh-huh."

"She's going to rest and get better for two weeks. She'll be here with Bailey by the time we get back from our camping trip next week." For which they'd tripled Rory's guards. Now three agents were going along instead of one.

Mikey's expression was older than his years warranted. "Then C.J. goes to Washington with Aunt Bailey."

He ruffled his son's hair. "You miss Aunt Bailey when she's not here, don't you?"

His son nodded.

"Me, too."

"I miss Mom more."

"I know." He pulled the boy close. "I feel the same way."

Sometimes Liam could still see Kitty barge in through the swinging doors behind his son to show him something she bought, to tell him a cute story about the kids, to give him a kiss when she was helping out waitressing. God, he'd give anything to have one minute of those times back again.

Instead, through those doors came his brother Aidan. Who'd been in the world's shittiest mood since he got back from the lake. Scowling, snapping, cranky as Angel got when she was tired. Aidan blamed it on worry about the kidnapping attempt, but Liam knew there was more to his foul disposition.

"I can't find the fuc—" He caught sight of Mikey on the stool. "Sorry." He crossed to the boy and tugged on his Yankees baseball cap. "How are you, kid?"

"'Kay."

Liam said, "The kidnapping thing's got him shaky."

"How's C.J.?" Mike wanted to know.

"Um, I'm not sure. Ask Aunt Bailey."

"You like her."

Liam crossed his arms over his chest and leaned back against the counter. "Out of the mouths of babes."

"Yeah, I like her. She's a nice woman."

"Did you call her and ask how she is? Daddy says I should do that when somebody's sick."

"She's resting."

Mikey scowled. "So what?"

"Don't want to disturb her. Now, what do you say you come out and help me stack glasses at the bar?" Something Mikey liked to do.

Liam smiled. Aidan had a way of cheering up the kids that none of the rest of them had. But he couldn't seem to make himself feel better. He had it bad for Special Agent Ludzecky.

Mikey scrambled off the stool. "Cool." He took Aidan's hand.

"Thanks," Liam mouthed behind Mikey's back.

"No problem."

Liam watched his brother go. For a minute, a familiar sense of anger welled inside him. Aidan should do something about his feelings for C.J. Life was too short to pussyfoot around with indecision. Liam knew that better than anybody.

Fishing his cell phone out of his pocket, he punched in a number. Waited for an answer. Then said, "Paddy, I gotta talk to you."

C.J. WATCHED her sisters swarm around the clothes *Matka* had unpacked for her and hung in the closet of her old room. There was no other word to describe their actions. Like bees making honey, they homed in. And now they were going to have a freakin' fashion show.

"For Christ's sake, they're just clothes."

"Easy for you to say." This from tall and willowy Magdalena. "Not every girl has her wardrobe bought by the vice president's wife at her own personal store."

"I get the yellow dress first." This from Elizabeita, whose blond shoulder-length hair was up in a clip.

"Why?" Paulina asked, holding the sundress C.J. had yet to wear. Paulie's hair still fell to her waist in a thick heavy mass.

Lizzie snatched the dress away. "Because I'm the youngest."

"Lizzie baby, that line is wearing thin." Ana eyed Paulie from where she sat on another of the three beds, nursing her second child. "The dress won't fit you anyway, Paulie. Your boobs are too big since you had the twins."

"Fine." Paulie pulled out the pink capris and matching shirts. "These will."

Antonia, identical to Paulina, joked, "Think your stomach's flat enough, girlfriend?"

"Flatter than yours by a half inch."

C.J. was shocked to learn her twin sisters had a contest to see who could lose their *baby fat* fastest. She hadn't been surprised the two of them had kids at the same time, though Toni only had one. Paulie's boys were with their dad, and Toni's baby right now was outside with his Uncle Luke, swinging in a hammock under a big oak tree. Must be her brother was practicing for his own little treasures. All these babies . . . all these happy marriages . . . C.J. was struck with an awful thought: Was this why she'd avoided coming home? Because it was *hard* witnessing what she might never have?

She banished the thought and turned her attention to her youngest sister. Lizzie was beautiful in the dress, of course. It complemented her tanned back and shoulders. Not only was she the smartest of them all but the prettiest. "It looks fantastic on me." And the least modest.

"You can have it," C.J. said.

Lizzie stared at C.J. in the mirror. "I can?"

Ana said, "No, you cannot, young lady."

Sofia added, "Caterina may need it to seduce some handsome agent back in D.C."

For a minute, the memory of deep blue eyes flashed through her mind. She imagined the look in them if Aidan saw her in that dress.

"What's this?" Magdalena asked. She'd bent down into the closet where Luke had stowed C.J.'s suitcase. When she stood she was holding a stuffed animal.

A white bear, with a pink ribbon. C.J.'s mouth dropped open.

"Look at her," Paulie said.

She recovered her wits. "Must be one of Angel's toys got in there by mistake."

Maggie stared down at it. "There's a note."

C.J. reached out. "Give it to me."

"No way . . ." This from Sofia. "Read it, Mags."

The others chimed in. They could be vicious when they wanted to be. They'd driven Luke nuts about his girlfriends when they were young.

"It just says, 'I'll never forget you.' "

"Ohmigod." Lizzie whirled around. "There *is* somebody. I'll bet it's that cute agent, Mitch. We've seen him on TV with Bailey."

"No," Paulie put in. "It has to be that other one, Grayson. He's more her type."

"Forget it." C.J. kicked her sheet off her bare legs. They'd even dressed her in their pajamas. This set was flowered capris and a ruffled top. "There's no guy in my life."

"Then who's never going to forget you, missy?" Elizabeita again.

When her son fussed, Ana stood and began to walk him. "You were moaning in your sleep last night."

"I jumped down twenty feet off of a Ferris wheel and got hurt. I'm in pain."

All of them froze. It would have been funny—five women in various states of undress and another with a crying baby— if their faces hadn't filled with fear. Usually, C.J. was cautious about what she said to them. But she *had* been dreaming about Aidan since she got home three days ago and didn't want them to know. And they'd caught her off guard. She should have been more careful because she'd heard them talking about watching the whole ordeal with Rory on TV. Still, no one mentioned it outright.

Lizzie broke the silence. She crossed to the bed, sat down and took C.J.'s hand. "Doesn't it scare you, Cat? To put your life in danger like that?"

She held her sister's hand tightly. "Not as much as it scares you. I'm sorry I said anything."

"It was on the news, anyway." There were tears is Ana's eyes now.

"Damn that reporter." C.J. was looking for someone to blame. "She's harassing us."

Sofia came to sit beside her, too. "We know you need to do this, but we just wish you were safer."

"I hate worrying you." C.J. bit her lip. "I remember what it was like with Luke."

"Well," Magdalena said, "at least we're talking about it. *I* hate the silences and you not coming home much. Sometimes I can't sleep at night—"

Matka appeared in the doorway wearing one of her housedresses and a stern look on her face. C.J. didn't think she loved anybody more in the world than this woman. *"Sciskac glos."*

They quieted immediately. Six beautiful faces turned toward the door where their mother stood.

"Owszem, Matka."

"Tak Jest."

All but Lizzie acquiesced. Raising her stubborn chin, she stood and plopped her hands on her hips. *"I'm* not shutting up. I want her to quit that damn job and live a normal life."

"That is not something for you to decide, *bobchee*."

Lizzie sniffed. "We got Luke to quit."

Crossing to her youngest, *Matka* smoothed down Lizzie's hair. "Kelsey got Luke to quit."

"See. Then what we need is a man C.J. would leave the Secret Service for."

C.J. could feel the blood rush to her face.

"Hmm," Ana said. "I think I was right about the dream."

Maggie was still holding the stuffed animal. "And I'm right about the bear."

C.J. pulled the covers up over her head and wished she could stay buried under them.

IT WAS MIDNIGHT when Aidan entered his apartment from his shift at the pub. He was too keyed up to go to bed, so he wandered around the place that had once been Bailey's. It was nicer than the studio he used to rent, so when she moved in with Clay, he took over her apartment for the last six months, then renewed the lease. He'd made it his own, though.

The first thing he'd done was install a dark room. There had been a big pantry in the kitchen, with easy access to the plumbing. He got permission to renovate from the landlord, and his brothers helped him make it over with blackout curtains, ventilation, a safelight, a wet bench in a flat sink. He enjoyed working in this medium for some of his more creative shots, but of course, the digital camera was easier to use and print copies.

In the kitchen, he got a beer and studied the far wall of family portraits. He'd done a montage of his nieces and nephews, had spent hours finding just the right juxtaposition and sizes. There was a big color photo of Ma and Pa, Bailey and his brothers. Another of Liam with Kitty. He stared at Liam's expression. He hadn't seen that look of contentment on his brother's face in three years. Patrick and Brie seemed happy in their photo, too. Aidan had taken it years before the trouble had started. Dylan was up there, with Stephanie, in black and white because it seemed more suited to them. Staring at the gallery of photos he wondered again why everybody had married but him. He'd just never found the right girl.

Until now.

Stop, he told himself. That was a stupid thought. He'd only known her a month. He didn't love her.

No, but you could. You feel it in your gut.

In the living room, he sank down onto the stuffed couch Bailey had left and stared at the landscapes he'd hung on the longest wall. There was room for some photos from the lake. If he could bear looking at them. Damn, he didn't want to do this. Be preoccupied with her. She'd been right, after all, that he could never watch her risk her safety for the rest of his life. *That* he also knew in his gut.

Picking up the TV remote, he heard footsteps, then his apartment door open. It had to be Paddy. He had an emergency key. But all three of his brothers swaggered into the living room like a posse looking for its quarry. Oldest to youngest, dressed similarly in jeans and pub shirts.

"Hey, buddy," Patrick said, leading the way, carrying a big brown bag. He sank onto the end of the couch.

"Hey." Liam took a chair and propped his feet up on a hassock.

Dylan dropped down on the floor by the TV. "How's it hanging?"

"Swell. What are you doing here at this hour?"

"Closed the pub a little early. Business was slow." Pat took a six-pack of Molson out of the bag and tossed one to each of them. Aluminum popped in the quiet apartment.

Liam spoke first. "We're bummed about the FBI report."

News had come today from Jack Masters that the strand of hair on Rory wasn't Bailey's. It was female and of Asian descent.

"That implicates Annie-O," Aidan said.

"Mitch says the FBI found her; she's still straight—and has an alibi for the day of the kidnapping." Dylan seemed the most knowledgeable on this.

"What about her cousin Sasha? She's not adopted or anything, is she?"

"No, she's Asian, too. But the FBI contacted the family. They were out of town at the time of the fair."

"What next?"

"They're going deeper in the gang stuff. The GGs."

"Who were responsible for the death of our half sister." Liam's voice was sad.

"Fuck," Dylan said. "I hope it's not them again."

Aidan asked, "Is this why you came tonight? To commiserate?"

"No." Pat leaned forward. "We're here because you're moping around like a lovesick pup."

"And you're grumpy as hell." Dylan lifted a dark brow. "We're doing an intervention."

"And we're concerned." This from Liam.

Aidan zeroed in on that brother. "You blabber to these guys?"

His chin raised, Liam looked him straight in the eye. "There's a time and place to keep secrets. This isn't one of them. We think you're making a mistake with C.J. Life's short, bro."

"All the better to spend it with the *right* woman."

Liam's eyes were wise. "Talking yourself into something you don't really want won't help."

"You said those exact words to me, didn't you?" Patrick was frowning. "When I wouldn't compromise with Brie."

Often with these guys, all Aidan's charm evaporated. "I don't appreciate this shit. Either drop it or leave."

"Fine, we're wrong. You mind's made up." Dylan held out a DVD Aidan hadn't seen him bring in. "Let's watch this."

Something wasn't right about the three of them giving in this fast. When they were younger, they'd used all kinds of ploys to torture him. "Yeah, sure, just so we're clear."

As Aidan punched the remote, his brothers murmured their consent.

"Uh-huh."

"Sure."

"We're backin' off."

The TV booted up and Dylan slipped a DVD into the machine. Some previews played and they laughed at Tom Cruise finding yet another impossible mission, made lewd comments about the umpteenth *Charlie's Angels*, but agreed the producers could make the same movie over and over if those chicks cavorted across the screen.

Aidan relaxed and, truthfully, appreciated the camaraderie. But his mood got shot to hell when the feature started. "What's this?"

Dylan's expression was innocent as *In the Line of Fire* came on-screen. "I never saw this movie."

"I did."

"Yeah, but you won't mind watching Renee Russo again, though," Patrick added. "With all that red hair."

Liam's gaze zeroed in on him. "Problem, little brother?"

The gauntlet was thrown, Aidan knew it. None of them would cave at the challenge or they'd never live it down. Damned if he was going to be the wuss.

Sinking back into the cushions, he watched the opening salvos Eastwood threw to Russo in the most accurate Secret Service movie ever made. Watched her put him in his place. "I wonder if all female agents are so tough?" Dylan asked idly.

Aidan's fist curled around the can of beer. He *wasn't* taking the bait.

The scene where Eastwood and Russo shed their armaments to jump into bed was next. Vests hit the floor. Cuffs jangled. Guns and beepers thumped into the pile.

"Think those vests come off easy?" Liam asked.

Aidan watched stoically until Russo appeared in a black dress at some formal event. Superimposed over her, he could see C.J. in that dress, with her breasts straining out the top just fine.

"You're drooling, kid." Patrick's tone was smug.

"Not over Russo." This from Dylan.

Liam asked, "Ready to give in?"

Aidan lost the battle and bolted out of the chair. "Fuck you, I'm going to bed." He stomped into the bedroom and crossed to the windows facing the back. There was a little yard where he used to play ball with Rory. Sometimes he missed Bailey and Rory so much it hurt. Sometimes he wished he had a son, who'd never leave him. And a wife.

"Aidan." Patrick's voice in the darkness.

Aidan grunted.

"We were just jabbing you."

"I know. It's okay."

"We weren't off base, were we?"

"You know you weren't. I talked to Liam about it and Dylan guessed. They told you."

His oldest brother crossed the room, stood behind him, and placed a hand on his shoulder. "Remember what else you said to me about Brie, besides talking myself into things?"

"Which time?"

Patrick chuckled. "Guess I shouldn't feel bad about interfering. You asked me if I wanted to look back on my life and wonder if I could have made it work with her."

"What do I know? I'm all talk."

"You know a lot."

He faced his brother. The moonlight cast Pat's face in shadows. For his whole life, Pat had been there for him, especially when his father wasn't. Now he looked tired—worn out. "It's not going so well, is it?"

"We're okay. There's still a lot of friction over her job. But I got Isabella out of our reconciliation."

"Your beautiful daughter."

"We're gonna make it."

"Good."

"Don't you want all that, kid?"

"I do." He swallowed hard and admitted, "She says she doesn't."

Pat waited a beat. "You want to look back on this when you're old and wish you'd at least gone after her and tried?"

He just stared at his brother. Did he?

"You're not gonna get a better chance. She's off work. A half hour away. We got the address."

"How'd you do that?"

"Dylan found out. He's got connections. It wasn't that hard."

"I don't know." He turned back to the window. "I don't wanna get slammed down again."

"You can pick yourself up, if it happens." Another squeeze on the shoulder. "And we'll be here if you need us."

He turned to see his brother heading for the door.

"Patrick," Aidan called out.

"Yeah?"

"Thanks."

"You gonna do it?"

"I'm not sure. But thanks for caring. All of you."

"Caring?" Pat said, the big-brother tone back. "Who said we cared? We just can't stand seeing you be such a wimp. We taught you better than that."

Aidan chuckled. And felt better.

FIFTEEN

THE GIRLS had dragged C.J. outside with them on Thursday afternoon. Her sisters had been in and out of the house this week, and three were staying until Saturday. Luke had to leave tomorrow. All eight of them were in the small backyard, in the end of July heat, wearing swimsuits and Coppertone. Self-consciously she adjusted the skimpy top of the watercolor bikini her sisters insisted she wear. In truth, it had been fun being *girly* with them—fussing with their hair, experimenting with makeup, painting finger- and toenails. Hers were now a bright peach.

Luke stood in front of her chaise with the garden hose in his hands. They'd been using it as a sprinkler to stay cool while sunbathing, though C.J. couldn't get out of the lounge chair and run through it with her crutches like the others had been doing.

"Okay," she said. "Not too strong, though." She closed her eyes and stretched out, prepared for a refreshing shower.

He blasted her with the water.

"Son of a bitch." Her hands went up to protect her face, but she took in water anyway. She sputtered and wiped the hair out of her eyes. "I said not too hard."

"You're as easy as you used to be, Cat," he said dropping down in the chair next to her. "I thought you'd toughened up in the big bad service."

She nodded to the crutches. "If I didn't have those, I'd take you."

He snorted.

"We're going to fix lunch," Paulie and Toni called out as they headed inside.

Ana wanted to check on the baby, Maggie went with her and Lizzie had to make a phone call for work.

C.J. watched the exodus with interest. "Did they leave us alone intentionally?"

"Uh-huh."

"What are you supposed to do?"

"Find out about the guy who gave you the bear. The one that you're dreaming about every night."

Closing her eyes, she angled her face to the sun. Its rays beat down on her. Warmth seeped into her. "Don't pry."

"I don't have to. I already know who it is."

He did, of course. He'd alluded to Aidan when he visited her at the cottage. The only damage control she could do was to say, "I won't talk about it."

"Then I will."

"I'll go inside."

Deftly, he reached over and snagged her crutches. He tossed them out of reach.

"Hey, that was mean."

"I must be cruel only to be kind."

"You? Quoting Shakespeare? What's the world coming to?"

"You can insult me all you want, but it won't stop me. Just listen. I gotta go home tomorrow, so shut up."

"You're all charm, Lukasz."

He gave an exasperated sigh. "When I met Kelsey, I liked what I did as much as you do."

She didn't say anything.

"But when it was clear I couldn't have both her and the service"—his voice softened—"I chose her. I don't regret it one bit."

"I know that, Luke. And I thank God every day you're safe and happy." She reached over and grabbed his hand. "But the same isn't true for me. You love teaching. I tried another job before I got into the service, but I didn't like it as much as this one."

"Why did you join?"

"Your doing it made me interested. I started reading up on the organization."

"You went to the training academy in North Carolina without anybody knowing. We thought you were down south on sabbatical from the UN."

She tried to distract him. "With all that's going on, I'm overdue for my refresher course at Beltsville." Every two out of eight weeks, protectives had to go back for qualifications in fitness, driving, shooting at a second facility that offered advanced training for recruits and pros alike. "You've been there, right?"

"Don't change the subject. Why didn't you talk about this all to me first?"

"I was sure you'd object, particularly since you knew the danger."

"*Know* the danger. You could at least look into a safer position in the service. Then you could have this guy and your work."

No response again.

"You liked being in Intelligence in New York. From what I hear, it's fascinating."

"It was. But I told you why I left. Anyway, it's a moot point. I love the VPPD, guarding Bailey and the kids. It's every agent's dream."

"Will you follow them into the White House if they go?"

"I don't know. Agents are usually cycled out every three to six years."

"Stepping up to the PPD would be a different rotation. She could ask for you again."

"Okay, if she does, then I'd get the *top* job, Luke. Why would I give that up for a fling?"

"I watched you around him, *kochanie*. It's more than a fling. You could care about him; you already do some."

"All right. I care about him. It could be more. Which is precisely why I will not put myself into a position where I have to choose him or my job."

"You're not even going to give it a shot?"

"No. I could lose my spot on the VPPD if anybody finds out I screwed the protectee's brother."

"Nice language."

"Give me a fucking break."

They laughed. He reached out and linked his hand with hers.

"Don't you ever miss it, Luke?"

"Yeah, of course I do. A lot sometimes. But nothing's a hundred percent. There's drawbacks to everything."

"I've chosen my side."

Luke shrugged. "I just hate to see you give up what I got: a great marriage and kids on the way."

She cocked her head. "This doesn't mean I won't ever have that."

"But you won't have it with Aidan O'Neil. When you're ready, he won't be available. A guy like him is gonna get snagged and soon."

Her throat closed up.

"Doesn't that break your heart a little bit?"

Once again she was silent. This time, she *couldn't* talk.

"Okay. Done here." He slid out of the chair and retrieved her crutches, setting them near the chaise. "I gotta go call Kelsey."

"Say hi for me."

Leaning over he kissed her head. "I just want the best for you, baby. And if you weren't so sad I wouldn't have pushed it this far."

"Thanks for caring. *Kocham Ciebie.*"

"*Kocham Ciebie.*"

Luke strolled into the house, and C.J. turned her face away. He'd stirred up too many emotions inside her and she was feeling raw. The image of Aidan with another woman having his babies cut deep. A tear slipped from her eyes, and she dashed it away, grateful her brother had left. God knew what he'd do if he saw her cry over the guy.

AIDAN WAS CRANKY the day after his video party with the guys. He'd tossed and turned all night long, unable to get Paddy's words out of his head. He was wiping down the bar and washing a few dirty glasses on Thursday at about four when his cell phone rang.

He checked the caller ID. Unavailable. "Aidan O'Neil."

"O'Neil. This is Luke Ludzecky."

Aidan's heart started to beat at a clip. "Is she all right?"

"Physically, she'll go off the crutches tomorrow. Emotionally she's a wreck."

"She took a pretty bad spill. Sometimes it's tough to get over the trauma."

"Remember the talk you and I had on the dock?"

"Yeah, sure." He was sick of brothers telling him what to do. "Look, Luke, I did what you wanted me to do."

"I know. I don't want you to do it anymore."

"What?"

"I don't want you to leave her alone."

"Why?"

"She's miserable here and it's because of you. I think you should come up here for a few days. I'll square it with *Matka*. You can stay in my old room."

"Hold on. You're moving too fast."

"No, *you're* moving too slow. And just so you know, I'm not being altruistic here. I want Caterina to quit the Secret Service. I think you might be her ticket out."

"Let me get this straight. You don't like me, but you want me to come up there and what, seduce your sister?"

"More information than I need, buster." Then Luke chuckled. "And you're okay. But listen, we never had this conversation. She isn't to know I called you hoping you could get her to quit."

"I don't like dishonesty, Luke." Especially with women he cared about.

"Put your nobility aside, Sir Galahad. Don't you want her safety more than your principles?"

"It hasn't really gone that far."

"Yeah? Then why do you sound like you just got back from a funeral, and why is she crying over you as we speak?"

"Crying? C.J.'s crying?"

"Don't tell her I told you. Just come."

"All right."

"And one other thing. If you hurt my baby sister, I just might have to kill you."

Aidan said, "Oh, that's just great," but was smiling when he got off the phone.

HE CAME bearing gifts. Knowing he needed her mother's approval, Aidan rang the front doorbell with present in hand. The August morning was a perfect jewel with a cloudless sky and slight breeze; he took it as a good omen.

The door opened and it had to be *Matka* standing before him. She was just as he'd pictured her from C.J.'s comments—a plain-dressed, sturdy woman whose expression was knowing. "You must be Mr. O'Neil."

Quickly, he got the picture out of his camera bag and

into her hands. She looked down. As she stared at the photo, her grip on the gilded frame tightened. After a moment, she wiped a tear that trickled down her face. When she raised her head, she was smiling. "I have never seen a more beautiful picture of the two of them. They were always close. So, what do you call it, in tune? This captures that, and the love between them."

"Thank you."

"You took this?"

"Yes."

An expression of motherly concern. "So you're the Bear Man?"

"Bear Man?"

"I found a teddy bear in her suitcase. You are the man who will never forget my Caterina?"

"Yes." He raised his chin. "I am."

She let him in; they passed a living room and a parlor as she led him down a corridor to her kitchen. "I will make lemonade."

Aidan stood in the doorway, at a loss for how to react. "That would be good."

The room was small, like the whole house, but spotless with gleaming Formica countertops and windows that invited light to spill into everything. Spices grew in pots on the windowsill. The faint wiff of some kind of soup permeated the air.

He crossed to the windows in the dining area and when he looked out into the backyard, he felt like somebody had knocked him back ten paces. "Oh, my God."

Matka peered out the window over the sink and smiled.

"They're absolutely beautiful. I've never seen anything like them. All of them together, it's . . . stunning."

C.J. and her sisters were stretched out on blankets and chaises. Slathered with oil. Piles of hair on their heads, shot with varying hues of gold. Each of their swimsuits was skimpier than the next. Tinkles of girlish laughter wafted in through the open window. When he realized some of it was from C.J., his whole body warmed. At that and the why-bother scraps of material she wore.

"Close your mouth, young man."

"Yes, ma'am."

"Here."

He took the lemonade, allowed himself a hardy drink of the tart liquid. He nodded to the outdoors. "I have to photograph them."

His comment lit up *Matka*'s eyes and spread a wide smile across her face. "That would be nice."

"I'd prefer doing it without them knowing."

"I will take you upstairs. There is a little porch overlooking the yard." She started away. "Come with me."

"Mrs. Ludzecky?"

Her brows arched.

"Don't you want to know anything about me?"

"Your picture tells me who you are. Besides, my Lukasz said you should come."

"Does she know?"

"*Nie*. There will be fireworks."

He removed the film camera from its carrying case and held it up. "Then let's do this first. And fast."

Upstairs and undetected, he took pictures for ten minutes. "Ah, baby," he said to his camera. "Can you believe it? Just look at them."

He was able to zoom in on Caterina, but all of them together was what captured his artistic interest. One coating another's back with oil. One lying on her stomach, kicking her feet in the air, paging through a magazine. Two of them still enough to be sleeping on the chaises. C.J. herself sitting up, sipping a drink through a straw. He could do a whole gallery show on them.

And from *Matka*'s porch, he could hear their chatter.

"Honest to God, Caterina, he kissed me right in one of the Italian painting rooms of the Met."

"Jared of course was the last to kiss me," another said. "But it's different now, since the baby. Nothing's spontaneous anymore. We have to *plan* when we're going to fool around."

They took turns, confessing he guessed, who was the last man each of them kissed.

Finally one socked another in the arm and nodded to C.J. "Your turn, Caterina. Who was the last to lay one on you?"

C.J. glanced away. Unfortunately, her gaze lifted and landed on him. Thankfully, he'd just put the camera back in his case. She stilled, watched him. Then she said, "He's, um, standing on *Matka*'s porch."

The resistance, the tension, the sadness C.J. had felt as her constant companion dissipated at the sight of Aidan here, looking down at them like some Greek God taking pleasure in his subjects. He was tanned and the light blue shirt he wore with dark shorts fit him so well, it hurt to look at him. She stood.

The girls flocked around to her, forming a semicircle, staring up at him.

"Could he be more gorgeous?" Lizzie asked.

"Look at those shoulders." This from Sofia.

Each sister had a similar remark. Some were salacious.

Aidan gave them a half grin and a little wave.

"Get down here." C.J. tried to sound stern. Mostly though, she felt a surge of inner joy. She took deep breaths to contain it.

His effect on her got worse when he was on the ground, and out in the sun, closer. The rays caressed his hair, kissed his skin. Self-conscious of her half-dressed state, C.J. picked up one of Luke's shirts that she'd borrowed and slipped into it. The other girls didn't cover up.

"You're not staying," she said.

"Listen, honey, I have to—"

"Not you." She motioned to her sisters. "Scoot."

As they filed past him, their looks were long and level.

They made approving noises, Toni patted his shoulder, Paulie tested his biceps. Lizzie said, "Go for it, handsome."

By the time they were out of the yard, he was blushing. Beautifully. "Well." His look was puppy dog. She imagined it got him a lot of mileage.

"Come on." C.J. preceded him to a picnic table under the shade of an oak tree.

He sat on the surface and she joined him. She curbed the urge to take his hand and hold it against her heart.

"Why are you here?" But, by God, she knew.

Clearing his throat, he placed a hand on her arm, as if he had to touch her. "I changed my mind. We have to see what's between us."

"No, Aidan. And your coming here just makes it harder."

"You don't know the half of it, baby."

She giggled. "I'm serious."

"Oh, so am I." When she didn't say any more, he did. "I can't walk away, Caterina. I thought I could, but I can't."

"What do you want from me?"

"This weekend. Go with me somewhere for a few days. Afterward, we'll decide if we can end it for good."

C.J. the agent warred with Caterina the woman.

Problem was, she'd been in girl mode for almost a week, and it was tough shaking the role.

And she could still hear Luke's warning . . .

But you won't have it with Aidan O'Neil. When you're ready, he won't be available. A guy like him is gonna get snagged and soon.

And for Christ's sake, she'd *cried* over the guy. That was reason enough to consider his proposal.

Or not to.

But in the bright light of day, surrounded by the love and security of her family home, C.J. couldn't suppress Caterina. "All right, I'll go."

He expelled a heavy breath. "Thank you, Lord."

C.J. surfaced. "But not on your terms. It's just this weekend, Aidan. I'm willing to take these few days with you. But don't expect any more."

"We'll make that decision on Sunday."

"I've already made it. I won't go with you under false pretenses."

"But you'll go with me." It was the little bit of awe in his voice that cinched the deal.

"I want to, yes."

He stood. "In that case, we won't waste one second of the time we have together." He held out his hand.

And Caterina took it.

SIXTEEN

THE SCENERY from Queens to the Finger Lakes at the beginning of August was breathtaking. Verdant greens and exploding flowers scrolled by as they drove up Route 17. Ordinarily, Aidan would have wanted to stop to take pictures, but the view *inside* the car was even more pleasing, so he kept driving. Caterina sat next to him, blooming like the wildflowers he'd brought her all those times. It wasn't only how she was dressed—in white shorts and a peach camisole kind of top that made his hands itch—but her hair was down and fluffy like she'd curled it, skimming lightly tanned shoulders. He detected a hint of color on her cheeks and lips, and she'd even painted her nails a pretty peach. Today, she was all girl.

And not just in looks. Her whole manner had softened, as if once she took off the suit, earpiece, radio, gun and handcuffs of her own free will, she'd shed the agent with them. The transformation mesmerized him.

Trying not to be too sappy about how she looked, about the time they had together, he gave her an appreciative smile. "Okay, your turn to ask a question."

They'd gotten a half hour into the drive, and he'd suggested they play Twenty Questions. In the guise of passing the time, it was a conspicuous ruse for getting to know things about each other that they hadn't had the opportunity to find out before today.

Caterina had readily agreed. She'd already answered his queries about her father, Stash Ludzecky. The man had loved his children in his own way, but had been stern and stereotyping. Luke, particularly, had had trouble with him. Caterina recounted his untimely death, and how unresolved issues with him had affected her and Luke the most.

"What about your pa?" she asked. "Tell me about him."

Aidan's grip tightened, he hoped unnoticeably, on the wheel. "He was a good father. Provided as well as he could for us, though we weren't anywhere near well off. But he's headstrong, as you know, and he and Mama hit a bad patch."

He went on to explain his parents' separation, and subsequent reconciliation, but not before Pa had slept with another woman and had a child, Moira. He told Caterina about his half sister's gang activities and how his mother had taken her in, despite the circumstances.

"That explains Bailey's gang interest."

He smiled.

"What?"

"You always call her Ms. O'Neil."

She laid back against the seat and let another layer peel off. "Not in my head."

"What do you call *me* in your head, Caterina?"

Amber eyes glistened in the sunlight streaming through the window. "I don't use that kind of language in mixed company."

Laughter bubbled out of him. He hadn't realized she could be fun, or had *any* sense of humor, let alone a good one.

"I called you Aidan," she confessed. "Right from the first." When he glanced over, he saw a scowl on her face.

"Why the frown? You're not having second thoughts are you?"

"No. I'm taking this one weekend with you without any recriminations. And without any interruptions." They'd turned off both their cell phones.

One weekend? They'd see about that. Already she was charming him to the point that he couldn't fathom ending their relationship after the forty-eight-hour deadline they'd given themselves. At noon on Sunday she planned to be out of his life.

"I scowled because I know about your fight with your father."

He hadn't expected that, and the dainty blow came like a left jab to the head. "Y . . . you do? How?"

"In the chapel, when you were praying that night he was rushed to the hospital. I heard you . . . talking to God, I guess. I'm sorry I eavesdropped."

"It's okay."

"I wanted you to know, because if we're going to get . . . close, there shouldn't be secrets between us."

"Oh, we're going to get close." Now was the time to tell her Luke had called him and encouraged him to come to Queens to see her. "I—"

"Tell me about the argument. What exactly happened?"

He agreed, mostly because he was afraid she'd be pissed about Luke and Aidan being in collusion to get her out of her job. So he recounted the whole, sordid story of his fight with Pa.

After he finished, she squeezed his arm across the gearshift. "Liam was right. Your father's heart attack isn't your fault. He had a physical condition that led to his attack. In any case, you should be able to pursue whatever profession you want to."

"Like you did? Despite your family's objections."

"How do you know that about me?"

"From things you let slip. From the expression on your

face when you talk about them. And Bailey mentioned that you didn't see much of them."

She sighed. "I guess I'm not really the one to give advice on family." This time she grabbed his hand and held it. "Why does your father object to your photography?"

"Not a real job, too risky, mostly it's my family duty to work at the pub with my brothers."

"He didn't feel that way about Bailey."

"She was a girl, and when she was single, she spent a lot of time waitressing, helping out where we needed it. Once Clay came along, my parents pitched a fit about him because he put her in jail years ago."

She smiled. "I like hearing those stories about them." She studied him. "There's more between you and your father, though, isn't there?"

"Yeah. Pa and I were born on the same day. We've had kind of a bond because of that. And because I was the youngest boy, he had more time to spend with me."

"Would he give his blessing if your brothers wanted to do something else?"

Aidan thought about that. "Probably not. I guess he just assumed we'd all stay on."

"It's a shame, Aidan. You're so good at photography. I hope you don't give it up."

"Ah, there's the rub."

"What do you mean?"

"When I can't sleep at three in the morning, I question my talent. Truth be told, I think part of the reason I don't make the break is Pa's objection, but the other half is the down and dirty terror that I'm *not* as talented as I think. It's a tough profession to sustain."

"Afraid of failure?"

"Maybe."

"From what I've seen, you're magic with your camera."

He had to tell her. "I have a confession to make. I took pictures of you when you didn't know it."

She gave him a sideways glance. "The yoga ones. I already know about those."

"There were more." He shrugged, and nodded to the back seat where his photography gear sat. "Most recently in your backyard. I got some stunning shots of you and your sisters. All beauty pageant material. Don't worry. I won't do anything with them." He grinned. "They're for my own personal enjoyment."

A blush crept up her body, starting with her chest and coloring her face. "I'm not sure how I feel about that."

He slid his hand off the wheel to rest on her bare knee. The soft skin, the light scent of lotion she used on it—apricots—shot sparks straight to his groin. "You *feel* wonderful."

Instead of responding, she covered his hand with hers. To keep it there. For a while, they were quiet. It was pleasant, normal, just watching the little towns pass by, anticipating what the weekend held for them.

They stopped for a snack about midafternoon at a small ma-and-pa shop on Route 17. There was a picnic area across the street; it was deserted, so they ate at a table and stretched their legs. The sun shifted through leaves and even the grass gleamed greener than usual. Aidan knew his senses were heightened because of her.

They asked and answered more questions while they nibbled on their food. Background about families: C.J. laughed at stories about Bailey's childhood antics. College experiences: She had some interesting dorm tales. They shared niece and nephew stories: Aidan's feelings for Rory, and how he missed the boy. Her attachment to her sisters' kids, her excitement about Luke's impending fatherhood.

After they finished eating, the wind picked up; they just sat there, letting the breeze blow over them. "I know you run," she said. "Is that your favorite kind of exercise?"

With a slow and sexy smile, he stood and took the can of soda out of her hand. Gently, he drew her to her feet. She was still limping some, but her ankle was better and she no longer used the crutches. He pulled her to him. "Ah, darlin', my *favorite* kind of exercise takes place in a king-size bed."

"Aidan," she said, checking over his shoulder, to the side. She was so *used* to being wary. "We're right out in the open."

"And anonymous. Besides, there's not a person in sight." He moved in further, whispered, "I need to be close to you for a minute," and slipped his arms around her waist. She was solid and strong, and her scent was like Eve's. He buried his face in her hair. Breathed her in. "Can I photograph you at the lake?"

"All right." She was nosing into his shoulder and sniffed him. "You smell so sexy. Right from the beginning I couldn't get your scent out of my mind."

"It's Aramis."

"No, it's you."

He tipped her chin up. "I love your eyes. The shape. Those thick lashes. Their unusual color."

"Six others have eyes just like mine."

"No, Caterina, no. Not just like yours. Yours are special." He anchored his hands at her hips. "You're special."

She whispered, "You make me feel that way."

"Just a taste. For now." He brushed his lips over hers. She arched into him, tried to increase the pressure. He held back. Teased. "No, no, sweetheart. We're out in public."

"I don't care anymore."

"We . . . gotta . . . take . . . this . . . slow." Each word was punctuated by his mouth finding her cheekbone, her jaw, her neck.

Her arms tightened around him. "We've already kissed hotter than this."

"You thought that first kiss was hot?"

"Oh, yeah."

In her ear, he said, "When you're ready, I'll show you hot like you've never seen before." He drew away. She swayed into him. "Come on. Let's get to the lake."

Grumbling about his being a tease, she let him take her hand and they walked back to the car.

After their contact at the picnic table, Aidan decided to push for more intimacy with her. "Tell me about the guys in your life. You're so pretty, there have to have been a ton."

C.J. turned her face away to look out the window. The scenery was lovely, but it dulled at Aidan's question. "I'm not sure I want to get into this."

"Why?"

"I've had some bad experiences with men."

"They must have been members of some moron club."

She chuckled.

"Proszè?"

Her heart quickened at his use of the Polish word. Her control over what this man did to her was dissipating by degrees and she felt like a candle melting in Aidan's sun. "I did the usual stuff in high school. Dated, met a special boy, got busy with him my senior year."

"Was your hair longer like your sisters'?"

"Yeah, down to my waist. How'd you know?"

"I can picture it, *you* as a teenager. The guy must have thought he'd died and gone to heaven."

"I don't know about that. We saw each other in college, too, since we both went to school in the city. But it fizzled out."

"Anybody serious after that?"

"A teacher. He was a nice guy. We lived together for a while, but he couldn't take it when I decided to go for the service." She recounted other stories of guys who couldn't handle her job after she'd gotten to be an agent. Though it was painful for her to talk about, she did it for Aidan, to re-inforce the idea of how nearly impossible it was to have a long-term relationship with a member of the Secret Service.

"Something's missing."

"Why do you say that?"

"You told me at the lake that you'd had bad experiences with men that hurt your career."

She felt the agent returning. *Close off. Don't share. Be cool.*

He must have felt it, too. "It'll stay with me, Caterina. I won't tell anybody anything about this weekend. Share this with me. I sense it's important to us."

So she told him about David.

His response was hot and quick. "Goddamn fucking son of a bitch."

She laughed. "Don't hold back, Aidan."

"I could track him down in New York, beat him up. My brothers and I can handle the job."

She could picture the O'Neil posse going after the conservative David Anderson. "Actually, I heard he's leaving the city for the field office in D.C. Ironic. I loved the work I did in New York. The Intelligence Division there is very busy."

"What did you do?"

"Mostly analyze threats that come in for the president, vice president or any of the dignitaries at the UN. We take every threat seriously and report our findings to headquarters. There's a huge database for tracking down people. And since I majored in languages and worked at the UN, I was good at deciphering accents, that kind of thing."

"You speak different languages?"

She nodded.

"Say something sexy in French."

"Je veux que m'ils aient touchè."

He winked at her. "I want you to touch me, too."

"You shit. You speak French."

The outrage on her face made him burst out laughing. "From college. I had a knack for it and it stuck, *ma jolie femme.*"

More moments of comfortable silence.

Then, he said, "Intelligence work sounds less dangerous than protective duty."

"People think so but the fact is no agent has ever died on

protective duty. They've been shot, but nothing fatal. There *have* been deaths in investigation, undercover, going in on the stings and in the field offices, too."

"Did you do either of those things?"

"Undercover assignments never appealed to me. I worked mostly on running down threats." She smiled. "I did do protective duty there. Field offices provide UN security when needed."

He seemed thoughtful. She wondered what he was thinking. Then decided she didn't want to know. So she said, "Your turn. I want to hear about these redheads."

Slashes of color accented his cheekbones. "You know about the redhead thing?"

"You and your brothers are open books, O'Neil. You jab each other all the time about your Titian-haired beauties."

"I didn't sleep with Sonia that night," he said abruptly.

"So you said the day of the picnic."

"Or any night we were at the lake."

"I didn't ask."

"I just wanted you to know that since I met you, there's been no one. I couldn't get a certain blond babe out of my mind."

"Babe? Oh, my God. No one's ever called me that."

"Don't bet on it."

"You're changing the subject. Come on. I want the details."

He told her tales of the women in his life. Some were funny. Some heartbreaking. Some stupid. The whole Twenty Questions thing worked its magic, because by the time they neared the cottage she did feel closer to him.

"We're almost there. One last question we each have to answer. A personal one." He cleared his throat and the devil danced in his blue eyes. "Real personal."

"Why doesn't that surprise me?"

"If you had to compare sex to something, what would it be?"

"You first."

"All right. It's like a meal to me." He ran his hand over her bare knee. "The appetizers should be tasty, but not filling. Little bites. Something to arouse the palate." He sniffed. "And they have to smell great. Right now, apricot sounds appealing."

"Oh, Lord. Why'd I ask?"

"Hush. Then the wine. I'd drink it in. Taste its lush body and full flavor."

She swallowed hard.

"Naturally, the main course would take the longest. The different textures. Mouth involved. Tongue. The sensations of each . . . bite go through your whole body. And when it's over I'd feel sated. But it would take a long"—he ran his hand over her knee—"long"—he inched up to her thigh— "long time to get there because I'd savor and indulge in every single morsel."

A moan escaped her. "Stop! I get the message."

"And then, Caterina, there's dessert."

"Oh, God, no please. No dessert. Not now."

His chuckle was smug. "I guess I can hold off on that particular delicacy . . . until later. Your turn."

Her competitive side kicked into gear. She had to match his wit, be as clever. Ah yes . . .

"Sex is like popcorn."

"There's a new one."

"The kind you air pop."

"I can't wait to hear this."

"First, you get the ingredients together. Then you put the kernels in the popper. It takes a lot of heat to get them ready to . . . pop."

"I'll remember that."

"The process starts slow. Real slow. Just a few bursts, here and there. Then, the level rises. Slow . . . slow . . . slow . . ."

"God, not too slow I hope."

"Shh. But you have to be very careful, because once in a

while, the kernels don't pop like they're supposed to and the corn doesn't reach the top. It just simmers there, but sadly, doesn't go over."

"You been buyin' the wrong brand then, baby."

Biting the inside of her cheek, she went on. "Sometimes, it gets to the top and tumbles over gently. Easily."

"Easy can be good, as long as it goes over."

"But sometimes—and this is rare—it bursts right out of the chute and over the top. Fast, furious. Uncontrollable."

"Oh, Lord, open the window. I can't stand this."

"You asked."

Satisfied she'd turned the tables on him, she lay back against the seat. He was silent, too. Then he said, "Caterina?"

"Yes?"

"You ever have Cracker Jack?"

The laughter was shared. So was the intimacy.

But when they pulled into the driveway to the cottage, the intimacy waned and C.J. started to feel edgy. When she'd been here before, she was Agent Ludzecky. "What did you tell Bailey about wanting to use the cottage?"

"Just that I was coming back up for a while. I didn't say I was bringing anyone with me," he added quickly.

"She can never know about this. Give me your word."

"I give you my word."

"Is the cottage still open? I know we left in a hurry and all the agents went back then, too."

"Yeah. A cleaning service is coming in to clean and close the place down next week. Everything's still up and running."

"Good."

He leaned in toward her. "It will be."

His comment made her smile. And, because of their blatant sexual teasing on the drive up, she was surprised when they entered the house, that he took only his bags to the room he'd used on their stay in July, and led her to the master bedroom.

She cocked her head. "What's going on?"

Crossing his arms, he leaned against the doorjamb all cocky and arrogant-looking. His shorts and T-shirt hung with masculine grace on him, and his color was high. "What, did you think I was going to jump you as soon as we got behind a closed door?"

She did. "Maybe."

"Not my style. We're going to go for a swim, have a drink, and then go out to dinner and dancing."

"What if I don't want to do those things?" she asked, sidling up to him.

"Not gonna happen yet, babe." He kissed her nose. "Anyway, anticipation is important. Like with the appetizers, remember? Or the popcorn taking its time to get to the top." His smile was thousand watt. "Now go into the bathroom and put on that bikini one of your sisters gave you while I change these sheets."

C.J. scowled. She'd been *anticipating* this all day. Still, she walked into the bathroom and changed.

Into the bikini.

"WHAT ARE you thinking?" Aidan asked C.J. as he sat across from her at a white linen–covered table at Starlight's, a restaurant on the tip of the lake close to the Hammondsport side. They'd both dressed up, him in a blue blazer and light blue shirt, highlighting the color of his eyes. They weren't cool like the sky tonight, but hot like flame. She knew why. Her body was humming too from the afternoon.

She gave him a siren's smile. She'd worn the gauzy yellow dress, earrings and had fussed with her hair, so she figured flirting was appropriate. "That you're a nice guy."

"Not exactly how I want you to be thinkin' about me tonight, lass."

"Oh, man, you're good."

"I am."

God, she loved this cocky side of him. She sipped her merlot and ran her tongue over her lips. His gaze narrowed on the gesture. All right, she was teasing him, too. But he'd been the one to delay the sex. It was kind of fun, though. She took another bite of her lobster and sighed. He was eating the same thing with asparagus and the twice-baked potato, but he showed little interest in the succulent meal. His attention was focused completely on her. That alone was heady.

"Okay, I'll bite. Why am I nice?"

"I know why we came to this side of the lake."

He averted his gaze, embarrassed now, by a kind thing he'd done.

"You didn't want to run into the pretty cop." She shook her head. "That's nice, considering how hot she is for you." The memory made her frown. "She was all over you at the picnic."

He grasped her hand and brought it to his mouth. Kissed her fingers. "I'm sorry you had to see that."

Probably it was the wine. Or the gesture. Or the stunning romanticism of the atmosphere—a table on the terrace overlooking the lake, a warm breeze and stars dotting the sky. But something made her say, "I couldn't believe how much it hurt."

"I'll never do anything to intentionally hurt you." At her skeptical look, he added, "You don't have faith in men, I know. But I can be counted on."

It was important—for both of them—to say, "This, us, is only for the weekend, Aidan."

"Then count on me for now. Trust me for the weekend."

The waiter appeared and removed their plates. They ordered triple chocolate decadence for dessert. The band began to play "When a Man Loves a Woman" and Aidan stood. "We've got time for a dance before dessert."

He came around and helped her out of her chair. "My foot's okay," she said.

"I know. This is just another excuse to touch you."

"Your fault," she whispered as she rose. "You could have been . . . touching me all this time, but you wanted to wait."

"Oh, God, I'm dead meat. I had no idea how lethal you could be when you flirted."

C.J. crossed to the dance floor with him. This, too, was outdoors, under the canopy of sky. He took one of her hands in his and slid his other around her waist. She nestled into him, resting her head on his shoulder. Silently they swayed, listening to the soulful tune.

He inched closer to her.

She hooked her arm tighter around his neck.

His mouth glazed her ear.

She tangled her legs with his.

When the music ended, Aidan drew back and stared down at her with a look so profound it made her throat tight. "It's time, love."

She smiled. "I think so, too." She glanced at the table. "What about dessert?"

He said into her ear, "We didn't get that far in our conversation today. As I said, I'll have to show you."

"The *chocolate decadence* we ordered?"

"Oh. We'll take that with us."

"Fine by me."

They didn't talk as they waited for the dessert—which seemed to take forever—and the check. He led her out of the restaurant and helped her into the front seat. He stole a kiss as he leaned in and buckled her seat belt. In the process, his knuckles grazed her breasts and she sucked in a breath. Once inside, silence again. He held her hand as he drove. His face was taut in the light from the oncoming cars, and she realized the teasing, flirty man was gone. He was trying to control what was building inside him during the day.

So was she. She didn't speak, just held on to him.

Five minutes . . .

Ten . . .

Fifteen by the time they finally pulled up to the house.

He swerved into the driveway a little too fast and stopped on a dime, making her pitch forward. He got out of the car and slammed the door. His urgency sent an embarrassing thrill through her. Dragging open the passenger door, he unclasped her belt and drew her out. He walked ahead of her to the front door, opened it, shut that hard, too.

Then he shocked her by sliding an arm beneath her knees, one around her waist and lifting her to his chest.

"Aidan, what are you doing?"

"Be still."

"I'm too heavy."

He disproved her words by taking the steps two at a time. She had no idea he was so strong. At the top of the stairway, he took her mouth ravenously, and she felt the primitive possessiveness of it, the way he carried her, his whole manner, in every nerve ending. "Hurry," she said against his lips.

He strode down the hall, kicked open the master bedroom door and went inside. Standing her by the bed, he cupped her face in his hands. She just watched him.

"Mine," he whispered roughly. "All mine."

HIS HANDS were shaking. Roiling inside him were emotions he didn't know he could feel. He'd made a mistake stringing this out, teasing her, giving her time to get used to the intimacy that was about to happen. Still, he tried to be gentle.

"This is so soft," he said, slipping one strap of the gauzy yellow sundress off her shoulder and running his fingertips over her skin. It was warm to the touch. He kissed his way across her collarbone. "Soft and supple."

At his words, her body melted even more, as if it was readying itself for him. He nosed the other strap off. Pressed his lips to her skin to feel her heat with his mouth. The straps gone, the front of the dress was supported only by her breasts, so he tugged it down, revealing cleavage . . .

a swell and curve . . . her nipples. Now, she was bare to the waist. She'd worn no bra, he knew that from watching her all night. She was lovely, lovely flesh, which the moonlight caressed through the open doors to the deck and skylights. He raised his hands and cupped her. Her breasts were firm and toned, befitting her. He massaged her with his palms, watching her gorgeous amber eyes close, watching her bathe in the sensations he was causing. A smile flirted with her lips; he took her nipples between his fingers.

Her back arched. "Aidan . . ."

He lowered his head and let his mouth replace his hands. She startled and made a throaty sound. It sent desire whipping through him. His words of praise, of need, of what he was going to do to her were a harsh whisper.

One quick yank brought the dress to the floor; he knelt before her like a servant and drew off the yellow lace panties that covered her. When she was fully bared to him, his hands shook even more. His legs got weak. He stayed on his knees and kissed her stomach, brushed his lips over her curls. She jolted into him and said, "I'll never last."

"No, you won't." Mercilessly, he increased the pressure with his mouth.

She came on one long, glorious groan of pleasure.

When she was done, she gripped his shoulders, her breathing ragged. He stood. Her cheeks were flushed, her eyes shining brighter than the stars. Reaching out, she undid the buttons of his dress shirt, disposed of that, and slid her fingers to his belt.

The jangle of his buckle.

The rasp of his zipper.

The thump of his shoes.

Wordlessly, she pushed the clothes down, knelt, too, in front of him, and rid him of everything he wore.

Then she took her turn, kissing his abs, running her mouth along one hip, then another. She murmured words that he couldn't grasp, so steeped he was in what she was doing to him. She bit one hip lightly; he jerked and grew harder. His body bucked when she took his penis in her hands, then her mouth.

He gasped for breath. Began to sweat. Blood rushed to his center, and he had to hold on to her shoulders for support. His world dimmed.

On the brink, he heard her say something, but again, couldn't make out the words. The interruption did give him one moment of sanity. "Get up."

"No."

So he bent down and forced her away, to her feet, then drew her onto the bed, stretched her out. He fumbled for the condoms in the dresser drawer, where he'd put them earlier. He winced as he sheathed himself too fast, too rough, but his heart had begun to thud, almost painfully. And he was clumsy. Kneeling on the bed, he gave her a searing kiss, then covered her body with his. At the meeting of skin, bone, every part of their bodies possible, his pulse beat wildly.

"I don't know how you like it . . ."

She pulled him close.

"What position . . ."

Her hands clasped his butt.

"What makes you . . ."

"Aidan, please. Just come inside me!"

He did. With one long thrust.

She arched into him. For a brief second he bemoaned his lack of finesse, of originality, of pretty words. Then, he couldn't think at all. He simply plunged and plunged and plunged. He heard her cry out, his head filled with the scent and feel of her, and he lost himself in all of it.

"THIS IS WHY they call it chocolate decadence," she murmured as she lay back into the pillows while Aidan did sinful things with the gooey confection.

"Oh, yeah."

Eyes closed, she enjoyed the sensation of his tongue licking the sweetness off her breasts. Suckling, just for good measure. "You're so beautifully formed, here."

A dot of cold on her navel . . . his tongue lapping it up. More on her hipbone, with the same method of removal.

"I'm going to be a sticky mess."

"We can take a shower together. Better yet a Jacuzzi. There's one in the master bath."

She knew about the tub, of course, from her sweep of the place when the Secret Service came up here with Bailey, but she'd forgotten that. She forgot the very fact that she was an agent. Before she could fret, he said, "Grasp the headboard with your hands.

"Why?"

"I want to see you like that."

She did what he asked. After he worked his way down and back up her body, he said, "Keep hold, and turn over."

"We'll get the sheets . . . Oh!"

"Just say, 'Yes, Aidan.' "

"Yes, Aidan."

Her face in the pillows, she learned everything there was to know about his special brand of dessert.

HE TOOK the snapshots quickly, before she could change her mind . . .

Caterina in the tub, flaky bubbles keeping her decent. Her hair was piled on her head, a few tendrils escaping. She held a glass of champagne in her hand, from a bottle he'd found in Bailey's small fridge, so he didn't even have to go downstairs to fetch it.

Caterina back in bed, wearing a baby-pink slip of a thing she said her sisters gave her to take up here. God bless sisters! The camera's eye caught the folds of silk that flowed like water over her body, which had been sculpted by years of working out. Her breasts strained against the fabric, making the photo even more sensual.

Caterina . . . at the dressing table, taking down her hair, brushing it in long, graceful strokes. He was entranced by the totally feminine ritual.

Caterina . . . asleep, exhausted from what they'd done together. It was the first time he'd seen her so relaxed. Her lips bore the evidence of his ardor, a bit swollen and red. There were a few bruises on her arms.

He switched off the camera, kissed her on the forehead, climbed into bed and turned off the lights.

"FAIR IS FAIR," she said, picking up Aidan's digital camera from where he'd left it on the night table. "I'm taking some pictures, though I won't make you come alive, like you do with this thing."

"You make me come alive, babe, with just a look."

She smiled when he drew back, zoomed in and took a close-up of his face. His blue eyes were filled with satisfaction and his smile was almost a smirk.

Shrugging into a robe, he brought his coffee out on the bedroom deck. There she caught the wind ruffling his hair . . . the indolent way he leaned against the railing, facing her with a Cheshire cat grin. "Why not?" he said wickedly. "I got the cream."

Another face shot, up close, tracking the dark growth of beard on his jaw. She shivered, remembering the abrasion of it brushing her inner thigh . . .

He made a naughty comment for the camera, then took it from her hands and led her to the chaise in a corner of the deck that even the prying eyes of Rachel Scott couldn't see if she'd still been around. It was private.

Wonderfully private.

Simply wonderful.

SEVENTEEN

AFTER A LATE morning nap, they packed a picnic and went for a gentle walk on the property outside the gated area. They Ace-bandaged her ankle, so she could make her way through the grass and foliage. Aidan was so besotted with her, he even liked that they were dressed similarly, in sneakers, khaki shorts, white T-shirts, though hers fit her a lot better than his. When they stopped at a clump of wild-flowers, this time varying shades of red, he picked some and handed them to her.

She arched a brow.

"From me," he said, meaningfully. All pretense was gone now, and he felt freed from the constraints she'd put on them.

Spreading a blanket on a patch of grass, they made small talk as they enjoyed the natural setting around them. A deer and some squirrels scampered by.

"I worry about my sister," he said after a while. He'd slid down, extending his legs and crooking his arm, for his head to rest on his hand.

Cross-legged, Caterina looked out over the lake. "It must be tough, having someone you love constantly in the public eye."

"There have been threats against her personally, haven't there?" She was about to speak, when he said, "Liam read about it. He said you guys won't reveal the number of threats received daily against the president and his family. So threats must be made against the vice president, too."

The breeze rippled her hair, and she tried to tie it back, but gave up. "That's why there are so many of us with her and the kids, Aidan."

"I know." He shook his head. "She's really worried about Clay's trip."

"The service would prefer he hadn't gone, too."

He plucked a strand of grass and put it in his mouth. "Tell me about who you guarded in New York. When you were doing protection from the field office."

She described her assignment to an ambassador from the Middle East, a king of a small country, the former vice president's kids a couple of times when they came to New York to see Broadway shows. After a while, she shifted restlessly. "Enough of me. Tell me what you want for dinner and I'll make it for you."

"You can cook?"

"Hush your mouth. Of course I can." She sniffed. She was a girl, all right. "*Matka* would skin me alive if I didn't keep up my culinary skills."

"Okay, I want something Polish."

"That shouldn't be hard."

"And you have to make it naked."

"Don't press your luck, mister."

"Have it your way. I'll take pictures of you cooking and alter them digitally. From memory."

She stilled and stared at him.

"You know I don't mean that, sweetheart."

"What are you going to do with the pictures you've been taking . . . after?"

His felt his throat constrict. "I don't know."

"Promise me you'll throw them out. For real, this time. Not like the yoga ones."

"No."

She drew in a breath and stood. As she looked down at him, the agent peeked out. "You'll destroy them, even if it isn't now. When you meet somebody else, she isn't going to like having the pictures of one of your flings around."

He rolled to his feet, like a jaguar springing into action. Grasping her shoulders, he yanked her to him. The kiss wasn't gentle. It wasn't nice. It was angry, *he* was angry, at her, for making that damn point all the time. He knew why she did it, to keep them focused on the temporariness of this weekend, but now, after hours of intimacy, that quite frankly blew the top of his head off; her remark pissed him off royally.

She let him kiss her like that. When he was done, she drew away, picked up the basket and said, "That doesn't change anything."

SHE COOKED, but not naked. She'd memorized *Matka*'s recipe for pirogies and started the ravioli-like dish about four that afternoon. When they'd returned from the picnic, he was upset and went running. Since she was none too steady herself—about their fight and about what would happen after this weekend—she'd done some yoga first, trying to center, trying to find the inner peace it usually brought.

She couldn't. So she just had to hold it in, hold *on*, and do what she needed to do no matter how much it hurt her heart. If he sensed weakness on her part, he'd go in for the kill.

By the time he returned, she was halfway through making dinner and the kitchen smelled like her mother's. That soothed her and kept a lid on her emotions. He entered the house soaked with sweat, took a bottle of water from the fridge and gulped it down.

Her hands covered with dough, she watched him. It took a lot to withstand his glare. "Did it help?"

"Some."

She bit her lip. The reality of causing him pain was almost as bad as giving him up. It wound the emotional spring inside her even tighter. "Don't ruin the rest of our time together because you're not happy about it ending."

His look was lethal. "You can just do it, can't you? Walk away."

She raised her chin. "We said we would."

He studied her as if she was an alien species.

"I have no choice." There was a catch in her voice.

"There's always a choice."

"Not with this."

"All right, fine." He slammed the bottle on the counter. "I'm going to shower."

He got halfway to the door, and she called out, "Aidan?"

He stopped but didn't look back.

"It hurts me, too. A lot."

Still facing away from her, he said evenly, "Then come upstairs and prove it."

The lovemaking that followed their tiff was raw enough to burn away some of the strain between them. By silent consent, they didn't talk about their imminent separation while they ate dinner.

"These are incredible. *Matka* taught you well, sweetheart."

Her heart, not so sweet, turned over in her chest every time he called her that, or even babe, which her feminist side revolted against. How could she live without that now that she knew what it felt like to be so close to someone?

In bed that night, they didn't make love again. Instead, they stared up at the stars and talked about ordinary things that ordinary people talk about. Problem was, C.J. thought as she cuddled into his chest and her eyes began to close, this tender time together was as intimate as the sex had been.

THE LAKE rolled over and over, tossing whitecaps willy-nilly. They crashed against the shore, splashed water onto the dock. The trees were wind-whipped and fiery. Rain battered the wooden deck that surrounded C.J. as she watched Mother Nature wield her power. The roar was enough to wake the dead, but Aidan still slept in bed where she'd left him.

C.J. was glad. She didn't want him to see her cry. Sob. Rage like the weather. She'd been keeping it together until the dream. Of Aidan, with his redheaded wife and two blue-eyed kids, at a fair, in a car on the Ferris wheel. At the top of the ride, he kissed his spouse thoroughly. His hand draped over the side of the car, and when he uncurled his fist, little pieces of paper floated to the ground. They were the shreds of the pictures he'd taken of C.J. at the lake. The scene was so real, it had startled her awake.

But Aidan making a family without her *would* happen. Just like they would go their separate ways in a few hours. She couldn't prevent either. She wasn't going to try to find a way to make it work between them because she was scared. How could you give up everything for a man? How could you let yourself trust someone completely with who you are? What if, like the others in her life, he let her down? Then what would she have? No, she was too much of a coward. The irony didn't escape her—she could put herself in the path of a bullet without flinching but she dodged emotional fire by turning tail and running.

Yet . . . how could she let Aidan go and make that other family after the physical and emotional intimacy of the last thirty-six hours? As rain pelted her face and soaked her robe, she regretted what she'd done earlier with him, the intimacies that had piled up like hidden treasures in her mind.

They'd awakened at eight when the storm started.

I want to do things with you that I've never done with another man.

Ah, love, I want that, too.

The hour that followed, with the total relinquishing of control, and the physical acts that took on an almost reverent quality, were the wrong things to do. Wrong, wrong, wrong. Added to the rest of their time together at the lake, and how close they'd gotten, she was very afraid he'd fallen in love with her.

And that she'd fallen in love with him.

What could be worse for a woman who had to walk away in a few hours?

"Honey, what are you doing out here? You're getting soaked."

She sucked in a breath. No, no, she needed more time to collect herself. She hadn't quite shaken the remnants of the dream.

Naked, he walked out into the rain. He grasped her arm, turned her around. "Your teeth are chattering."

"A-are they?"

"Come inside."

When she hesitated, he took control and once again scooped her up into his arms. He carried her indoors and into the bathroom. He removed her wet clothes, sat her on the toilet, and turned on the Jacuzzi faucets. As the tub filled, he snagged a towel off the bar and wrapped it around her; took another to dry her hair. All the while he kissed her cheek, her nose, murmured soothing words.

Oh, God, he knew. He knew what sent her into the storm. Would he use it against her? The notion terrified her. How strong could she be?

He helped her into the tub, then climbed in behind her. The heated water, the jets that caused the swirls and bubbles, relaxed her muscles, had her sinking back into him. He held her close, kissed her hair. And bathed her with long sensuous swipes of the washcloth and loofah.

When the water turned cold, he stood and helped her out. He dried her like a loving maid and bundled her into one of the terry cloth white robes hanging on a hook in the bathroom. Donning one as well, he took her hand, brought her downstairs, fixed coffee and when they were seated at the kitchen table, sipping the hot brew, his face grew serious.

"You know what's happened between us this weekend. Last night. Upstairs just now."

Shaking her head, she said, "It doesn't matter."

"Of course it does. It changes everything."

"No."

"Caterina, if you think I'm letting you go now, you're crazy."

"You promised."

He stopped at that. Only for a minute. "Look. I have a plan. We can be together and you don't have to quit the service. But you'd have to leave the VPPD. Bailey and Clay would be glad to arrange another protective assignment if they knew we wanted to be together."

"The job I have is a plum of the service."

He raised his chin. "Wouldn't you give up that specific assignment at least, for me? And risk a knock on your reputation?"

His bravery in asking her, his courage in confronting her, kept her honest, too. "Maybe I would, Aidan. But I know you could never handle what I do. What I might *have* to do in a protective assignment. Think about how it felt to see me jump off the Ferris wheel. You said you couldn't handle *that*."

"I found out this weekend I can to do whatever's necessary to keep you in my life."

He was so strong, but not as strong as he thought. "You think that now, but you'd worry yourself to death. You'd be alone doing it, too, because agents travel so much. Eventually you wouldn't be able to handle the stress. Unofficial statistics say eighty-five percent of agent/civilian relationships split up."

"Tim Jenkins is doing just fine with his family. I talked to him about it when Clay came up."

"He's leaving the VPPD."

"All right then. We'll be the fifteen percent that makes it."

She gave him more arguments. But he wouldn't budge. And she couldn't imagine putting him through what he so foolishly vowed he could withstand. So, her heart breaking, she stood and held out her hand. "Come with me."

He was frowning, but he followed her to the den, to the house computer. She booted it up, did a Google search and clicked into the news site she wanted. "Sit. Watch this. Afterward, if you can honestly tell me you can deal with something like what you see on-screen, if I were in this situation, I'll listen."

THERE WERE CROWDS cheering outside the Hilton hotel as President Reagan and his team of agents left the building. People yelled, and one called out, "Mr. Reagan, Mr. President," and Reagan waved, smiling. The door to the limo opened, and he and his agents were about six feet from it when two shots rang out.

Then four more were fired.

Press Secretary Brady and a police officer went down.

The camera zeroed in on Reagan. Suddenly he was shielded by a Secret Service agent. Tim McCarthy, Aidan knew. The big blond guy took a step and then spread his arms and legs out in a body block to protect the president. He allowed himself to be totally vulnerable.

He took a shot in the stomach, doubled over and went down. There were screams, the president was pushed into the limo and another agent fell on top of him.

The camera panned to the ground ... blood all over Brady.

It zoomed in on McCarthy, who seemed to be in shock. He held his hand to his chest, while other agents loosened his tie, pulled back his coat. His face was in a frown, his mouth slack. He didn't moan or shout or even groan with pain. He was stoic and stalwart as he'd been trained to be.

Caterina said from behind Aidan, "There was live coverage of this on TV. Imagine me there, Aidan, taking that bullet like McCarthy did, and you're at the pub, razzing your brothers and this comes on the screen. How would it feel? What would you do? You couldn't handle it. No man could. Admit that now to me. Tell me the truth."

When he looked up at her, he knew she had her answer.

His cheeks were wet.

THEY PACKED in silence. Aidan wanted to punch his fist through the wall at what she'd done to him. Showed him the worst thing that could happen to her, to any Secret Service agent, by the very nature of the job. And she'd done it cold-bloodedly.

Maybe he didn't love her like he thought.

He slammed his duffel bag onto the foyer floor just as the clock chimed twelve. Their Cinderella hour.

It was done. But instead of the prince getting his girl and living happily ever after, Aidan and C.J. would be left only with memories. And pictures that he would, now, destroy.

He stormed through the house checking the doors to see if they were locked, cleaning up any evidence that he and C.J. had been here. When he walked into the den, he noticed they'd left the computer on. Of course, once she'd delivered the killing blow, she'd walked out of the room without saying anything. Aidan had bolted off the chair and kicked the wastebasket across the room.

He picked up the mess he'd left and went to turn the computer off. He closed down the Reagan shooting video, and the current news page popped up on the computer's browser window. He glanced at it . . . and gripped the sides of the desk. "Oh, my God."

"What's wrong?"

He looked over to find her in the doorway. "It's Clay. The embassy where he's staying in Zanganesia has been taken hostage."

Right before his eyes, soft and sexy Caterina turned back into the cold and calculating agent. She whipped the cell phone off her hip and turned it on. Sent for messages. Then she punched in a number. She waited. "Mitch, it's C.J."

He saw her wince and could imagine the retort from the other end. Something like, "Where the *hell* have you been?"

"I, um, went away for a few days. To clear my head . . . I know, I know, I should have stayed in touch. I just found out about Vice President Wainwright."

Aidan could hear a raised voice from the other end. Her face was sober, her tone serious, her back stiff.

"I was cut off. I said I was sorry. That's not important now. How bad is the situation?"

Again she winced. "All right, I'll be there this afternoon. Yes, my ankle's fine." After she hung up, she faced Aidan. "The situation is critical." Her voice held little emotion. "Zanganesian militants—now they're terrorists—have Clay and three agents hostage, along with some embassy personnel. Everybody's in chaos back in New York."

"What do they want?"

"When Clay consulted with them on how to deal with their street crime problem a year ago, the government cracked down primarily on eighteen- to twenty-year-olds. Many of them were involved in drugs. Apparently, these terrorists are part of a drug cartel. They want Clay out of the picture, the release of those arrested and for the government to amend the new laws." She frowned.

"What?"

"Intel gathering suspect two of the terrorists have sons who are in prison."

Swallowing back his own misery, he stood. "Bailey will need us both now. I checked everything in the house. We can leave any time."

She carried her own bags to the car, and they got in without talking. Before they took off, she stayed his hand. "Would you like me to drive? I know you're close to Clay, too."

"I'm fine," he said, putting on his sunglasses. "I'm just fine . . . Agent Ludzecky."

EIGHTEEN

AIDAN ARRIVED in the city alone. He'd dropped C.J. at her mother's house; she said she'd get her belongings and make it to the city on her own. That way, Aidan could go to his sister first, and he could avoid showing up with Agent Ludzecky, both of whom were MIA for the weekend. Nice of her to think of him. Fucking *nice* of her.

They'd listened to the radio on the way home for news of Clay. She'd also gotten regular updates from Mitch on her cell. When Aidan had pulled the car onto her mother's street, she started to say something, but he held up his hand. "Don't."

They hadn't even said good-bye.

Keeping his mind blank, he dropped off the rental car and took a taxi to Bailey and Clay's brownstone. A crowd milled in front of the town house and because the sky was gray and there was a soft mist in the air, it took him a minute to realize the people were reporters. One must have recognized him. She came toward him and stuck a microphone in his face. A cameraman stood behind her. "Mr.

O'Neil, Rachel Scott for WNYC News. Do you have any comment on the situation with Vice President Wainwright?"

"No. I just heard about it. Let me by."

Planted in front of him, she blocked his way. "How is your sister handling the hostage crisis?"

He drew himself up. "How do you *think* she's taking it? What's wrong with you people? She's pregnant and—"

"Are you worried about her losing the baby?"

Then it clicked who this person was. Rachel Scott. He moved in closer to her and she took a step back. "Look, lady, haven't you done enough? It's your fault Rory almost got kidnapped. Now you want to badger Bailey when she's at her worst. You're leeches, you—"

"Excuse me." Mitch Calloway inserted himself between Aidan and Scott. "Mr. O'Neil has no comment." Mitch grabbed him by the arm. "Come on, Aidan."

Damn. Sheepishly, he followed Mitch in the path he cleared. "Sorry. I wasn't thinking. I know I'm supposed to keep my mouth shut when they descend like that."

"Forget it. I'm just glad you're here. Bailey's been as strong as a saint. Your brothers are worried about her keeping everything inside." He cleared his throat. "So am I."

"Are the guys here?"

"Yeah, they closed the pub today."

At the front door, Agent Gorman let them in. Her expression was sober. "Hi, Aidan," she said moving to the side. "Glad you're back."

Nodding, he entered the living room. It looked like a Secret Service command center. There were agents everywhere—here, in the kitchen, dining room. Phones rang. The low mumble of voices drifted out of the den.

"Where is she?" he asked.

Mitch said, "In the bedroom, trying to rest."

Aidan took the stairs two at a time and made his way to the master suite. Ludicrously, he recalled moving Bailey into this town house when she and Clay got married. After knocking softly on the door, he wedged it open.

His sister was sitting on the bed in a nest of pillows, next to Patrick, who had his arm around her. Dylan slouched in a chair near the wall, one leg propped up on his knee, his foot bobbing up and down. Aidan was surprised to see Pa in another chair, asleep now.

Bailey looked over to the doorway. "Aidan?"

"Hi, honey." He crossed to the bed. Pat moved away from her, slid off the mattress, and Aidan took his place, encircling his sister in his arms. "I'm so sorry, B."

Bailey turned her head into his chest and gripped his shirt with both hands. "This is so awful."

"I know." He smoothed his hand down her hair. "How are you holding up?"

"I'm scared."

Glancing down at her stomach, he asked, "How's the little guy doing?"

"Okay."

Lying back on his shoulder, she said, "Thank God Rory's at camp and they're incommunicado. We contacted the agents there about what happened with Clay but asked them not to even tell Liam what's going on."

"Good thinking." She didn't say more. "You can let down, you know. It's just us."

"Would do her good to cry." This from Dylan. "She's been a rock."

"No. I need to be strong." Her gaze narrowed on the TV, where CNN coverage of the scene in Zanganesia was continual.

The lights in the tiny embassy were off. There were silhouettes of men with guns stationed around it—not the good guys. Static from radios and shouts in the darkness were live and vivid.

Then the screen split to show the anchor interviewing Clay's press secretary, Mica Proust.

The woman looked exhausted. "Yes, of course we believe it will end safely."

"Why are they doing this?" Bailey asked. "The United States doesn't even have the prisoners. They're in Zanganesian jails."

Dylan leaned forward and linked his hands between his knees. "Probably because they blame Clay for influencing the laws over there. They figure they can make a statement by holding him, and also get their prisoners freed."

"But the Zanganesian government won't change their laws because of Clay."

"The militants might think their actions will keep the United States from interfering in the future."

Bailey shook her head. "We'll certainly interfere now."

"Terrorists aren't always logical, honey." This from Patrick, who was grim-faced.

"Logical or not, they should know that the United States doesn't negotiate with terrorists, damn it!"

"Any word on Bailey O'Neil, the vice president's wife?" the anchor asked.

"Oh, fuck. I *wish* they wouldn't keep asking about me." Her picture flashed on-screen. It was one taken when she was pregnant with Angel. Her hands on her stomach, she was smiling broadly. "Or showing that."

Mica's gaze turned hard. "I talked to her an hour ago. She's doing as well as can be expected. She's a strong woman, you know."

The anchor ended the interview and more discussion ensued between her and a few political analysts about what the terrorists hoped to accomplish. At one point, the anchor glanced off to the side. She frowned. Nodded. Then she faced the camera, with the other side of the screen still focused on the embassy.

"This is just in. We have a video from WNYC News. It's of Ms. O'Neil's brother entering the vice president's town house in New York."

"Goddamn it." Aidan's hand fisted as footage of him and Rachel Scott appeared on the screen. How the hell had she gotten it to CNN so fast? He watched himself tower over her and verbally attack her. Thank God Mitch intervened.

Dylan stood and began to pace. "I hate this kind of blatant exploitation of people dealing with a crisis. Aidan's worried as hell. Anybody can see that."

"I'm sorry, B." Aidan swallowed hard. "I shouldn't have said anything to her. I wasn't thinking."

"It's okay. You look so upset."

"I am."

"Sorry to ruin your weekend."

"I wish I'd been here."

"It just happened last night."

"Still." He kissed her head. "I'm staying for the duration." He looked to the guys. "What about the pub?"

Pat said, "We closed for today. Tomorrow's Monday." When the place wasn't normally open for business. "By Tuesday this situation will be over." He smiled weakly at Bailey. "I believe that, lass."

"Thanks." Bailey moved away from Aidan and stood. "I have to use the bathroom." She eyed them. "Don't talk about me while I'm gone."

When she left them alone, Pat turned to Aidan. "So, where were you that you didn't see any TV and you had your phone off?"

"I don't want to discuss it." He nodded to the TV. "Especially now."

Dylan started to speak and Aidan warned him off with a glare.

When Bailey came out of the bathroom, she looked peaked. "I need to eat. I'm feeling weak." She glanced over to see Pa was still asleep. "He needs food, too. We all do."

"I'll get you a plate, babe," Dylan offered.

"No, I want to go downstairs and check with Mitch."

She frowned. "I can't believe C.J. didn't come back to New York. I know she's recuperating at her mother's but she has to have heard about Clay. She didn't even call." Bailey shook her head. "I'd feel better if she was here."

Patrick darted a quick glance at Aidan. "Did you ask Mitch about it?"

"No, I will now."

Leaving Pa asleep, they went downstairs. The noise level diminished considerably when they appeared on the stairway. Aidan checked the TV, but nothing had changed. Mitch came out of the kitchen. "Ms. O'Neil, can I help you?"

She pressed her hand to her stomach. "We need food."

"Come on out, there's a spread."

Bailey started for the kitchen when the front door opened. And in walked C.J.

The agent.

Gone was Caterina. Her hair was up, earpiece in place. Aidan could see the glint of her gun when the jacket of her severe suit pulled back. She didn't even look at him, but crossed to Bailey. "I'm sorry, Ms. O'Neil. About the vice president."

Bailey hesitated, then threw herself into C.J.'s arms. She still didn't cry, just hung on as if she was taking strength from her own, familiar personal agent.

Surprise crossed C.J.'s face. Then she simply hugged Bailey back.

C.J. HAD GOTTEN a double whammy when she walked into the vice president's town house. First, Bailey had behaved out of character by throwing herself into C.J.'s arms. Though she was surprised, C.J. did what she'd done a hundred times with her own sisters, just held on. When her gaze settled on Aidan, the second blow hit her full force.

Never in her life had she known such a strong need to

comfort someone as she had for Aidan at that moment in time. His face was desolate and C.J. wanted to hold him like she was holding his sister. She wanted to give him comfort with her soul, her mind, her body. She had to close her eyes to keep the emotion back.

Finally, Bailey drew away. "I'm sorry. I know you don't like breaking formalities. I'm just so glad you're here."

"Took her a while," Pat said, a tinge of big brotherly suspicion in his voice.

Dylan glanced at Aidan. "Yeah, it did."

"What can I do for you, Ms. O'Neil?" C.J. asked.

"Just your being here helps. We were on our way to get some food. Have you eaten?"

She and Aidan hadn't stopped on the four-hour drive to the city. And she couldn't eat at her mother's because her stomach was tied up in Boy Scout knots. "No, I haven't. Let's go get something."

Mitch had gone back into the kitchen; he was leaning against the counter holding a plate heaped with food. When he saw C.J., he nodded. "Agent Ludzecky." He'd never betray her with an "It's about time" comment. But his annoyance over her absence was in his eyes. He smiled at Bailey. "The buffet's in there, Ms. O'Neil. Guys."

All of them headed for the dining room except C.J.

Mitch watched her as he chewed his food. "You'd better eat. It's going to be a long night."

"No news?"

"Some." He set down his plate, crossed the kitchen and moved her into the living room. Now his face was lined with concern. "The Zanganesian terrorists refuse to negotiate. The government's not letting it out, but the terrorists have given Prime Minister Tikasia some kind of timeline for releasing the prisoners. If Zanganesia doesn't meet their deadline, they say they're going to kill the vice president."

"What?"

"U.S. SWAT teams are all over place. They've called in the Big N for consultation."

"If anyone can get Clay out of this, it's Joe Nash." She respected the CIA agent who specialized in hostage crises. More than once she'd watched him work miracles. She prayed he had one up his sleeve for this family. "I feel so bad for Bailey."

"She asked for you several times." His gaze was direct. He was waiting for her to explain her absence.

"Mitch, can you leave that alone right now? I'm sorry I was out of touch. It won't happen again, but technically I was on medical leave and I wasn't required to check in."

"Aidan O'Neil got here just before you did."

"Really?"

A long silence. Before she could respond, she heard Bailey call from the dining room. "C.J., come and eat with us."

After she chose half of a turkey sub from the buffet, the only seat left at the dining-room table was next to Aidan. She pretended not to notice his scent as she sat down next to him. She tried not to watch the muscles in his arms bunch as he ate. Mostly, she struggled not to remember what it had been like to be close to him. As she'd told him at the lake, their time was over. Back to business as usual.

When she finished with supper, Bailey stood. "I'm going to lie down."

"I wonder if Pa's up yet," Pat said.

"Yeah, I'm here." Pa O'Neil stood in the doorway, looking older and more tired than he had at the lake. "Ma's coming over, too. She just called."

And so they would set up another vigil, like they had when Paddy O'Neil had a heart attack and subsequent surgery. A lot for one family to handle. But they were strong people. She glanced at Aidan. He busied himself with his meal and didn't look at her.

"Ma's bringing Angel, right?" Bailey asked.

"Un-huh. Go lie down. They'll come up as soon as they get here. You and your little one need rest, lass."

"Want me to come?" Aidan asked.

"Us, too." Both Patrick and Dylan suggested.

"I want you two"—she pointed to her oldest brothers—"to go home to your families. You were here all last night."

"We can stay." This from Patrick.

"I know Brie called you a few times."

He shrugged. "Isabella's sick."

"And Hogan called you, Dyl."

"Yeah, he's worried about Clay."

"Go, both of you. Your families need you."

Aidan said, "Go ahead, guys. I'm here for the duration." He glanced briefly at C.J., then dismissed her. "We'll be fine."

C.J. blinked so she didn't react to his coldness. *Get used to it,* the agent inside her said. *This is how it's going to be. It's what you asked for.*

So she would. She'd be strong for Bailey. This job was, after all, her life.

AIDAN SLID OFF the bed and stuck his feet into a pair of sandals. It was five a.m. and cool, so he slipped on a long-sleeve shirt over the T-shirt he wore. Thank God Bailey had finally fallen asleep after spending time with Angel. In the dim glow of the TV, which they'd left on for news of Clay, his sister's skin was pale and translucent. Her hand rested on her stomach.

Sitting on the edge of the bed, he watched the crawler on the news station. Some expert named Nash had been called to the scene. More SWAT teams were in place. Then his heart stopped. Son of a bitch! Shit! The government had gotten an ultimatum from the terrorists. They warned they would kill the vice president at dusk today U.S. time if no progress in negotiations was made. Panicky, he glanced at Bailey. "Please let her sleep," he prayed and switched off the TV. She might need it. The grim reality hit him hard, and he felt foolish for moping about Caterina and his own problems.

Quietly, he left the room and went downstairs. Half of the agents had gone to hotels to sleep. He heard C.J. and Mitch talking earlier; they'd stay here at the town house and alternate shifts of sleeping. Must be she was in bed in one of the spare rooms, because when he came to the doorway, Mitch was in the kitchen. Looking haggard. Aidan noticed a pack of cigarettes on the table. Man, he wanted one. He'd smoked in college and sometimes, when things were stressful, he and Dylan indulged in one or two.

"Hey," Mitch said.

"I saw the crawler."

"Just leaked out. That damn paparazzi. Why do they have to tell the world everything?"

"Did you know before it came on the TV?"

"We were called. Orders were not to tell you, though."

"You guys are great at keeping secrets." His stomach roiled. "Sorry, I'm bummed. I can't imagine what Bailey will do if something happens to Clay."

"Joe Nash is an expert at what he does."

"So are the terrorists."

"Not these guys. They—"

As he poured himself coffee, Aidan interrupted Mitch. "No, I don't want to beat it to death. That doesn't help. I'm going outside for a while." He nodded to the smokes. "Mind if I have one?"

"Go ahead."

Aidan shook out a cigarette and made his way to the backyard. An agent standing post spoke to him, then Aidan crossed to a swing Clay had put in for him and Bailey to sit under the stars—and neck, Bailey had said with a devilish glint in her eyes.

Aidan dropped down onto the swing, lit the smoke,

coughed and sipped his coffee. He thought about Clay Wainwright and how the light would go out in Bailey's eyes, maybe forever, if something happened to her husband.

A few minutes later, he heard a voice from the darkness. He'd recognize it anywhere. "Aidan? I saw you from the window upstairs."

He waited until she came into view. "You're supposed to be sleeping."

"My break's up." She came closer. "Are you *smoking*?"

"Yeah, my bad." He drew in a puff. "Bailey and I used to sneak cigarettes when we were young. It was fun being bad then, too." He swallowed hard. "Nothing's fun right about now, is it?"

"Mind if I sit with you?"

"Why not?"

Her weight settled into the swing. He could see her better now, in the moonlight. She wore her suit, but the jacket was off. The gun holster crossed her chest like a brand.

Because it hurt to just look at her, he stared down at her feet. "Those shoes have to be the ugliest things I've ever seen."

"Not Jimmy Choos, that's for sure."

He butted out the cigarette on the ground. "God, that tasted awful."

She fished in her pocket and handed him a breath mint. "Here."

The peppermint refreshed his mouth. "I know about the dusk deadline."

"Mitch said you did." A hesitation. "I'm sorry, Aidan. We have to believe Nash can pull this off."

"Yeah." He swallowed hard. "I was just thinking about Clay and Bailey."

"Tell me."

"He fell hard and fast for her right after they met up again on the task force. She kept him at a distance for a long time."

No response.

"Sounds familiar, doesn't it?"

"Do you need to talk about us, now?" No anger. Only concern for him.

"No. As you said earlier, there's nothing more to say."

"Then tell me about Clay."

He told C.J. how Bailey and Clay met up again after eleven years, how once he was with her again, he was smitten. "He and I had some knock-down-drag-outs about Bailey."

"Clay Wainwright? He doesn't seem the type."

"Believe me, where my sister's concerned, he's all passion." He sighed. "That's what happens when you fall in love with someone."

No response. What the hell could she say? The night stillness was broken only by the crickets, chirping away.

The inactivity made him antsy. "I gotta move." He stood and wandered to the back of the lot. Leaning against a tree, he pulled a few leaves from a low branch.

She came up to him and touched his arm. "Is there anything I can do? For you?"

He stared down at her hand, strong and competent, on his sleeve. When he raised his eyes, he said, "How about us going upstairs and fucking our brains out?"

"If that's what you need now, I'll find a way to make it happen."

"No," he said, turning from her. "No mercy fuck. What we had was too special."

"I should go in."

"Yeah, you should. Do me a favor, though?"

"Anything."

"Don't make any more of those kinds of offers. Next time, especially if things get worse, I won't be able to say no. And I'd hate myself afterward."

"All right. I'm sorry if I said the wrong thing." A pause. "I just care about you."

He watched her walk away. He tried to rein in his fury over her, and over Clay, but when she got inside, he whirled around and smashed his mug against the tree, sending cold coffee and ceramic chunks flying.

He was still standing there a few minutes later when C.J. came running back out. "Aidan!"

He met her halfway. "What?"

"Oh, Aidan." She cupped his face with her hands.

"What? Tell me."

"The Zanganesian terrorists just released a video. It supposedly shows Clay . . ."

His heart rate tripled in his chest.

"It says he was executed at dawn."

NINTEEN

"THE VIDEOTAPE doesn't prove that it's Clay's body . . ."

"The president called and said the tape is uncon-
firmed . . ."

"Joe Nash doesn't believe they killed him . . ."

The comments filled the living room, but Aidan sat
stone-faced in front of the TV, his hands linked between his
spread legs. Since C.J. had rushed out to the backyard to tell
him the news, he was more introverted than she'd ever seen
him. Gone was the carefree, gregarious brother of the Second Lady. The somber man before her was grieving.

She had to struggle to focus on the TV and not on him.
Over and over CNN ran the grainy tape of a body lying on
the ground, hooded and unidentifiable. Behind it stood a
man in a mask, holding a rifle, speaking in Zanganesian.
The translation scrolled across the bottom of the screen.
"The vice president of the United States has been executed. We will kill every American inside the embassy unless our prisoners are released."

After thirty minutes of watching the newscast, Aidan

looked up at Mitch. "What should we do? About my sister?"

"Don't wake her yet. Let's give it an hour." Her coworker's face was almost as grim as Aidan's. "If there's still no confirmation—one way or the other—we'll tell her then."

"*I'll* tell her." His voice was raw. "It'll be best to hear it from me." He frowned. "What about Jon? If he sees this, he'll believe . . ."

"The president has been in touch with Clay's son."

Unable to stand idly by and watch Aidan suffer alone, C.J. dropped down on the couch next to him and—fuck it—she took his hand, clasped it between both of hers. "I'm so sorry."

He gripped her so tightly, pain shot up her arm. Mitch pretended not to notice what they were doing. They all sat there, watching the damned video replay its deadly message, searching for clues in the scene that Clay might still be alive.

Then President Langley preempted the video. In calm, reassuring tones, he reiterated what he'd told Mitch when he called during the night. Something was wrong, though. C.J. could tell by Langley's tight jaw and the sadness in his eyes that he wasn't revealing everything he knew. She prayed he wasn't lying about Clay.

Mitch's phone rang, making the three of them jump.

He answered it. A pause. "No! Fuck!"

Aidan's whole body tensed. C.J. moved in closer and linked her arm with his.

Covering the phone, Mitch said, "It's not Clay. But it's been confirmed that one agent is dead, and two others are wounded."

"*What?*"

C.J. asked, "Who was killed?"

"Tim Jenkins."

Her hand went to her mouth and she gasped. The brutal image of the baby-faced agent who was more competent than any she knew, dead in a tiny foreign country, made her stomach cramp.

This time, Aidan took her hand. Not only was a good man dead, but this was bad news for Clay. "I'm sorry about your colleague."

"Me, too."

The room was funereal as the reality of Jenkins's death sunk in, and as they kept vigil for news of Clay.

A half hour . . .

Forty-five minutes . . .

It was nearing the one-hour deadline Mitch had set for them to wake Bailey. And no one had called to say Clay Wainwright was alive.

Aidan stood abruptly. "I'm going to check on Angel."

C.J. rose, too. "I'm coming with you."

Mitch shot them a glance, said nothing and went back to staring stone-faced at the screen. C.J. followed Aidan to the staircase and climbed the steps behind him, watching his stiff shoulders, his tense back. She longed to soothe him, but she promised she wouldn't make any overtures. They entered the small bedroom and found Angel awake and standing up in her crib. Her face rosy, her curls damp, she babbled when she saw Aidan.

"She always does this," he said, his voice rough. "She wakes up and just waits for Bailey or Clay to come get her. Rory used to scream his head off in the morning." Leaning over the crib, he picked up the baby. "Hello, beautiful. How are you?" He held Angel to his chest. "They'll grow up without a father. Angel will never really have known him. The baby . . ." She could see his eyes mist. "Rory adores him."

"I know."

"He'll never be that happy-go-lucky boy again, will he?"

Sugarcoating this wouldn't be right. "Not for a while."

His hand smoothed down Angel's hair; he stared at C.J. "You think they did it, don't you? That they already killed him."

"I think it's a strong possibility. One you need to pre-
pare yourself for."

He kissed Angel's head. "I can't believe it."

Angel chose that moment to babble, "Da-da-da."

Tears leaked from Aidan's eyes. "I can't do this."

C.J. crossed to him, put her arm around his shoulder,
and laid her head against it. "Yes, you can. You have to do
this for your sister." She whispered, "And I'll help you."

There was movement at the doorway. Bailey stood
there, sleep-tousled and totally unaware that her life was
about to fall apart.

"Aidan, what are you doing in here with Angel?" She
cocked her head. "C.J.? You both look awful." Then she
grabbed the doorjamb. "Oh, God, oh no. Something's happened, hasn't it?"

Handing Angel to C.J., Aidan crossed to his sister and
grasped her shoulders. "Yes, honey, it has."

HEARING THE DISTANT phones in the background, Aidan
stared down at Bailey and for a minute thought he was going
to be sick. How could he tell her this? "Let's sit down, B."

"No." She gripped his arm. "Just tell me now, like you
used to when something went wrong. Quick and to the
point, A."

Feet pounded on the stairway behind them. Over Bailey's shoulder, Aidan saw Mitch striding down the corridor
to Angel's room, holding his cell. "President Langley's on
the phone. Not only is Clay alive, but he's escaped. He's
safe, Bailey."

Bailey collapsed against Aidan. He held her close; in his
peripheral view, he saw C.J. clinging to Angel.

"Are you sure he's safe?" Bailey asked.

"Here." Mitch held out the phone. "The president wants
to talk to you."

Her hands shaking, Bailey took the phone. "Hello,

Mark. Yes, yes." She bit her lip. "I . . . I'm so . . ." She began to cry as she listened. When she started to sob, she handed the phone to Aidan.

He took it and kissed her cheek. "Mr. President, this is Bailey's brother, Aidan. She can't talk right now."

The president's deep voice came across the line. "I'm sorry they put her through this."

"Well, they didn't put her through much. We didn't wake her up. I was just about to tell her about the videotape when you called."

Langley chuckled. "There'll be hell to pay over that one. Bailey doesn't like to be kept in the dark."

"Just so Clay's all right."

"Calloway has the details. Tell Bailey to call me later when she's composed. Oh, and tell her I've got a second call into Jon in Paris. I want him to hear this from me ASAP."

When Aidan clicked off, he saw Angel babbling from the crib, and Bailey crying in C.J.'s arms. Agent Ludzecky's cheeks were wet.

Bailey drew back and swiped at her face. "I—I'm just so relieved." She drew in a heavy breath. "I have to call Jon. He needs to be told right away his father's okay."

Aidan explained that the president was doing just that.

Mitch was smiling. "Come on downstairs and I'll fill you in on the details."

Lifting the baby from the crib again, Aidan held her close as they trekked down the steps with a lighter tread than when he and C.J. climbed them a few minutes ago. He said a quick prayer of thanks for Clay's safety. They sat in the kitchen and while C.J. fixed a sippy cup and cereal for Angel. Mitch spoke directly to Bailey, who'd taken the chair across from him. She was pale but in control.

"We received a message yesterday that the terrorists threatened to kill Mr. Wainwright at dawn if their demands weren't met."

Bailey flushed. "You didn't tell me?"

"I couldn't. The FBI's directive was clear."

"Go on," she said, but Aidan could tell she was miffed. Long ago she'd extracted a promise from Clay and the Secret Service not to keep anything from her.

"Mr. Wainwright was beaten, Bailey. We heard this right after you went to sleep."

His sister's eyes rounded. "How badly was he hurt?"

"All we know is that he's safe. He should be on a DC-11 by now and calling you any time now."

"You don't know the extent of his injuries?"

"He's well enough to travel. He can walk around, talk. The agents said to tell you he was all right."

"What about the death report?"

"About six a.m., a tape hit national TV showing a body lying on the ground." Mitch described the gruesome sight in detail.

Bailey shuddered.

"He's okay, honey," Aidan told her.

"How did he get out?" C.J. asked, holding the cup for the baby, then spooning the cereal into her mouth.

Mitch smiled. "On the vice president's last trip to Zanganesia, he'd been nice to the staff. Complimenting the food and service. Thanking them. Lower-level jobs are held by natives, and some of the more haughty visitors to the embassy treat them badly."

"Clay wouldn't do that."

"And it saved his life. A man named Famita brought him food, then ice for his bruises. Mr. Wainwright showed him pictures of Angel and Rory and the man showed him his grandchildren. It appears that when Famita got wind that the terrorists were going to kill Mr. Wainwright, he smuggled the vice president out and to his own home. They got in touch with the local FBI from there."

"Smuggled him out? How?"

"The terrorists had the vice president in a wine cellar. Famita stole the key, and he and two of his sons conked the guard over the head. They snuck Clay out in a laundry truck."

"Sounds like a movie."

"I assure you it was real." He shook his head. "These people were not Al-Qaida quality terrorists, thank God. Basically they were a bunch of militants and drug dealers."

"What happened to them?"

"SWAT teams went in when there was no activity for a while, and when no demands were reiterated. Apparently the terrorists left when they discovered Mr. Wainwright escaped." He cleared his throat. "I assure you the government will track them down."

"Will Famita's family be safe in Zanganesia now?" Bailey asked.

"Probably not. So Clay insisted they come to the U.S., at his expense. They're under the FBI's protective custody until that can be arranged."

Closing her eyes, Bailey leaned her head back against the chair. "I can't believe this happened and no one was hurt."

Mitch's face grew somber. "People were hurt, Ms. O'Neil. One of Clay's agents was killed and two were injured."

Bailey gasped. "Who?"

"Tim Jenkins."

Tears again. She covered her face with her hands. "Oh, no, his wife has a baby on the way."

"I'm sorry."

"Clay must be devastated."

Just then Mitch's phone rang. He clicked on. "Yes, Mr. Vice President. She's right here."

Bailey stood, took the phone, and walked into the living room. From the kitchen, they could hear soft sobs, mumbles, relieved laughter.

Aidan leaned back against the chair, dazed from the events of the morning. He watched C.J. feed Angel and coo to her. The sun streamed in and caught the highlights of their hair. He pictured her as his wife, feeding their own child at the breakfast table.

Then going off to some foreign country to protect a dignitary. And getting killed like Jenkins.

He shook his head. She was right all along. He could never handle her job.

THE EMOTION of the morning left them limp as rag dolls. Bailey slept when Angel went down, and even Aidan took a nap. C.J. was too wound up to rest, and devastated about Jenkins's death and the other agents' injuries. Mitch was stretched out on the couch in the living room trying to catch a few winks. He hadn't slept all night. She was in the kitchen with Gorman and Girard and three agents the field office had sent over, mourning the loss of their colleague.

"Remember when he got on the VPPD?"

"He was so excited about the new baby . . ."

"He was only thirty-five . . ."

"He was leaving, you know. At the end of Clay's term . . ."

Unspoken, and underscoring their grief, was the knowledge that what had happened to Jenkins could happen to any one of them. It was a sobering afternoon.

As if that wasn't bad enough, the events of the last few hours had hit Aidan like a sledgehammer. If the McCarthy tape wasn't enough to kill their relationship, the death of an agent landed the fatal blow. C.J. could read it on his face and in the stiff movements of his body.

That was good. He'd finally seen the light.

Curses, loud and vehement, came from the living room. C.J. bounded out of her chair along with the other agents. Rushing into the room, they saw Mitch standing before the TV. "I can't fucking believe this."

"What is it?"

He pointed to the screen.

Hell, there was that damn reporter again. They listened to her opening. In just a few hours, she'd put together a piece on the Secret Service—and on Tim Jenkins.

"The Secret Service is a noble calling. Now a twenty-seven-hundred-agent organization, and part of Homeland Security, it began in the 1800s as a branch of the Treasury Department, formed to catch counterfeiters. Late in the nineteenth century, the department instituted informal protection of the president and in 1902, the service officially took over full-time responsibility for presidential safety." She faced the camera gravely. "Luckily for Vice President Clay Wainwright, in 1962 a law was passed making it mandatory for the vice president to have Secret Service protection."

Scott gave a grim smile. "But how many of these brave men and women go into the service thinking they'll die, like Tim Jenkins did last night? There had never been a death of an agent protecting a president or vice president until yesterday, but there *have* been fatalities. The first Secret Service agent to die in the line of duty, Joseph Walker, was investigating land fraud in 1907. The first female agent to die was Julia Cross, while trying to break up a ring of counterfeiters. Six agents were killed in the Oklahoma City bombings, and one died during 9/11."

Then Tim Jenkins's face came on-screen. C.J. groaned. Several of the guys swore. "Special Agent Timothy Jenkins was born in 1972 in a small town in Connecticut. He married his high school sweetheart . . ."

C.J. was mesmerized watching the footage of Jenkins's young life, his wedding picture, his smile when he graduated from the Beltsville training academy, shots of him and his sons. But there was something wrong about this newscast: It felt like such a violation of the family's privacy, an exploitation of their fresh grief. Logically, she knew the press could, and sometimes should, report the news without bias or emotion. There was an amendment to assure that right. But this wasn't just news. It was sensationalism, especially so soon after Jenkins's death. She'd had the same feeling about them exposing Bailey's whereabouts on the lake.

When the broadcast ended, the room was church quiet. Everybody seemed stunned.

C.J. heard a rustle behind them and turned to find Aidan on the stairs. He'd obviously been there watching the tape. Without saying anything, he strode through the room and out the front door.

The day dragged on. Patrick, Dylan and Bailey's parents came and went. The president called back. Jon phoned and asked if he should come home. Bailey's friends at ESCAPE checked in to see how she was doing. At seven p.m., there was a commotion outside. Bailey, who was pacing the living room waiting for her husband, went running to the foyer, but Mitch blocked her before she reached it. "I know you want to go out there and greet him, Ms. O'Neil, but I can't let you do that."

Bailey brought herself to her five-seven height. "Listen, Mitch . . ."

C.J. knew she was going to argue this one, but it became a moot point as the door opened and, like a hero returning from war, a battered Clay Wainwright strode through it. Bailey flung herself at him and though he winced—he had purplish bruises on his face and arms—he held her tight.

Every agent in the room busied himself; C.J. suspected they were as moved as she was.

When Bailey finally let go of Clay, he kissed her head, drew he to his side and led her into the room. Up close, C.J. could see his face was discolored and puffy; his eyes were a muddy blue. His gaze took in all the agents. "I want to say how sorry I am about Tim. I liked him very much." He swallowed hard. "He died saving my life."

Murmurs all around.

Clay cleared his throat. "And I want to reiterate how much I appreciate what you do for me and my family." He went to each agent and shook their hands. When he came to C.J., his expression grew even more serious. "No words can convey how much I'm in debt to you, Agent Ludzecky— C.J." And then he did something he'd never done before. He hugged her. When he drew back, he said, "You saved my son from kidnapping. I can never, ever express my gratitude deeply enough."

"I was just doing my job, sir."

"I know." Smiling, he moved back to Bailey. "Now, I'd like some time with my wife." He looked to Mitch. "Could you get me everything you have on Rachel Scott?"

"The reporter?"

"Yes, the one that's dogged my family during their worst times. The one who led the kidnappers to Rory. And the one who completely sensationalized Tim Jenkins's death in the TV show I saw on board the plane. She won't be a happy camper once I'm through with her."

After the vice president and Second Lady went upstairs, Gorman said, "Man, I wouldn't want to be on his bad side."

Mitch's phone rang again. "What now?" he wondered aloud and answered it.

C.J. waited.

"Are you kidding? Hell, they don't need this. All right, we'll wait for him." He clicked off and faced the rest of them. "You won't believe this. There's been a threat against Bailey's life. It came in at the field office here in the city."

"What did it say?" C.J. asked.

"I quote, 'The vice president didn't die, but his wife will. Just like the agent you saw on TV.'"

TWENTY

THE FIELD office personnel arrived like a band of brothers, six of them flanking the outer perimeter of the house, while two went inside. No one was taking any chances with the vice president's safety or with Bailey's welfare. Aidan was glad, though he felt like he was caught up in an espionage movie. He wished he could take pictures of the agents, dressed in severe dark suits, earpieces, serious expressions. He'd portray them as modern warriors, closing ranks to protect their own. Instead, as they came inside, he sat in the living room and watched the action unfurl. Heading the pack was an older guy, nearing fifty, but in top shape. There was something different about him. Besides his air of authority, he wore a suit which seemed better cut and made of more expensive fabric than that of the other agents. Across the room, Dylan, who'd come by earlier, was studying the guy, too.

Mitch and C.J. greeted the two new agents. The older one held out his hand. "Mitch, nice to see you again."

They shook. "You, too, but not under these circumstances."

"Goes without saying." Then the agent turned to C.J. Something flared in his eyes and his facial expression softened. "Caterina, hello."

Caterina? What the hell?

C.J. nodded. She let the guy take her hand. He didn't shake it, but held it between two of his, much as C.J. had done with Aidan when they thought Clay might be dead. From this jerk, it was a come-on. She kept her face blank. Too blank. "David. It's been a long time."

David. As in David Anderson? The schmuck who ran her out of town? Aidan had the urge to jump off the couch and punch his lights out.

Anderson straightened and stepped back with effort, as if he was forcing himself away from her; he turned to Mitch. "Where's the vice president?"

"Right here." Clay was at the bottom of the staircase, with Bailey in tow.

When the threat came in, Aidan had gone up and told them about it. Bailey had taken the news on the chin, but Aidan could tell she was upset; a lot had happened to her world lately. Clay had been furious at yet another thing to deal with concerning his family.

Anderson approached Clay. "Special Agent David Anderson, sir."

Clay shook his head. "Yes, the hotshot agent of Manhattan. I understand you helped identify the Brooklyn nut who was after my predecessor."

"I did. With the help of my team." He glanced to C.J. "Agent Ludzecky was on it at the time and was invaluable in tracking down the accent of the perpetrator."

"That's our girl." The comment was said with such affection, it would be hard to interpret it as sexist.

The other agents, Dylan and Aidan were introduced.

Clay thanked the field office people for coming, then said, "Let's sit down."

Aidan joined Dylan at the entryway to the kitchen. There was limited seating in the living room and the pow-wow about to take place was important. Aidan was an on-looker to the action, but C.J. was central to it. He had a flash that this was how it would be from now on—he'd always be on the outside of her life.

Anderson took charge. "I have a copy of the audiotape we received. The original's been sent to Headquarters Global Threat Analysis Center."

C.J. said to Bailey, "It's where every threat on our protectees is analyzed."

"Didn't you work there before you came to us?" Bailey asked.

"Yes, when I left New York." She glanced at Anderson. "And before I got on the VPPD."

Anderson took over the explanation. "In addition to the voice-analysis equipment, which is more sophisticated than ours in New York, they do extensive forensic analysis."

"Like CSI without the commercials," Mitch put in.

Dylan said, "I read somewhere that most written threats are tracked down and you find the person."

"That's true, through FISH."

Before Anderson could explain the acronym, his brother did. "Forensic Information System for Handwriting analysis."

Aidan poked Dylan in the ribs. "Stop showing off."

Anderson gave C.J. a sideways glance and she smiled back. Aidan didn't understand the exchange. He wondered what other freakin' subtext was going on between them that he didn't get.

"In any case," Anderson continued, "voice threats are harder to track, though we do have the database for them. We enter the tapes to see if we can get a match to past threats made on any protectees. Voice print, accent, those kinds of things are studied."

Bailey nodded. "I want to hear the tape."

"Are you sure?" Clay asked. "It'll be chilling to hear aloud. Very different from being told what's in it."

Frowning, Bailey raised her brows. "And you know that how?"

A guilty look on Clay's face answered the question.

"You've received threats you didn't tell me about, haven't you?"

He said nothing.

"Damn it, Clay. We agreed from the outset not to keep things from each other."

"Let's not fight now, sweetheart. Just know hearing the threat is even more upsetting than being told about it."

She raised her chin.

Clay said to Anderson, "Go ahead."

Clearly the voice was disguised. Tinny. Lots of background noise. It only lasted a few seconds. "The vice president didn't die, but his wife will. Just like the agent you saw on TV."

When Anderson switched the recording off, he turned to C.J. "What do you think?"

"The voice analysts will know better when they filter out the background and get rid of the muffling device, but my guess is it's an Asian accent."

"How do you know that?" Dylan asked.

Again, Anderson answered. "She majored in linguistics in college. Worked at the UN. We were lucky to get her in the service." The pride and affection in his voice made Aidan's fists curl. Who the hell was he to be proud of her?

"You know what this means?" Anderson asked Clay.

"Yes." He turned to Bailey and said, "The threat to you and the attempted kidnapping of Rory could be related to the terrorists in Zanganesia, which is an Asian country."

* * *

WHEN THE MEETING ended, David stood and shook hands with Clay. Then he crossed to C.J. "I'd like a word with you, Agent Ludzecky, if I could."

"Yes, of course."

David faced his team. "Those of you not on duty now should go home and get some sleep." Several field agents were assigned to the house full-time until the Wainwrights went back to Washington.

C.J. glanced at Aidan. His mouth was set in stern lines of displeasure. She hated the thought that David being here, working with her, might hurt him.

David touched her arm. "Where would be good?"

"Outside."

"Lead the way."

They excused themselves from the others. She saw Dylan say something to Aidan. Aidan shook his head but didn't take his eyes off her as she walked out with David.

When they reached the picnic table, he sat on the surface. C.J. remembered another table, in the park, where Aidan had kissed her. Banishing the memory, she studied her former boss and the man who had changed her life, feeling oddly detached. He was handsome, with that George Clooney thing going for him, but he seemed older, and more restless than when she worked with him.

"So," David said with a flirty smile. "Are you still mad at me?"

"Mad?" she asked. "No, I guess not."

"The few times I've seen you since you left New York you seemed angry." He arched a brow. "Though I don't know why; you got the brass ring. The VPPD is a step up from our field office."

She angled her head at him. "Well, I suppose you could see it that way. Still, I got transferred against my will, out of a job I loved because of *your* feelings for me. My brother said I should have brought you up on sexual harassment charges."

"Why didn't you?"

"You know very well why. You knew what I'd do when you told me the truth about why you wanted me out of there."

His forehead furrowed. "What do you mean?"

"Damn it, David. I was young and inexperienced as an agent. You were the boss of the office, and well liked, though now I'm wondering why. I was intimated when you made your big confession."

"I didn't know that."

She didn't believe him for a second. "Then try this one. I wondered if I'd done something wrong to bring about this attraction. We were close. We spent a lot of time together. And I respected you then. You were my mentor, my idol and my friend, or so I thought." She shook her head, unable to believe how naïve she'd been. "In the end, I knew we could never go back to that, and I could never be comfortable in that office with you after what you'd said. So I left."

"I was trying to be honest. To preclude something happening between us."

"So was I. I cared about your wife, and your girls—who reminded me of my sisters—so I left without making a fuss."

The muscles in his jaw tensed.

She could still see pretty Joan Anderson, slim, dark-haired, at her husband's side. The perfect wife. And his three lovely girls. "How are they, by the way?"

Leaning back, bracing his arms on the tabletop, David looked up at the sky. "Joan had an affair."

Guess she wasn't perfect. "I see."

"It's not that uncommon for agents' wives to cheat." His voice was neutral, as if he was describing a case. "The travel, the long hours, the reticence in talking about our work. You know all that."

"She adored you."

"She complained I was distant. That the service took precedence over her and the girls. I got *more* distant when you left."

"What happened with her?"

"She met a schoolteacher at a PTA event. Had a fling, she said."

"Are you still together?"

"Yes. I left for a while. But the girls were young, so we reconciled. We're struggling again. I'm not sure life can ever be the same after infidelity." He shook his head. "Funny, isn't it? I gave up an affair with you for Joan and she had an affair because I became morose and moody. *About* you."

C.J. crossed her arms over her chest. "What do you mean you *gave up* an affair with me?"

His look was very male. "You know what I mean."

"David, I would never have had an affair with you."

"You cared about me."

"Of course I did. But not that way. In any case, I'd never steal another woman's husband."

"What about now?"

"You're still married."

"If I wasn't?"

"Oh, for God's sake, stop it. We already played this out once. I don't need an encore."

Lithe and graceful, he came off the table toward her. She stepped back but he caught her by the arms. His grip was strong and possessive. He drew her close, very close, so her breasts brushed his chest. "I've missed you." He tucked back a strand of her hair. "For years, I've dreamed about you. Watched your career progress from afar. Been ludicrously proud of you. Fuck it, Caterina, I made a mistake staying with Joan. And the twins are in college now. We could be together." He cleared his throat. "I'm taking a new job in Washington."

"So I heard."

His hands ran up and down her arms, shoulder to elbow. "Despite what you said, I don't believe the only things you felt for me were respect and admiration. I don't believe all I was to you was a mentor."

She pushed on his chest and stepped back. "It's true. Under no circumstances can we be together. I don't love *you*."

"Who is it?"

"What?"

"Your emphasis was on you. Who *do* you love?"

"No one. And even if I did, it's none of your business."

He practically snarled. "You and Calloway are pretty chummy."

"Stop it."

She started to turn away but he grabbed her again and forced her to face him. So she said, "Not everyone is as weak as you and gets involved on the job, David."

As soon as she said the words aloud, she winced. She'd gotten involved, deeply, on this job.

"You never said you thought I was weak before."

She hadn't. What was the point? She was getting transferred no matter what. Because she felt like a hypocrite, she said, "I don't want to hurt you now and I didn't want to hurt you then. But a relationship between us is not going to happen." She felt her heart speed up at being put in this position. "I'll try to limit our contact in D.C. and I hope you'll do the same."

"All right. I've done enough to you already. I apologize for bringing it up again. I guess I misunderstood everything."

"Apology accepted. And for the record, I'm not sure I'd handle the situation you put me in the same way today as I did five years ago." This time, she strode away.

When she reached the back door to the house, something made her look up. She saw Aidan in the window of the spare room. Which had a clear view of the backyard.

She wondered how much he'd seen.

* * *

AIDAN HAD SEEN enough in Bailey's backyard to drive him to the pub late that night. As some current pop rock played from the jukebox, he sat at the bar, staring down at his beer. Bridget had been called in to cover for him during the hostage crisis so he could be with Bailey, but when Clay came home, Aidan had left the town house. Freed from responsibility, he was downing a Molson. And shots of tequila. The mixture almost numbed him, almost blocked the images of C.J. and David Anderson, the fucking asshole who cost her her job in New York, together in Bailey's yard.

And how she let him put his hands on her.

From the other side of the bar, Patrick walked toward him. He wiped the counter in front of Aidan. "Cryin' in your beer?" He glanced at the shot glass. "Hard stuff?"

"Maybe." Aidan gulped back the shot and slapped down the empty glass. "I'll have another."

"Suit yourself." Patrick poured a second shot, then braced his hands on the bar. "Since Pa's heart attack you been acting like a different person. I'm thinkin' it's more than stuff with C.J. that we already talked about. What's going on, kid?"

"You got all night?" Aidan asked. He downed the second shot.

Patrick stared at him. "I could, if you needed it."

Aidan was tired of withholding what had happened with his father, with C.J., from his brothers. So he said to Patrick, "I been keeping stuff from you."

His gaze narrowed. "Wanna tell me now?"

"I guess." Aidan shrugged. "I caused Pa's heart attack."

"What the hell are you talking about?"

Aidan described the fight he had with Pa over Aidan wanting to leave the pub and how that caused the heart attack, at least in part. Nothing anybody said had convinced him he hadn't contributed to it.

When he finished, Pat just shook his head. "Bullshit. Pa had clogged arteries. *That* caused his heart attack." He snorted. "Besides, if he was going to have heart failure over a fight with one of his sons, he'd have been dead a long time ago from the rows we get into."

Aidan hadn't thought of that. Pa and Patrick often went head to head. It had started with Moira, and now they fought over what brand of beer to order. "Maybe. I forgot about that."

Pat concentrated on his task of washing glasses. After a while, he asked, "You really want to do this photography?"

"I don't know what I want anymore."

"For what it's worth, I say go for it. We'll survive at the pub. Liam could quit his part-time job and earn enough here to live on."

"Maybe."

Another silence. "Tell me what's goin' on with C.J. You guys were really weird around each other the whole time we waited to hear about Clay."

Running his finger around the rim of the beer glass, Aidan pictured C.J. as she'd been at the lake. Then he saw Anderson towering over her. What had he said to her? "I was with her when the hostage situation happened."

Pat stopped washing. "I suspected as much. And?"

"On Sunday, she said she wouldn't see me anymore."

"I knew she said it wasn't a go before. But the weekend didn't change anything?"

"No. She was all weepy about it, though."

"How about you?"

"I feel like shit."

"This sounds serious."

"For me, very. For her, who knows? I saw her playing nice with her old boyfriend before I came over here." He pounded his fist on the bar. "It doesn't matter anyway. Right from the beginning, she said I couldn't handle her job. I thought I could so I went after her, like you guys said

I should. And after what happened between us at the lake, I tried to argue her out of ditching me. But now . . . I guess she's right. This thing with Jenkins . . ."

"He got killed, Aidan." Pat's dark eyes flared with hot emotion. "Maybe the guys and me were wrong to push you together. How could a man watch his wife put herself in a situation like that?"

"I don't know. I can't imagine it."

"Me, either."

"Hell, Paddy. You can't handle Brie's job and she just runs a business."

His brother stared over Aidan's shoulder. "There's more to our problems than what I been tellin' you. But we're working on things." He wiped the bar. "What are you gonna do now?"

"Nothing. There's no way to get around the facts." He held up the shot glass. "Except with this maybe. I'll have another shot of the sweet lady."

"No, you won't." Pat undid the towel around his waist. "Let's close up. Go get some breakfast. Food always makes you feel better than that crap."

Aidan watched Pat. Maybe going with his brother would keep him from thinking about Caterina at the lake, Caterina in his arms.

And Caterina with David "Hotshot" Anderson.

TWENTY-ONE

CLAY WAINWRIGHT often tricked people into believing he was just an average guy. But today, seated in his den at his town house with the entire O'Neil clan, he seemed every inch the vice president of the most powerful country in the world. Despite his battered face and casual slacks and sport shirt, he was in command, forceful and angry as hell. From across the room, C.J. watched him wield his power.

"Mary Kate, Patrick, I wanted to update you on what's been happening here."

Pa O'Neil sat stiffly his chair. "No offense, Clay, we like you now, but kidnapping and hostage situations aren't what we'd hoped for our daughter."

A muscle leaped in Clay's jaw. "I know, and I'm sorry my job has put her in harm's way. Mitch and I have hammered out a plan to keep her and the kids safe. Rory gets back from the camping trip tomorrow, then the next day is Jenkins's funeral in Connecticut. Bailey, the kids and I will leave for Washington immediately afterward." He glanced over at his wife, who nodded to him. "The residence on Observatory Way can be a veritable fortress and I'm going to keep her, Rory and Angel there until the FBI gets to the bottom of this."

"What if they don't, Clay?" This from Bailey's mother. "You can't lock them up forever."

"I can assure you three government agencies—the Secret Service, the FBI and the CIA—are on top of this and will have some answers soon."

"What do you think, Bay?" Dylan asked. He was leaning against the wall next to Aidan.

"I'll do whatever's necessary to protect Rory and Angel and little Paddy, here." She lifted her chin. "I agreed to everything Clay and Mitch think is best, except I'm going to Tim Jenkins's funeral."

Jenkins's body had been brought back by his colleagues when they returned from Zanganesia on the DC-11 with Clay. Calling hours would be held tomorrow, and the funeral was the next day. C.J. steeled herself against the images of putting one of her friends in the ground. She would go and do her duty and stay strong, as was expected of her.

Clay faced his wife squarely. "The jury's still out on your attending the funeral, Bailey." His voice deepened with concern. "Everybody will expect you to be there. After a death threat on your life, you should *not* go."

"Make this work for me, Clay, because I'm going."

C.J. saw Aidan's lips thin. Lips she'd kissed until they were swollen. Lips which had made her tingle everywhere. Memories of him had haunted her since their sojourn at the lake, but particularly since Jenkins's death. She'd traded a life with Aidan for what? Endangering herself every single day, risking death like Tim?

Mitch said, "We can seal off the church and cemetery with agents. Most of them will want to be at the funeral anyway. C.J. and I won't leave Ms. O'Neil's side."

Clay's jaw tightened. "Mark Langley will be there, too.

It will be even more dangerous with the president of the United States in attendance."

"Or more under control just because he's there." Bailey stared hard at her husband. "In any case, this is my decision, Clay, not yours. I'm going."

"I thought it was *our* decision."

Bailey folded her arms over her chest.

Shaking his head, Clay finally said, "All right. But I don't like it."

He turned to Bailey's brothers. "Thanks for what you did holding Bailey's hand through this ordeal." He zeroed in on Aidan. "And Aidan, I appreciate your going to the lake with her."

"I'll never forget my time at the lake," he said, not glancing at C.J.

Most everyone chuckled, thinking Aidan was being sarcastic about experiencing all the cloak and dagger of protection firsthand, and then the excitement of the attempted kidnapping.

C.J. knew better.

Clay transferred his gaze to her. "And C.J., thank you again for saving Rory from the kidnappers." His voice was strained and held a hint of vulnerability.

"You've already thanked me, Mr. Vice President."

Pa O'Neil got up, crossed to her and hugged her. "He's my boy, too," Pa said, drawing back. "I don't know what I'd do if . . ." He shrugged and turned away.

"We can never thank you enough," Clay reiterated. "If you ever need anything from me, don't hesitate to ask."

"Be careful. I might hold you to that, sir." Agents rarely joked with protectees but she was trying to diffuse the tension in the room.

Once again Clay spoke to the whole clan. "I hope our plans help you sleep better at night."

A knock on the door. Gorman poked her head in. "Mr. Vice President, Agent Masters is here."

"We're ready for him now. Send him in." Clay got up and circled the desk.

Patrick and Dylan exchanged looks. Aidan stared ahead. C.J. pivoted so she didn't have to watch him. They hadn't had any private conversations since Clay returned. Mostly Aidan had avoided her and she tried to stay out of his way. She had no idea what he thought about her and David in the yard last night. She'd considered catching him alone and explaining that the encounter had been innocent. But ultimately, she decided it would just make things harder between them.

Jack Masters entered the spacious den. About forty, tall, he moved with confidence and authority. C.J. had worked with him in Washington and respected him.

Clay said, "I asked you to come today to update me, and fill in the O'Neils as to what the FBI is doing to keep Bailey and the kids safe."

The agent took a seat. "As you know, we isolated the gender and nationality of the kidnappers through genetic testing of DNA on the strand of hair found on Rory's clothes. The two people C.J. saw were dressed as boys, but at least one was female."

"And Asian, right?" Clay said.

"Aren't the Anthrax girl gang member and her cousin Asian?" Dylan asked.

"Yes, they're Chinese. But they both have alibis for the day of the kidnapping. Annie-O was in school at a community college course all day long. Sasha Sanders wasn't even in Penn Yan. Her parents took her to visit friends in Corning. We checked on both alibis. They work."

"So who was it?"

"One theory is that the kidnappers were tied to the terrorists."

"Holy Mother of God." Mary Kate made the sign of the cross.

Dylan pushed off from the wall, went to his mother and

placed a hand on her shoulder. "How exactly would that have played out?"

"The scenario goes like this: Mr. Wainwright was supposed to be accompanied by Ms. O'Neil to Zanganesia, where the terrorists planned to take her and the vice president hostage. When they got wind of her canceling, they put a secondary plan into place to kidnap Rory, especially when they learned he'd be outside of Washington and more easily accessible. But when Agent Ludzecky foiled that attempt, the terrorists went ahead and took Mr. Wainwright as a hostage. This hypothesis presupposes that their agenda all along was to scare Mr. Wainwright off from influencing Zanganesian laws further and to release those arrested to this point. The end result was the same whether they had you, Mr. Vice President or Ms. O'Neil or Rory."

Dylan asked, "The terrorists still haven't been found, right?"

"No. They've gone underground." His gaze turned flinty. "But after what happened with Jenkins, we'll get them. I can promise you that."

"Then Bailey's still at risk because of them."

"If they were involved in the kidnapping attempt, yes. It's one reason Ms. O'Neil needs stringent protection."

"Do you think it was them?" Pa O'Neil asked.

"No. It's just one avenue we have to consider. We can't afford to ignore any possibility." He shook his head. "But in my professional opinion, these terrorists weren't organized enough or competent enough—witness Clay's escape—to have plans for the kidnapping and the death threat way over here, in addition to what they were doing thousands of miles away."

Dylan scowled. "So the death threat and the kidnapping attempt may not be related? That's hard to believe."

"Too hard. Too much coincidence. I believe there's definitely a link between those two things, but neither involves

Zanganesia. I think the kidnappers-slash-threat-makers are out to hurt Ms. O'Neil. They could do that by snatching Rory or doing her bodily harm."

"Who the hell are they?" Pa asked.

"Our best guess is that both these things are related to Ms. O'Neil's old gang activities." Masters looked at his notes. "Since the Anthrax girl is out, we're back to the GGs."

"We've been over this a thousand times." Bailey sounded exasperated. "Mazie Lennon's still in prison for murdering Taz. And the other girls are on the Watch List and haven't been active again." She angled her head. "Did you get the sealed records from juvenile court?"

"Yes. In the process of disbanding the GGs, three young girls were rounded up and put in juvie. They're out now and have left town or gone straight, like the older ones."

"Then why do you suspect the GGs still?" Bailey asked.

"Because of Mazie Lennon. We've been watching her and viewing the tapes of her visitors in the last few months at Lancaster State Penitentiary. One was a young Asian boy."

"Well," Clay said. "That's a lead. And a connection."

"We can't track him down, though, even through the routine previsit information and identity checks given to everybody."

Clay gripped a pen on his desk. "Maybe C.J. can tag the boy as one of the kidnappers."

"I looked at the pictures, Mr. Wainwright. It could be him, but I can't be sure. Everything happened so fast and of course, I had a bad angle."

"Question Lennon, then." Clay practically barked the words out.

"We've got that scheduled for tomorrow. With the hostage crisis, some of our attention was diverted."

"Understood." Clay nodded to Masters. "I want you to handle this personally, Jack."

"I will, Mr. Vice President. Be assured that we're working hard on the case and running down every lead. We'll find the perpetrators." His gaze encompassed Mitch and C.J. "Meanwhile, stay close to them. Keep them safe."

Mitch's look was hard. "You can count on it."

After the FBI agent left, Mica Proust, Clay's press secretary, stuck her head in the door. She'd flown to New York this morning with his chief of staff, Jack Thornton. "Vice President Wainwright, we'll be starting in a few minutes."

Clay had called a press conference about the hostage situation. It was his responsibility to assure the public he was unharmed. Since Bailey needed to be there, too— the kidnapping had been sensationalized and they wanted to show the American people she was unharmed—Clay had decided to hold the gathering on the front lawn of the town house. Secret Service agents swarmed the area, it had been secured three times over and sharpshooters had been placed on rooftops.

The vice president's gaze turned cold. "I'm assuming Rachel Scott isn't here."

Mica nodded. "Thorn went over to the station and met with the president of WNYC. He caved, though he made some noise about freedom of the press."

"I'm not curtailing anyone's freedom." Clay's expression got even colder. "I'm asking for more responsible journalism from them. I don't want Rachel Scott doing the stories about us. The station can choose somebody else to cover our activities."

"In any case, she isn't outside right now, but my guess is her lawyers will be dealing with this at some point."

"Bring 'em on!"

"Yes, sir."

"Did you contact Hank Sellers about the story I'd like him to do?"

Clay had formed an unlikely relationship with a *Village Voice* reporter two years ago after he'd put a positive spin on Clay and Bailey's surprising marriage.

"He'll be here at four."

"Why are you seeing Sellers?" Dylan asked.

"I want something out there from me personally. I want to let the public and the stations know that I'm disgusted with Scott and her brand of journalism. Somebody has to take a stand on the paparazzi."

"I see."

Clay studied Dylan. "I never thought to ask you if you'd want the interview from me for your column."

"No, not now, anyway. I'd need more input, research, et cetera, to use it for my column. Maybe when this is over, *CitySights* might pursue it. Go ahead with Sellers. He's a good guy."

Clay stood. "Patrick, Mary Kate, we'll see you before we leave of course." He smiled at Bailey's brothers. "You, too, guys." Together he and Bailey went to tackle the press.

"So," Aidan said scanning the room. "They'll be gone in two days. You all will. For good."

Again, C.J. averted her gaze.

"They're coming back for yours and Pa's birthday." Dylan winked at his mother. "Can't miss the big four-oh and seven-oh."

Mary Kate went into mother mode. "Forty years old, and not married. You should have yourself a nice girl with you at your party, Aidan."

C.J. felt her throat close up. Aidan would find himself a nice girl. Marry her. And she'd have his babies . . . just like in the horrible nightmare C.J. had at the lake.

Aidan faced his mother with a phony smile. "Okay, Mama. I'll do my best to find myself a *nice* girl."

The words cut like a knife and regardless of what anyone thought, C.J. strode out of the room.

THE CAMP was cleaned up, and twenty little boys were ready to go back to their homes after spending a week in the wilderness. The excursion had been full of swimming, hiking, campfires and camaraderie. Many of the scouts had finished badges. Liam was glad for the respite from the politics of Bailey's life, but now it was back to reality. A grim reality.

Before any parents arrived, Liam drew Mikey and Rory off to the side for some privacy, as much as you could have with three agents standing guard a few feet away. This talk couldn't wait. He'd put it off as long as possible because Rory would be upset and Mikey could go further into his funk. His son had been happy and carefree on the camping trip and Liam hated to spoil his mood.

He smiled at the two of them sitting on top of the picnic table, their green T-shirts imprinted with "Boy Scout Troop Number Four—Liam's Lads." "I gotta tell you guys something." He thought about saying they needed to be brave, but why the hell should they suppress their emotions? "Rory, your daddy went to Zanganesia on a goodwill tour, do you remember that?"

Rory tugged on the camp cap he wore. "Yeah, I know. That means he's making friends, right?"

He was supposed to. "Yeah."

Mikey went white. "Something happen to Uncle Clay?"

"He's safe at home now, but something *did* happen." Liam explained the hostage situation as simply as possible, downplaying the threats and the violence as much as he could.

Rory's eyes filled. "He's okay, right?"

"Yes, honey. He has some bruises but he's going to be fine."

"He got beat up?" Mikey's tone was horrified.

"The terrorists roughed him up some, but the important thing is he's okay."

"We gonna go back to Washington now?" Rory said. " 'Cause it's safer?"

"You are. The day after tomorrow."

Mikey's eyes turned bleak and his little body sagged.

"I know you're going to miss Bailey and Rory, son."

"And C.J."

"Yeah, and C.J. I'm sorry. But school will be starting soon and you'll see your friends. You'll have a lot to do then and you won't miss them so much."

Disbelieving eyes stared up at him. Damn it to hell! The kid kept losing people he loved. It seemed like he'd get close to somebody and something would happen to them or they'd go away. Liam wondered how much more Mikey could take. So he tried to reassure him. "Grandpa's okay now, too, Mike. He'll be around to keep you company."

Mikey's face was passive. Accepting.

Liam picked up his son and hugged him tight. Mikey headlocked his neck and clasped his legs around Liam's waist. The boy seemed so frail. Cleary was a big kid and had a lot of self-confidence, but Kitty always had to assure Mikey he'd grow up brawny like his dad. Since her death, Liam couldn't sway him as much as she could. He admitted he couldn't fill a lot of the gaps Kitty had left in their lives.

They were quiet on the drive back. Jerry Grayson drove the Suburban and another car followed with the other two agents. Usually on trips, there were shouts and howls from the backseat, and some bickering between the boys. On the way up, the three of them had sung camp songs. Nothing today. Alone with his thoughts, Liam worried about Mike and about Bailey. And about his brother-in-law who'd become a friend to him and the best thing that happened to the country in a long time.

The town house appeared to be under siege when they pulled up to the curb. Rory said. "Look at all these people!"

Mike stared mutely out the window.

Mitch Calloway opened Rory's door and bent his head in.

"Hi, Mitch." Rory hugged him and Mitch smiled. Bailey had told Liam once that normal protocol observed with the agents broke down because of Rory's open affection with them.

They were ushered inside, and Bailey met them at the door. "Hey, buddy, I missed you."

Rory flung himself at her. "Mommy."

Clay came to the entrance to his den. "Hey, Champ."

Untangling himself from his mother, Rory raced to his father and leapt into his arms. Liam caught a glimmer of tears in the kid's eyes. When he drew back, he said, "Wow, they *hit* you bad."

"They did."

"Did it *hurt*?"

"Yep, it hurt." He walked to the couch, holding his son close. "Let's sit a minute."

Liam knew what was coming so he grasped Mikey's hand, led him to a chair and dragged the boy onto his lap. They'd agreed to let Clay reveal this last piece of information.

"I have some bad news, Rory. You remember Tim Jenkins?"

"Uh-huh. He plays cards with me sometimes, but made me promise not to tell."

Clay swallowed hard and glanced across the room to Bailey. She nodded. "I'm sorry, son, but Agent Jenkins died trying to protect me in Zanganesia."

"Huh?" Rory scowled and again the tears came. "Agents aren't supposed to get killed, Dad. You said so."

"I know." Clay's voice was strained. "This happened because of some very bad people."

Liam ran his hands up and down his son's arms. "Mikey, did you hear that? About Agent Jenkins?"

Turning around, Mikey stared up at him, his eyes even bleaker than before. "Yeah, it means C.J. could get killed, too."

There was a noise at the doorway. Liam looked up to

find Aidan standing at the front entry. From the expression on his face, it was obvious he'd heard Mikey's remark. And it was also obvious that things had progressed—a lot—in the doomed relationship between Aidan and his pretty Secret Service agent.

TWENTY-TWO

THE SUN was too bright for this, the grass too green. Aidan would have backdropped the scene at the cemetery with an ashen gray sky and drizzling rain as the Catholic priest stood over the flag-draped coffin and offered words of comfort. "Tim Jenkins was a family man. He was also loyal to his country in a way few individuals are. He gave his life, as did Christ, to save another."

Aidan listened to the priest drone on. His gaze kept straying to Celia Jenkins, who sat in front of the oak coffin, her hands resting on her very pregnant belly. She wore a black dress, heels and hat. An older gentleman and woman flanked her. Another elderly couple sat to their right. But Aidan couldn't take his eyes off the spouse of a Secret Service agent who died. He could never do what she was doing. Whatever lingering doubts he'd had even after seeing the shooting of Tim McCarthy on TV vanished in the wake of Jenkins's death.

The priest assured the crowd that Tim was with God and out of earthly danger. He said his sons could be proud of their dad's life, and Celia Jenkins should take pride in her husband's sacrifice.

Bullshit . . .

Celia Jenkins cried nonstop.

The sons looked like they'd been poleaxed.

Bailey was crying, too. She'd turned her face into Clay's shoulder. Langley's wife, Michelle, clung to him. But it was Clay's face that got to Aidan the most. It was ravaged; what was happening today was because Jenkins had been protecting *him*. Bailey said he put up a front for everyone else, but he'd been inconsolable when they were alone.

His sister and Clay were hard to watch, so Aidan turned his attention to the agents. Over a hundred of them had come to the services. They stood like soldiers at attention, even those not on duty. Those that were sported earpieces and radios, guns and handcuffs, maybe even vests for heightened security, given the brass was here. The agents might look like robots, but they weren't. They were living, breathing humans capable of being gunned down with an Uzi, like Tim Jenkins.

Aidan looked back to the coffin that would soon be buried in cold, dark ground. How could this job be worth that sacrifice? He wondered if C.J. was afraid now. The thought chilled him. To dissipate it, he glanced down the row where his brothers stood. Their presence comforted him. They were somber-faced and dressed in suits and ties, here for Bailey. Not unlike the Secret Service, they'd come to protect their sister. Aidan wondered if C.J. knew he'd be here.

He took a peek at her, standing in a group of other agents, forming a tight perimeter around the Second Couple. To anyone else, her face was blank, her posture typical of her position. But he could see she held herself stiffer, her head at an odd angle. Her hands were curled at her sides. His stomach clenched at the sight of what he'd lost.

No, not lost. She'd thrown him away, really, in favor of

the job that had put a perfectly nice man in an oak box. But today wouldn't alter her decision in the long run. After a tragedy, people forgot their acute feelings of loss, their vows to live their lives better in the future. As the days rolled into one another, life would return to normal, and people would go back to their old ways. He'd seen it after 9/11 leveled his beloved city.

The priest concluded his prayers and Aidan watched Clay stride stiffly to the casket and take the now-folded flag from the soldier, who'd been part of an honor guard of ten. Clay's anguish played across his face and his hands shook as he presented the flag to Celia Jenkins. Afterward, he hugged her. Aidan imagined he said, "I'm sorry."

When the service ended, Aidan approached Bailey from one side. C.J. stood on the other. Up close, he could see she did indeed wear the bulletproof vest the agents donned in crisis situations. His stomach did somersaults at the sight of her prepared for battle.

Bailey hugged him, then focused red-rimmed eyes on CJ. "I . . . I don't know what I'd do if something like this happened to you or Mitch."

Aidan had to will back his own reaction to Bailey's fears. Verbalizing the connection between what happened to Jenkins and what could still happen to C.J. made the nightmare worse. And C.J. looked so sad he could barely stand it. Bailey hugged her, and over his sister's shoulders, she locked gazes with him.

Before he could say anything, two men approached and the connection was broken. When the women drew apart, Bailey turned to them. "Director Basham," she said.

"I'm so sorry, Ms. O'Neil. I know how much Clay liked Tim." The head of the Secret Service cleared his throat. "We all did."

Bailey nodded. "Thank you."

Basham turned to C.J. "You okay, Agent Ludzecky? Sure you're recuperated?"

"Yes, sir."

The man next to the director stepped forward. "Ms. O'Neil. I'm Joe Stonehouse."

After Bailey greeted him, C.J. said, "Joe, hello."

"Hello, Caterina." The man hugged her. "I expected you'd be here."

"I didn't know you would be."

He cleared his throat, and his face was grave. "I brought Jenkins into the D.C. office."

"Oh."

She introduced Aidan to the men. "Aidan, this is Director Basham and this is Joe Stonehouse. A former agent. He worked with my brother."

"With Luke?"

"Yes, we quit at the same time."

Ah, that's right. Aidan had heard those stories. Both Luke Ludzecky and Joe Stonehouse left the service for the women they loved. Apparently it wasn't impossible. For a moment, the notion incensed him. These men had sacrificed their jobs for the sake of their relationships. C.J. wouldn't do that for him.

The director excused himself, and Joe drew C.J. away to speak with her. Aidan made small talk with his sister until Clay motioned her over to where he stood with the president and First Lady. Mitch accompanied Bailey.

When Aidan looked back, he saw Stonehouse walking away from C.J. Aidan had one more thing to do before she left today. Bailey had told him earlier she'd asked for the night off to go visit her mother; she'd fly to Washington tomorrow. Aidan didn't plan to see her again for a very long time.

He came up behind her and put his hand on her shoulder. "Caterina."

She turned and her face was no longer blank. It was lined with grief. When she saw him, her expression turned even more grim. "Aidan."

"I've come to say good-bye."

They both glanced at the coffin. There were a lot of good-byes today. "I'm glad you did." She clasped her hands behind her back, as if she was afraid she'd touch him.

"I have something for you."

Her brows arched. In the sun, her hair seemed lighter, her complexion paler. She seemed fragile, like she had that morning at the lake when she'd had the meltdown.

Reaching into his pocket, he removed what he'd bought for her, something he needed to give her. He took one hand, placed the velvet bag in it and closed her fist. "Open it later." He squeezed her fingers, then turned away.

He knew she was staring at him. But he didn't look back. This time, it was really over.

MATKA OPENED the door to their little house in Queens and C.J. burst into tears standing right there on the front stoop.

Her mother said, "Here now, *kochanie,*" and took C.J. into her arms. It was such a relief to let it out, to vent the feelings she'd stuffed since Aidan dropped her off here a week ago.

With the ease of a parent who'd had years of experience comforting children, *Matka* drew her inside, onto the old, faded living-room couch, and pulled her close. The smell of her mother's talcum powder made C.J. feel safe. "Cry it out, little one, cry it out."

She did. For Tim Jenkins. "Oh, *Matka*, he was so young, with so much of life ahead of him." For Tim's wife. "She's pregnant with her third child." For Bailey and Clay. "They were overcome with grief, and guilt, I think." And for herself and Aidan. Which she couldn't talk about, but just remembering made her cry harder, like her insides were spilling out with each sob that wracked her body. When she quieted, she just stayed there against her mother's safe bosom.

Matka said nothing for long moments, making small comforting circles on her back. Then she asked, "What is that, Caterina?"

"What, *Matka*?"

"What do you have your hand around? Inside your shirt."

Her throat closed up. She hadn't realized she was clutching Aidan's parting gift. "It's . . . it's a medal. St. Michael."

"The Archangel."

"What?"

"St. Michael the Archangel. After God created the angels, Lucifer decided he wanted to rule the world. The angels took sides. Michael stood with God to defeat the devil and the dark ones."

"I . . ." Hiccups. "I knew he was the patron saint of law enforcement."

"Because he fought evil, just like you do, my brave child." She could feel her mother's sigh. "He is supposed to protect you."

She pictured the silver medal she'd opened in the train on her way to Queens. And cried when she saw what it was. "Michael has his foot on Lucifer, a sword at the devil's throat."

"Good triumphing over evil."

C.J. didn't say more, just kept the precious gift pressed against her heart.

After a while, *Matka* spoke again. "He gave it to you, didn't he?"

She nodded. *Matka* knew she'd gone to the lake with Aidan, of course. C.J. didn't realize her mother was aware of how they felt about each other. "How did you know?"

"My daughter does not spend the weekend with a man unless she cares about him. He must care about you, too."

"Stop, *Matka*, please. I can't get into this. I can't bear it."

"It is not what I'm saying that is hard for you to hear, Caterina. You know that."

"Just hush, then, please. Let me stay here with you for a few minutes."

"Always," her mother said and held on tight.

AIDAN'S BROTHERS had kicked him out of the pub at ten o'clock tonight. He'd slept little over the past week, given the hostage situation and what had happened with C.J. Without turning on lights, he stumbled into the apartment, shed his clothes beside the bed and fell facedown on the mattress.

He startled awake at a noise. He checked the red dials on the clock. One a.m. Again, the sound. His head cleared and he realized it was the front doorbell. Panic struck him like lightning. This couldn't be good. He bounded out of bed, threw on a robe and raced to the door, down the staircase. *Please don't let there be something wrong with Bailey or Clay or the kids,* he prayed as he dragged open the door at the bottom of the steps without even checking to see who was behind it.

She stood bathed in the moonlight, like a specter come to life, wearing some white shimmering thing. Her hair was down around her shoulders, glistening, too, in the beams that kissed her head. She carried a garment bag with her. She didn't speak, but her expression told him what he needed to know.

One last time, let me be with you one last time.

Wordlessly, too, he stepped aside and she entered the foyer. He preceded her up the steps. When they were inside, he locked the door to his apartment and led her to the bedroom, switching on only one tiny light in the corner.

He faced her.

She dropped the bag on the chair.

He dropped his robe.

Still, no words. This final good-bye would be said in silence.

Aidan hadn't known the last time he'd made love to her it would *be* the last time. Now he knew, and he'd take this gift she offered and treasure each moment of it.

C.J.'s pulse rate tripled as Aidan stood before her, naked like Adam. In the early hours of this morning, she'd be his Eve. She unzipped the one-piece jumpsuit she wore, the only thing the girls left behind that fit her. Somehow she couldn't come to him tonight in her Secret Service suit. It was packed in the bag she'd brought, to be donned when she went back to her real life. And left him behind.

Her clothes slid to the floor, and his eyes widened—she wore no underwear. Only the medal that he'd given her nestled close to her heart. She stood before him waiting.

He moved lithely and reached for her; lifting the medal, he kissed it. Then he brushed his fingers over her breasts, her abdomen, lower. She closed her eyes to savor his touch, to remember the slight calluses on his thumb. She breathed in his scent, memorized it, as he leaned in close and pressed butterfly kisses to her forehead, jaw and lips. She understood that tonight wouldn't be frenzied. It would be cruelly gentle and brutally tender.

Encircling her arms around his neck, she pressed her body to his, tangled their legs. He held her close, kissed her shoulder, nosed into her hair. He would smell jasmine, from Lizzie's shampoo. Lotion to complement it. For a long time they just stood there, melded to each other. Then he drew her to the bed. Eased her down. Joined her.

She was so lovely, Aidan wanted to caress her all night, her hair, her breasts, the triangle of curls between her thighs. Moans and groans, sighs escaped her and he tried to record them in his memory bank. Store them for later, when she was gone.

Somehow, he found himself on his back. She took his arms and brought them over his head, so his hands could grasp the headboard. It was reminiscent of their time at the lake, when he put her in this position so he could make love to her without interference. He gripped the bars and blanked his mind.

She kissed him everywhere. His body swelled when she tongued his nipples. Her mouth went lower, brushing, stopping to suck. When it closed over his penis, his upper body arched off the bed. He allowed her touch as long as he could, then he managed to pull her up. They met on their sides, face-to-face, hands linked, as he entered her.

C.J. gasped as he slid so deftly into her. He was full and heavy and she felt him throb. She didn't hurry the process, though. Just tucked him inside her and kept him there. Then his mouth came down on hers. He changed the angle of his head, teased open her lips and slid his tongue into her. Again, so gently she wanted to weep.

At last he began to move. Slow . . . slow . . . too slow. The sensation was building like a wave on the lake, nearing the peak but not quite. All she could do was ride the gentle crest until it was upon her, tumbling over her, taking her under.

Aidan felt her come and increased the pressure by degrees: gliding in and out, pushing, pushing. *Remember this love, remember how it feels, how one we are,* he thought and plunged in deep and hard.

As soon as she was finished, he let himself go. Pleasure burst upon him, blocking out reason, drawing him in and drowning him in the woman joined to him.

They stayed connected for a long time. But before they dozed off, he brought his mouth to her ear and whispered, "*Kocham Ciebie*, Caterina."

"*Kocham Ciebie*, Aidan," she said sleepily.

When he awoke at seven, she was gone.

TWENTY-THREE

Clay had been right. The vice presidential residence was a fortress, nestled inside the Naval Observatory grounds, on Embassy Row in north Washington. The home had been built in 1873 as the house of the superintendent of the observatory, and had been taken over officially for the vice president during Gerald Ford's term. Complete with alarms, motion detectors, magnometers, closed-circuit TVs and surrounded by uniformed guards on the larger perimeter, it was the safest place for Bailey and the kids. The Secret Service command post was across the street.

The vice president's and Second Lady's personal agents occupied a space in the basement with desks, computers and a huge communication center. Thanks to Marilyn Quayle, who didn't want the agents upstairs or right outside the house where their presence intruded, the office down here had been built to cover inside security.

"Good to be back?" Mitch asked, his eyes on one of the TV monitors. Rory was in the family room, watching TV with Hower at his feet. Another screen showed Angel asleep in her crib.

C.J. was reading the latest report from the FBI on the attempted kidnapping. "Yeah, it is."

"You saw quite a bit of your family in New York."

"I know." She put down the papers. "I mended some fences."

"Hmm. You seem restless."

"I am, I guess. Change is hard for me. We were away for a month. I still haven't acclimated to being back."

On the monitors, C.J. watched Bailey lead Rory up the sweeping staircase to his bedroom with the peaked roof, near the turret of the old Victorian house. The dog shuffled along with Rory, and would sleep on his bed, guarding him, too.

C.J. hadn't had a private conversation with Bailey since they'd returned from New York. In the entire week they'd been back, she'd tried to avoid any personal discussion with the Second Lady, because she was so attuned to Aidan that C.J. was afraid she sensed something was going on between them.

Aidan. She stared down blindly at the report. His medal lay inside her shirt, pressed against her heart. If she closed her eyes, she could still smell his cologne, feel his hands on her, relive the moment he was inside her, groaning out his release. She didn't regret their last time together and hoped he didn't, either. She'd have the memory of that stolen night forever.

Mitch took a bottle of water from the fridge. "Want one?"

"No, thanks."

"What *do* you want, C.J.?"

She *didn't* want to have this conversation. Though nothing had been said outright, things had been strained between her and Mitch since she'd denied any relationship with Aidan at the lake, then she'd shown open affection for him during the hostage crisis. "Excuse me?"

"As your friend, not colleague, not the agent in charge on this detail, what do you want out of life?" He waved his hand at the basement. "All this? Forever?"

She scanned the interior. "No, not forever. For a while, though. I just got on the VPPD. I'd like to stay for a few years, then go back to Intelligence." Taking a bead on Mitch, she asked, "What about you?"

"I'm getting tired of it all. Jenkins's funeral made me realize life is short. If Clay gets reelected, I'm not sure I'll stay on."

"Well, we all have to cycle out at some point."

"No, I mean for good."

"That cute brunette over at Afterwards Books and Cafe have anything to do with this?"

"Maybe. Since my divorce there hasn't been anybody else. And she has this great kid I'm crazy about. I'm pretty sure—"

The house phone buzzed.

Mitch was closest so he picked it up. "Yes, Ms. O'Neil?"

"Mitch, could you ask C.J. to come up here and meet me in the library?"

"Sure."

C.J. stood. "We can talk more later if you want."

"I hope so," he said ominously.

They'd talk, maybe, but C.J. wouldn't tell him anything concrete about Aidan, despite his suspicions. Professionally, she couldn't confirm she'd had an affair with him. *Knowing* would be a whole different story, and Mitch would have to do something about her breach of ethics if she confessed she slept with their protectee's brother.

Besides, her relationship with Aidan was over and it would be foolish to ruin C.J.'s career by going public now. She refused to think about what she'd lost.

Like the other downstairs rooms, the library had twelve-foot ceilings and a fireplace. Clay and Bailey had left a lot of the furnishings in place when they moved in—most of them formal—but they'd put their own things in a few rooms. This was one of them. Warm fabric couches, plush rugs and homey oak wood accents filled the area. Books lined shelves that went on forever.

"Hi," Bailey said. Tonight she wore a red top over maternity jeans. Despite the circumstances, she looked healthy and rested.

"Hi. Everything okay?"

"Yes." She sat on the couch and C.J. took a chair. "Missing my family, I think. When Clay's gone at night like this, it's worse. And I spent so much time with them lately, it's hard to be alone." She smiled. "Besides, you and I haven't had much of a chance to chat since we got back."

C.J. cleared her throat. "Have you heard from your family?"

"Yeah. Mama calls every day and the guys alternate. They're still worried about the kidnapping attempt and the threat to my life, of course."

"Do they know we isolated the background noise on the tape?"

"I told them it was a restaurant." She sighed. "Annie-O works in a restaurant."

"Masters said her alibi for the day of the kidnapping is airtight. And from everything we've garnered about her, she's gone straight and staying that way."

"It's not her, I guess." She angled her head. "I'm glad, really."

"They're running down the rest of Anthrax and the GGs to see if any of them work in restaurants."

"That I didn't know."

"We'll catch them, Ms. O'Neil."

"I believe you will."

"At least your family can take comfort in the progress made so far."

Bailey frowned. "I'm worried about Aidan."

"You are?"

"Uh-huh. He's overly protective right now, and harps on me about making sure I don't do anything stupid. But something else is wrong. He sounds like he usually does when he has *girl* problems. Mama says he's dating some redhead, but he won't talk about her to me."

C.J. thought, *Great, he's found nice girl, a redhead.*

It only took him a week? Fucking son of a bitch.

Bailey stared out the window for a moment, as if lost in thought. "Did I ever tell you about how supportive Aidan was to me when I got together with Clay?"

"Didn't Aidan deck him once?"

"How would you know that?"

"I, um, just heard it, I guess."

A giggle. "Yeah, he knocked Clay flat on his ass when he thought Clay was using me. But afterward, they got to be friends. Aidan tried like hell to get me to give up my job at ESCAPE and marry Clay."

Of course he did. "And you gave it up."

"Not without a struggle. I couldn't imagine forsaking my antigang work for a man."

No response. C.J. was afraid she knew where this was headed. Hell, had *everybody* guessed about her and Aidan?

"But when I realized I couldn't have both, I picked Clay."

"Do you ever regret it?"

"I found something else I loved as much here in D.C. Working on committees to help at-risk kids, getting educational programs and reforms passed through channels. I'm happy. But it wasn't easy to give up ESCAPE. I feel the loss sometimes, like when I saw Suze Williams."

C.J. adjusted the cuff of her starched white shirt so she didn't have to look at Bailey. God, was the woman going to ask her outright about Aidan and forgo these veiled comparisons?

A cry came from the baby monitor on the table. "Oh, dear. Angel's awake. Sorry to cut short this chat."

Sorry? C.J. couldn't wait to escape. When they reached the staircase, Bailey stayed her arm. "C.J.?"

"Yes?"

"You loved the work you did in Intelligence in New York, didn't you?"

Shit. "Um, yeah."

"I thought so."

C.J. started toward the basement steps.

"One other thing."

She halted.

"Clay meant it when he said he'd do anything for you in return for saving Rory from the kidnapping."

"It was my job."

"Still, if you ever needed something from us—a recommendation for another position, someone to defend your actions, we'd both be there for you."

Tears threatened and C.J. had to turn away. Her back was to Bailey when the Second Lady spoke again. "Do you understand what I'm saying?"

"Yes, Ms. O'Neil, I do. Thank you."

"I want you to be happy." The next words would be, *With my brother.* Bailey didn't say them aloud, but she might as well have. The message was loud and clear.

WHAT ARE YOU going to do with the pictures you've been taking . . . after?

I don't know.

Promise me you'll throw them out. For real, this time. Not like the yoga ones.

No.

You'll destroy them, even if it isn't now. When you meet somebody else, she isn't going to like having the pictures of one of your flings around.

As he sorted through the stack of digital prints he'd run off on his computer, Aidan recalled the conversation he'd

had with C.J. on their picnic at the lake. She was right, he
wasn't going to keep them. He was going to send them to
her. Drop them off at the post office before he picked up
Sandy, his date. He'd already addressed the envelope with
the information he'd gotten from her brother in a phone
call yesterday . . .

After Luke gave him the address, he'd asked, "So, is
this good news?"

"We're not together, Luke. She ended it, but she's right,
I can't handle her job."

"You couldn't talk her into giving it up?"

"She wasn't buying it."

"Then maybe you're *not* the man for her . . ."

Aidan had hung up angry. What did the guy know, anyway? He thought Aidan could talk C.J. into quitting the
service. Instead, he'd just been a fling . . . a fucking *fling*!

He reached for another stack of photos from the printer
and they fell to the floor. As he bent to retrieve them, he
swore vilely at the glimpses of her that he promised himself he wouldn't ever look at again . . .

Caterina and six other blond beauties in the backyard of
the family home . . .

Caterina in that watercolor bikini that barely covered
her . . . in a white terry towel . . . in the bathtub . . .

He remembered teasing her that he was going to alter
the ones of her cooking. But he hadn't taken any shots in
the kitchen that day. They'd fought bitterly, and he'd been
angry, so she made him dinner alone.

It killed him to see the images of her, so he scooped
them up in a messy pile. But the picture that came out on
top stopped him. What the hell? He dropped down into a
chair. He hadn't seen these, but he remembered now how
she'd said fair was fair and snatched the camera from him.
He glanced through them. They were the photos of him
from that night. And at other times, too. Some of the shots
were of him asleep, one where he was on his side, the sheet

dipping dangerously low. Another of him staring out at the water. One of him sweaty and drinking from a bottle of water. One of him lounging out on the deck. There were twenty all together, and every single shot conveyed the same message.

They were taken by a woman in love.

Kocham Ciebie, Aidan.

Of course he'd said he loved her first.

And he did—love her.

Damn her. How could she take pictures of him like this and insist it was over? How could she make love with him that last night as if her very breath depended on him, and then be gone just hours later?

He stuffed the photos—all of them—in the envelope. To get rid of them completely, he added the disc card he'd copied them onto from his laptop and the camera itself. See how she liked seeing them. Pissed off, and hurt, he sealed it.

Hell. He knew in his heart that he couldn't send the pictures to her. Despite how angry he was, he wasn't going to subject her to what he'd experienced when he saw her feelings reflected through the camera lens. He left the whole package on the table and went to the bathroom to take a shower and get ready to meet Sandy.

God, he was dreading this date.

"THAT YELLOW DRESS looks terrific on you, C.J."

She smiled at Ben Holmes, a security expert at headquarters who'd been trying to get her to date him for a long time. After the encounter with Bailey last night, C.J. had panicked and decided she needed to go out with other men. It would get around that she was seeing Ben, and Mitch and Bailey would know she was done with Aidan. And maybe she'd have fun. Ben jumped at the chance when she called and told him this was her night off.

"Thanks." She smoothed down the front of what she'd come to think of as Aidan's dress. "I got it at a boutique on Keuka Lake."

"Man, it must have been fun to spend a month there." He gave her a boyish grin. He was cute, really, with a buzz cut and nice brown eyes. "Except for getting hurt. But hell, you saved the Second Son."

"I love that kid. I'd die if something happened to him."

"What else did you do at the lake?"

Her hand went to her throat, but the medal wasn't there. It seemed blasphemous to wear the charm out on a date with another man, but still, she felt naked without it. She hadn't taken it off even to shower and sleep since Aidan gave it to her. Until now. Even without the physical reminder, images of the two of them stayed with her: how they'd frolicked in the water together, watching the sunset from bed, making it fast and furious against the kitchen wall.

"C.J.?"

"Mostly we worried about the openness on the lake, the boats, that kind of thing."

Their dinner arrived, and C.J. pretended interest in her steak. "So how are things at headquarters?"

"You heard about the tapes?"

"Yeah. Nothing in the data bank to match the voices?"

"Nope." After a few more minutes of discussion, he reached over and grasped her hand. "Let's not talk shop, okay? I finally get you alone, and I want to know you better."

Let's play Twenty Questions. To get to know each other better.

They finished their meals with small talk about their lives before entering the service.

Ben asked, "So, want to go dancing? There's this great club in Georgetown that just opened up."

"Um, I have to . . ." Shit. She had nothing to do. And if

she was going to date, to get over this awful feeling of being with another man, she had to try to harder. "Sounds like a plan."

The club was swank, with its art deco interior and a variety of music. She was having fun on the dance floor until the band began to play "When a Man Loves a Woman" and Ben took her in his arms.

"What's wrong?" he asked. "You tensed up when that song started."

"Nothing's wrong."

Leaning over, he kissed her lips gently. "Good, 'cuz I'm really hoping you invite me up to that apartment of yours when I take you home."

She smiled, though she felt sick and stupid. "Maybe."

AIDAN SHOULDN'T have gone up to Sandy's apartment because she was all over him on the couch and he could barely stand to be touched by another woman. But he'd come here for a reason, so he tried to participate. He ran his fingers through her red hair, but he couldn't help thinking it was too lank for his tastes. He preferred the thick wavy texture of a certain blond mane.

"Aidan," Sandy whispered in his ear. "You feel so good."

She didn't. She was too skinny.

He tried to turn off his mind by throwing himself into a kiss. Son of a bitch! This wasn't working! Maybe he wasn't trying hard enough. He had to find a way get his stride back with women. What did he used to do? He drew back and said, "Could we have some wine first?"

"First?" Her blue eyes danced. "Now that's the best thing you've said to me tonight." She rose, went to her kitchen and returned with two merlots. Clinking her glass with his, she said, "I was beginning to think there was someone else."

There is. "No, there's not. I just like to take things slow."

"Okay." She leaned over and gave him an openmouthed, wet kiss with mega tongue action. "Just don't take too long."

In the end, he couldn't have sex with Sandy. And he was furious on the subway ride home. At himself, and especially at C.J. Damn her for haunting him. Damn him for letting her.

You couldn't talk her into giving it up . . .

She wasn't buying it . . .

Then maybe you're not *the man for her . . .*

Okay, so maybe he should have tried harder.

And maybe she needed a push.

Or maybe he just wanted her to face what she'd given up. If he had to confront the tangible proof of what they'd had together, why shouldn't she?

He strode into his building, pounded up the steps of his apartment and stomped into the kitchen. Grabbing the envelope off the table, he stormed back out, and took the subway to the post office that had twenty-four-hour automated service.

With a drop in the slot, he mailed the pack of memories to C.J.

BECAUSE IT was C.J.'s day off, and she'd gone grocery shopping and to the dry cleaners, she had her hands full when she approached her first-floor apartment in Foggy Bottom.

Someone jumped out of the bushes.

"Oh, my God," she said, dropping everything and reaching for her gun. Too late she realized she wasn't carrying today.

She didn't need the piece anyway. "Son of a bitch, Luke. You scared me to death. If I'd had my gun, I could have hurt you."

"*Proszè*, little girl. You think you could have taken *me*?"

Despite how miserable she was, she had to smile at his ingrained arrogance. Besides it was good to see him. The e-mails they exchanged were not satisfactory contact with him. After a hug, she asked, "Did you bring Kelsey?"

"No, she had curriculum work to do before school starts."

They bent down to get her belongings.

He said, "You mail's here." It was sticking out of the box.

"Grab it, will you?"

She let them both into her place, led him back to the kitchen and deposited her groceries and laundry on the table. "Want something?"

"Yeah, I'll take a beer." He looked around. "This place is homey." He'd never visited her here. "Like the old you."

"Don't start."

"I'm not. I mean it. Lots of great oak wood, stuffed couches. The place shouts comfort and . . . *haven* maybe." He shook his head. "I remember needing one myself when I was in the service."

"I guess."

While she put the food away, they made small talk about Kelsey's pregnancy, *Matka* and Lizzie's new boyfriend. C.J. went to the bedroom to put her clothes in the closet. She scowled at the bed on her way out. On it sat a cuddly white teddy bear with a big pink ribbon. Not only hadn't she been able to part with it, but last night, after the date with Ben, she was miserable and missed Aidan so much, she took the stuffed animal out of the closet where she'd stowed it. She fell asleep clutching the silly thing to her chest.

What does that tell you?

That I'm weak and stupid, and maybe a masochist.

Hiding the bear under the pillow, she returned to her living room to find her nosy brother fiddling with a bulging brown envelope.

"What's that?" she asked.

His expression was smug. "You tell me."

"I have no idea. Who's it from?"

"The love of your life."

She felt her face drain of color. "I don't know what you're talking about."

"It's from Aidan O'Neil, the man you're in love with. Don't bother to deny it. I still read you like a book, and besides, I've talked to him a couple of times."

She sank onto a chair. "Why are you in contact with him?"

Luke snorted. "Take a wild guess."

"Who called who?"

"First, I called him when you were staying at the house after you got hurt." His face flushed, betraying the fact that he knew he'd done something wrong. "I, um, suggested that he come up that weekend."

"What?" Her hand slid inside the shirt where Aidan's medal lay. "It wasn't his idea to come to Queens that day?"

"Don't get your panties in a twist. He needed a nudge. He's crazy about you." Luke sipped his beer, his eyes twinkling. "I told him to try to talk you into quitting the service."

"You had no right."

"Big brother prerogative."

"Bullshit."

He arched a brow and she caught a glimpse of the ladykiller brother she knew and loved. "Shall I count the ways you've interfered with my dates in the past? You and the girls?"

"Luke, please, this is serious. Not some teenage crush. I can't even think about a life with him. And you're just making it hard for me."

Because she knew her eyes were filling with tears, she got up and went to the fridge.

Because he knew it, too, he followed her. From behind, he put his hands on her shoulders. *"Kochanie,* this is eating you up. I can't stand by and let it happen."

Her shoulders shook.

"And I can't believe he's such a wuss that he'll really let you go."

"He's not a wuss. He's sensitive, and listens to me, to what I want. Unlike you."

"What a bunch of crap. If he was any kind of man, he'd be here today, instead of sending you packages. And I told him so, too."

She pivoted. "When?"

"When he called to ask for your address, to send that, I guess." He left her, crossed to the table and picked the envelope up. "Open it."

"No." She had a bad feeling about this. Like she had when she met Aidan. She hadn't listened to the inner warning then, and look where that got her. She'd learned to take hunches about him seriously.

"Okay, I'll see what it is."

"Luke."

"*Nie*. Now hush."

The fight drained out of her. She was tired and cranky and all right, lonely. Let Luke do what he would. She got herself a beer and in her peripheral vision, saw him shake the contents of the envelope out onto the table. Overcome with curiosity, she crossed to stand behind him. "What are . . ." She froze with the bottle halfway to her mouth.

Luke leafed through the photos he'd taken from the envelope. They were pictures of her and Aidan at the lake. He turned his face away. "These are private. I'm sorry. I just glanced."

C.J. stared down at the table.

Luke stood up and held out the chair. "Tell you what? Sit and look at every single one of these. If you can still tell me you're done with him, I promise I'll never bring his name up again. And I won't interfere anymore."

"Honest to God?" she said.

He rolled his eyes. "Yeah."

Okay, she could do this. She sat down.

Oh, God!

The pictures of her and her sisters . . .

The yoga shots . . .

The ones with her in bed . . .

Outside on the deck, on the dock, in the boat . . .

Earlier ones of her with Rory at the picnic . . .

What was this? Photos at the fair? Her mind cleared and her heart began to beat at a clip. Slowly she set the pictures from that day out on the table next to each other.

"Oh, Lord! Luke."

"I told you."

"No, it's not that. Come see these."

Crossing to her, he peered over her shoulder. "What are they?"

"Aidan took photos the day of the kidnapping atempt."

TWENTY-FOUR

JACK MASTERS stared down at the pictures C.J. set out for him. She and Luke had called and said they needed to see him ASAP. When he found out it was about the kidnapping, on which his teams were working nonstop, he told them to come right over to FBI headquarters. His huge corner office was equipped with state-of-the-art computers, monitors and beeping phones, just like in the movies. Only this was the real deal.

"Here are some of the pictures Aidan O'Neil took at the fair in Penn Yan. I picked out the ones with the two Asian boys in them."

Masters's expression was grave. "They're always around Rory."

"Now, look at this picture I downloaded from the Watch List. It's Sasha Sanders, Annie-O's cousin."

He studied the photos and came to the same conclusion she had. "She's the boy at the fair. Since some of these are close-ups—thank you, Mr. O'Neil—I can see the resemblance. Of course, we have to make a positive ID."

"Caterina and I got Annie-O's picture from the list, too." Luke shook his head. "The other *boy* isn't her. There's no resemblance."

"I'm not surprised," Masters said. "We got a room full of people to testify where she was that day, if necessary. It's one of the reasons we didn't pursue Sasha any further than we did. If her cousin wasn't involved, why would she be?" Jack studied the first concrete lead they had. "Put it together with the Asian accent on the death threat and a female Asian strand of hair on Rory, and Sasha Sanders's involvement fits right in."

"What about her alibi, Jack? Her parents claim she was out of town the day of the kidnapping."

Masters's eyes narrowed. "Parents have been known to lie for their children."

"Didn't you check it out?" Luke asked.

"I sent an agent down to Corning to talk to the Sanderses' friends. They swore the family was with them. They said specifically that Sasha was there that weekend. We had no reason to believe they were lying. We had no reason to dig deeper." He held up the photo. "Until now. If these are the kidnappers, which seems highly likely, given what you saw, Agent Ludzecky, and because one of them is sure to be a match to Sanders."

"We should double-check it with the boy that went to see Lennon."

"I can do that now." He called up that picture on his computer. "Shit, the boy at the prison isn't Sanders." He did some more manipulation of the keys. "Bingo. It's the other one."

C.J. scrutinized the photographs of the second boy. "Nothing's familiar about him, or her."

Masters swerved around in his chair. "We can blow the photos up on our computers and put them through the profiling bank. We can also use imaging software to change the appearances, like from boy to girl, different hairstyles, facial hair, et cetera. We'll get a positive ID of Sanders and a line on who the other one is." He cocked his head. "Do you have the disc card the pictures were on?"

She hesitated. "Can't you just scan them into your computer and do all that?"

"I could if I had to. But I'd rather not spare the time. They wouldn't be as clear, either, as the ones off the disc. Don't you have the original card?"

C.J. picked up the envelope. "Yeah, I do. It's in here."

"Give it to me."

C.J. threw a panicky glance at her brother.

A scowl from Masters. "What's going on? We've got a breakthrough that could solve the case. Why are you balking?"

Luke started to speak, but C.J. stayed him with a hand, palm out. She faced the FBI agent directly. "With these pictures were others of me . . . with someone. I imagine they're on the disc, too." Had she realized things might go this way, she could have deleted them. "They're private, Jack."

"Hell, I don't care what you do in your spare time. Besides, I can be discreet."

"If the pictures got out, they could ruin my career because of who I'm with."

"A man or woman? 'Cause if it's the latter, nobody would care, C.J."

"No, it's a man."

"Jesus, he's not a married politician or something like that, is he?"

"No, he's neither."

"Then who is it?"

"I'd rather not say."

Masters studied her. "I'm the FBI. I can find out that kind of information on you in the snap of my fingers if I need to. Everybody leaves some kind of trail."

They had—at the places they stopped, the night at dinner on the lake. Sighing, C.J. saw her career going down the tubes. Worse yet, the embarrassment to Bailey and Clay.

"The person I'm with is Ms. O'Neil's brother, Aidan."

"The one who took these pictures?"

"Yes. I know what I've done is unethical. But, besides hurting my career, it could embarrass Ms. O'Neil and I don't want to do that."

"Still, you brought this in."

"Of course I did."

He exhaled sharply. "I could subpoena the disc. Best I look at it now. Maybe we can work something out."

Reluctantly, she handed him over the card.

But she had to walk away while he went through every single photo on the disc. Jack seeing what had transpired between her and Aidan was such an invasion of privacy. To her, it was sacred. Now a practical stranger was witnessing their intimate time together. The irony of the situation didn't escape her. She'd been so adamant that no one know about their assignation at the lake. Now this public exposure—which could get even more public.

Luke came to the window and circled his arm around her. "Sorry, baby."

"My fault."

They could hear Masters fiddling with the keys. Outside, D.C. was hustling and bustling, warm and humid. After an interminable time, Jack said, "I got what I need."

They went back to the desk; he popped the disc card out of the computer and handed it to her. "You can have this back. Far as I'm concerned, I never saw anything that could hurt you or embarrass the Second Lady."

"Thanks, Jack."

"Too bad," he said, raising an eyebrow, "you two look happy as hell together." He turned back to the computer.

C.J. squelched the regret and focused on what Jack was doing with the photos. Imaging-enhancement software blew up the two suspects, then changes were plugged in. He kept playing with the photos, his hands flying across the keys, until one of the boys at the fair turned into Sasha Sanders.

"No question," Masters said. "That's definitely Sanders."

Shaking her head, C.J. frowned. "I don't get it. If this confirms one of the kidnappers is Sanders, but the other boy-turned-girl isn't Annie-O, who is it?"

Jack said, "We'll find out. I have a feeling Sasha Sanders will tell us who her cohort is." He booted up another program on the screen and sent the picture of the second person through it. "*If* we can't find a match in our files first."

As Jack got up and poured coffee, the computer clicked and clicked and clicked. Luke and C.J. sat on the couch, pretending to read today's *Washington Post*. Finally, there was ding from the machine. Jack said, "Hoo-rah! We got a match."

They hurried to the computer and looked over Jack's shoulder. C.J. said, "I still don't know who she is."

"Read her bio."

"Oh, Lord. Of course, there's the connection."

AT FIVE that afternoon, Mitch and C.J. sat with Bailey and Clay in his office in the Executive Office Building next door to the White House. The Second Lady's face was flushed and she gripped the chair arms as Jack Masters told them of the discovery he and C.J. had made only hours earlier. The vice president stood behind her, his hand on her shoulder.

"Are you sure?" Bailey asked, her voice gruff.

"We are. Our team in New York is on their way right now to pick her up."

"Quinn Pnu. I don't recognize the name as one of the GGs. She wasn't taken in for questioning when they arrested Mazie, was she?"

"No, she wasn't," Masters said. "She was picked up later and sent to juvie."

Bailey frowned. "You got the juvie records unsealed. You said the GG juvie girls went straight."

"They did. Pnu was *originally* a GG, the youngest. But she was never rounded up with the other juveniles. She got away. Later, she crossed over to the Anthrax gang."

"Ah, I see. That could happen, especially with a younger girl."

"For six months she ran with them. When the cops broke that group up, thanks to some leads the GGs eventually gave them for lighter sentences, Pnu was with them and went to juvie then. We'd gotten the juvie records from a family court judge for the GGs but not Anthrax. I sent for those this afternoon when she came up on the computer." He sighed. "She was thirteen when she got into the gang."

"Christ," Clay said. "She's only seventeen now and she planned out this whole kidnapping plot?"

"They age fast in gangs. Besides, she probably had help." He showed them the photos from the prison. "Here she is visiting Lennon at Lancaster. Dressed in her disguise as a boy."

Bailey took the pictures. "I don't remember seeing her at the fair. But I wouldn't have known who she was, anyway, as I've never seen a picture of her anywhere."

Jack said, "Don't forget, there were hundreds of people there that day, too."

"The service should have thought to get the juvie records on Anthrax," C.J. put in. "We might have recognized her at the fair."

"She was dressed as a boy," Masters said. "So probably not."

Mitch spoke up. "Still, we should have been on top of this, Ms. O'Neil."

The vice president held up his hand. "Stop this. You two foiled the kidnapping attempt, and now figured out who the kidnappers are. Apologies are in no way called for."

"Did Pnu do this because I helped break up her gang?" Bailey asked.

"That's one possibility. Since Lennon's involved, another scenario would be that Lennon forced Pnu to do it."

"Blackmail?" Mitch asked.

"Could be. If Pnu was an accessory to the murder of that young girl who was trying to get out of the GGs and we didn't know her part in it, Lennon might have held it over her head. At the very least, they probably planned the kidnapping together. Pnu's boy photo matches the boy who visited Lennon in Lancaster, though Lennon wouldn't give the person up when we questioned her. But there's no way this is all a coincidence. Lennon's got to be involved somehow." He thought for a minute. "And the death threat to you, Ms. O'Neil. As I said before, I believed all along they were done by the same person or group as the kidnappers. Keep in mind Mazie Lennon is certainly capable of murder."

Bailey cleared her throat. "But why now? I've been out of gang intervention for almost three years."

"Our agents will have to discern the reason. Though I have a theory on that, too." The FBI agent scowled. "Your stay at the lake got a lot of publicity from a TV station in New York. What's the anchor's name? Scott?"

Clay's mouth tightened. "Rachel Scott."

"Blackmail or not, both Lennon and Pnu had a grudge against Ms. O'Neil. When they saw on TV that she and the kids were at the lake for a prolonged period of time, they might have figured things would get loose because you were on vacation. Sanders being there was icing on the cake. It made Pnu's trip to Penn Yan easier. She and Sanders had a clear path to come after Rory as payback to Bailey."

Clay's expression turned grim. "From my way of thinking, Rachel Scott is to blame at least in part for the attempted kidnapping of my son and the death threat against my wife. If they hadn't been so irresponsibly placed in the public eye none of this would have happened."

"Let's just be glad we've identified the perpetrators." Masters checked his watch. "And we'll have them nailed, soon. Reports from the two groups of agents I sent out are long overdue." His phone rang. "Maybe that's one of them. Masters." A pause. "Yeah, did you get them?" A scowl. "Just her?" A deeper scowl. After some instructions to his agents, he clicked off. "The group of agents that went for Quinn Pnu couldn't find her at her last known address. They picked up Annie-O to question her. As we knew all along, she has an alibi for the times the events occurred. She claims she hasn't had any contact with Sasha Sanders since her parents moved her to the lake. And that she knew Quinn Pnu from years ago when Pnu was a kid in Anthrax. But by the time Pnu got out of juvie, Annie had gone straight."

"So if Annie-O wasn't involved," Bailey asked, "how did Sasha Sanders end up in the thick of it?"

"There has to be a link. As I said before, I don't believe in coincidences. Think about what we have here. Two girl gangs from New York are in the picture. A member of one has a cousin in the same town as the Wainwright cottage and they're not connected? I don't think so. My other agents are up in Penn Yan now to get Sanders." He glanced at his watch again and picked up his cell phone. "I'll call them now."

They waited as Masters made the connection.

"Carson, this is Masters. You're overdue. Anything on Sanders?" He listened for a long time. "Yeah, yeah. Does she know where Pnu is?" A long hesitation. "*What?* Damn it to hell!"

"What happened?" Clay asked when Masters hung up.

"Bad news. Pnu is allegedly here in D.C."

"*What?*"

"Just before my agents got to Sanders, Pnu called her and said she was in D.C.—to get another shot at Ms. O'Neil. She didn't know that Sasha had already confessed everything to her parents. They did lie, by the way. They'd left her with friends, and when they came home, Sasha got scared and she told them about the attempted kidnapping with Pnu. They panicked. They'd taken her out of New York to get her away from the girl and gang life. So they covered for her."

"That's incredible," Clay said.

"Then, when Pnu called, Sasha's parents didn't want to cover up a murder plot. As I said earlier, her father's a retired cop and after Pnu called, he contacted a lawyer friend of his in town who came right out. The lawyer was with her by the time the FBI arrived. They cooperated for a deal."

"Why was Sanders in on the kidnapping?"

"She told the agents she wanted to be part of the new gang Pnu was forming and that was her method of jumping in."

"Another gang is forming?" Bailey asked.

"No. It didn't happen. Pnu tricked her with that. Sasha found out right after the kidnapping attempt that the plans fizzled out for the new gang."

Clay asked, "How she'd meet Pnu, anyway?"

"We don't know the details of how they hooked up. The critical thing right now is that she told us that Pnu is in D.C. My agents are staying with Sanders, hoping that Pnu will contact her again. Meanwhile, we'll be checking credit cards, known gang members in the area, that kind of thing to pinpoint where she is. We'll also put the D.C. cops on alert for her." He faced Bailey. "Don't worry, Ms. O'Neil, we'll find her. But you'll need an armed escort besides your personal agents back to Observatory Way."

"And she'll stay inside the house until Pnu is caught," Clay put in.

"Of course I will."

Clay turned to his agents. "C.J. and Mitch, I'd like you two to move into the residence until this is cleared up. It will mean twenty-four-hour duty, but I'd feel better if you were with her day and night, in close proximity."

"I agree," Mitch said.

He looked to C.J.

"Yes, of course. We'll do anything until she's safe."

On their way back to the residence with double the guards, Bailey sat in the backseat of the bulletproof limo and turned to C.J. "In all the excitement, I didn't get to ask you how you got the pictures Aidan took at the lake."

"Aidan sent them to us." Technically, he sent them to *her*, but it was almost the truth.

"I'm surprised he'd think his photos would help us. He takes shots of everything and rarely knows what he has on disc."

C.J. thought fast. "Truthfully, I'm surprised he didn't make the connection before this." Except that he had a lot on his mind. "Maybe when he got back to New York and printed them off, he realized what he had—pictures of the fair on the day of the kidnapping." Well, it *could* have gone down like that. There was no note with the pictures. C.J. didn't know exactly why he sent them to her.

"Still, something's off about it all."

"Let's just be glad he got them to us. This thing could be over soon."

BEHIND A TWO-WAY mirror that gave them a view into an interrogation room, C.J. and Mitch flanked Bailey and Clay. It had been a long night and another long day, but they'd picked up Quinn Pnu at a bar on A Street. She'd tried to buy some blow from an undercover cop and he called it in. The D.C. police had their people on the lookout for her, so the officers identified who she was and brought her in.

The door opened and a girl—Pnu—was ushered inside. She wore a fringed suede top that bared her belly. A tattoo of a pitchfork was visible just above the waistband of jeans that could have been painted on her. An orange bandana wrapped around her head like a crown.

"She's flying her colors. The bandana's the trademark

of the old GGs." The Second Lady shivered and leaned into Clay. "It gives me the creeps to see all this again. After Moira and Taz dying because of their involvement in gangs."

"You don't have to watch this interrogation, love."

"Yes, I do."

C.J. touched her arm. "She can't hurt you."

"Only emotionally."

The girl had donned an attitude along with her gang paraphernalia. When she sat, she threw one leg up so her foot crossed the other knee. She lounged back and appeared bored.

"So," Masters said to her. "What are you doing in D.C., Quinn?"

"It's a free country, popo. I can go where I want."

"Not if you're planning violence against the vice president's family."

The young girl fiddled with her fringe. Eyes made up with kohl-like mascara glared at him mutinously. "Dunno what you mean."

He tossed pictures on the table between them. "We got you almost red-handed, lady."

Quinn peered down at the pictures. She rolled her eyes. "What the fuck are these?"

"Pictures of the people who tried to kidnap Rory O'Neil. These 'boys' are scouting out the vice president's son."

She jutted out her chest. "In case you hadn't noticed, I ain't no boy."

Masters lounged back in his chair, too. He had a reputation for being a closer, getting a confession from the suspect. "No? Aren't you smart enough to plan this?"

The girl's face reddened. The fingertips of her left hand began to drum on the chair's arm.

"Guess Sasha Sanders figured it out by herself."

A snort. But no more.

"Or maybe Mazie Lennon planned it."

Pnu's whole body stiffened. "Mazie's in prison."

"She's had visitors." He tossed some of the pictures on the table of Pnu dressed as a boy visiting Lennon. "The same person in the photos at the fair visited her in prison."

Pnu frowned.

"But if it wasn't you, then it has to be Sasha. I guess you don't have it in you. You're not tough enough. Now Sasha, she's tough."

"She's a baby. She couldn't plan dick with nobody."

"Then you *did* plan it? By yourself?"

A smirk.

Bailey said, "They never change. He's appealing to her pride as a gang member. She's going to give it up."

Masters leaned forward. "Why would you want to hurt Rory O'Neil? Because of his mother?"

No answer. But Pnu's lips thinned and her eyes narrowed.

"You found out Rory's mother was the Street Angel when she married Mr. Wainwright, didn't you?"

"Did I?"

"Bailey O'Neil never hurt you. All she did was try to help kids out of gangs."

"Nobody leaves gangs." Her chest started to heave under the tight T-shirt.

"The Street Angel got Taz Gomez out, though. And then Mazie killed Taz."

Pnu's eyes flared wildly. "It was the Angel's fault for dicking around with Taz. I hate the cunt. She put my girl in jail."

"So you tried to hurt her by kidnapping her son."

Quinn pretended interest in the toes of her boots.

"What were you going to do with him? Have a little fun?"

"Oh, God," Bailey gasped. She knew what gang girls did for fun.

"Was Mazie Lennon in on this with you?"

Her head snapped up. "Mazie didn't do nothin'."

"Quinn, we're just trying to help you. We might be able to cut you a deal if you tell us who else was involved in this kidnapping attempt." He waited a beat. "Now here's something I didn't want to tell you, but I'm going to have to, I guess. Sasha Sanders ratted on you. She told us about the kidnapping. And about the death threat."

Pnu bolted up at the new information. "Sasha ain't no hater."

"Sit down!" When she did, she shifted around, curled and uncurled her hands. "Tell us about it, Quinn. You're toast anyway."

The girl pounded her fist on the arm of the chair.

"How did Sasha get involved? Did she start a new gang?"

"That punk? Gimme a break. When the cunt broke up the GGs I went over to Anthrax. Me and Annie-O hung out for a while. I met Sasha then. Annie was thinkin' about letting her in the gang. Then the cops was pressing Anthrax, so the three of us decided to get a new posse. Before we could do it, Annie was arrested and I went to juvie. When we both got out, her little cousin was still livin' in New York, and wanted to be part of our new gang, so we told her gettin' back at the Street Angel could be her way of jumpin' in."

"Annie-O wasn't involved, you know that."

"Sure she was."

"No, Quinn, if she was, you wouldn't give her up. Gang girls don't give up their homies. Annie refused to be part of the plot against Ms. O'Neil, didn't she? She wouldn't participate and told her aunt and uncle what was happening to her cousin. That's why you're trying to sell Annie out. After she did her time, she decided to go straight. So you lured Sasha in. When you told her parents about it, they moved to Penn Yan to live. To get away from you."

An ugly laugh. "Didn't help. Her and me are homegirls, now."

"You and Lennon and Sasha."

"I didn't say nothin' about Maze being in on this."

"She won't give Mazie up," Bailey said. "It's their code of honor. Since Sasha already snitched on her—she wasn't entrenched enough in gang life not to—and Annie-O refused to hook up with her, Quinn feels she can finger both girls."

Masters switched tactics. "So you just wanted to hurt Ms. O'Neil."

"Yep."

"Why now?"

"Me and Sasha been makin' noise about doing it all along. Thinking of a plan."

"How did you know Bailey was at the lake?"

"I saw the cottage on the fuckin' TV. I caught a train that night to Penn Yan. Stayed with Sasha 'cuz her 'rents were out of town. We figured the Angel might be at the fair, so we dressed up as boys—like I did when I went to see Maze."

"Why the death threat, Quinn?"

Her laugh was maniacal. "Just makin' things interesting."

Clay said gravely, "I think we've seen enough."

"All right." Bailey rose and arched her back. "I feel bad for those girls, all of them, but at least it's over and Rory's safe." She glanced at the glass and a little of the old Street Angel peeked out. "How sad. I wish I could have . . ." She let the sentiment trail off.

As if to switch moods, Bailey turned to her husband and, in front of the four agents in the room, gave him a sloppy kiss on the mouth. "Bye, honey. See you for dinner."

They chuckled at Bailey acting as if they were just an ordinary couple saying good-bye until suppertime.

Mitch and C.J. escorted Bailey out of FBI headquarters, and Clay went to his office. It took only ten minutes for the agents to get Bailey back to the residence.

Once inside, Mitch said, "After you rest, Ms. O'Neil, we need to decide which one of us—C.J. or me—will be going down to the Beltsville training center."

"Did we talk about this already?" she asked.

"Just before your father got sick, but with everything going on, you probably forgot about it. C.J. and I are both weeks overdue for our periodic refresher, but we were told to stay with you until this whole kidnapping thing was finished. One of us will need to go now."

"Maybe after Dad's and Aidan's party? It's only ten days away. Don't you want to see my family again? They'll worship the ground you walk on now you got the lead on Quinn and Sasha."

C.J. drew herself up. It was time to take this to the next level. "Ms. O'Neil, I'd like to be the first to go for the refresher. A session starts in a couple of days." She'd checked the dates. "Gorman can go to New York with you two in my place."

Bailey studied her. "But Pa's taken a shine to you. If you went to the party with us, you could see him and Mikey. And of course Aidan would . . ." Her words trailed off.

Mitch was watching C.J. "I think it might be the right thing if C.J. went first. When would you leave?"

"Thursday."

Bailey cleared her throat. "Are you sure this is what you want, C.J.?"

She practically choked out the words. "I think it's best."

"All right then." Bailey looked disappointed.

Mitch looked relieved.

And C.J. felt like shit.

TWENTY-FIVE

THE LUNCH crowd had just left Bailey's Irish Pub and Patrick was restocking the liquor bottles, Dylan was straightening the chairs and Liam was writing out the dinner menu on the chalkboard. All of them showed signs of worry for their sister: a furrowed brow, a curse at something stupid, a quietude that just didn't happen when the O'Neil men got together. Usually there was a ball game blaring from the TV and razzing back and forth. Aidan kept to himself because he was worried about Bailey, and about C.J. protecting her from a death threat.

As he wiped the bar, his father hurried out of the back room. "I got good news." Pa's face was animated and he hadn't had good color like this since he got sick.

"About Bailey?" Aidan asked.

They others came down to the end of the bar and crowded around Pa.

"Yeah. The lass just called. They found out who the kidnappers are, picked them up and got a confession outta both of them." He explained about Sasha Sanders, Annie-O and Quinn Pnu. He grinned at Aidan. "It was your pictures from the fair that clued the Secret Service in, son."

"How did they get the pictures you took up there?" Dylan asked.

"I sent them on when I . . . realized what I had." Not exactly the truth, but Aidan didn't care. His heart was beating fast. "Then she's not in danger anymore?" Which meant C.J. wasn't, either. At least for now.

"She's good as gold. The FBI kept her under some kind of house protection until they got the kidnappers in custody." He chuckled. "Bet she didn't like bein' locked in like that."

Patrick scowled. "Damn it to hell! That gang stuff still comes back to haunt her. I knew we never shoulda let her get involved with that."

Pa rolled his eyes. "As if we could stop her." He scanned them. "Least you boys got some common sense."

Maybe, Aidan thought. *Maybe not.*

"She wants to talk to you. Said you should call on her cell."

Dylan asked, "Did she say if Rachel Scott was responsible for the gang girls finding out where she was?"

"Didn't mention that."

"I'll call her later." Pat's smile was wide. "Brie'll want to talk to her."

"So will Mikey," Liam put in. "I'll wait."

"Me, too." Dylan frowned. "I have some questions that might take a while."

Aidan straightened. "I'll call her now." His cell was in his jacket so he followed his father to the back room of the pub.

When they got behind closed doors, Pa stopped and faced him. "Something's eatin' at you, isn't it?"

"No, Pa. I'm okay."

"Is it the problems with Bailey? You two were always peas in a pod."

"Well, I was worried about her, sure."

"Is it the damn photography thing?"

"No, Pa," he said, exasperation bubbling out of him. He'd kept a tight control on his emotions because of the danger Bailey and C.J. had been in, but freed from those restraints, the rest came out. "If you gotta know, it's a woman!"

"That redhead?"

"I don't wanna talk about it."

His father shook his head. "Seems like you not *talkin'* about stuff is part of your problems."

Pa stormed off and Aidan stared after him. *Fuck.*

He found his cell and punched in his sister's number. No answer. Into the voice mail, he said, "Hey, kid, it's me, A. I hear we got cause to celebrate. Call me back."

Holding his phone in his hand, he stared at it. He could call C.J. under the guise of checking on Bailey, since he hadn't been able to reach his sister. But hell, that wouldn't solve anything. It wouldn't make the pain in his heart go away.

Nothing short of a miracle would.

C.J. ENTERED the library where the Second Lady was reading to Rory. For once, the boy was quiet, and Bailey held him close to her side as they turned the pages. Hower, who'd been sleeping by the window, barked when she arrived and scurried to her. She bent down and took a few seconds to nuzzle the animal. "Ms. O'Neil, can I talk to you for a minute?"

"Of course. Would you like Rory to leave?"

"No." It would be better to have him as a buffer. "I, um, need a favor."

Rory gave her a mischievous grin. "My dad said he'd give you the moon 'cuz you saved me from the girl gang and caught them, too." •

"I don't need anything that big in return."

"What is it?" Bailey asked.

"Do you have any photos Aidan took of you and your family other than the ones at the lake? Some he might have developed from film? I've only seen his digitals."

"Why do you want them, C.J.?" Rory asked.

Bailey ruffled Rory's hair. "Hush, buddy. C.J. has her reasons. She doesn't have to share them with us." She arched a brow. "Unless you want to."

"No, I'd rather not." She had to do one last thing for Aidan, but she didn't want to broadcast it.

Crossing the room, Bailey took out a bulging leather album from the bottom shelf of the bookcases. "These are the most recent pictures before the lake. Both digital and film are in there. I've got tons of them from the past."

"No, this is enough."

Rory was still eying her suspiciously. "How come you won't go to Papa's and Uncle Aidan's party? Mike says they like you, especially Uncle Aidan."

C.J. ignored the comment and addressed the question. "I have training I have to attend."

The kid grimaced. "Like school? When you could go to a party?"

"Yes." She held up the album. "Is it all right if I take this? I'll return it tomorrow."

"Of course. No hurry."

Before Rory interrogated the truth out of her, C.J. absconded with the pictures. She didn't look at the photos, though, until she was home and tucked into her cozy couch, where she felt safe. Since she was going to be thinking about him anyway, she brought the white bear and sat it beside her on the couch. The weight of the medal near her heart made itself known. Aidan was everywhere in the room.

Most prominently in the photo album. His essence was in each photo . . . one she'd seen on his computer of Bailey

and Angel . . . a shot of Bailey and three of her brothers . . .
Liam with Mikey sound asleep on the couch . . . Hogan
and Dylan wearing ball caps . . . Brie, Pat's wife, with a
beautiful baby girl. Each successive picture captured the
subject in a way that might be invisible to the naked eye.
Each revealed a deep love for the members of his family.

When she'd picked out the ones that best showcased his
talent, she closed the album. On a whim, she kissed the
cover. "You're so talented, love. You need to be doing this
for a living."

To that end, she took the pictures to a photo mart, had
them copied and purchased another album. Back at home,
she lovingly filled that one.

Then she got out a sheet of stationery, and wrote:

> *Dear Mr. O'Neil,*
> *Happy seventieth birthday. I'm sorry I can't be*
> *there, but I'm sending you this album because inside*
> *are pictures of what's most important to you—your*
> *family. I believe this is a perfect gift for you. But I*
> *confess I have an ulterior motive. I think you'll know*
> *why I'm giving this to you and I have faith you'll do*
> *the right thing.*
> *Sincerely,*
> *Caterina Ludzecky*

She closed the album and wiped her eyes—she hadn't
even realized she was crying. She couldn't give Aidan the
wife and family he wanted. But this was one thing she
could do for him, the one thing no one else seemed to be
doing for him, and certainly not something he was doing
for himself. It was a birthday gift for Pa, but also a parting
gift for Aidan, and a final good-bye.

Surely he would see it as such.

* * *

THE SACK of flour Aidan carried into the kitchen fell to the counter with a thud; it burst open, and a cloud of powder puffed up then filtered down. His face and shirt were covered with a fine white dusting. "Fucking son of a bitch."

Liam glanced over at him. His brother had been in a foul mood for days. Then again, so had Liam. "The abominable snowman."

At the sink, Aidan tried to clean himself off. "Yeah, you ever see him?"

"I didn't mean the white part. I meant the *abominable* part."

"Screw you."

Shrugging, Liam went about his business at the stove. Even the comforting smells of old-fashioned chicken noodle soup heating up didn't help. Given his own pervasive depression these days, he didn't want to tangle with Aidan.

Grumbles and more curses from the sink. Then he felt a presence behind him. "See if I got it all."

Liam turned around. Aidan still had flour in his eyebrows. Reaching over, he got a towel and cleaned off his brother's brows. "There, now you're your normal ladykiller self."

"What the hell is that supposed to mean?"

"It's *supposed* to be a joke. Not that you have any sense of humor these days."

"Oh, yeah, spoken by St. Liam of the Perpetual Grimace."

Liam let the anger come. "You know what, fuck you. At least I got a reason not to smile. The love of my life *died*. I lost her and couldn't do anything about it. You, on the other hand, let yours go because you're a chickenshit and now all you do is mope around about it."

"I don't have to take this crap from you."

"Somebody's gotta tell you. Jesus, Aidan, take control of your own life."

"Oh, like you—"

"Don't say one more word about my life or I'll take you down, you crybaby."

A snort. "Your life? What life?"

That was it. Aidan started to walk away and Liam grabbed his arm and yanked him around.

"Let me the fuck go!"

"Like hell."

Aidan pushed on Liam's chest. He stumbled backward and hit the side of the stove. The whole pot tumbled off the opposite side and its contents spilled on the floor with a bang. Soup splashed up the side and made a river on the floor.

"Son of a bitch! I spent all yesterday making that." When Aidan didn't say anything, Liam pushed at *his* chest. His brother went backward this time. "Proud of yourself?" Liam asked and kept moving toward him. Kept pushing.

Aidan fell against the counter; pots and pans clattered to the floor and echoed in the huge kitchen. He raised his fist, swung. Liam ducked and momentum carried Aidan into the wall where a corkboard also crashed to the floor.

Whirling around, Aidan raised his fist again.

Liam got in his face and grabbed his wrist. "You wanna take me on, little boy, we'll go outside."

"What's going on in here?" Patrick's voice, from the doorway.

"None of your business." Liam moved in even closer to Aidan.

Each of his arms was grabbed, and he was dragged back.

Dylan's voice came over his right shoulder. "Liam, geez, this isn't you. You never fight."

"I'm sick of his whining. If he wants the girl, he should go after her. If I could get Kitty back for even an hour, I'd—" He cut himself off when he realized what he'd said. His whole body sagged and he closed his eyes. "Shit." He shrugged off his brothers and stalked to the other side of the room; bracing his arms on either side of the window, he faced the backyard. "I'm sorry," he finally said. "I don't know what got into me."

Pat asked, "Things worse with Mikey?"

Ashamed of his selfish outburst, Liam turned around. "Yeah, ever since Bailey went back to D.C., he's withdrawn more and more. One night he even cried for C.J. Then he went back to school and the teacher says he'll hardly talk, even when he's called on." Liam shook his head. "I don't know what to do."

"He needs counseling," Dylan said. "You gotta get him some help."

"I guess. Too much loss." He glanced over at Aidan who stood against the wall. "I'm sorry I took this out on you. Your life is your own. I got no business interfering."

Aidan shrugged a shoulder. "It's okay. I shouldn't have said those things about your life." He drew in a breath. "Besides, you're right. I'm acting like I have no control over this situation with C.J."

"And bitching about it," Dylan, The Taunter, put in.

"Stop," Patrick said. "I don't wanna get hurt breakin' them up." He turned to Liam. "I'm thinking you need some help, too."

"I know. I'm depressed now because it's finally sunk in what my life is going to be like and I hate it. I'm lonely. And this celibacy shit sucks!"

All of them laughed; the release of tension felt good. "There you go," Dylan said. "What you need is to get laid."

Liam chuckled. Then sobered. "But it's more than that." He glanced at Patrick, who so often hit the nail on the head. "You're right, Pat. I should to talk to somebody."

"Brie and I will help—moneywise, with the kids."

Dylan crossed the room and put his hand on Liam's shoulder. "I got the name of a counselor that Hogan and I went to. She worked wonders with him."

"Maybe." Liam faced Aidan. "We square?"

"Yeah." Aidan shuffled his feet.

Liam stuck his hands in his pockets.

They were like little boys making up on the playground after a fight.

Aidan finally said, "You did me a favor. I needed a kick in the pants."

"Anytime," his three brothers said in unison.

TWENTY-SIX

C.J. DROVE the Beast, the first car in a motorcade consisting of four big black vehicles, decorated with American flags and flanked by several motorcycles with white-helmeted agents. She wended her way through streets of brick-front buildings at a slow speed, so people could catch a glimpse of the president of the United States of America.

A loud boom exploded behind her. She glanced in the rearview mirror and saw a ball of fire ready to bite the car in the ass. Jerking the wheel to the right, she said to the female next to her, "Evasive maneuvers," and began darting in and out of the traffic. The motorcycle cops cleared the path, and as fast as she could go, given the traffic, she dipped around the other vehicles and swerved into a side street between two buildings. Gunning the motor, she sped off. When she hit the open paved lot, she gunned the car up to seventy miles per hour. Another quick jerk of the wheel and the car spun around 180 degrees. She drove a few yards, then came to a screeching halt. The tires screamed and rubber burned at the tight stop. She'd executed the J-turn without a flaw.

"Wow," the trainee said, "that was great. I couldn't do it."

C.J. peered over at her. God, the girl was green. It was hard to believe little Ella Thomas would *ever* be able to drive a protectee's limo or any hard car. "Thomas, do you or do you not want to be in the Secret Service?"

"Yes, ma'am, I do."

After completing the initial round of training in North Carolina, required for all Secret Service personnel, Thomas was at Beltsville for her second—the advanced eleven-week course designed for special agents. All the rookies called C.J. ma'am, even though she was here for training herself and was only thirty-two years old. But any agents at the compound, and especially those on the PPD or VPPD, were treated like instructors. C.J. had been asked to take trainees along with her on some maneuvers she herself was required to practice, like this one today, conducted on the streets of a town that resembled a Hollywood back lot. Adding to her aura of authority was the fact that the facility administrators had snagged her as soon as she arrived and asked her to give a seminar later in the week for the entire population on how her team foiled Rory's kidnapping and the intelligence that went on behind finding the perpetrators.

"If you do want to be one of us," she said to the girl, "you'll have to be able to execute maneuvers like this without even thinking about it."

"Yes, ma'am."

The door to the Camaro, the model of car used in training, opened. The special agent in charge of Beltsville instruction, Finn Flannigan, had a clipboard in his hand. As she got out, he said, "Good job, C.J. Your reflexes are still top-notch in the motorcade." He gave her a half grin. "Then again, you've been driving around the cream of the crop. Congrats, by the way, on saving the day."

"Thanks, Finn. I was just doing the job I was trained here to do."

The teacher beamed at the compliment. "Appreciate that." He checked his chart. She'd been in Maryland three days and had completed about a quarter of her qualifications. "What do you want to do next?"

"Water rescue."

In the event of protectees' cars going into a lake or their planes going down in the ocean, protectives were trained for underwater rescue and getting the subjects safely to land.

"Water rescue recertification isn't until tomorrow." He checked his watch. "You could do your quals in fitness now. Should be a piece of cake. You're in great shape."

A memory hit her, like an uppercut to the chin . . .

You're in such good shape. Perfect shape.

At the time, she and Aidan were both naked and he was *testing* every muscle in her body for strength, flexibility and suppleness. His hands were magic and she'd basked in his touch.

"You scowled. Don't you want to do the fitness thing now?"

"No, I do. Something just crossed my mind."

C.J. bade good-bye to Finn and the trainee, who was still looking at her with stars in her eyes. When she first trained here, C.J. had felt like that way about the experienced agents she came in contact with. All she'd wanted out of life was to be one of them.

What do you want in life? Aidan had asked, as they drove from Queens to the lake. *I mean, you know, in the future. A husband to love you to pieces, and kids?*

She'd said yes, eventually she wanted that.

Not now though. What she wanted now was to protect the vice president's wife, and in order to forget Bailey's brother, C.J. was going to lose herself in the training she needed to do the job. By the time she left Beltsville, she planned on being over Aidan O'Neil completely.

Kocham Ciebie.

All right, maybe not completely, but enough to stop dreaming about the way he laughed, and how his face looked when he was taking pictures, the color of his hair when the sun hit it.

And the raw intimacy of making love with him.

"Arrgh . . ." she growled as she headed off to change her clothes.

Once she was dressed in black sweats and sneakers, she checked in with the agent in charge of the fitness group, and began her endurance qualification. Breathing hard as she ran, she remembered that Aidan ran, and how sexy he looked sweaty and spent from the exercise. Then she remembered how other activity made him sweaty and spent . . .

Oh, baby, you blew the top of my head off.

She was straddling him, and brushed damp hair from his forehead. *I want to do that, and more.*

"Stop!" she said aloud to herself. "Don't do this."

With a blank mind, she finished the rest of the run in record time. Then she headed to the obstacle course. She climbed the ropes, swung out over the pond, and shimmied up to the other side. There she scaled a wall painted with the Secret Service star and the agency motto, *With trust and confidence,* on it.

You can trust me, Caterina. I'll always have your best interest at heart.

Aidan, there's no future to trust you in.

Don't bet on it, baby.

Well, she'd won the wager. And she was breaking records with her fitness and skills qualifications. So why did she feel like such a loser?

* * *

"PA, I GOTTA talk to you." Since it was still warm in early September, Aidan's father was seated outside the pub, on the small back porch, some kind of book on his lap. He looked healthy and . . . at peace. Aidan figured this was a good time to talk to him. He was done coasting in his life. The fight with Liam had brought everything into focus.

"Sit," Pa said.

Instead, Aidan stood by the post and leaned against it. "Since your heart attack, I've been walking on eggshells around you."

His pa gave a snort.

"I felt guilty that our fight caused your heart attack." He blew out a heavy, disgusted breath. "Then I took you out on the lake and you cracked your head on the bottom of the boat."

"Christ the Lord, boy, how many times do I have to tell you none of it was your fault?"

"I know that now. It just took me a while to come around."

"Seems like everything does."

"What do you mean?"

"I been wondering why you waited so long to talk to me about the photography in the first place."

He shrugged. "I don't know. I guess I was afraid you'd be mad." He shook his head. "No, that's not true. At least not all of it. I think it boiled down to me not having enough confidence in my work. Maybe I was using you as an excuse." He straightened and took a bead on his father. "But I'm gonna do it now, Pa. I'm gonna pursue photography full-time."

"Okay."

"If the guys need me, I'll work at the pub part-time."

"Okay."

"And I might be moving—"

"I said okay, son."

"You did?" Aidan scowled at him. "Why is it okay? You've been against this."

He gripped the book he held. "I know. I had a lot of time to think about things since I got sick. I've been selfish. I wanted my boys with me, you especially. And I had a feeling that your interest in takin' pictures would make you leave us."

"You didn't mean that stuff about it not being a real job, just a hobby?"

"No, I meant it. Then."

"Now?"

"I can see it's not just a hobby."

"What changed your mind?"

"This." He held up the book and Aidan noted it was a leather photo album. "Is that one of Bailey's?"

Pa shook his head.

"Where'd you get it?"

"It's a birthday present for me. And for you in a way."

"From who?"

"See for yourself." He handed Aidan the book.

Immediately Aidan recognized the photos he'd taken of his family. He turned the pages, smiling at each one. This was a nice gift for his father. "I gave Bailey these pictures, Pa."

"Didn't give them to me." He sighed. "Can understand why, I guess." He shook his head. "Wish I'd seen them sooner."

"Why?"

"Because when I looked at them, I could hear little Angel laugh, see the sadness on Mikey's face even when he's asleep. They show how you love your brothers, your Ma . . . me. You have a gift, son, and you should pursue it."

Aidan swallowed back the emotion. He hadn't realized, even though he would have gone ahead with this career now, how much his pa's blessing meant. More so, how important his acknowledgment of Aidan's talent was to him. "I . . . I don't know what to say."

"I'd say thank you to that little secret agent of yours."

"What do you mean?"

"Look at the letter in the end."

Aidan flipped to the back of the album. The note was from C.J. In her no-nonsense handwriting. Carefully he read each word.

But he also read in between the lines.

When he looked up at his father, he couldn't help the smile that spread across his face. "Hot damn," he said to Pa.

"That's my boy."

"So once we received the threat we started isolating factors about the call." C.J. stared out at the nearly one hundred members of her seminar on intelligence gathering and how it unraveled with the attempted kidnapping of Rory O'Neil. "This is the fun part."

A male recruit gave her a wave. "It was a voice threat right? Not a written threat."

"Yes."

"It's impossible to conceal your identity in a written letter, isn't it?"

Show-off. The kid was cute, though, and had eyes almost the color of Aidan's. "Yes, we can hone in on specific things with written threats." Quickly she recounted the ink and paper analysis used, the FISH section of the department and the database that held the past input with which they'd compare the current threat.

"After zeroing in on the restaurant noise, and the Asian accent, we were pretty sure Annie-O had been the culprit." She winked at them. "Just goes to show you how you shouldn't jump to conclusions." She explained that Annie-O had been cleared and Quinn Pnu was being indicted. Sasha Sanders, at fourteen, was being handled by juvie, but her cooperation in nailing Pnu would go a long way in keeping her out of the system.

Another hand from one of the recruits. "Did you really jump off a Ferris wheel to save Rory O'Neil?"

"I really did. And I don't recommend it."

"How long was your recovery?" a woman asked.

Just long enough to fall in love.

"About a week. Then the vice president was taken hostage and I went back to New York to be with Ms. O'Neil."

They peppered her with questions, and even the instructors had some queries . . .

"What's the most difficult thing about the VPPD?"

"Do you go into the classroom with Rory?"

"What's it like to guard a baby?"

"Is Ms. O'Neil nice? She's so mag in what she's done as the Second Lady."

"She's very nice." For some reason C.J. added, "Her whole family is."

You went to the other side of the lake, to avoid hurting Sonia . . .

I'm worried about Liam. He needs help.

And rocking Angel, keeping Bailey company when Clay was away, playing endlessly with Rory and Mike.

"Agent Ludzecky? Which do you like better, intelligence work or protective work?" This from Ella Thomas, who had been in her car earlier in the week.

"Stupid question," Mr. Blue Eyes said. "Of course it's the protection."

"No," C.J. answered. "It's not that cut and dry. I like the protective division. It's exciting, interesting and you're really standing next to history being made."

"What's the downside?"

"Not so much a downside, but more an upside to Intelligence. The work I did in the New York office was challenging, and rewarding, in a different way. My mind was active, as opposed to hours of watching other people and doing nothing. That can be excruciatingly boring, by the way. And in Intelligence, I liked figuring out the puzzle. Solving the crime. To break it up, and get the adrenaline rush we seem to need, we supply the protection for dignitaries visiting the UN."

There was a lot of buzz back and forth from the rookies about which kind of jobs they wanted in the service. C.J. sat back and let them talk. Her own mind was busy with one thought: She'd had a position that she loved, in the same city where Aidan lived, and had only left it because she'd been forced out by her boss.

Who was leaving the field office in New York City.

THE COMPUTER KEYS clicked under Aidan's fingers. Since his talk with his dad, and admitting some things to himself about his own insecurities, he'd gone online daily researching opportunities in Washington, D.C., for photographers with his credentials. He investigated employment in magazine work and photojournalism.

And because of his fight with Liam, and the suggestion his brothers had made about Liam getting himself and Mikey counseling, Aidan realized *he* needed help, too. So he'd begun scouring the Internet for information on the significant others of men and women who worked in dangerous jobs. First, he looked for specific articles on government personnel: Secret Service, FBI and CIA agents. There had been a few things written by the wives of agents, but nothing, of course, from men whose women were in the business.

He had, however, found a chat room where people gathered to talk about this very issue. He clicked into the site.

WifeforYou was online. She was married to an FBI agent. She talked about raising kids virtually alone, but when hubby came back, they got another kid on the way. *Furlough babies,* she called them.

NotforMe was divorced from a police officer. She had nothing good to say about people who endangered their lives when they had families to consider.

Smitten was one of his favorite contributors, for obvious reasons. He was living with a female firefighter and had solid advice about dealing with her job. He and Aidan had exchanged several private e-mails.

There were sad stories from women whose military husbands had left them, CIA agents who'd turned alcoholic and one man's lover who'd been killed in the 9/11 attacks on the World Trade Center.

As Aidan watched the comments scroll by, someone brought up the idea of support groups for those people trying to make a life with today's heroes. Aidan typed in with: *I don't suppose there's any kind of group like this for the federal government, is there?*

The agent's wife with the kids typed, *Hey, yeah, there is. One's starting in Washington, D.C., this fall for the CIA, FBI, the Secret Service. After Tim Jenkins died, there was a rush of concern from spouses.*

This was kismet, Aidan thought after she e-mailed him the information. The person running the group was Joe Stonehouse. Luke's old boss. He'd been at Jenkins's funeral and talked to C.J. Because he felt strongly about this topic, he was flying from his home in upstate New York to D.C. once a week for a trial eight-week seminar.

Aidan got off-line and took out his cell phone. For some reason, he'd saved the number he needed in his phone book.

In a few minutes, the call was answered. "Hello." A beautiful feminine voice. "This is the Ludzecky residence."

"Mrs. Ludzecky?"

"Yes, who's this?"

"Aidan O'Neil. I'm—"

A throaty feminine laugh. "Oh, I know who you are. Luke's told me about you. We were hoping to hear from you."

"You were?"

"Yeah, let me go get Luke."

As Aidan waited, he thought about life, and how, when

you really wanted something, someone—God maybe?—kept throwing ways to get it in your path.

Two days before Pa O'Neil's birthday, when the vice president's family and their agents were headed to New York, C.J. stayed at the gun range long after she qualified for Rapid Accurate Firing.

Bang, bang! The bullets from her .357 semiautomatic hit the target's heart. She was used to the ricochet and held her ground. The acrid smell of smoke assaulted her.

More shots. Ouch! Right in the target's groin. Served the villain right.

Kneeling down, goggles and earplugs in place, she set up with the M16, then MP5 and fired.

By the time she finished, she'd been off the charts with her scores in shooting. Somehow, the pleasure she took in that was minimal, just like when she aced her written tests. Her success in this training had felt so-so.

She left the gear behind and headed out to get some dinner. Twenty feet from the range, she was approached from the left. Ella Thomas again.

"Agent Ludzecky, I was wondering if I could ask you something."

"Yeah, sure. And you can call me C.J."

"The other women trainees and I were talking last night about how great it was watching you work. You do everything right. You held your own with the guys in the workshop. And you made it to the top. We wondered if you'd wanna come and talk to us about what it's like to be a female in the agency."

C.J. was about to brush Thomas off with a comment that life in the Secret Service for a woman was just like it was for a man, but she felt like a hypocrite, because in so many ways, it wasn't. And she'd been e-mailing her sisters a lot since she got here, which made her miss contact with them even more, so an all-girl evening might be fun. "I guess I could. When?"

"We're getting together for pizza right now."

"Now's fine," she said, and followed Ella over to the housing complex and up the steps to her suite.

They walked inside her quarters and C.J. found ten women seated on the floor, couches and chairs. They were chatting, flipping through magazines, sipping drinks. Dressed in a variety of jeans, sweats and shorts, they could have been any group of college coeds.

But they weren't. They were training to take a bullet for someone else.

They greeted her warmly.

C.J. accepted a soft drink and a slice of pizza with everything on it and sat on a chair somebody vacated for her. After she ate the spicy pie, she asked, "So what do you want to know, ladies?"

A short-haired woman took the lead. "There's got to be prejudice against women on the job. Most of the PPD and VPPD are men, right?"

Shrugging, C.J. said, "Most Secret Service agents are men. But women get the same opportunities. I got on the VPPD, which is a plum position." She told them how she'd substituted for Bailey's guards when an agent from the field office was needed. And what the heck, she added, "However, there were rumors I'd slept my way to the top. I wouldn't guess a man would be accused of that." Then she blasted David Anderson—nameless—and confessed to leaving a job she loved under duress. She quickly explained why she went along with it, though, so these young women wouldn't think it was the right thing to do, or that they should take that crap from anybody. After discussing the whole situation with Luke and Aidan, C.J. was pretty sure she would handle it differently if it happened to her today.

"It must work the other way, too," a pretty brunette

stated. "Do you think you got to guard the vice president's wife because you're a woman?"

"No. Marilyn Quayle had male agents, and Jackie Kennedy has a special affinity to Clint Hill. Granted, Ms. O'Neil asked for me, but I don't think it's because I'm female. We clicked, personality-wise, when I subbed on her detail several times." She smiled thinking of Rory and Angel. "And I'm sure the fact that I adore the kids came through. Not everyone can guard children."

Other questions surfaced: physical fitness of a man compared to that of a woman, spending all day as one of the guys, then going home and turning back into a woman, the rigor and loneliness of consistent travel.

Finally, little Ella said, "I want to know some personal things. You don't have to answer if you don't want to."

"I won't." She smiled. "Shoot."

"Isn't it hard on your love life being an agent?"

She thought of Aidan's beautiful blue eyes darkening with desire. And filled with hurt when she left him.

"Yes, it is. You must have heard the stories that agents have difficulty sustaining personal relationships."

"Is it worse for a woman?"

"I'm not sure, but I would think so. If their significant others are men, guys tends to be more protective." She pictured the look on Aidan's face when he saw the tape of Tim McCarthy getting shot. "It's hard to imagine a husband watching his wife put herself in the line of fire. Those kinds of things get televised live."

"No harder than a wife watching her husband," someone else put in.

Maybe she was right. The women batted that around for a while.

The brunette asked again, "I heard that the service unofficially recommends women not change their names when they get married because chances are the union won't last."

Another added, "Divorce rates are among the highest for Secret Service agents. I read where a good percentage turn to booze because of the loneliness."

Which was exactly why C.J. had made the decision she had about trying to sustain a relationship with Aidan.

Though the conversation was making her sad. And a bit angry. Was this really what life had to be like for women in the Secret Service?

"Have you had any serious relationships since you've been an agent, C.J.?" Ella asked.

She told them about the string of guys who couldn't accept her job.

"So there's really no hope of falling in love and making it work."

She fingered the medal around her neck, the one she hadn't yet been able to take off since the disastrous date with a man other than Aidan. "Well, I fell in love. Once."

"How did it end?" another asked.

It hasn't. No, no, that wasn't right. It had. "Same old, same old. He recognized the fact that he couldn't handle the danger I put myself in." She shook her head. "Of course, I helped him down that path." Maybe too much.

A cute little redhead that Aidan would like the looks of lifted her chin. "I refuse to believe it has to be that way. If two people love each other, they should be able to compromise."

C.J. felt defensive—and embarrassed by being such an emotional coward. "It's not that easy."

"It's doable, though, isn't it?"

She thought long and hard about what kind of advice she should give these girls. *Don't count on it. Be a robot and be prepared to give up everything, especially a man.* That message was so cynical. And if women in the ranks kept preaching that mantra, how would things ever change? Yet, should she mislead them? Or was it just her limitations that caused her own situation?

In the end, she said, "You know what, maybe you're right. At the very least, if you think you can have both, you should go for it." She recalled one of her favorite quotes. "You miss one hundred percent of the shots you don't take."

Like she had. She'd missed her chance with Aidan because she'd been afraid to take the risk.

The redhead looked at her. "If you believe that now, is it too late for you and the guy you fell in love with?"

That question haunted her as she left the young women to finish their pizza party. It was humbling to witness another generation of female rookies who were braver, in some ways stronger, than she was.

EPILOGUE

෨෪

BAILEY'S IRISH PUB was festively decorated with crepe paper and signs that read, "We love you, Pa," and "Happy 70th Birthday, Grandpa," and not-so-festively festooned with black balloons and signs for Aidan that read "Over the Hill," thanks to his brothers, he guessed. The place smelled like home-cooked food and laughter rang out from every corner. Combined with the buzz of voices and the drone of Irish music in the background, it was apparent that everybody was having a swell time.

Aidan was leaning against the bar when his sister broke away from Clay and Dylan and some guy Aidan didn't recognize and crossed to him. Her pregnancy was showing more these days and she wore a pretty blue dress that looked good on her. Aidan himself wore a gray silk T-shirt and matching gray slacks. He wondered if C.J. would like the outfit.

Bailey said, "Hey, A. How are you?"

"Great."

Her gaze narrowed on him. "Yeah, you seem better this

time. When I left to go to Washington the last time, I thought you might throw yourself off a bridge."

"Not quite."

"Is it because you got the stuff about photography ironed out with Pa?"

"That's part of it." He'd thought it through about how to be honest with Bailey. "You and I gotta have a discussion, sis, but not before I talk to somebody else first."

"Hmm." His sister's grin was mischievous, which meant she knew something. "Does this have anything to do with C.J.?"

The beer he held sloshed over onto his hand. Shit, had C.J. talked to Bailey? He said, cautiously, "Why do you ask that?"

"Because she phoned Clay from Beltsville and told him she wanted to call in her marker."

"Marker?"

"Yeah." Bailey toyed with the straw in her soft drink, and drew out the moment. "After she foiled the kidnapping, and helped figure out who was after us, both Clay and I promised her we'd do anything in our power for her if she ever needed us."

"I wonder what she wanted." To be transferred from VPPD, maybe, because of him? Was that a good sign or a bad one?

"I wish she'd come today," Bailey added. "Pa would have liked having her here. He took quite a shine to her at the lake."

"Me, too." God, he was starved for information on her. How could he get it without telling Bailey too much before he talked things over with C.J.? "When is she coming back from Beltsville?"

"I'm not sure. Ask Mitch. I know she called him about her schedule. He said she told him the female recruits are picking her brain about what it's like to be a woman in the Secret Service."

He'd give his right arm to know what she was telling them. If it was bad—like that crap she'd been spouting about agents *never* having a personal life—she'd just have to eat her words. Aidan was biding his time until his and Pa's birthday was over and until C.J. returned from Maryland to put his plan into action. No matter what, he was going to get her back and was hoping to start the process soon.

Patrick and Brie approached them. "Hey, guys," Brie said, kissing Bailey's cheek. "We haven't had a chance to talk since you've been back."

Pat's wife seemed tired. "How are you, Brie?"

"Exhausted. The baby's been sick and she's up at all hours."

"And then Brie goes to work." Pat's response was strained.

Brie stiffened, but her tone was gentle when she said, "So do you, honey."

"I know." He kissed her head. "I'm sorry."

At least they were trying. Like people in love *should*. Aidan had learned that lesson. And C.J. damn well better learn it, too.

"Who's the guy talkin' to Clay and Dylan?" Pat asked.

"Hank Sellers. The reporter from the *Village Voice*."

True to his word, Clay had given an interview to his old friend about irresponsible journalism. He'd cited WNYC News coverage of Bailey and how incensed he was about their giving up her location and plastering her face on TV. When it came out, the article had caused a flurry of complaints from the station. Rachel Scott had tried to contact Clay but he refused her calls. Dylan had taken a personal interest in the whole thing, probably because he was in journalism, too.

Clay had also gotten good news that one of the militants in Zanganesia was captured, and they were hoping to use him to find the others. After Jenkins's death, the FBI and CIA had been relentless in going after his killer.

Aidan was distracted by Mikey, who came racing across the room with Rory. Liam followed at a distance with Cleary, who said hello, then detoured to the jukebox. Mikey embraced Bailey.

Liam kissed her cheek. "I think he misses his aunt."

Bailey drew the boy to her and gave him a warm hug. "You okay, buddy? You haven't said much to me since I got here."

Mikey just stared at her. Bailey's comment was an understatement. The boy was hardly talking at all. Then he asked, "Where's C.J.?"

They were surprised at his question and before anyone could respond, they heard from behind, "I'm right here, Mikey."

Aidan whirled around.

Caterina stood a few feet away. And tonight she *was* Caterina. Dressed in a pretty print dress that hugged every curve and even had ruffles around the bottom, she looked so feminine he almost swallowed his tongue. Her hair was curled and, Jesus, she even had makeup on. She crossed to them on strappy sandals that made her hips sway. When she bent over to hug Mikey, he could see his medal nestled in the swell of her breasts.

"Close your mouths, guys," Bailey said to her brothers.

Liam smiled. "C.J., you look terrific."

"Yeah, you do." From Pat.

Mitch, who'd been standing by the door, approached her. "Hey, Ludzecky."

She didn't respond to anyone, but kept her eyes trained on Aidan. "Hi, Aidan." No *Mr. O'Neil* this time.

"What are you doing here?" he blurted out.

"I wanted to wish you and Pa a happy birthday."

Pa? She never called him Pa. What did she mean by that?

His gaze narrowed on her. "You're not dressed for duty."

"She's not on duty." Mitch scowled, but there was

something . . . affirming in his demeanor. Aidan couldn't make sense of all these vibes.

"Hey, guys." Bailey nodded to the other side of the room. "Let's go see Pa. He's sitting by himself." She made sure everybody moved away. Before Aidan knew it, he and C.J. were alone.

"We need to talk," she said, softly, but so seductively he got hard in a second.

"Not here." He grabbed her hand and dragged her out to the back area. He made his way to a small room with a bed, slammed the door and locked it.

"What are you doing?" she asked, her eyes wide.

"Just this," he said, and moved in on her.

A ZIPPER unzipped.

Her dress unbuttoned.

His shirt opened.

She kicked off her shoes.

He stripped her of her panty hose. Panties ripped.

She yanked at his belt.

All the while, he took her mouth. She returned the kiss with ardor.

Now that C.J.'s decision had been made, she couldn't get close enough to this man. When he opened the front clasp of her bra and she spilled into his hand, she moaned and ran her fingers down his bare chest. They detoured to his butt.

"Oh, God," he said, "I've missed you."

She took bites out of his shoulder. "Me, too. I've missed *you.*"

Reaching between them, she freed his penis from his pants and took him in both hands. He let out a fierce growl.

"Fuck, Caterina, don't *do* that."

She said, "I love you, Aidan." And repeated it in Polish.

"Oh, God, that's it." He hiked her up and growled, "Wrap your legs around me."

She did.

He plunged inside her.

Plundered her.

Her back against the wall, he thrust and thrust until she screamed her pleasure. He covered her mouth to catch the sounds and as soon as she was done, he groaned out his own release.

The whole thing had lasted . . . maybe ninety seconds.

Breathing like bellows, they clung to each other. Face in each other's neck. Still joined. She inhaled him, felt the hard planes of his body. Reveled in the feel of his flesh.

He drew back, but he didn't let her go. "So, now that's over, tell me what you're doing here."

She raised her chin and said simply, "I've decided that we've got to try to make this work between us."

He scowled.

"What?" She hesitated. "Oh, God, have you changed your mind?"

"Of course not. I decided the same thing, but I wanted to tell you first."

Her smile was Jezebel's. "Tell me now."

"I talked to Pa." He kissed her nose. "I can't tell you how grateful I am to you for sending him the album of my pictures. I was going to go after a photography job anyway, but your gift made it a hell of a lot easier."

"I'm glad."

"I'm looking at photography opportunities in D.C. I can come there after I wean myself from the pub, and you can work something out with Bailey, and your job. I don't know what, though."

She grinned. So typical of him to meet her halfway. "I know what. I've already decided I don't need to be Bailey's agent anymore." She leaned in close. "Especially if I can be her sister-in-law?"

"Oh, God, oh, yes. Her sister-in-law." He kissed her again. "My wife."

"I like the sound of that."

"But what about your job?"

"I'm thinking about coming back to New York and working in the Intelligence Division. David is leaving the field office, and his position is open."

"Or you could stay in Washington, and just give up the VPPD. But you could still work in protective there if you want. Clay could minimize the damage to your reputation from our . . . from us."

She cradled his jaw in her palm. "Then again, there *are* opportunities for protecting dignitaries at the UN if I was still interested in doing some work in that area."

"You don't have to make that big of a change, sweetheart. I'm joining a support group for significant others of the agents. I'll learn to handle what you do."

"But I've got a meeting with Clay tomorrow to ask for his help with reassignment here."

They both laughed at what they were trying to do for each other.

"So?" she asked. "What are we going to do?"

Aidan pulled her close again. "I don't know. So long as we stay together, either way works for me." He brushed back her hair. "I love you."

"I want you to. Forever." She smiled and yanked on his hips. "Speaking of which?" She arched a brow as she must have felt him respond. "I really missed you. Think you can go another round?"

"Are you kidding? I been saving it up for you, sweetheart."

"Just so it's for me and not some redhead." She kissed him.

"Always," he said hiking her up again. "Just for you."